ESSAYS IN ZEN BUDDHISM
(THIRD SERIES)

THE COMPLETE WORKS OF D.T. SUZUKI

Edited by

CHRISTMAS HUMPHREYS

(President of the Buddhist Society, London)

DAISETZ TEITARO SUZUKI, D. LITT.
(Late Professor of Buddhist Philosophy in the Otani University, Kyoto)

ESSAYS IN
ZEN BUDDHISM

(THIRD SERIES)

New Age Books
New Delhi (India)

ESSAYS IN ZEN BUDDHISM

ISBN: 978-81-7822-431-2
(Set of Three Books)

First Indian Edition: Delhi, 2017

Published by
NEW AGE BOOKS
A-44, Naraina Industrial Area, Phase-I
New Delhi (India)-110 028
E-mail: nab@newagebooksindia.com
Website: www.newagebooksindia.com

Library of Congress Cataloging-in-Publications Data
Suzuki, D. T.
ISBN 978-81-7822-431-2
Includes Foreword, Appendices, Index, Illustrations
Buddhism

Printed and published by
RP Jain for NAB Printing Unit
A-44, Naraina Industrial Area
Phase-I, New Delhi-110028. India

CONTENTS

		Page
	PREFACE	12
	EDITOR'S FOREWORD	14
I.	FROM ZEN TO THE GAṆḌAVYŪHA	18–74
	1. Zen and the Philosophy of Identity	18
	2. The Early Masters and the *Avataṁsaka*	20
	3. Zen and the Chinese mentality	22
	4. Bodhidharma on the Unconscious (*wu-hsin, mu-shin*); Tao-shin on the 'Abandoning of the Body'	23
	5. Hui-nêng on the Unconscious (*wu-nien, mu-nen*)	30
	6. Shên-hui on the Unconscious (*wu-nien, mu-nen*)	37
	7. Tai-chu Hui-hai on the Unconscious	40
	8. Chao-chou on Zen	44
	9. Lin-chi on Zen	48
	10. Other Zen Masters of T'ang and Sung on Zen	52
	11. Zen and the Study of the Sutras	63
	12. The *Avataṁsaka* and the *Gaṇḍavyūha* Distinguished, and Their Message	70
II.	THE GAṆḌAVYŪHA, THE BODHISATTVA-IDEAL, AND THE BUDDHA	75–106
	1. A Complete Change of the Scenery in the *Gaṇḍavyūha*	75
	2. Some Ideas Characterizing the Sūtra	78
	3. The Doctrine of Interpenetration	87
	4. The Bodhisattvas and the Śrāvakas	91

5. Causes and Conditions of the Differentiation 95
6. Parables 97
7. The *Gaṇḍavyūha* as Giving the Essence of the Mahāyāna 99
8. The Buddha as Conceived in the Sutra and by Zen Masters 101

III. THE BODHISATTVA'S ABODE 107–166
1. Whence and Whither 107
2. 'The Mind that has no Abode' in the Mahāyāna Sūtras, and the Zen Masters 111
3. The Vairochana Tower as the Abode of the Bodhisattva 120
4. Sudhana's Song of the Abode 124
5. The Description of the Tower 132
6. Similes Explaining the Admission of Sudhana into the Tower 142
7. The Coming and Going of the Bodhisattva 144
8. The Vairochana Tower and the Dharmadhātu 147
9. The Fourfold Dharmadhātu 150
10. The Bodhisattva's Jñāna and Adhishthāna Explained 156
11. The Bodhisattva's Native Land and His Relatives 159
12. Zen Masters on the Abode of the Bodhisattva 164

IV. THE DESIRE FOR ENLIGHTENMENT (AS DEFINED IN THE GAṆḌAVYŪHA SŪTRA) 167–221
1. The Meaning of *Bodhicittotpāda* Defined 167

2. Sāgaramegha and the *Daśabhūmika* on the Desire for Enlightenment and the Constituents of Enlightenment 178
3. Maitreya's Sermon on the Bodhicitta 185
4. The Sermon Continued 191
5. Further Analogies Concluded 201
6. The Main Points Concerning the Bodhicitta Gathered up 214
7. The *Daśabhūmika* on the Desire for Enlightenment 218

V. The Significance of the Prajñā-Pāramitā-Hṛidaya Sūtra in Zen Buddhism 222–238
1. The Sanskrit Text of the *Hṛidaya* and its English Translations 222
2. The Analysis of the Sūtra 226
3. As the Psychological Document of Zen Experience 233

VI. The Philosophy and Religion of the Prajñāpāramitā 239–331
Preliminary 239
I. The Philosophy of the Prajñāpāramitā
1. Prajñā as the Directing Principle 243
2. The Prajñā Compared to the Bird's Wings and the Jar 244
3. The Prajñā as Mother of Buddhas and and Bodhisattvas 246
4. Prajñā = Sambodhi = Sarvajñatā 247
5. Prajñā as Seeing Things Yathābhūtam 251
6. Prajñā and Śūnyatā 255
7. Prajñā and Māyā 264
8. Prajñā and Intuitions 269

9. The Prajñā as Unattainable, and Relativity 272
10. The Prajñā and Irrationalities 277
11. The Unattainable and the Unattached 280
12. Reality as Seen from the Other Side 283
13. The Prajñā as Handled by Zen Masters 287

II. THE RELIGION OF THE PRAJÑĀPĀRAMITĀ 295
1. Where the Prajñā Functions 295
2. Upāya ('Skilful Means') 298
3. The Bodhisattva and the Śrāvaka 302
4. Śūnyatā Seen but Not Realized 307
5. Some of the Significant Opposites 313

III. RECAPITULATION 321

VII. BUDDHIST, ESPECIALLY ZEN, CONTRIBUTIONS TO JAPANESE CULTURE 332–366
1. The Buddhist Life 333
2. Non-ego, Emptiness, and Suchness Defined 338
3. The Three Methods of Buddhist Realization 343
4. Zen Characterized 346
5. Zen and Sumiye 350
6. Eternal Loneliness, and Bashō 355
7. Zen and the Art of Fencing 359
8. Takuan and Yagyū the Swordsman 362
9. The Tea-room 364

APPENDIX, ON JAPANESE BUDDHISM 367–378
Nara Buddhism 367
The Shadows Cast 369

Dengyō Daishi 370
Kōbō Daishi 371
Aristocratic Buddhism 372
Against the Spirit of Buddhism 372
Creative Buddhism: 1. Coming of Kūya Shōnin 373
Creative Buddhism: 2. Nichiren Appears 375
The Rise of Zen Buddhism in Kamakura Period 376
After Kamakura 376
Conclusion 378

VIII. THE ZEN LIFE IN PICTURES 379–385

INDEX 387

ILLUSTRATIONS

Plate		*Opposite page*
I	The Śakya Trinity	16
II	Ch'ing-liang the Zen Master	17
III	The Greeting of Amida with his suite of Bodhisattvas	32
IV	Śakya Trinity	33
V	Shoichi the National Teacher, the Founder of Tofukuji	64
VI	Samantabhadra and the Rakshasis	65
VII	Manjusri in a grass-robe	80
VIII	Samantabhadra	81
IX	The Solitary Angler	112
X	The 'Pa-Pa' Bird	113
XI	Hotei (Pu-tai) and two fighting cocks	128
XII–XIV	Three Landscapes	129
XV	(*a* and *b*) Han-shan and Shih-tê (by Mincho)	160
XVI	(*a* and *b*) Han-shan and Shih-tê (by Indra)	161
XVII	The Dancing Pu-tei	176
XVIII	Bodhidharma crossing the Ocean on a reed-leaf	177
XIX	The Three Laughing Ones by the Hu-ch'i	192
XX	Tsai-sung Tao-chê (The Pine Planter)	193
XXI	The Sixth Patriarch as a bamboo-cutter	208
XXII	(*a* and *b*) Hsien-tzu and Chu-t'ou	209
XXXIII	Hsien-tzu the Shrimp-catcher	240

Plate		Opposite page
XXIV	In the Morning Sun	241
XXV	Facing the Moon (ascribed to Mu-ch'i)	256
XXVI	Facing the Moon (ascribed to Pei-chien)	257
XXVII	Samantabhadra and the ten Rākshasīs	288
XXVIII	Kuan-yin carrying a fish-basket	289
XXIX	Samantabhadra as a courtesan	304
XXX	Bodhidharma and the Emperor Wu of Liang	305
XXXI	Ma-tsu, Pai-chang, and Huang-Po	336
XXXII	A Zen Master and a layman	337
XXXIII	Niao-k'ê and Pai Lê-t'ien	368

PREFACE

In this Third Series of *Zen Essays* I have tried to trace the relationship which exists between Zen and the two chief Mahāyāna sūtras, the *Gaṇḍavyūha* and the *Prajñāpāramitā*, and then the transformation through which Indian Buddhism had to go while adapting itself to Chinese psychology. The Chinese are a practical people quite different from the Indian, who are highly endowed with the power of abstraction as well as an inexhaustible mine of imagination. It was natural that the Mahāyāna teachings had to be so transformed as to make them appreciated by the Chinese. This meant that the *Prajñāpāramitā* and the *Gaṇḍavyūha* were to be converted into Zen dialogues.

As regards Zen contributions to Japanese culture, a special volume has been written.[1] Apart from Buddhism, apart from Zen after the Kamakura era, Japanese cultural history has no significance, so deeply has Buddhism entered into the lifeblood of the people. My attempt here is merely tentative. The section on 'The Zen Life in Pictures' is also a suggestion; a fuller and more systematic treatment awaits another opportunity.

A few facts are to be mentioned concerning the matter treated in this Series, which have come up while it was in the press. (1) The Tun-huang MS. of the *Sayings of Shên-hui* mentioned in p. 21 fn. and p. 37 fn. has already been reproduced in facsimile, while its printed and fully revised edition will be published before long. (2) Dr. Keiki Yabuki has published a book giving detailed explanations of the Tun-huang MSS. collected in his *Echoes of the Desert*. He supplies us with a wealth of useful information regarding them. (3) All page references to the *Gaṇḍavyūha* are either to the Idzumi MS. or to the R.A.S. one. (4) The Tun-huang MS. of Hui-nêng's *Tan-ching* (p. 15 fn.) will be printed and

[1] See *Zen Buddhism and its Influence on Japanese Culture*, 1938.

made accessible to the general public. It will be accompanied by the Koshoji copy of the same. The latter is an old Japanese reprint of the fifteenth or sixteenth century, the Chinese original of which was probably printed some time in the tenth or the eleventh century. Quite likely it is the 'older edition' referred to in a preface to the current edition of the *Tan-ching*. Its historical importance is beyond dispute.

The author's thanks are, as usual, due to his wife, Beatrice Lane Suzuki, for reviewing the whole MSS. and reading the proofs, and to Mrs. Ruth Fuller Everett, of Chicago, who also kindly read the proofs.

Reference to the generous encouragement of the author's friend, Yakichi Ataka, is not to be omitted just because he is always ready to respond unhesitatingly to all the requests of the author and to make the teachings of Zen Buddhism universally approachable within the limits of literary interpretation.

DAISETZ TEITARO SUZUKI

EDITOR'S FOREWORD

DAISETZ TEITARO SUZUKI, D.LITT., Professor of Buddhist Philosophy in the Otani University, Kyoto, was born in 1869. He is probably now the greatest living authority on Buddhist philosophy, and is certainly the greatest authority on Zen Buddhism. His major works in English on the subject of Buddhism number a dozen or more, and of his works in Japanese as yet unknown to the West there are at least eighteen. He is, moreover, as a chronological bibliography of books on Zen in English clearly shows, the pioneer teacher of the subject outside Japan, for except for Kaiten Nukariya's *Religion of the Samurai* (Luzac and Co., 1913) nothing was known of Zen as a living experience, save to the readers of *The Eastern Buddhist* (1921–1939) until the publication of *Essays in Zen Buddhism* (Volume I) in 1927.

Dr. Suzuki writes with authority. Not only has he studied original works in Sanskrit, Pali, Chinese and Japanese, but he has an up-to-date knowledge of Western thought in German and French as well as in the English, which he speaks and writes so fluently. He is, moreover, more than a scholar: he is a Buddhist. Though not a priest of any Buddhist sect, he is honoured in every temple in Japan, for his knowledge of spiritual things, as all who have sat at his feet bear witness, is direct and profound. When he speaks of the higher stages of consciousness he speaks as a man who dwells therein, and the impression he makes on those who enter the fringes of his mind is that of a man who seeks for the intellectual symbols wherewith to describe a state of awareness which lies indeed 'beyond the intellect'.

To those unable to sit at the feet of the Master his writings must be a substitute. All these, however, were out of print in England by 1940, and all remaining stocks in Japan were destroyed in the fire which consumed three quarters of Tokyo in 1945. When, therefore, I reached Japan in 1946, I arranged with the author for the Buddhist Society, London—my wife and myself as its nominees—to begin the publication of his Collected Works, reprinting the old favourites, and printing as fast as possible translations of the many new works which the Professor, self-immured in his house at Kyoto, had written during the war.

This undertaking, however, was beyond the powers of the Buddhist Society, and we therefore secured the assistance of Rider and Co., who, backed by the vast resources of the House of Hutchinson, can honour the needs of such a considerable task.

Of Zen itself I need say nothing here, but the increasing sale of books on the subject, such as *The Spirit of Zen* by Alan Watts (Murray) and the series of original translations of Chinese Zen Scriptures and other works published by the Buddhist Society, prove that the interest of the West is rising rapidly. Zen, however, is a subject extremely easy to misunderstand, and it is therefore important that the words of a qualified Master should come readily to hand.

CHRISTMAS HUMPHREYS
President of the Buddhist Society, London

PLATE I

SAKYA TRINITY

Ascribed to WU TAO-TZU, OF T'ANG
Owned by Tofukuji, One of the
Chief Zen Monasteries, Kyoto

Sakyamuni, the central figure, sits as tradition goes, on a grass seat, and white clouds rise around the rock on which the Great Sage has his seat spread. He wears a reddish robe and his arms are held before his chest to form a mudra, reminding one of a Shingon figure. Mañjuśrī sits on the lion and Samantabhadra on the elephant, both with more or less personal decorations, though in easy postures. They are all incomparably serene and dignified, with an atmosphere of power and spirituality.

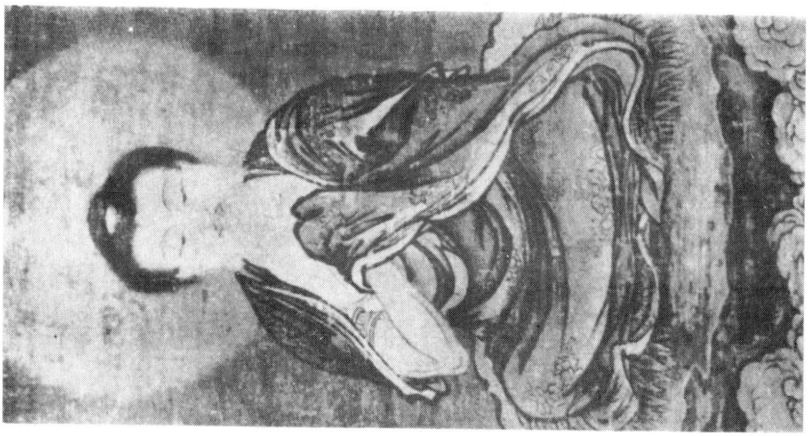

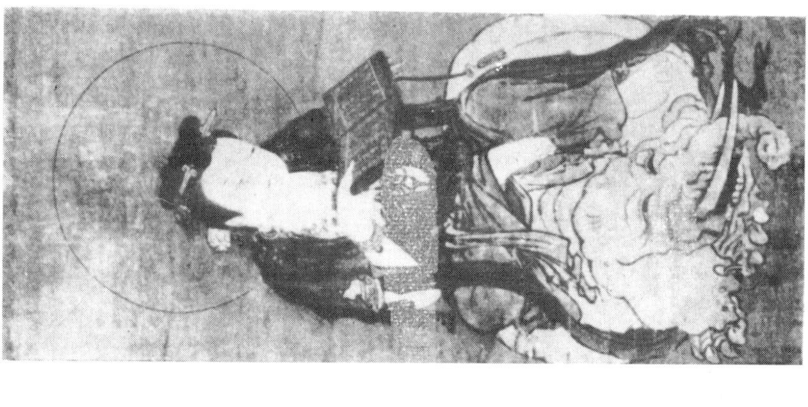

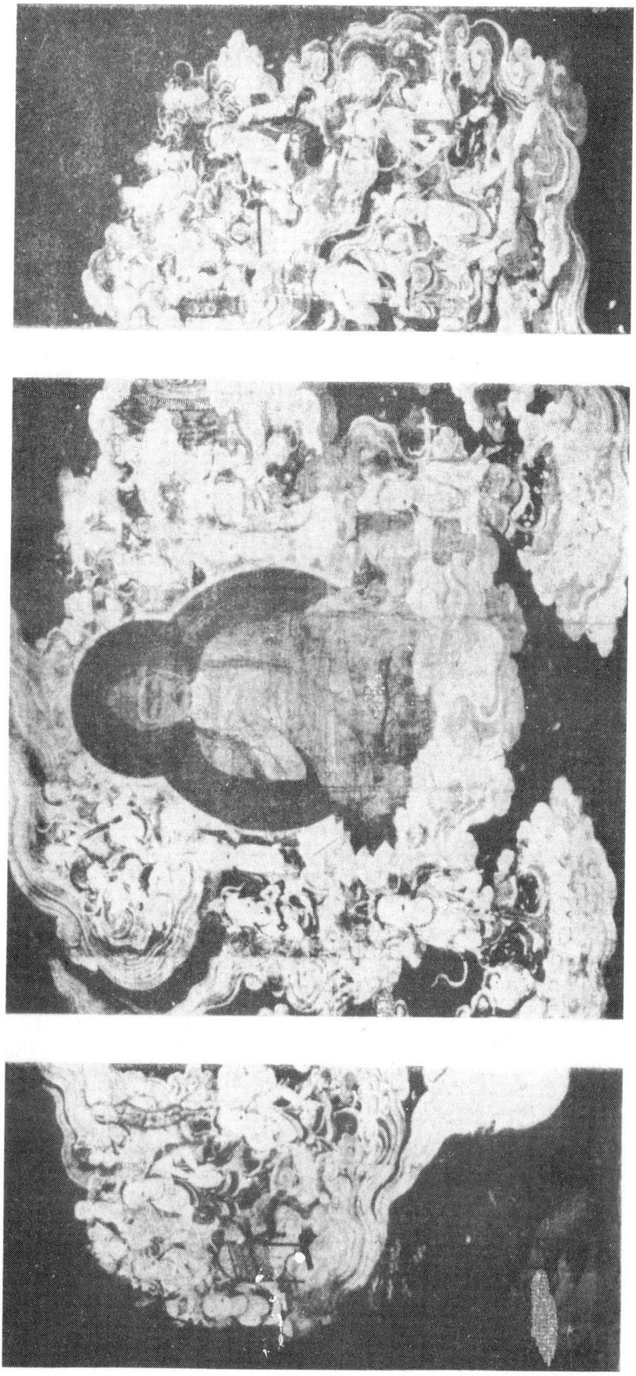

PLATE II

CH'ING-LIANG THE ZEN MASTER

Ascribed to MA YÜAN

(*Late in the 12th Century*)

In fact this can be any Zen master. The main thing that concerns us here is that a Zen interview may take place at any time and anywhere, no formal lecturing in the Hall is needed, no congregational meeting is to be announced. A monk-student may accost the master while the latter is working in the garden, or walking among the pines, or reading the sutras before the Buddha, or lying on a sick-bed, and ask him, "Where is the Way?" or "What is the Buddha?" Zen always keeps itself in the most iniimate manner with life. There is no conceptualism in Zen. Hsüan-sha (835–908) was one day treating General Wei to tea, when Wei asked, "What is meant by the statement that people do not know it even when they are daily making use of it?" Sha offered him a piece of cake saying, "Please take it." Wei accepted it, ate it, and resumed the question. Thereupon the master said, "We just make use of it everyday and yet fail to know it." And no doubt here is one of the strong points we can make out for Zen dicipline. It is no more quiet-sitting, no being absorbed in meditation, no whole-hearted sinking into idealistic somnambulism. I wish to emphasise forcibly this aspect of the Zen life against the Indian idea of mere tranquillisation.

Ch'ing-liang the Zen master, (as Fa-yên Wên-I, see *Zen Essays*, I, p. 275,) once told his attendant-monk to get more soil for his lotus. When he brought it in, the master asked, "Did you get it from the east of the Bridge, or from the west of it?" The monk answered, "From the east of the Bridge." The master asked again, "Is that a truth? Or is that a falsehood?"

The master asked a monk, "Where do you come from?" "I come from the Pao-ên." "Are the monks there all getting on well?" "Yes, they are." "Sit down and have a cup of tea," finished the master.

Another monk was asked, "Where do you come from?" "I come from Szu-chou where I paid my respect to the Great Image of the Buddha." "Will he come out of the Pagoda this year?" "Yes, he will." The master turned aside and, addressing another monk beside him, said, "You tell me whether he was at Szu-chou or not."

I. FROM ZEN TO THE GANDAVYŪHA

I

IN THE beginning of its history Zen had no special affiliation with the *Gaṇḍavyūha Sūtra* such as it had with the *Laṅkāvatāra* or the *Vajracchedikā*. The *Laṅkāvatāra* was given by Bodhidharma to his chief Chinese disciple, Hui-k'ê, as the sūtra containing a doctrine closely related to Zen, and after Hui-k'ê the sūtra was studied chiefly by Zen followers. The *Vajracchedikā* came to be known among them at the time of Hung-jên and Hui-nêng, about one hundred and fifty years after Bodhidharma. Shên-hui, however, who was one of the principal disciples of Hui-nêng, goes so far as to declare that it was indeed the *Vajracchedikā* that was handed by the father of Zen to Hui-k'ê.[1] Though this statement may not be historically correct, we may safely assert that the *Vajracchedikā* came to exert great influence upon the study of Zen about this time, i.e. late in the seventh century. The connection of the *Gaṇḍavyūha* with Zen did not begin until the time of Têng-kuan (738–839), the fourth Patriarch of the Avataṁsaka School of Buddhism in China, who studied Zen under Wu-ming, a disciple of Shên-hui. Têng-kuan was a great philosopher and endeavoured to incorporate the teaching of Zen into his own system. After him came Tsung-mi of Kuei-fêng (780–842), who also studied Zen and produced the great commentary on the *Engaku-kyo*,[2] 'Sūtra of Perfect Enlightenment', which he interpreted according to the philosophy of his school. He also wrote a book on the different ways of understanding

[1] According to a recently recovered MS. containing sayings of Shên-hui. The MS. will be edited and published before long by the author of the present *Essays*.

[2] *Yüan-chiao-ching*.

Zen which, except for the introduction, is unfortunately lost. The idea was to point out the essentials of Zen and to distinguish them from the misinterpretations which were then prevalent not only as regards Zen itself but as regards its relationship to Buddhist philosophy. Thus through Tsung-mi Zen came to be related to other sūtras than the *Laṅkāvatāra*, the *Vajracchedikā*, and especially to the *Gaṇḍavyūha*.

While scholars of the Avataṁsaka School were making use of the intuitions of Zen in their own way, the Zen masters were drawn towards the philosophy of Identity and Interpenetration advocated by the Avataṁsaka, and attempted to incorporate it into their own discourses. For instance, Shih-t'ou[1] in his 'Ode on Identity' depicts the mutuality of Light and Dark as restricting each other and at the same time being fused in each other; Tung-shan[2] in his metrical composition called 'Sacred Mirror Samādhi' discourses on the mutuality of *P'ien*, 'one-sided', and *Chêng*, 'correct', much to the same effect as Shih-t'ou in his Ode, for both Shih-t'ou and Tung-shan belong to the school of Hsing-szŭ[3] known as the Ts'ao-tung branch of Zen Buddhism. This idea of Mutuality and Identity is no doubt derived from Avataṁsaka philosophy, so ably formulated by Fa-tsang.[4] As both Shih-t'ou and Tung-shan are Zen masters, their way of presenting it is not at all like that of the metaphysician. Perhaps Lin-chi's 'Fourfold *Liao-chien*'[5] too may be traced back to the system of Fa-tsang.

The influence of Avataṁsaka philosophy on Zen masters grew more and more pronounced as time went on, and reached its climax in the tenth century after the passing of Tsung-mi, the fifth patriarch of the Avataṁsaka School in China. It was Fa-yen Wên-i,[6] the founder of the Fa-yen branch of Zen Buddhism, who incorporated the philosophy of the Avataṁsaka into his treatment of Zen. Though he did not belong to their school he must have been greatly impressed with the works of Tu-shun (died 640) and Fa-tsang

[1] 699–790. [2] 806–859. [3] Died 740. [4] Died 712.
[5] *Liao-chien* means 'to consider', 'to estimate'. [6] 885–958.

(died 712), and other Avataṁsaka philosophers; for there is evidence of his having made his pupils study their writings as an aid to the mastery of Zen. He also wrote a commentary on Shih-t'ou's 'Ode on Identity', which is, as I said before, based on the metaphysics of the *Avataṁsaka*.

The culmination of this movement, the syncretic movement to unite Zen with the philosophy of the *Avataṁsaka* or of the *Saddharma-puṇḍarīka*, was reached when Yên-shou of Yung-ming[1] wrote his *magnum opus* the *Tsung-ching-lu*, 'Records of the Spiritual Mirror', in one hundred fascicles. In this he attempts to melt all the differences of Buddhist thought in the doctrine of Mind-only—understanding by 'Mind' an ultimate reality which is aware of itself, and is not the seat of our empirical consciousness. This doctrine of Mind-only is not to be confused with the Vijñaptimātra philosophy of the Yogācāra, for Yên-shou follows the thought-current running through the *Laṇkāvatāra*, the *Avataṁsaka*, the *Śraddhotpāda*, etc.[2]

2

Properly speaking, Zen has its own field where it functions to its best advantage. As soon as it wanders outside this field, it loses its natural colour and to that extent ceases to be itself. When it attempts to explain itself by means of a philosophical system it is no longer Zen pure and simple; it partakes of something which does not strictly belong to it. However rational the explanation may be, Zen is then adulterated. For this reason, the masters have been jealous to see that it was not associated with any school of metaphysics, whether Buddhist or Taoist or Confucian. Even when Bodhidharma handed the *Laṅkā* over to Hui-k'ê, the latter and his followers refused to write anything on it in the

[1] 904–975.

[2] It may incidentally be mentioned that a Zen master's commentary on the *Avataṁsaka* was written as early as the seventh century, for a catalogue of the Chinese Tripitaka records that Shên-hsiu, who died in 706, wrote thirty fascicles on the *Avataṁsaka*.

nature of a commentary or an exposition. Though Hui-nêng seems to have edited the *Vajracchedikā* according to his own light, his descendants altogether neglected it, and their sermons and dialogues developed in quite a different direction. Of course, they make frequent references to all kinds of sūtras and śastras, quoting passages from them freely, but they are always careful not to get involved in the letter, not to be tinged with the philosophical ideas forming the background of these writings.

The *Avataṁsaka Sūtra* was quoted by Zen masters even prior to Tu-shun, for, according to the *Masters and Disciples of the Laṅkā*, Hui-k'ê extensively refers to the sūtra in support of his view that the One circulates throughout a world of particulars, while Tao-hsin, a contemporary of Tu-shun, also quotes a passage from the sūtra saying that a particle of dust contains innumerable worlds within itself. Being Zen masters, they made no attempts to systematize their Zen intuitions; they were satisfied with quoting for authority passages which harmonized with their ideas. Therefore, their quotations were not limited to the *Avataṁsaka*; wherever they found statements they could use they did so, for example from *Saddharma-puṇḍarīka*, *Vimalakīrti*, *Vajracchedikā*, *Laṅkāvatāra*, *Prajñāpāramitā*, *Dharmapada*, etc. But in the case of the *Avataṁsaka*, the reference is more than local and specific, it is concerned with the entire thought pervading the sūtra. It is likely from this fact that Zen masters regarded the sūtra from the first as one which supported their experiences even to the extent of the *Laṅkā* and *Vajra*. But as their position was to uphold the spirit and neglect the letter altogether, they did not go so far as to formulate a Zen philosophy after the *Avataṁsaka*. They were always careful to abide with facts and not ideas. For they say, quoting the *Avataṁsaka*:

'It is like a poor man counting up day and night treasures which do not belong to him, while he has not a cent to his name. So with much learning. Again, for a while you may read books, but be careful to set them aside as soon as possible. If you do not quit them, you will get into the habit of learning letters only. This is like seeking ice by heating running water, or like seeking snow by boiling up hot water. Therefore, it is sometimes said by the Buddhas that [ultimate truth] is explicable and sometimes that it is not explicable. The fact is that there is nothing explicable or inexplicable in Reality itself, which is the state of all things that are. When this one thing is thoroughly grasped, all the other thousand things follow. So it is said in the *Saddharmapuṇḍarīka* that [Reality] is neither real nor unreal, neither such nor not such.'[1]

3

The sūtras, especially Mahāyāna sūtras, are direct expressions of spiritual experiences; they contain intuitions gained by digging deeply into the abyss of the Unconscious, and they make no pretension of presenting these intuitions through the mediumship of the intellect. If they appear to be at all ratiocinative and logically demonstrative, this is merely accidental. All the sūtras attempt to give the deepest intuitions of the Buddhist mind as they presented themselves to the early Indian Mahāyāna followers. Therefore, when the sūtras declare all things to be empty, unborn, and beyond causation, the declaration is not the result of metaphysical reasoning; it is a most penetrating Buddhist experience. This is why so many scholars and philosophers of Buddhism who endeavour to understand or interpret these intuitions according to rules of logic fail in their endeavours; they are outsiders, so to speak, in Buddhist experience, and consequently they are bound to miss the mark.

The sūtra intuitions and those of the Zen Master are the same in so far as they are all Buddhist. Whatever differences there may be in expression are owing to the psychology of the Indian and the Chinese genius. Inasmuch as

[1] A sermon given by Hui-k'ê as recorded in the *Masters and Disciples of the Laṅkā*.

Zen is a form of Indian Buddhism transplanted into China, its experiences are fundamentally the same as those of Buddhism. But the psychological differentia of the people assert themselves when the experiences begin to be localized in harmony with the new conditions under which they are to develop. The process of this differentiation is clearly traceable in the sermons of the Zen masters as they are separated further from the direct influence of the first master from India. As Zen takes hold of the Chinese mentality, its expressions grow typically Chinese, and one even begins to suspect their essential identity with the original. When the differentiation has progressed so far as to make it look as if it were going to revolt against itself, the masters hurry to repair the damage and to reconcile it with its own source. This is really the meaning of that movement which manifested itself strongly in the eighth and the ninth century, for instance under Tsung-mi or Fa-yen.

Let me give examples of the gradual change which took place in the expression of Zen intuition during the five hundred years which followed the introduction of Zen into China by Bodhidharma, a monk from India who died presumably in A.D. 528. In the following pages are quoted sermons given by Zen masters of the various schools which arose during those years. In them we mark the shifting of the sūtra type of discourse to that of the Chinese Zen type.

4

Let us start with Bodhidharma, the father of Chinese Zen, who writes on *Wu-hsin* (literally, 'no-mind'):[1]

[1] This is taken from Dr. Keiki Yabuki's *Echoes of the Desert* (folio 77) containing collotype reproductions of some of the Tun-huang Buddhist MSS. kept in the British Museum. This Discourse ascribed to Bodhidharma is not mentioned in any of the Zen histories we have at present and there is no way to decide its authenticity. The MS. is not in the best style of writing.

Wu-hsin is one of those difficult Chinese words which are untranslat-

'The ultimate Reason itself is without words, but to give expression to it words are borrowed. The great Way has no form, but in order to come in contact with the uncultivated it reveals itself in form. Now let us suppose that there are two persons engaged in the discussion of the Unconscious. The disciple asks the master:

'D.: Is [the ultimate Reason] conscious or unconscious?

'M.: It is unconscious.

'D.: If it is unconscious, who is it that does all the seeing, hearing, remembering, and recognizing?[1] Who is it that recognizes the Unconscious?

'M.: Just because of the Unconscious, seeing, hearing, remembering, and recognizing are possible; just because of the Unconscious, the Unconscious is recognized.

'D.: How is it possible for the Unconscious to see, to hear, to remember, or to recognize? The Unconscious would be incapable of all this.

'M.: Though I am of the Unconscious, I can see, hear, remember, and recognize.

'D.: If you can see, hear, remember, and recognize, you cannot be of the Unconscious; you must be a conscious being.

'M.: To see, to hear, to remember, and to recognize—these are the very acts of the Unconscious. Apart from the seeing, hearing, remembering, and recognizing, there is no Unconscious. I am afraid you do not understand this, and I will see to it that the matter is explained step by step and you are led to see into the truth. For instance, seeing being done, it is said that there is a seeing, and this is because

able. *Wu* is a negative term and *hsin* comprises various meanings. It is 'mind', 'heart', 'soul', 'a regulating principle', 'a mental attitude', 'consciousness', 'voluntariness', etc. In the present case, *Wu-hsin* is 'unconsciousness' in its ordinary, empirical sense, and at the same time it means the Unconscious as underlying all our activities mental and bodily, conscious and unconscious. In this translation the term is freely translated according to the sense it acquires in the context.

[1] Literally, 'the seen, heard, thought, and known', *dṛiṣṭa-śruta-mata-jñāta* in Sanskrit, comprehensively sums up the activities of mind, that is, consciousness. It is most important not to confuse the Unconscious with the unconscious referred to in psychology and biology.

there is the not-seeing; the seeing thus is even of the Unconscious. ·Hearing being done, it is said that there is a hearing, and this is because there is the not-hearing; the hearing is even of the Unconscious. Remembering being done, it is said that there is a remembering, and this is because there is the not-remembering; the remembering is even of the Unconscious. Recognizing being done, it is said that there is a recognizing, and this is because there is the not-recognizing; the recognizing is even of the Unconscious. A work being done, it is said that there is a doing, and this doing is indeed not-doing; the doing is even of the Unconscious. Therefore, we say that seeing, hearing, remembering, and recognizing—all these are of the Unconscious.

'D.: How can we know that this is of the Unconscious?

'M.: You examine into the matter more closely and tell me if Mind has any perceivable form. If you say that it has, such will not be real Mind. Is it to be considered existing within, or without, or midway? Mind is not to be located at any of these three points. Nor is it to be perceived as existing in any other possible places. Hence the Unconscious.

'D.: O master, if it is the Unconscious that prevails everywhere, there should be neither guilt nor merit. Why do all beings transmigrate in the six paths of existence and constantly go on through birth and death?

'M.: This is because all beings are so confused in mind as to conceive the illusive idea of [an individual] reality in the Unconscious, and, creating all kinds of deeds, erroneously cling to the notion that there is really a conscious mind. For this reason, they transmigrate in the six paths of existence and constantly go on through birth and death.

'It is like a man's seeing in the dark a table or a piece of rope which he takes for a departed spirit or for a snake, and getting terrified at his own imagination. In like manner all beings illusively cling to their own creations. Where there is the Unconscious, they erroneously imagine the reality of a conscious mind. Thus various sorts of deeds are performed, and there is really transmigration in the six paths of existence. Such beings are advised to see a good friend, great [in his spiritual insight], and to practise meditation which will lead them to the realization of the Unconscious. When this is done, all their karma-hindrances vanish and the chain of birth and death is cut asunder. As the sunlight once penetrating into the darkness dispels all that is dark, all their sins are destroyed when they realize the Unconscious.

'D.: Being an ignoramus, my mind is not yet quite clear as to the functioning of the six senses as they respond everywhere [to the stimulation].[1]

'M.: Various contrivances are carried on by words.

'D.: Evil passions and enlightenment, birth-and-death and Nirvāṇa—are these indeed of the Unconscious?

'M.: Assuredly they are of the Unconscious. Just because of all beings' erroneous clinging to the idea of a conscious mind there are all kinds of evil passions and birth-and-death, enlightenment, and Nirvāṇa. If they are awakened to the Unconscious, there are no evil passions, no birth-and-death, no Nirvāṇa. Therefore, for the sake of those who harbour the idea of a conscious mind, the Tathāgata talks of birth-and-death; enlightenment is opposed to evil passions, and Nirvāṇa to birth-and-death. All these names are mutually conditioning. When the Unconscious is attained, there are neither evil passions nor enlightenment, neither birth-and-death nor Nirvāṇa.

'D.: If there is neither enlightenment nor Nirvāṇa, how do we account for the enlightenment which is said to have been attained by Buddhas of the past?

'M.: This is talked of because of conventional phraseology. As long as absolute truth is considered, there is no such thing. Therefore, it is said in the *Vimalakīrti* that there is no body in which enlightenment is to be realized, no mind by which enlightenment is to be realized. Again, it is

[1] Something is missing in this question and as it stands it yields no sense. The master's reply too does not seem quite to the point.

said in the *Vajracchedikā* that there is not a thing, not a reality which one can claim to have attained, that all the Buddhas' attainment is really non-attainment. Therefore, let it be known that all things rise when a conscious mind is asserted, and that all things cease to exist when the Unconscious is realized.

'D.: O master, you say that the Unconscious obtains everywhere. Now, wood and rock are of the Unconscious; are not then [all sentient beings] like wood and rock?

'M.: But the Unconscious realized in my conscious mind is not that of wood and rock. Why? It is like the celestial drum, which, while lying still, spontaneously and without conscious efforts, produces varieties of exquisite sound in order to teach and discipline all beings. It is again like a wish-fulfilling gem (*maṇi*) which, without conscious effort on its own part, creates spontaneously varieties of form. In like manner, the Unconscious works through my conscious mind, making it understand the true nature of Reality; it is furnished with true transcendental wisdom, it is the master of the Triple Body, it functions with the utmost freedom. So, we read in the *Ratnakūṭa* that the mind functions by means of the Unconscious without being conscious of it. How can we then be like wood and rock? The Unconscious is the true Mind, the true Mind is the Unconscious.

'D.: How shall we discipline ourselves then with this [relative] mind of ours?

'M.: Only let us be awakened to the Unconscious in all things, in all our doings—this is the way of discipline, there is no other way. Thus we know that when the Unconscious is realized, all things cease to trouble us.

'Hearing this, the disciple all at once had an illumination and realized that there is no matter outside mind, and no mind outside matter; in all his behaviour and activities he acquired perfect freedom; all his net of doubts was torn to pieces, and he felt no obstructions.'

Tao-hsin,[1] generally regarded as the Fourth Patriarch of

[1] Died A.D. 651.

Zen Buddhism in China, gives the following sermons on 'The Abandoning of the Body'.[1]

'The method of abandoning the body consists first in meditating on Emptiness, whereby the [conscious] mind is emptied. Let the mind together with its world be quietened down to a perfect state of tranquillity; let thought be cast in the mystery of quietude, so that the mind is kept from wandering from one thing to another. When the mind is tranquillized in its deepest abode, its entanglements are cut asunder. How unfathomable! How abysmal! The mind in its absolute purity is the Void itself. How almost unconcerned it appears! Like death there is no breathing. It abides in the utmost purity of the Dharmakāya, and is no longer subject to a future becoming. When a [conscious] mind is stirred and confusion takes place in it, one cannot escape suffering another form of existence. Therefore, let a man discipline himself first of all in the realization of a perfect state of quietude in his mind and also in its world. This is the way the discipline ought to be carried out.

'But in this discipline there is really nothing to take hold of as a definite achievement, and this non-achievement is what is achieved by the discipline, for Reality is grasped by non-striving, and non-striving is truth itself. Therefore, we read in the sūtra, "Emptiness, non-striving, desirelessness, formlessness—this is true emancipation!" For this reason, Reality is non-striving.

'The way to abandon the body is to have a penetrating insight into its provisional nature, when the mind together with its world becomes transparent and its functions illuminated.

'Further, said the master, according to Chuang-tzŭ, "Heaven and earth are one finger, and ten thousand things are one horse." [But this is not exact.] The *Dharmapada* says: "The One is not to be thought one. In order to destroy the idea of multiplicity, the One is said to be one, but this is

[1] This is recorded in the *Masters and Disciples of the Laṅkā* recently recovered at Tun-huang and published at Peiping, 1932.

meant for the shallow-minded." [This being so,] we can state that Chuang-tzŭ fails to go beyond oneness.

'According to Lao-tzŭ: "How unfathomable! How abysmal! Within, there is Essence!" With Lao-tzŭ, an outside form is got rid of, but he still holds on to a mind within. The *Avataṁsaka* states, "Do not cling to dualism, because there is neither one nor two!" The *Vimalakīrti* states, "Mind is not within, nor without, nor in the midway—this is realization." For this reason, we know that Lao-tzŭ still stands with the idea of a mind-essence.'

In another place Tao-hsin explains what is meant by quietude and Emptiness in the following manner:

'Reflect on your own body and see what it is. It is empty and devoid of reality like a shadow. It is perceived [as if it actually exists], but there is nothing there to take hold of. Prajñā rises in the midst of these shadowy objects, where it is fixed it has no ultimate abode. Remaining itself immovable, it enters into relations and endlessly suffers transformations.

'Out of the midst of Emptiness there rise the six senses, and the six senses too are of Emptiness, while the six sense-objects are perceived as like a dream or a vision. It is like the eye perceiving its objects; they are not located in it. Like the mirror on which your features are reflected, they are perfectly perceived there in all clearness; the reflections are all there in the emptiness, yet the mirror itself retains not one of the objects which are reflected there. The human face has not come to enter into the body of the mirror, nor has the mirror gone out to enter into the human face. When one realizes how the mirror and the face stand to each other and that there is from the beginning no entering, no going-out, no passing, no coming into relation with each other, one comprehends the signification of Suchness and Emptiness.'[1]

[1] The translation is a free one.

5

It can readily be seen that Bodhidharma and Tao-hsin are speaking of the same subject from different angles of understanding. Bodhidharma's *Wu-hsin*, 'the Unconscious', is 'the Empty', 'the Serene', 'the Abysmal', etc., of Tao-hsin. The one uses psychological terms while the other is inclined to Prajñā philosophy. While Bodhidharma's discourse on *Wu-hsin* may be regarded as still in accordance with the Indian way of thinking, Tao-hsin's is more or less tinged with Taoist thought. Nothing properly of Zen, however, has yet made its appearance with them. It was with Hui-nêng and his successors that Zen began to be distinctly Chinese both in its expression and in its interpretation.

The consciousness of Zen specifically as the 'immediate understanding' of the Unconscious[1] dawned in the mind of Hui-nêng. If Bodhidharma used the term, *wu-hsin*, for the Unconscious, Hui-nêng replaced *hsin* by *nien*. *Nien* is generally 'memory', 'recollection', 'thinking of the past', etc., and is used as equivalent to the Sanskrit *smṛti*. Therefore, when it is used in connection with *wu* as *wu-nien*, this is *asmṛti*, that is, 'loss of meaning' or 'forgetfulness', and in this sense it is used in the Sanskrit texts. The use of *wu-nien*, however, in the sense of 'unconsciousness', and pregnant with a deep spiritual significance, as far as I can gather, begins with Hui-nêng. *Wu-nien* is not here mere forgetfulness, or not remembering what one is doing; it is not a simple psychological term. When Hui-nêng makes the *Wu-nien* the most fundamental fact in the life of Zen, it corresponds to the Triple Emancipation—*śūnyatā*, *animitta*, and *apraṇihita*[2]—for the realization of the *Wu-nien* means emancipation for Zen followers. And the term is essentially Chinese.

The other idea original with Hui-nêng is the doctrine of 'Abruptness' (*tun*), i.e. of immediate understanding of

[1] *Tun-wu, wu-nien.*
[2] Emptiness, no-form, and non-striving.

Reality. According to him, Zen realization is characterized by abruptness or immediacy, for this is the nature of Prajñā itself. The doctrine of 'Gradualness' (*chien*) maintained by his rival, Shên-hsiu, ought not to be applied to the intuition which takes place in Zen meditation. Prajñā acts intuitively, and what it perceives is perceived at once, without any mediation or deliberation or interrupting process. 'In my teaching,' so says Hui-nêng, 'there is no distinction between Dhyāna and Prajñā;[1] Dhyāna is the body of Prajñā, and Prajñā is the function of Dhyāna. When you have Prajñā, Dhyāna is in Prajñā; when you have Dhyāna, Prajñā is in Dhyāna. They are one and not two.' By thus diving deeply into the abyss of Reality, Hui-nêng instructed his followers to see the intuitive light of Prajñā flash through the hard crust of an empirical consciousness. The mere sinking into the deep abyss was not the object of Zen discipline; unless Dhyāna culminated in an immediate intuition (*tun-wu*), there was no Zen in it. Let us now see what Hui-nêng has to say about the Unconscious (*wu-nien*).[2]

'Good friends, our teaching, since days of yore, whether of the "Abrupt" school or of the "Gradual", is established on the foundation of the Unconscious (*wu-nien*), while formlessness (*wu-hsiang*) is its body and not-abiding-anywhere[3] (*wu-chu*) is its root. What is meant by formlessness? It means not to get attached to form while admitting it. To be unconscious means to be innocent of the working of [a relative mind]. Not-abiding-anywhere is the original nature of a living being. [Consciousness as we perceive its working] moves ever forward, never halting in its progress through divisions of time as one thought succeeds another uninterruptedly. In order to get down, however, to the Dharmakāya [which is the Unconscious], the stream is to be cut through for once, for then we shall be separated from the

[1] *Ting* and *hui*.

[2] The following passage is taken from the Tun-huang MS. of the *Tan-ching* incorporated in the Taisho Edition of the Tripitaka, No. 2007.

[3] *Wu-hsiang wei t'i, wu-chu wei pên.*

PLATE III

THE GREETING AMIDA WITH HIS SUITE OF BODHISATTVAS

Ascribed to YESHIN SODZU

In the Koya Museum

According to the Pure Land teaching, Amida accompanied by twenty-five Bodhisattvas comes to greet the entrance of a pious soul into the Land of Purity at the moment of his early death. The holy host comes with music on violet-coloured clouds. They all seem to be perfectly happy over the fact that a new recruit has been added to their spiritual kingdom. Perhaps this is the way all good spirits are rejoiced when an act of goodness is performed in the universe. Again perhaps this was the way the Bodhisattvas came from all the ten quarters to join the spiritual assemblage of Sakyamuni the Buddha at Jetavana, which is most elaborately described in the *Gandavyuha*. In the Mahayana the universe is the Dharmadhatu where each single dharma, however insignificant, is intimately related to all other dharmas, individually and collectively, morally and physically. Therefore, not only Amida but all the Buddhas in the ten quarters are seriously concerned with the spiritual welfare of each individual soul. So we see that the idea of the Greeting Amida is translatable into terms of our earthly life.

PLATE IV
ŚAKYA TRINITY

By Motonobu Kano

Here is another Sakya trinity with Mañjuśrī on a lion and Samantabhadra on an elephant. They are shorn of all forms of personal decoration such as are noticeable in most pictures of this character. The central figure is an embodiment of eternal serenity; but the two side-figures are not distant and unapproachable; there is even something of humanity in them, whose counterparts may be found among the masters made familiar to us by Zen artists. This indicates a strong tendency and practice among Buddhists generally to bring down the Bodhisattvas among them so that they can be friends in every possible way. That this has actually been achieved is seen in some of the following pictures.

Rūpakāya [i.e. this physical body], and there is here no abiding of thought anywhere on anything. If thought abides anywhere on anything for once, the whole series ceases to flow unclogged—this is called being in bondage. When there is no abiding of thought anywhere on anything—this is being unbound. Thus, not-abiding-anywhere is the root [of our life].

'Good friends, to be separated from all the external form is to be formless. When this is realized, the nature and body [of the Unconscious] is found pure and devoid of impurities. Hence formlessness is the body.

'Not to be defiled by any external objects—this is known to be one with the Unconscious, that is, to be detached from objects though they are present in consciousness; for consciousness is not engaged in weaving thoughts concerning them. When thus all [irrelevant] thoughts are discarded, consciousness is cleared off from all its defilements. When this consciousness is once for all swept clean, there will be no future becoming. Let students of Buddhism take heed not to go astray in this matter. When the meaning is not well grasped, not only they themselves become confused but others take share in the confusion and will be led to blaspheme the teaching. Hence the Unconscious is established as the foundation.

'When people are merely dependent on names, they contrive to have varieties of thought about the objective world, and these thoughts lead further on to evil intentions. All erroneous ideas that characterize this worldly life take their rise here. So it is that our teaching is established on the foundation of the Unconscious. Let people be advised to get rid of their one-sided views in order not to give rise to entangling thoughts. When thoughts are not at all aroused the Unconscious itself will cease to be obtrusive.

'When we speak of annulling (*wu*), what is it that is to be annulled? What is meant by thought or consciousness (*nien*)? To annul means to be separated from dualism, to be freed from all worldly thoughts. Consciousness rises from Suchness; Suchness is its body, and consciousness is the functioning of Suchness. Consciousness, inevitably from the nature of Suchness, functions to see, to hear, to recollect, and to comprehend, but Suchness itself is not defiled by multiplicities of objects, it forever remains free, master of itself. So we read in the *Vimalakīrti*, "When all external objects and conditions are adequately discriminated, the ultimate inner principle retains its immovability." '

Wu-nien, the Unconscious, according to Hui-nêng, is the name not only for ultimate reality but for the state of consciousness in which the ultimate presents itself. As long as our individual consciousness remains severed from Reality which is at its back, its strivings are ego-centred consciously or unconsciously, and the outcome is a feeling of loneliness and pain. Consciousness must be made somehow to relate to the Unconscious, if it is not; and if it is, the relation must be realized, and this realization is known as *Wu-nien*, literally, a state of 'thoughtlessness'.

Chinese or Sanskrit terms when translated literally are frequently subject to gross misunderstandings. *Wu-nien* is one of them, for 'thoughtlessness' will surely be a most undesirable state of mind as the goal of Zen discipline, in fact as the goal of any spiritual exercise. Even 'the Unconscious' may not be a very appropriate term. Let us further listen to Hui-nêng, who goes on to explain what he means by *Wu-nien*, 'the unconscious':

'Good friends, to have an insight for once is to know what Buddhahood means. When the light of Prajñā[1] penetrates the ground nature of consciousness, it illuminates inside and outside; everything grows transparent, and one recognizes one's own inmost mind. To recognize the inmost mind is emancipation. When emancipation is attained, Prajñā-Samādhi obtains. To realize Prajñā-Samādhi means to have the Unconscious.

'What is the Unconscious? It is to see all things as they are and not to become attached to anything; it is to be present in all places and yet not to become attached anywhere; it is to remain for ever in the purity of self-nature;

[1] *Prajñā* is another significant idea with Hui-nêng.

it is to let the six sense-robbers run out of the six sense-gates into the world of the six sense-objects, and yet not to become defiled therein, nor to get away therefrom; it is but to retain perfect freedom in going and coming. This is to realize Prajñā-Samādhi, to be master of oneself, to become emancipated, and is known as living the Unconscious. If no thought rises on anything whatever, this means the cessation of consciousness, and such is in the bondage of the Dharma, it is a one-sided view.

'He who understands the teaching of the Unconscious has a most thoroughgoing knowledge of all things. He who understands the teaching of the Unconscious sees into the spiritual realm of all Buddhahood. He who understands the "abrupt" teaching of the Unconscious reaches the stage of Buddhahood.'

The doctrine of the Unconscious (*wu-nien*) together with that of immediate understanding (*tun-wu*) was the chief topic of interest in the days of Hui-nêng and his followers. 'Immediate understanding' is the Chinese translation of Prajñā, and 'the Unconscious' is the Chinese way of describing the realization of Emptiness (*śūnyatā*) and No-birth (*anutpāda*). In one sense the Laotzŭan teaching of Non-action (*wu-wei*) may be said to be living in the Unconscious of Hui-nêng. It is true that Buddhist philosophy has *Wu-shêng*, *Wu-yüan*, *Wu-tso*, *Wu-kuang-yung*,[1] etc., and *Wu-nien* can be regarded as coming from these conceptions.[2] There is no doubt, however, that Taoism had something to contribute to the establishment of Zen Buddhism, which we consider distinctively an elaboration of the Chinese genius.

[1] *Anutpāda, apraṇihitā, anabhisaṁskara, anābhoga.*

[2] In the *Aṣṭaśahasrikā* (Mitra Edition, p. 5), we have: *Punaraparaṁ bhagavan bodhisatvena mahāsatvena prajñāpāramitāyāṁ caratā prajñāpāramitāyāṁ bhāvayatā evaṁ śikṣitavyaṁ yathāsau śikṣyamāṇas tenāpi bodhicittena na manyeta. Tat kasya hetos tathā hi tac cittam acittaṁ prakṛitiś cittasya prabhāsvarā.* Further on (p. 19) we read: *Kena kāraṇena āyuṣman subhūte tatrāpi citte aśakto 'paryāpannaḥ. Subhūtir āha: Acittatvād ayuṣman sāriputra tatrāpi citte aśakto 'paryāpannaḥ. Na manyeta* and *acittatva* may be regarded as corresponding to the Chinese *wu-nien* and *wu-hsin*. There is another Sanskrit term, *manaskāra*, which is generally rendered by *tso-i*, and the negation, *amanaskāra*, by *wu-tso-i*. *Wu-tso-i* conveys essentially the same ideas as *wu-nien*.

6

Shên-hui[1] was one of the great disciples of Hui-nêng, and it was his school that flourished most immediately after the death of the master, for he bravely erected the standard of 'the abrupt school' against 'the gradual school' of Shên-hsiu, the rival of Hui-nêng. The following passages are quoted from the sayings of Shên-hui:[2]

'Chang Yen Kung[3] asked: Master usually speaks of the Unconscious (*wu-nien-fa*), advising people to discipline themselves in it. Is this Unconscious to be regarded as existent or non-existent?

'A.: The Unconscious is not describable as either existent or non-existent.

'Q.: Why is it not describable as either existent or non-existent?

'A.: When it is said to be existent, this is not in the sense which people of the world give to it. When it is said to be non-existent, it is not in the sense which people of the world give to it. For this reason, the Unconscious is not to be considered either existent or non-existent.

'Q.: What kind of thing do you call it, then?

'A.: The term "thing" is inapplicable here.

'Q.: If so, what term is applicable?

'A.: No designation is possible. Hence the Unconscious. It is beyond characterization. The reason why it is spoken of here at all is that questions are asked about it. If no questions were ever raised, there would be no talking about it whatever. For instance, when the mirror has no objects

[1] 686–760. He was one of the most noteworthy characters in the early history of Zen thought.

[2] Professor Hu Shih, of Peiping University, published in 1930 Shên-hui's sayings as recovered from the Tun-huang cave. The present author's is also one of the ancient MSS. preserved in the cave, but it differs from the Hu Shih edition in several respects. The quotation here cited is taken from the author's own; the reader who is already in possession of the Hu Shih will notice certain dissimilarities recognizable even in these translations.

[3] Cf. Hu Shih, pp. 115–16.

before it, there will be no images in it. That images are now perceivable in it is due to the fact that it stands before objects. Images are therefore there.

'Q.: If the mirror has no objects before it, is it illuminating, or not illuminating?

'A.: I just spoke of its illuminating objects, but whether it stands before an object or not, it is ever illuminating.

'Q.: If it has no form, if it is not to be described in any sense, as it is altogether beyond existence and non-existence, and yet if it is said to be illuminating, what does it illuminate?

'A.: When the mirror is said to be illuminating, it is because its self-nature has this quality of brightness. When the Mind of all beings is pure, the great light of knowledge which by nature belongs to it will illuminate all the worlds.

'Q.: If this be the case, when is it possible to have it?

'A.: Only by seeing into nothingness (*wu*).

'Q.: Nothingness—is this not something to see?

'A.: Though there is the act of seeing, the object is not to be designated as a "something".

'Q.: If it is not to be designated as a "something", what is the seeing?

'A.: To see into where there is no "something"—this is true seeing, this is eternal seeing.'

A little further on Shên-hui continues:

'Q.: What is meant by the Unconscious (*wu-nien*)?

'A.: Not to think (*nien*) of being and non-being, not to think of good and evil, not to think of limit and no-limit, not to think of measurement, not to think of Bodhi (enlightenment), not to fix your thought on Bodhi, not to think of Nirvāṇa, not to fix your thought on Nirvāṇa—this is to attain the Unconscious.

'This Unconscious[1] is no other than Prajñāpāramitā, and Prajñāpāramitā is no other than Ekavyūha-Samādhi.[2] Good friends, if those who are still in the stage of the

[1] The MS. has here *wu* (un-) only, which the translator takes for *wu-nien*, i.e. 'un-conscious'.

[2] The term occurs in the *Śaptaśatikā-Prajñāparamitā* taught by Mañjusri. See my *Zen Essays*, Second Series, p. 162fn.

learner conceive a thought (*nien*) in their minds, this thought may lead up to enlightenment; but when even such a thought is no more stirred in their minds, enlightenment itself will be no longer—which is no other than the Unconscious. In the Unconscious there are no states;[1] if there are any states [to be referred to as something definable in one's mind], they are not in accord with the Unconscious. . . . Those who see into the Unconscious have their senses cleansed of defilements. Those who see into the Unconscious are moving towards Buddha-wisdom. Those who see into the Unconscious are known to be with Reality. Those who see into the Unconscious are in the Middle Path, in the ultimate truth itself. Those who see into the Unconscious are furnished at once with merits as numerous as the sands of the Gangā. Those who see into the Unconscious are able to create all kinds of things. Those who see into the Unconscious embrace all things within themselves. . . .

When a man has a most decided realization he remains unmoved as solidly as Vajra, and because he has seen into the Unconscious, he sits in perfect quietude even when in the clash of armies a forest of swords cuts him to pieces. Even when the Buddhas like the sands of the Gangā come to greet him, not a thought of happiness is stirred in his mind. Even when beings like the sands of the Gangā are destroyed all at once, not a thought of grief is stirred in his mind. For this strong-willed man has attained Śūnyatā (emptiness) and Samacittatā (equal-mindedness).'

The Lord Szŭ-tao wanted to know if this teaching of the Unconscious was meant for holy men or for ordinary people. He was evidently doubtful as to the value of such an exalted teaching for the latter. Answered Shên-hui, the master, 'The teaching of the Unconscious belongs to holy men, but if the ordinary man disciplines himself in it, he is no more an ordinary man.'

[1] *Ching-chieh*, that is, particular states of mind definable in one way or another; enlightenment too is one of such states, and is to be transcended by those who really wish to attain the Unconscious.

The term *wu-nien* is given not only to ultimate reality itself, where all individual consciousness finds its final abode, but to the functioning of Reality in our minds. It is by this functioning that our empirical psychological consciousness is enabled to dive down into the abysmal depths of Reality. And this functioning is not to be separated from Reality, the Unconscious. Consciousness so called may thus be regarded as the field where the Unconscious functions. But when we have cut ourselves off from the source by imagining that our consciousness is an independent and ultimate reality, we have gone astray and know not where to go or where to stop—the result being a state of utmost spiritual unrest. However this may be, the Lord Szŭ-tao wishes to know what *wu*, 'to annul', means and what *nien*, 'to think of', means.

'A.: "To annul" means to annul the notion of duality, "to think" is to think of Suchness.

'Q.: What is the difference between one who thinks and Suchness itself?

'A.: There is no distinction between the two.

'Q.: If there is no distinction, why this thinking of Suchness?

'A.: "To think of" is the function of Suchness, and Suchness is the body of this thinking. For this reason, non-thinking [or to be unconscious, *wu-nien*] is said to be the principle [of Zen teaching]. When this is attained [the Unconscious], with all its seeing, hearing, recollecting, and knowing, remains for ever quiet and empty.'

7

With Tai-chu Hui-hai,[1] the Unconscious still continues to be one of the deeply absorbing subjects for discussion. While there is nothing especially new in his point of view, the following may be culled from his work called the

[1] A disciple of Ma-tsu (died 788).

Tun-wu Ju-tao Yao-mên Lun.[1] Hui-hai distinguishes between *hsieh nien* and *chêng nien*[2] and says that in the Unconscious there is right thought but no wrong thought.

'Q.: What is right thought?

'A.: Right thought is to be conscious of Bodhi, enlightenment.

'Q.: Is Bodhi attainable?

'A.: No, it is unattainable.

'Q.: If it is unattainable, how can one think of it?

'A.: As to Bodhi, it is no more than a provisionally made-up word, and there is no [corresponding individual reality to be the object of sense-] attainment. Nor is there any one who has ever attained it in the past or ever will attain it in the future; for it is something beyond attainability. Thus there is nothing for one to think of, except the Unconscious itself. This is called true thought.

'Bodhi means not to have any thought on anything [i.e. to be unconscious of all things]. To be unconscious of all things is to have no-mind (*wu-hsin*) on all occasions. . . . When this is understood, we have the Unconscious (*wu-nien*), and when *Wu-nien* is realized, emancipation follows by itself.'

In this passage, Hui-hai evidently identified *Wu-hsin*, no-mind, with *Wu-nien*, no-thought, and as they mean the same thing, they can be translated as 'the Unconscious' or 'to be unconscious' according to the case. *Wu-hsin* was used by Bodhidharma and *Wu-nien* by Hui-nêng and Shên-hui. Hui-hai, here using them as synonyms, explains Bodhi (enlightenment) and Moksha (emancipation) by them. Whatever this is, the ultimate end of Zen discipline consists, to use more popular phraseology, in not having any attachment to anything, because everything belonging to this world of particulars is predictable in one way or another and not at all final. Final reality is above all categories, and therefore beyond thinkability or attainability;

[1] 'Discourse on the Entering into Truth by Means of Immediate Understanding.' This is one of the most interesting and illuminating works on Zen Buddhism when it was about to attain its full development after Hui-nêng.

[2] Wrong thought, right thought.

hence it cannot be described except as 'unconscious' both in its adjectival and nominal sense. To illustrate the way in which Hui-hai used to demonstrate to his disciples and inquirers his doctrine of the Unconscious or of 'do-nothingness', the following is given as an example:

'The master used to say to his pupils: "I do not understand Zen, nor is there any special teaching to give out for your sake. Therefore, there is no need for you to be standing here for so long. It is best for you to get the matter settled with yourselves." But pupils came to him ever more increasingly, asking him questions day and night. So there was no help for him but to get up and answer their questions one after another. His flowing eloquence was something wonderful.

'One day a company of several monk-scholars called and said, We wish to ask you a question; would you kindly enlighten us?

'Master: The moon is reflected in the depths, and you pick it up as you like.

'Scholars: Who is the Buddha?

'M.: Facing you right in the depths. Who can it be but the Buddha himself?

'The scholars did not know what to make of him. After a while they asked again, What is your teaching whereby you convert people?

'M.: I have never had any teaching whereby to convert people.

'S.: This is the way with all Zen masters.

'The master now asked: Learned gentlemen, what do you teach to convert people?

'S.: We discourse on the *Vajracchedikā Sūtra.*

'M.: How many times have you already discoursed on it?

'S.: More than twenty times.

'M.: Who preached this Sūtra?

'A monk-scholar raised his voice, and said: O master, you are not joking, I hope. You know well it was the Buddha who taught it.

'M.: [According to the Sūtra,] if you declare the Buddha

to be the teacher of a doctrine, this is reviling him, and you do not understand his teaching. And if you declare this Sūtra not to be the Buddha's teaching, this is reviling the Sūtra. Learned Sirs, enlighten me on this [dilemma].

'The scholars made no answer. After a while the master questioned thus. According to the Sūtra we have: "If any one should see me through form or seek me through sound, such a one walks on the wrong road, and would never see the Tathāgata." Tell me, Reverend Sirs, who is the Tathāgata?

'S.: This is where we feel lost.

'M.: While there is no such thing as is to be called "enlightened", why do you speak of getting lost?

'S.: Please tell us about it, O master.

'M.: Reverend Sirs, you say you have discoursed on the Sūtra more than twenty times, and yet you do not know the Tathāgata?

'The monk-scholar made a second bow and craved for the master's instruction.

'M.: Tathāgata means the Suchness (*tathatā*) of all things.[1] How can you forget it?

'S.: Yes, I know that it means the Suchness of all things.

'M.: But, Reverend Sirs, your "yes" is not necessarily final.

'S.: Why can it not be final? It is what is plainly declared in the Sūtra.

'M.: Are you of Suchness or not?

'S.: Yes, we are.

'M.: Are wood and rock of Suchness?

'S.: Yes, they are.

'M.: Is your Suchness the same as the Suchness of wood and rock?

'S.: They are not two.

'M.: If so, where is the difference between yourselves and wood and rock?[2]

[1] This is quoted from the *Vajracchedikā* itself, hence this reproof.

[2] Cf. §38 in Hui-hai against studying sūtras. A similar argument is advanced by Shên-hui in his *Sayings* as regards the Dharmakāya and the bamboo-grove, Prajñā and the yellow blossoms. See also Hui-hai, §§10 and 16.

'The monk-scholar failed to answer this, and had to admit the unsurpassability of the master. After a while he asked again:

'S.: How can one attain Great Nirvāṇa?

'M.: Have no karma that works for transmigration.

'S.: What is the karma for transmigration?

'M.: To seek after Great Nirvāṇa, to abandon the defiled and take to the undefiled, to assert that there is something attainable and something realizable, not to be free from the teaching of opposites—this is the karma that works for transmigration.

'S.: How can one be emancipated?

'M.: No bondage from the very first, and what is the use of seeking emancipation? Act as you will, go on as you feel—without second thought. This is the incomparable way.

'S.: The master is really a wonderful personage.

'So saying, they bowed and retired.'

8

As this is not meant to be a history of Zen thought in the T'ang dynasty (A.D. 618–922), I shall not quote many more masters except Chao-chou T'sung-shên (778–897) and Lin-chi (died 867) and some others. For these will sufficiently show where Zen teaching was drifting, and how finally Zen masters themselves attempted to bring it into harmonious accord with the Indian phraseology and way of thinking in the sūtras.

The following was once given out by Chao-chou T'sung-shên[1] in one of his sermons:

'The Bronze buddha is not to be placed in the furnace, the wooden Buddha is not to be placed in fire, the clay Buddha is not to be placed in the water. The true Buddha sits in the interior. Bodhi and Nirvāṇa, Suchness and Buddha-nature—all these are outer clothings too tightly

[1] In his *Sayings* (*wu-lu*).

fitting the body. They are also known as defilements (*kleśa*). When no questions are asked, there are no defilements. In the limit of reality, in the ground of absolute truth, there is nothing there to which you get yourselves attached. When no thoughts are stirred within yourselves, no faults are committed anywhere. In order to reach the depths of Reality, only sit down quietly, say, for twenty or thirty years, and if you still fail to understand, cut off this old man's head. All things are like a dream, a vision, an ethereal flower, and to run after them is an altogether idle occupation. When you can keep your thoughts from wandering about, all things will go on well with you. Nothing comes to you from the outside, why then get busy with these? What boots it just to go around like a sheep sticking its nose into every corner, picking up any old thing, and putting it into its mouth? When I was with Shih-t'ou, he used to say whenever anybody asked him a question, "Close your mouth, no barking like a dog!" I follow his example and say, "Close your mouth, no barking like a dog!" There is defilement when the ego is asserted, there is purity when it is not asserted. You are like a hunting dog, and only wish to have something in your mouth. If so, when can you come to the understanding of Buddhism? Thousands, nay, tens of thousands of people all go about seeking Buddhahood. There is none indeed who can be called a true man. If you wish really to be disciples of the King of Emptiness, beware of becoming incurably sick in mind. Even before the world was, this Reality is; this Reality remains undestroyed when the world is no more. Ever since my interview with this old man, I am no other person than myself—I am master of myself. It does not profit you to seek this man in the outside world. When he is right here do not fail, by turning round and looking in the wrong way, to interview him.'

Chao-chou's 'Sayings' consists mostly of 'questions and answers', and not many sermons are to be found in it. What sermons there are, are very short and to the point.

. . . . .

The master once came up to the pulpit, and for a while remained silent. Finally he said, 'Are you all here, or not?'

'All here, master.'

'I withhold my discourse until another one turns up.'

'I will tell you when no one turns up,' said a monk.

'Difficult indeed to know the man,' the master remarked.

Another time the master told the monks: 'When a thought moves, multiplicities of things rise; when no thoughts are aroused, multiplicities vanish. What do you say to this?'

A monk remarked, 'How about it when thoughts neither rise nor disappear?'

The master said, 'I grant you this question.'[1]

The master on another occasion declared: 'When you say it is all bright, it is not quite so; the pathway is still dark as at twilight. Whereabouts are you?'

A monk said, 'I am on neither side.'

'If so, you are in the midway.'

'If in the midway, that means to be on either side.'

'You seem to have stayed with me for some time, since you have learned to make such a statement. But you have not yet gone beyond the triple statement. Even though you may say you have gone beyond it, I declare you are still in it. What would you say to it?'

'I know how to use the triple statement.'

Said the master, 'Why did you not say so before this?'

Another time Chao-chou's remark was: 'The Great Way is right before your eye, but difficult to see.'

A monk asked, 'What form does it take so that we can see it before us?'

'To the south of the River or to the north of it just as you please.'

[*Continued on page 50*

[1] Cf. the teaching of the Unconscious (*wu-hsin* or *wu-nien*) as expounded by Bodhidharma, etc.

'Have you not some means [to make us understand it more explicitly]?'

'What did you ask before this?'

Once Chao-chou came out into the hall and said to the monks: 'The truth of this matter is difficult to grasp; and even an extraordinary personality who is free from the ideas of relativity finds it hard to transcend the entanglements. When I was with Wei-shan, a monk asked him, "What is our Patriarch's idea of coming from the West?" The master said, "Pass me the chair over there." When a real master comes, he deals with people straight from his transcendental understanding.'

At that time a monk came forward and asked Chao-chou, 'What is our Patriarch's idea of coming from the West?'

Said the master, 'The cypress-tree in the courtyard.'

'Don't try to demonstrate the matter by means of an objective fact.'

'No, I do not.'

'What is our Patriarch's idea of coming from the West?' the monk persisted.

'The cypress-tree in the courtyard.'

The master further said: 'It is now ninety years ago that I was with Ma-tsu the great master, and every one of his fully qualified disciples, numbering more than eighty, was a real master indeed. But how is it now? The so-called masters are like so many secondary branches and vines growing further away from the main stems. As they descend further and further away from the great sages, each generation becomes worse than the preceding. Nan-ch'üan used to say, "Walk right into the midst of dissimilarities." Monks, how do you understand this? Nowadays I observe yellow-mouthed, inexperienced ones showing themselves openly in public and discoursing on varieties of subjects. They receive offerings and are reverently treated by their followers, even numbering as many as three or five hundred; they claim to be worthy masters and call others their pupils.'

• • • • •

Once Chao-chou asked Nan-ch'üan, 'Please say a word that goes beyond the four statements and one hundred negations.'[1]

Nan-ch'üan uttered not a word but went back to his own quarter.

Chao-chou said, 'Our old master ordinarily talks glibly enough, but when he is asked, he utters not a word.'

The attendant remarked, 'You had better not say that.'

Chao-chou gave him a slap.

Nan-ch'üan then closed the gate leading to his quarters, and scattering ashes around, said to the monks, 'If you can say a word, the gate will be opened.'

There were many who expressed their views, but the master Nan-ch'üan was not pleased with any of them.

Chao-chou gave the exclamation, 'O heavens!'

Nan-ch'üan then opened the gate.

9

Lin-chi was one of the greatest masters of the ninth century, and it is his school which is still flourishing in Japan and China, though in the latter country Zen itself is somewhat on the wane. Lin-chi's 'Sayings' are regarded by many as the strongest Zen treatise we have. One of his sermons runs:

'The main thing in the study of Buddhism now is to understand it in the proper way. When there is the proper understanding of it, a man is not defiled by birth-and-death; wherever he goes he enjoys perfect freedom. He may not seek to achieve anything specifically excellent, but this will come by itself.

'Friends, the ancient masters all had their way of helping others; as to my method, it consists in keeping others away from being deceived. If you want to use what you have in yourselves, use it, do not stand wavering. What is the trouble with students these days that they are unable to

[1] Briefly, 'What is the Absolute?'

reach realization? The trouble lies in their not believing themselves enough. As you are not believing enough, you are buffeted about by the surrounding conditions in which you may find yourselves. Being enslaved and turned around by objective situations, you have no freedom whatever, you are not masters of yourselves. If you cease from running after outward things all the time, you will be like the old masters.

'Do you wish to know what the old masters were like? They were no other than those who are right before you listening to my discourse. Where faith is lacking, there is constant pursuing after outward objects. And what you gain by this pursuing is mere literary excellence which is far from the life of old masters. Make here no mistake, O my friends!

'If you miss it in this life, you will have to go through the triple world for ever so many kalpas. If you run after and cling to your own enjoyments, you will be reborn in the womb of an ass or a cow.

'Friends, as far as I can see, my insight into Reality and that of Śākyamuni himself are in perfect agreement. As we move along, each according to his way, what is wanting to us? Are we not all sufficient unto ourselves? The light emanating from each one of our six senses knows no interruptions, no obstructions. When your insight is thus penetrating enough, peaceful indeed is your life!

'Reverend Sirs, there is no rest in this triple world, which is like a house on fire. It is no abode for any of you long to remain in. The devil of impermanence may visit any of us at any moment regardless of rank and age. If you desire to be like the old masters, do not look outward. The light of purity which shines out of every thought you conceive is the Dharmakāya within yourselves. The light of non-discrimination that shines out of every thought you conceive is the Sambhogakāya within yourselves. The light of non-differentiation that shines out of every thought you conceive is the Nirmāṇakāya within yourselves. And this triple body is no other than the person listening to my discourse this very moment right in front of each of you. The reason why these mysteries are possible is because one ceases to pursue outward objects.

'According to scholars, this triple body is the ultimate reality of things. But as I see into the matter, this triple body is no more than mere words, and then each body has something else on which it depends. An ancient doctor says that the body is dependent on its meaning, and the ground is describable by its substance. Being so, we know that Dharma-body and the Dharma-ground are reflections of the [original] light. Reverend Sirs, let us take hold of this person who handles these reflections. For he is the source of all the Buddhas and the house of truth-seekers everywhere. The body made up of the four elements does not understand how to discourse or how to listen to a discourse. Nor do the liver, the stomach, the kidneys, the bowels. Nor does vacuity of space. That which is most unmistakably perceivable right before your eyes, though without form, yet absolutely identifiable—this is what understands the discourse and listens to it.

'When this is thoroughly seen into, there is no difference between yourselves and the old masters. Only let not your insight be interrupted through all the periods of time, and you will be at peace with whatever situation you come into. When wrong imaginations are stirred, the insight is no more immediate; when thoughts are changeable, the essence is no more the same. For this reason, we transmigrate in the triple world and suffer varieties of pain. As I view the matter in my way, deep indeed is [Reality], and there is none who is not destined for emancipation.

'Friends, Mind has no form and penetrates every corner of the universe. In the eye it sees, in the ear it hears, in the nose it smells, in the mouth it talks, in the hand it seizes, in the leg it runs. The source is just one illuminating essence, which divides itself into six functioning units. Let all interfering thoughts depart from Mind, and you experience emancipation wherever you go. What do you think is my idea of talking to you like this? I simply wish to see you stop wandering after external objects, for it is because of this hankering that the old masters play tricks on you.

'Friends, when you come to view things as I do, you are able to sit over the heads of the Enjoyment- and Transformation-Buddhas; the Bodhisattvas who have successfully mounted the scale of ten stages look like hirelings; those who have attained the stage of full enlightenment resemble prisoners in chains; the Arhats and Pratyekabuddhas are cesspools; Bodhi and Nirvāṇa are a stake to which donkeys are fastened. Why so? Because, O Friends, you have not yet attained the view whereby all kalpas are reduced to Emptiness. When this is not realized, there are all such hindrances. It is not so with the true man who has an insight into Reality. He gives himself up to all manner of situations in which he finds himself in obedience to his past karma. He appears in whatever garments are ready for him to put on. As it is desired of him either to move or to sit quietly, he moves or sits. He has not a thought of running after Buddhahood. He is free from such pinings. Why is it so with him? Says an ancient sage, "When the Buddha is sought after, he is the cause of transmigration."

'Reverend Sirs, time is not to be wasted. Do not commit yourselves to a grave mistake by convulsively looking around your neighbourhood and not within yourselves. You make mistakes by trying to master Zen, to master the Way, to learn words and phrases, to seek for Buddhas and Fathers and good friends. There is just one parenthood for you, and outside of it what do you wish to acquire? Just look within yourselves. The Buddha tells us the story of Yajñādatta. Thinking he had lost his head, he wildly ran after it; but when he found that he had never lost it, he became a peaceful man. O Friends, be just yourselves, stop your hysterical antics. There are some old bald-headed fools who know not good from bad. They recognize all kinds of things, they see spirits, they see ghosts, they look this way and that way, they like fair weather, they like rainy weather. If they go on like this, they are sure one day to appear before the King of Death, who will ask them to pay up their debts by swallowing red-hot iron balls. Sons and daughters of good families become possessed of this uncanny fox-spirit and go wildly astray even against their original sanity. Poor blind followers! Some day they will have to pay up their board.'

Here we see Lin-chi as a great smasher of the conventional Buddhism whose ideas are ordinarily couched in Indian phraseology. He did not like the round-about way in which Buddhist experience was treated by philosophers and learned doctors. He wanted to reach the goal directly. He destroyed every obstacle that was found in his approach to Reality. He wielded his Vajra right and left, not only against those intellectualists but against the Zen masters of his day. He stands so majestically among his contemporaries, and no doubt his attitude appealed greatly to the Chinese mind. Chinese psychology is practical and does not like to be hampered by too many conventionalities, intellectual and otherwise. It produced Lao-tzŭ and Chuang-tzŭ, and asserted itself again with Zen, especially in the Lin-chi method of handling Zen. Quite refreshing and vivifying it is to see Lin-chi all naked and shorn of trumperies in his wrestling with Zen.

But at the same time it will be well to remember that this Zen attitude towards Buddhist lore and philosophy tended to slight its study in an orderly manner, to neglect the sūtras and what metaphysics there is in them.

10

In the following sections more Zen masters will be quoted who lived between late T'ang and early Sung. The object is to see the trend of development of Zen teaching when it gradually superseded the other Buddhist schools in China. At the same time we will notice in what relation their sermons and 'questions and answers' stand to the sūtra teaching which is characteristically Indian.

Chih-chang[1] said to his monks, 'I am now going to talk on Zen; you will all come forward.' When they came forward, he continued, 'Do you hear the way Kwannon lives in full response to varieties of situations?'

A monk asked, 'What is Kwannon's way of living?'

The master snapped his fingers, and said, 'Do you hear?'

The monk said, 'Yes.'

The master exploded, 'A company of stupid fellows—what do you want to find out here?'

So saying, he drove them out with a stick, and laughing aloud went away to his quarters.

Liang[2] was a great scholar, learned in the sūtras and philosophic treatises. When he saw Ma-tsu, the latter asked, 'You are evidently a learned student of the sūtras and philosophic treatises, are you not?'

Liang said, 'Yes, I am supposed to be so.'

Ma-tsu: 'How do you discourse on the sūtras?'

'With mind (*citta*).'

' "Citta is like an actor and Manas a jester";[3] how does Mind (*citta*) understand discoursing?'

Liang, raising his voice, declared, 'If mind is unable to discourse, do you think space can?'

The master remarked, 'Indeed, space can discourse.'

Of course Liang could not accept him, and wishing to leave, was about to depart, when Ma-tsu called out, 'O scholar!'

As Liang the philosopher turned back, the meaning of the whole proceeding dawned upon him, and he made bows to the master.

Ma-tsu, however, observed, 'What is the use of your bowing, you dull-witted fellow?'

Liang the scholar returned to his own temple and told this to his pupils: 'I thought no one could compete with

[1] *Chuan-têng-lu*, abbreviated *Chuan*, Fas. VII.
[2] *Chuan*, VIII.
[3] A quotation from the *Laṅkāvatāra*.

me in discoursing on the sūtras and philosophical treatises, but today, being questioned by Ma-tsu the master, all my proud learning has melted away like a piece of ice!'

Tai-tz'ŭ Huan-chung[1] one day came up to the pulpit and said, 'I do not know how to make answers; I only know where diseases are.'

A monk appeared before him, and the master came down from the pulpit and vanished into his room.

Fa-yen comments, 'Declaring himself to be a doctor in public, he knows now who is standing before him.'

Hsüan-chiao remarks: 'Does Tai-tz'ŭ really know diseases? Or does he not? The monk who appeared before him, was he really sick, or was he not? If he were sick, he could not get up and walk around as he did. If he were not sick, why did he appear before the master-doctor?'

Pai-ma T'an-chao[2] used to say: 'How delightful! How cheering!' When he was about to die, he cried, 'How agonizing!' or sometimes, 'King Yama has come to take me along!' The resident priest asked: 'How is it, Master? When you were once arrested by the governor and thrown into water, you were quite calm and serene; but what is the trouble with you now?' The master raised his head and said, 'Tell me when I was in the right, then or now?' The priest made no reply.

I-tuan[3] told this in one of his sermons: 'To talk is blaspheming, to remain silent is deception. Beyond silence and talking there is an upward passage, but my mouth is not wide enough to point it out to you.' So saying, he came down from the pulpit. Another sermon of his ran like this: 'However repeatedly you are peeled off and thoroughly cleansed, never stay where you are. Whatever contrivances you make, they are all temporary to meet the situation and people. As to the other side there are no such [contrivances].'

. . . . .

[1] *Chuan*, IX. [2] *Chuan*, X. [3] *Chuan*, X.

Yang-shan Hui-chi[1] gave among others the following sermon: 'You monks, turning back your light look within; do not try to memorize my words. Since the beginningless past you have turned your backs to your light, throwing yourselves into darkness. The root of false thinking goes deeply into the ground; it is hard to pull it out. The many contrivances are meant for the destruction of coarser imaginations. They are like the yellow leaves given to a child to stop its crying. They are in themselves of no value whatever. Again, it is like a shop where all sorts of goods are sold together with genuine golden wares. The goods light and heavy are delivered to suit the requirements of the customers. So, I say, Shih-t'ou keeps a shop dealing in solid gold only, but mine handles varieties of wares. If a man comes for a rat's droppings I let him have them. If he wants solid gold, I also meet his wish.'

A monk came out and said, 'I do not wish a rat's droppings, but give me, master, a piece of solid gold.'

Yang-shan said, 'One who tries to open his mouth while biting the point of an arrow is for ever unable to understand.'

The monk made no reply.

The master continued: 'When sought out and called for, there is an exchange of goods; but with no seeking, no calling, there will be no exchange of any sort. When I demonstrate Zen in its genuine form, nobody is able to accompany me however much he may desire it; much less a company of five or seven hundred. But when I talk this way and that, they crowd into my room and view with one another to pick up whatever leavings there are. It is like cheating a child with an empty palm; in truth there is nothing real. I now tell you most distinctly where the holy man's abode is. Do not attempt to work out your various imaginations on the matter. Only sincerely discipline yourselves so as to be in the ocean of your original nature. The sciences and miracles are not needed at all. Why not? Because such are the fringes of Reality. When you want to

[1] *Chuan*, XI.

know Mind, penetrate into the very source of things. Attain the source, and the rest need not bother you; some day you will come to a realization and know what I mean. But so long as you are kept away from the source, nothing else will be of any value to you; with all your learning and knowledge you are not there yet. Has not Wei-shan the master told us this? When all your imaginations, holy and worldly, are exhausted, Reality presents itself, true and eternal, in the unity of One and Many, and this is where the Buddha of Suchness abides.'

Yao-shan Wei-yen[1] was one day approached by a monk, who said to him, 'I have a doubt which I wish you would settle.' The master replied, 'Wait till the time comes for my sermon when I will settle it.'

The evening came, the master appeared in the hall, the monks were all gathered.

'Where is the monk who wished today to have his doubt settled?'

The monk came out of the gathering and stood before the master. The master thereupon came down from his chair, and seizing the monk said, 'O monks, here is one who has a doubt.' Releasing him then, the master went back to his room.

One evening Yao-shan climbed the mountain for a walk. Seeing the moon suddenly appearing from behind the clouds he laughed most heartily. The laugh echoed ninety *li* east of Li-yang where his monastery was. The villagers thought the voice came from their neighbours. In the morning the inquiry went eastwards from one door to another until it reached the monastery, and the villagers concluded, 'Last night the master gave us the greatest laugh of his life at the top of the mountain.' Li-ao, philosopher-governor of the Lang-chou,[2] who was one of Yao-shan's lay-disciples, composed a poem on the incident and sent it to the master:

[1] *Chuan*, XIV.

[2] See also my *Zen Essays*, Series II, Plate facing p. 209.

A lonely shelter is chosen,
His rustic taste is appeased;
None to greet, none to bid adieu,
Alone all the year round is he.
One eve he climbed
Straight up the solitary peak;
Revealed in the clouds the moon he saw,
And what a hearty laugh he gave!

Chao-chou Tai-tien[1] was a disciple of Shih-t'ou, and even after his retirement in Ling-chou he was besieged by monks. This is one of his sermons:

'Those who wish to master the truth must know first what is their own original Mind. This is attained when it is pointed out by means of its forms and manifestations. But most people nowadays, being unable to penetrate into the very essence of things, are falsely led to take a mere raising of the eyebrows, glancing this way and that way, remaining silent, or uttering a word, for the finality of Zen truth. In point of fact, this is far from being satisfactory. I will tell you now most plainly how to proceed in this matter, and you will listen attentively. Only when all your erroneous imaginations, thought-constructions, and experiences are put aside, will you come to the realization of your true Mind. This Mind has nothing to do with a world of defilements, with your being silent, with your holding on to quietude. Mind is no other than Buddha, and there is in it no artifice, no elaboration. Why? It responds to calls, it illuminates objects as they come, and its functions are cool and self-originating. The mysterious source of all these activities is beyond conception. And we call this mystery our own original Mind. Take heed, monks, not to let it wander away from your hold.'

When Yüan-chih and Yün-yen[2] were attending on their master Yao-shan, the latter said: 'Where human understanding fails to reach, refrain by all means from putting in

[1] *Chuan*, XIV.

[2] *Chuan*, XIV.

any words; if you do, horns will grow on your head. Brother Chih, what would you say to this?'

Yüan-chih without saying a word left the room.

Yün-yen asked the master, 'Why did not Brother Chih answer you?'

The master said: 'My back aches today. You'd better go to Chih himself and ask, for he understands.'

Yün-yen now sought out Brother Chih and asked, 'How is it that you gave no answer to our master just now?'

Yüan-chih remarked, 'It's best for you to ask master himself.'

Later, Yün-chü was asked by a monk, 'What did Yao-shan mean when he said, "Refrain by all means from putting in any words"?'

Yün-chü said, 'This is full of poison.'

The monk further asked, 'How is it so poisonous?'

Yün-chü simply replied, 'It strikes down dragons and snakes at one blow.'

Tung-shan Liang-chieh,[1] a disciple of Yün-yen and the founder of the Sōtō School of Zen Buddhism, said: 'Even when you say straightway that from the very beginning there is not a thing, this does not entitle you to be an inheritor of Zen tradition. I want you to say a word in this connection. What would you say?'

There was a monk who expressed himself ninety-six times to please the master. Each time he failed until he had his ninety-seventh trial. The master blurted out, 'Why did you not say that sooner?'

Later on, another monk learning of the incident came to the first monk and asked him to repeat the answer he had given to the master. For three years the second monk was in attendance upon the first monk in order to learn the secret from his own mouth. No chance, however, was given to the contriving attendant-monk. In the meantime the first monk fell sick. The attendant-monk made up his mind to get the desired answer by any means, fair or foul. 'I have

[1] *Chuan*, XV.

been with you for these three years wishing for you to tell me about your answer given to the master. You have persistently refused to acquiesce in my request. If I cannot get it by any honest means, I am going to get it this way.' So saying, he drew his sword and continued, 'If you refuse once more to give me the answer, I am ready to take your life.'

The first monk was taken aback and said: 'Wait, for I will tell you. It is this: "Even if it is brought out, there is no place to set it."'

The murderous monk made profound bows.

Nan-ch'an Ch'i-fan[1] said: 'As to fine words and exquisite phrases, you have enough of them in other places. If today there is any one in this assembly who has gone even beyond the first principle, let him come forward and say one word. If there is, he has not betrayed our expectations.'

A monk asked, 'What is the first principle?'

'Why do you not ask the first principle?'

'I am asking it this very moment.'

'You have already fallen on a second principle.'

Chin-lun K'ê-kuan,[2] seeing his monks depart, called out, 'O monks!' When they turned back, he said, 'Look at the moon.' They looked at the moon. The master remarked, 'When the moon looks like a bent bow, there is more rain and less wind.' The monks made no reply.

Hsüan-sha Shih-pei[3] sat quietly in his pulpit for some time without saying a word. The monks thought he was not going to give them a sermon and began to retire all at once. He then scolded them: 'As I observe, you are all of one pattern; not one of you has sagacity enough to see things properly. You have come here to see me open my mouth, and, taking hold of my words, imagine they are ultimate truths. It is a pity that you all fail to know what's what. As long as you remain like this, what a calamity!'

[1] *Chuan*, XIX. [2] *Chuan*, XIX. [3] *Chuan*, XVIII.

Another time the master again remained silent for a while and then said, 'I have been thoroughly kind to you, but do you understand?'

A monk asked, 'What is the sense of remaining quiet without uttering a word?'

The master said, 'How you talk in your sleep!'

'I wish you to tell me about the truth of Zen.'

'What is the use of snoring?'

'I may snore, but how about you?'

The master said, 'How is it possible to be so insensitive as not to know where it itches?'

The keeping quiet in silence for some time in the pulpit was a favourite method with many masters. To give another instance, Chih-fêng[1] practised it, and then saying, 'O monks, look, look!' would come down from the seat.

Shih-chin of Jui-yen[2] while in the pulpit kept his monks standing for some time, and finally said: 'I am ashamed of not having anything special today. But if you are merely here to follow my talk and listen to my voice, you had better indeed retire into the hall and warm yourselves by the fire. Good night, monks.'

Tsang-yung of Chang-ching[3] came up to the pulpit, and seeing all the monks assembled threw his fan down on the floor and said: 'Fools take gold for earth, but how about the wise? Future generations are not to be despised. It is not praiseworthy all the time to be too modest. Is there anybody wishing to come out before me?' A monk came out, and making bows withdrew his steps and stood still.

The master said, 'Anything besides that?'

'I wait your fair judgment.'

'A peach-stone one thousand years old!'—this was the sentence given by the master.

. . . .

[1] *Chuan*, XXVI. [2] *Chuan*, XXII. [3] *Chuan*, XXII.

Yên-jui of Yang-lung monastery[1] came up to the pulpit, the monks crowded into the hall; the master rose from his seat and danced and said, 'Do you understand?'

'No, master,' the monks answered.

Yên-jui demanded, 'I performed, without abandoning my religion, a deed belonging to the world; why do you not understand?'

Hsüan-fa of the Lo-han[2] once gave this: 'In this whole universe, extending to the furthest ends of infinity, there is not a bit of doctrine which I can give you as an object of learning, study, or perception comparable even to a particle of dust. This, however, is beyond you until you have had an insight into Reality. Do not make light of it. Have you not heard an old master say this, "If you are unable to understand the multiplicities of your actual experience, however clear your perception of your own self may be, your insight is not comprehensive enough"? Do you follow me, monks?'

A monk asked, 'When a proposition, not even as little as a particle of dust, is asserted, how do these multitudes of good and bad come into our sight?'

'Distinctly committing this to your memory, go and ask elsewhere.'

'The monks are crowding here, and who among them has gained an insight to this?'

'Who has ever lost it?' was the counter-question of the master.

Another monk asked, 'Who is the Buddha?'

The master asserted, 'You are a monk-pilgrim.'

When Tao-ch'ien[3] first saw Ching-hui, Hui was much impressed with him. One day Hui asked, 'What sūtras do you read besides your study of Zen?'

'I read the *Avataṁsaka Sūtra*.'

'The sūtra refers to the six aspects of existence; general

[1] *Chuan*, XXII. [2] *Chuan*, XXV. [3] *Chuan*, XXV.

and particular, same and different, existing and disappearing. To what doctrine does this belong?'

Ch'ien said: 'The passage occurs in the chapter on the ten stages of Bodhisattvahood. According to its theory, all things either of this world or of a super-world are considered to have these six aspects.'

'Is *k'ung* (*śūnyatā*, emptiness of space) furnished with these six?'

Ch'ien was at a loss how to answer the question.

Hui said, 'You ask me.'

'Is *k'ung* furnished with these six aspects?'

'*K'ung!*'

The answer opened at once the mind of Tao-ch'ien to a new light; filled with joy, he bowed to the master. The master said, 'How do you understand?'

'*K'ung!*' said Tao-ch'ien.

When later Tao-ch'ien presided over the Yang-ming monastery, he gave the following sermon:

'The Buddhist truth is in full manifestation, and why do you not comprehend it? O monks, if you want to understand the Buddhist truth, ask your Chan-san and Li-szŭ.[1] If you want to understand worldly things, go and ask the old master. Peace be with you. Good night.'

Tsung-chien of Kuan-yin shrine[2] sat quietly for a while in the pulpit and then, referring to the *Vimalakīrti*, said this: 'Mañjuśrī greatly praised Vimalakīrti as he sat in silence. Now I want to know: did the philosopher accept the praise, or not? If he accepted it, there was no philosopher worth the name. If he accepted it not, Mañjuśrī must be said to have wasted his praise. O monks, do you understand? If you do, you are real students of Zen.'

A monk came forward and said, 'What is the meaning of Vimalakīrti's silence and Mañjuśrī's praise?'

'You ask, I answer.'

'If such men made their appearance here, what would be the outcome?'

[1] I.e. men in the street.

[2] *Chuan*, XXV.

The master recited the following:

'Walking up the mountain path I come to the source of the stream;
While sitting in quietude I watch how the clouds rise.'

II

I have given here sufficient varieties of Zen sermons and *mondo* ('questions and answers') to show how Zen developed in its characteristic way during the three hundred years after Hui-nêng. We can say, after examining all these examples promiscuously culled from biographies of the Zen masters in T'ang and Sung, that Zen has succeeded to a certain extent in establishing itself on the basis of Chinese psychological experiences. Not only is this true in the terminology which the masters have adopted to express themselves, but in the way by which their experiences are made communicable. Zen Buddhism has achieved a unique development in the history of religion and of mysticism generally.

The one thing I wish especially to notice in this connection is that the Zen neglect of the latter and consequently of philosophy began to manifest an undesirable tendency in the tenth century. By this I mean that the study of scholastic Buddhism was regarded by Zen masters and especially by their followers, to a degree which was more than actually necessary, as a pair of worn-out straw sandals—an attitude which hindered rather than helped Zen realization. Such an attitude was justifiable in a sense, but when it is carried to excess, as was perhaps the case with ignorant followers of Zen, Zen turns into antinomianism, and licentiousness becomes confounded with the free movement of the spirit.

There is a history of Chinese Buddhism written early in the thirteenth century from the standpoint of the T'ien-tai sect. It is entitled *The Orthodox Transmission of the Śākya*

PLATE V
SHOICHI THE NATIONAL TEACHER, THE FOUNDER OF TOFUKUJI

Ascribed to MINCHO

This is an unusual portrait picture of a Zen master, seeing that most of the pictures of this nature known as *Ting-hsiang* (*Chin-so* in Japanese) are the "official" ones. The figure in full ecclesiastical robe sits in a chair, generally with a stick held slantingly in his right hand. The posture is quite stiff and formal with nothing betraying his inner feelings. This portrait of Shoichi places him on a natural rock, with his legs stretched out and with one of his hands reposing on his knee. He looks as if enjoying a rest after a walk in the temple grounds. The pine tree at his back stretches one of its branches over him. The serenity of his features suggests what is taking hold of his inner consciousness; the flow of the drapery folds which contrasts with the forceful lines of the rock and the tree is indicative of his attitude towards the objective world.

PLATE VI

SAMANTABHADRA AND THE RAKSHASIS

By AN UNKNOWN JAPANESE ARTIST

The idea comes probably from the *Saddharmapundarika* in which ten Raskshasis, female demons belonging to the Raksha family, promise to protect all the supporters of the sutra. The connection of Samantabhadra with these pious Buddhist demons is not explicitly told in any sutras, except as it took place in the imagination of the artist himself. The present picture is one of the fine specimens of the Bodhisattva with the lady-demons. Samantabhadra, with all the ornaments belonging to a Bodhisattva, sits in a most dignified manner on his lotus-throne on the back of an elephant. He is a fully-qualified Bodhisattva, he is like a royal prince; he is an object of worship here, but not a friend of the needy and humble, as we see him later. The Bodhicitta works in a twofold direction, upward and downward. Samantabhadra here is represented as he has reached the upward limit of perfection; when he becomes a courtesan, he is on the lowest ground with all his evil impulses among us.

Doctrine,[1] in which the author severely attacks Zen almost as the teaching of the devil.

'When Buddhist philosophy changes it becomes Zen; when Zen grows worse it turns devilish; when the devil is allowed to prosper, there is perversity of nature. The harm from depending too much on the sūtras and philosophical treatises is slight compared with the harm from positively ignoring them—an attitude which is a great hindrance to properly following the Buddhist life.'[2]

In another place the author of the Buddhist history gives the following quotation with which he is in apparent sympathy: 'The lecturing on the sūtras is becoming less popular than ever while the study of Zen is all the more flourishing now. The worst part of it is, indeed, that those ignorant villagers, after visiting the Zen monasteries and listening to sermons given by the masters, are inordinately delighted, and without giving much thought to the spirit of the teaching, declare themselves to be teachers, not only disparaging the ancient worthies but depreciating the sūtras and their contents with their own incoherent utterances. The stupid masses are deceived, and even respectable gentlemen who, however, have not much learning, are pleased with the empty talks of the Zen followers. . . .'

The criticism of Zen here cited may be considered somewhat one-sided as coming from a T'ien-tai scholar, but we can well imagine how things might be when Zen is degenerated. The peculiar Zen attitude towards the letter probably started with the immediate disciples of Hui-nêng whom they dignified with the title of the Sixth Patriarch of Zen Buddhism in China. For one thing, they made Hui-nêng an unlearned pedlar of wood, ostentatiously opposing his simple-mindedness against the scholarly erudition of his rival, Shên-hsiu. Their sayings and writings, including the one ascribed to Hui-nêng, contain many slighting remarks against the contemporary doctors and philosophers of Buddhism. Most of the latter were very

[1] *Shih men chêng t'ung*, in eight fascicles.
[2] The Kyoto edition, f. 413b.

likely mere learners of the letter, but those who came to interview the Zen masters are recorded to have experienced an ignoble defeat in one way or another. Besides, did the masters actually forbid the study of the sūtras? In Hui-hai's writings we have this:

A monk asked, 'Why do you not allow us to recite the sūtras which are regarded as recording other people's words?'

The master explained. 'It is like a parrot repeating human language without understanding what it means. The sūtras transmit the thought of the Buddha; if you read them without understanding the sense this is just repeating his words. This is why the sūtra-reading is not permitted.'

The monk asked again, 'Can the meaning be expressed by other means than words and letters?'

The master said, 'What you say is again repeating another's words.'

'Words are the same everywhere, and why are you so prejudiced against me?'

'You listen, O monk, for I will tell you. In the sūtra it is distinctly stated that "What I teach contains words full of meaning and not mere words; but what ordinary people talk are mere words and have no meaning. Those who know the meaning have gone beyond senseless words; those who have an insight into Reason have transcended the letter. The teaching itself is more than words and letters, and why should we seek it in numbers and phrases?" This being so, he who is awakened to Bodhi attains the meaning and forgets words, has an insight into Reason and leaves the teaching behind. It is like a man's forgetting the creel when he has the fish, or his forgetting the noose when he has the hare.'

Yao-shan was one day reading a sūtra when a monk appeared and asked, 'Master, you ordinarily do not allow us to read the sūtras, and how is it that you yourself are reading one?'

The master said, 'I just want to keep it before my eyes.'

'Cannot I follow your example?'

'In your case, your eyesight ought to be penetrating enough to go through the cow-hide.'[1]

This making light of sūtra-study on the part of the Zen masters shows its symptoms already at the time of Hui-nêng. According to his *Tan-ching* ('Platform Sermons') as we have it today, Hui-nêng did not know how to read, and when he was asked to explain the *Nirvāṇa Sūtra* and the *Puṇḍarīka Sūtra*, he said, 'I cannot read, you read it for me, and then I will tell you what is the meaning.' It is true that there are as many parrot-like followers of the scriptures among Buddhists as among Christians, but at the same time we cannot ignore the letter altogether, as it is one of the important vehicles not only of thought but of feeling and of spiritual experience.

The Zen masters were all right so far as they themselves were considered, but their ignorant and half-enlightened followers were always ready to go beyond the limits and to justify their own ignorance by claiming to imitate their masters. It was quite natural, therefore, to find some movement among the masters themselves to effect a reconciliation between Zen and sūtra-learning. This meant that the Chinese genius was to be nourished and enriched by the Indian imagination.

That the *Gaṇḍavyūha* together with other sūtras came to be systematically utilized for the philosophical interpretation of the Zen experience need not now surprise us. The *Gaṇḍavyūha* especially, with its rich and beautiful imageries, whose equal could not be found in the whole range of Chinese literature, provided a timely and fitting support to which Zen could be affixed for its sound healthy growth.

If Zen retained the idea that the dispensing with the letter accomplished the whole thing, its achievement in the history of Buddhist life in China could not be very great. Of course, to rise above fine phraseology and mere abstraction is in itself a weighty thing; for when this is

[1] Yang-shan once declared that the forty fascicles of the *Nirvāṇa Sūtra* are no less than the Devil's talk. (Quoted by T'ui-yin in his *Mirror for Zen Students*.)

successfully achieved, we can say that nine-tenths of the work is finished. But at the same time we must remember that there is a positive work for the Zen master to carry out. The insight he has gained into Reality must be organized into a system of intuitions so that it will grow richer in content. The insight itself is contentless, for to be so is its very condition. As soon as it begins to have something in it, it ceases to be itself. But this contentlessness of Zen insight is not an abstraction. If so, it turns into a metaphysical idea and is to be so treated, that is, according to the logic of epistemology. Hereby Zen loses its reason. In point of fact the insight is dynamical; in other words, it is characterized by fluidity. It thus gains its meaning by being connected with other intuitions, the *ensemble* of which really constitutes the Buddhist life. The study of the sūtras thus could not be neglected by the followers of Zen, however much they revolted against it.

To reduce all existence with its multiplicities into Sūnyatā (emptiness) is the great accomplishment of the *Prajñāpāramitā Sūtras*—one of the highest achievements carried out by the Indian mind. To hold up the realization of noble wisdom (*pratyātmāryajñānagocara*) as the foundation of the Buddhist life is the mission of the *Laṅkāvatāra* as far as the Zen interpretation of it is concerned, and this too is something the Chinese Buddhists before Bodhidharma did not quite fully comprehend. But if the Zen masters had not had something more for the consolidation of their work, the life of Zen could not have effected such a signal success in the general moulding of the spiritual life of the Far-Eastern peoples. The grand intuitions—grand not only in scope and comprehensiveness but in penetration—which make up the substance of the *Gaṇḍavyūha* are the most imposing monument erected by the Indian mind to the spiritual life of all mankind. Zen thus inevitably takes up its abode also in the royal palatial structure of the *Gaṇḍavyūha*. Zen becomes one of its incalculable Vyūhas. To describe it from another point of view, Zen develops into all the Vyūhas that are the ornaments of the Dharmadhātu.

12

In what follows I intend to describe the three important notions which according to the *Gaṇḍavyūha* distinguish the Buddhist life especially after the attainment of an insight into the truth of Zen. The three notions are Bodhisattva-hood, the Desire for Enlightenment or All-knowledge (*bodhicittopāda*), and the Bodhisattva's Abode (*vihāra*). They are fully treated in the sūtra.

Before this is done, the reader will most naturally desire to have some general information regarding the *Gaṇḍavyūha* or *Avataṁsaka*. Let, then, this concluding section be devoted to the description of the sūtra as to its subject-matter, style, construction, and translations.[1]

First about the title of the sūtra. The *Gaṇḍavyūha* and the *Avataṁsaka* have been more or less indiscriminately used for the Chinese *Hua-yen* and the Tibetan *phal-po-che* in these Essays. As far as the Chinese *hua-yen* is concerned, *gaṇḍavyūha* seems to correspond to it: *gaṇḍa* = *hua* = *flower*, that is, ordinary flower, *tsa-hua*, and *vyūha* = *yen*, that is, *chuang-yen* = ornament, array. According to Fa-tsang's commentary on the *Hua-yen*,[2] its original Sanskrit title is given as *chien-na-p'iao-ho*, which stands as nearly as the Chinese phonetics can for the transliteration of *gaṇḍa-vyūha*. Fa-tsang then explains *chien-na* to mean 'common flower' and *p'iao-ho* 'decoration'. *Avataṁsaka*, on the other hand, means 'garland', or 'flower decoration', and may be regarded as an equivalent to

[1] The original Sanskrit text of the *Gaṇḍavyūha* is still generally inaccessible. Some years ago, Professor Hokei Idzumi of Otani Buddhist College copied a Nepalese MS. in possession of Mr. Yekai Kawaguchi, which he later collated with another Nepalese MS. kept in the Library of the Imperial University of Kyoto. Five years ago, Prof. Idzumi permitted the author of the present *Essays* to make mimeographic copies of his MS., and there are at present about twenty such copies in circulation, mostly in Japan. Although the author has now rotograph copies of the Cambridge and the R.A.S. MSS., the *Gaṇḍavyūha* references in the present book unless specially mentioned are to the mimeograph copy (MMG) of 1928.

[2] *T'an-hsüan-chi*, Fas. III.

hua-yen. This term is found in the *Mahāvyutpatti*, §LXIV and §CCXLVI. In §CCXXXVII *avataṁsaka* is given as 'flower-ear-ornament'.

What is confusing here is that there is a Mahāyāna sūtra bearing the specific title *Gaṇḍavyūha* as one of nine principal Buddhist sūtras in Nepal. This belongs to the group of the Mahāyāna sūtras known in Chinese as belonging to the *Hua-yen-ching* (*Kegon-kyo* in Japanese), and in fact is the final chapter of the *Hua-yen-ching* both of sixty and eighty fascicles, and corresponds to the *Hua-yen-ching* translated into Chinese by Prajñā in forty fascicles. This final chapter is called in Chinese, and in Tibetan, the 'Chapter on Entering into the Dharmadhātu' (*dharmadhātupraveṣa* in Sanskrit).

To avoid confusion it may be better to apply the Sanskrit title *Avataṁsaka* to the entire group of the *Kegon* (*hua-yen*) and *Gaṇḍavyūha* to the forty fascicle *Kegon* only. Thus the *Avataṁsaka* will include the *Gaṇḍavyūha*, which latter, in spite of Fa-tsang's authority, is specifically the name reserved for the 'Chapter on Entering into the Dharmadhātu'.

In Nāgārjuna's commentary on the *Prajñāpāramitā*, *Gaṇḍavyūha* is quoted under the title *Acintyavimoksha*, which forms the sub-title to the Chinese forty fascicle *Kegon*.

There are three Chinese sūtras bearing the title *Kegon* or *Hua-yen* in sixty, eighty, and forty fascicles. The last as aforementioned corresponds to the Sanskrit *Gaṇḍavyūha*. The sixty fascicle *Hua-yen* contains thirty-four chapters, and the eighty fascicle thirty-nine. The first *Hua-yen* was translated by Buddhabhadra in A.D. 418–420, the second one by Śikshananda in 695–699, and the third—which corresponds to the Sanskrit *Gaṇḍavyūha*—by Prajñā, 796–797.

Long before the first translation of the *Hua-yen* by Buddhabhadra appeared, one of the first Buddhist missionaries from India is recorded as having rendered what appears to be the Sanskrit *Daśabhūmika* into the Chinese language in eight fascicles in the year A.D. 70. Unfortunately, this translation is lost. About ninety years later (A.D. 167), Chih

Lou-chia-ch'an came from Yueh-chih and translated into Chinese the *Tushāra Sūtra*, which is also part of the *Hua-yen Sūtra*. The *Tushāra* corresponds to the 'Chapter on the Names of the Tathāgata'. Still later, Chih-chien, Dharmaraksha, Nieh Ch'êng-yüan and his son Tao-chen, Chu Fo-nien and others produced a number of sūtras belonging to the *Hua-yen* group, until the time when, in A.D. 420, Buddhabhadra finished his great sixty fascicle sūtra in which all these separate sūtras, as well as many others, were included as belonging to one comprehensive *Hua-yen-ching* (*Avataṁsaka*).

From this fact we can gather that some of the chapters in the *Hua-yen-ching* were originally independent sūtras, and that the compiler or compilers of the larger sūtra thought it expedient to put them all together under one title so as to have them arranged systematically. The *Daśabhūmika* and the *Gaṇḍavyūha* (or *Dharmadhātupraveṣa*) for this reason still keep up their independence. The Tibetan *Avataṁsaka* is just as inclusive as the Chinese eighty or sixty fascicle *Hua-yen.*[1]

What is the message of the *Avataṁsaka*? The sūtra is considered generally to be the king of the Mahāyāna sūtras. The following is Fa-tsang's interpretation of the message, according to his monograph called 'The Meditation by which Imagination Becomes Extinguished and One Returns to the Source'.[2]

There is one Mind which is ultimate reality, by nature pure, perfect, and bright. It functions in two ways. Sustained by it, the existence of a world of particulars is possible; and from it originates all activity, free and illuminating, making for the virtues of perfection (*pāramitā*). In these two functions, which we may call existential and moral, three universal characters are distinguishable. Existentially viewed, every particular object, technically called 'particle of dust' (*anuraja*), contains in it the whole Dharmadhātu. Secondly, from the creational point of view, each particle

[1] For the detailed comparison of them, see Sakurabe's Otani Kanjur Catalogue, 1932.

[2] *Wang-chin-huan-yüan-kuan.*

of dust generates all kinds of virtues; therefore, by means of one object the secrets of the whole universe are fathomed. Thirdly, in each particle of dust the reason of Śūnyatā is perceivable.

Against this objective world so characterized the Bodhisattva practises four virtues: (1) the virtue of creative adjustment born of wisdom (*prajñā*) and love (*karuṇā*), (2) the virtue of morality by which the dignity of human life is preserved, (3) the virtue of tenderness towards others and of simple naturalness, and (4) the virtue of sacrifice or vicarious atonement. By the practice of these virtues the ignorant are saved from their delusions, passions are converted into rationality, defilements are thoroughly wiped off, and the mirror of Suchness is always kept bright and clean.

The disciplining of oneself in these virtues is not enough to complete the life of devotion, for tranquillization (*śamatha*) is needed to keep one's mind in perfect harmony with the nature of Reality; not to be carried away into a world of multiplicities, but to hold one's light of the Unconscious unspoiled and unobstructed. Tranquillization alone, however, may lead one to a state of self-complacency and destroy the source of sympathetic motivation. Hence the need of Vipaśyanā exercises. *Śamatha* means 'stopping', and *vipaśyanā* 'seeing'. The one complements the other. Fa-tsang observes that to understand the *Avataṁsaka* these six contemplations are needed: (1) to look into the serenity of Mind to which all things return, (2) to look into the nature of the world of particulars which are because of Mind, (3) to observe that there is perfect mysterious interpenetration of all things, (4) to observe that there is nothing but Suchness where all the shadowy existences cast their reflections, (5) to observe that the mirror of identity holds in it images of all things each without obstructing others, and (6) to observe that the relation of master and attendants exists in a most exhaustive manner throughout the universe so that when any one particular object is picked up all the others are picked up with it.

Aided by this monograph of Fa-tsang, we shall be able

to grasp the ultimate teaching of the *Gaṇḍavyūha* and also its relation to Zen Buddhism. When all is said, Zen discipline consists in realizing the Unconscious which is at the basis of all things, and this Unconscious is no other than Mind-only in the *Gaṇḍa* as well as in the *Laṅkā*. When Mind is attained not as one of the attainables but as going beyond this existence dualistically conceived, it is found that Buddhas, Bodhisattvas, and all sentient beings are reducible to this Mind, which is the Unconscious. The Indian genius makes it develop into a Dharmadhātu which is so graphically depicted in the form of the Vairochana Tower with all its Vyūhas and Alaṅkaras. In the Chinese mind, the heavenly glories resplendent with supernatural lights, so wonderfully described in the *Gaṇḍa*, are reduced once more into the colours of this grey earth. Celestial beings are no more here, but hard-toiling men of the world. But there is no sordidness or squalor in Zen, nor is there any utilitarianism. In spite of its matter-of-factness, there is an air of mystery and spirituality in Zen, which has later on developed into a form of nature-mysticism. Hu Shih, the Chinese scholar, thinks Zen is the revolt of Chinese psychology against abstruse Buddhist metaphysics. But the fact is that it is not a revolt but a deep appreciation. Only the appreciation could not be expressed in any other way than in the Chinese way.

II. THE GAṆḌAVYŪHA, THE BODHISATTVA-IDEAL, AND THE BUDDHA

I

WHEN we come to the *Gaṇḍavyūha*[1] after the *Laṅkāvatāra*, or the *Vajraccehedikā*, or the *Parinirvāṇa*, or even after the *Saddharma-Puṇḍarīka* and the *Sukhāvatīvyūha*, there is a complete change in the stage where the great religious drama of Mahāyāna Buddhism is enacted. We find here nothing cold, nothing grey or earth-coloured, and nothing humanly mean; for everything one touches in the *Gaṇḍavyūha* shines out in an unsurpassable manner. We are no more in this world of limitation, obscurity, and adumbration; we are miraculously lifted up among the heavenly galaxies. The ethereal world is luminosity itself. The sombreness of earthly Jetavana, the disreputableness of the dry-grass seat on which the Lion of the Śākya probably sat when preaching, a group of shabbily dressed mendicants listening to a discourse on the unreality of an individual ego-soul—all these have completely vanished here. When

[1] The *Gaṇḍavyūha*, or *Avataṁsaka*, comprehensively known as *Hua-yen-ching* in Chinese, represents a great school of Mahāyāna thought. Traditionally, the sūtra is believed to have been delivered by the Buddha while he was in deep meditation after the Enlightenment. In this sūtra the Buddha gives no personal discourses on any subject except giving the sanction, 'Sādhu! Sādhu!' to the statements made by the attending Bodhisattvas such as Mañjuśrī or Samantabhadra, or emitting rays of supernatural light from the various parts of his body as required by the occasion. The Sanskrit *Gaṇḍavyūha* exclusively treats of the pilgrimage of Sudhana under the direction of the Bodhisattva Mañjuśrī. The young pilgrim-aspirant for Supreme Enlightenment visits one teacher after another, amounting to more than fifty in number. The object is to find out what constitutes the life of devotion as practised by a Bodhisattva. The sūtra occupies more than one-fourth of the *Avataṁsaka* and is complete in itself, undoubtedly proving its independent origin. For further details see above.

the Buddha enters into a certain kind of Samādhi, the pavilion where he is situated all of a sudden expands to the fullest limits of the universe; in other words, the universe itself is dissolved in the being of the Buddha. The universe is the Buddha, and the Buddha is the universe. And this is not mere expanse of emptiness, nor is it the shrivelling-up of it into an atom; for the ground is paved with diamonds; the pillars, beams, railings, etc., are inlaid with all kinds of precious stones and gems sparkling brilliantly, and glittering with the reflection of one another.

Not only is the universe of the *Gaṇḍavyūha* not on this side of existence, but the audience surrounding the Buddha is not a mortal one. The Bodhisattvas, the Śrāvakas, and even the worldly lords who are assembling here are all spiritual beings. Though the Śrāvakas and lords and their followers do not fully comprehend the significance of the miracles going on about them, none of them are those whose minds are still under the bondage of ignorance and folly. If they were, they could not even be present at this extraordinary scene.

How does all this come about?

The compilation of the *Gaṇḍavyūha* was made possible owing to a definite change which took place in the mind of the Buddhist concerning life, the world, and especially the Buddha. Thus in the study of the *Gaṇḍavyūha*, what is most essential to know is that that the Buddha is no more the one who is living in the world conceivable in terms of space and time. His consciousness is not that of an ordinary mind which must be regulated according to the senses and logic. Nor is it a product of poetical imagination which creates its own images and methods of dealing with particular objects. The Buddha of the *Gaṇḍavyūha* lives in a spiritual world which has its own rules.

In this spiritual world there are no time-divisions such as the past, present, and future; for they have contracted themselves into a single moment of the present where life quivers in its true sense. The conception of time as an objective blank in which particular events as its contents succeed one after another has completely been discarded. The Buddha in the *Gaṇḍa* thus knows no time-continuity; the past and the future are both rolled up in this present moment of illumination, and this present moment is not something standing still with all its contents, for it ceaselessly moves on. Thus the past is the present, so is the future, but this present in which the past and the future are merged never remains the present; in other words, it is eternally present. And at the centre of this eternal present the Buddha has fixed his abode which is no abode.

As with time, so with space. Space in the *Gaṇḍavyūha* is not an extension divided by mountains and forests, rivers and oceans, lights and shades, the visible and the invisible. Extension is here indeed, as there is no contraction of space into one single block of existence; but what we have here is an infinite mutual fusion or penetration of all things, each with its individuality yet with something universal in it. The general fusion thus taking place is the practical annihilation of space which is recognizable only through change and division and impenetrability. To illustrate this state of existence, the *Gaṇḍavyūha* makes everything it depicts transparent and luminous, for luminosity is the only possible earthly representation that conveys the idea of universal interpenetration, the ruling topic of the sūtra. A world of lights transcending distance, opacity, and ugliness of all sorts, is the world of the *Gaṇḍavyūha*.

With the annihilation of space and time, there evolves a realm of imagelessness or shadowlessness (*anābhāsa*). As long as there are lights and shades, the principle of individuation always overwhelms us human mortals. In the *Gaṇḍavyūha* there is no shadowiness; it is true there are rivers, flowers, trees, nets, banners, etc., in the land of purity, in the description of which the compiler taxes his human imagination to its utmost limits; but no shadows are visible here anywhere. The clouds themselves are luminous bodies inconceivable and inexpressible in number,[1] hanging all over the Jetavana of the *Gaṇḍavyūha*—which are described

[1] *Acintya* and *anabhilāpya* are numbers of high denominations.

in its own terminology as 'heavenly jewel-palaces', 'incense-wood', 'Sumeru', 'musical instruments', 'pearl-nets', 'heavenly figures', etc.

This universe of luminosity, this scene of interpenetration, is known as the Dharmadhātu, in contrast to the Lokadhātu which is this world of particulars. In the Dharmadhātu there are space and time and individual beings as in the Lokadhātu, but they show none of their earthly characteristics of separateness and obduracy as are perceivable in the latter. For the Dharmadhātu is not a universe spatially or temporarily constructed like the Lokadhātu, and yet it is not utter blankness or mere void which is identifiable with absolute non-entity. The Dharmadhātu is a real existence and not separated from the Lokadhātu, but it is not the same as the latter when we do not come up to the spiritual level where the Bodhisattvas are living. It is realizable when the solid outlines of individuality melt away and the feeling of finiteness no more oppresses us. The *Gaṇḍavyūha* is this also known under the title, 'The Entering into the Dharmadhātu' (*dharmadhātupraveśa*).

2

What then are some of the chief changes of thought that have taken place in Buddhism enabling it to evolve a universe to be known as Dharmadhātu? What are those feelings and ideas which have entered into the consciousness of the inhabitants of the Dharmadhātu? In other words, what are the qualifications of Tathāgata, Bodhisattva, and Śrāvaka?

When these are specified, we shall know how the Mahāyāna came to be differentiated from the Hīnayāna, that is, why some Buddhists became dissatisfied with the way Buddhism had so far taken in its development after the passing of the Buddha himself. This development had run steadily towards exclusive asceticism on the one hand and towards the elaboration of philosophical subtleties on the other. This meant that Buddhism, instead of being a practical, social, everyday religion, had turned into a sort of mysticism which keeps its votaries on the giddy height of unapproachable abstractions making them refuse to descend among earthly entanglements. Such a religion may be all very well for the *élite*, for Arhats and Pratyeka-buddhas, but it lacks vitality and democratic usefulness when it is kept from coming in contact with the concrete affairs of life. The Mahāyānists revolted against this aloofness and unconcernedness of the Śrāvaka-ideal. Thus they could not help reviving and upholding the Bodhisattva-ideal, which marked the career of the Buddha before his attainment of supreme enlightenment; they then endeavoured to unfold to its furthest limits all that was to be found in the ideal. I have therefore selected the opening chapter of the *Gaṇḍavyūha*, where the Bodhisattva-ideal is contrasted in strong colour to the Śrāvaka-ideal, to show what was in the consciousness of the Mahāyāna followers when they developed their own thoughts and aspirations.

Towards the end of this Essay, I intend briefly to touch upon the further progress of the Bodhisattva-ideal among the Zen followers in China. They have induced even the Buddha himself to take an active part in the common life of the masses. He no more sits on a high seat decorated with seven kinds of jewels, discoursing on such abstract subjects as Non-ego, Emptiness, or Mind-only. On the contrary, he takes up a spade in his hands, tills the ground, sow seeds, and garners the harvest. In outward appearances he cannot be distinguished from a commoner whom we meet on the farm, in the street, or in the office. He is just as hard-working a person as we are. The Buddha in his Chinese Zen life does not carry his *Gaṇḍavyūha* atmosphere ostentatiously about him but quietly within him. A Buddha alone discovers him.

The following points may then be noted in the reading of the *Gaṇḍavyūha*:

1. The one dominant feeling, we may almost assert, that runs through the text is an active sense of grand inscrutable

PLATE VII

MANJUSRI IN A GRASS-ROBE

By Hsüeh-chien

The author was probably of Yüan. He was reputed, according to Japanese records, for his painting of Mañjuśrī. The Bodhisattva in this form is said to have appeared in a vision to a certain Lu when he visited T'ien-tai Shan in the Yüan-fêng period of Sung. This utter ignoring of the conventional symbolisation of the Bodhisattva is another example of "secularisation" which took place in China along with the growing popularity of Zen Buddhism. The present picture is one of the best specimens of the youthful "grass-robed" Mañjuśrī. Ch'ing-yü, of the King Aśoka monastery, writes: "Here, behold the teacher of the seven Buddhas! How, instead of riding on thy familiar golden-haired lion, showest thou thyself in this form?"

Mañjuśri generally represents Prajña, wisdom, which sees into the emptiness of all dharmas.

五臺山上雲蒸
飯面目分明
七佛師不誇金
毛獅子胡為
卻露此形儀
古績
草衣文殊像
阿育王山 業松
書于無畏堂

PLATE VIII
SAMANTABHADRA

By Ma Lin

The picture shows him in an easy posture, quite different from the way he appears in the preceding representations. Such pictures as this mark a gradual approach to the complete "secularisation" of the Bodhisattvas. The kakemono may be hung in the alcove and appreciated as a work of art. The subject is not necessarily meant for worship.

Samantabhadra generally represents Karuna, love. He lives in a world of particulars, in which respect he stands contrasted to Mañjuśrī.

mystery (*acintya*), going beyond the power of thinking and description. Everything one sees, hears, or observes in the Dharmadhātu is a mystery, because it is incomprehensible to the ordinary sense of logical measurement. Jetavana of so many square miles abruptly expands to the ends of the universe—does this not surpass human conception? A Bodhisattva comes from a world lying beyond even the furthest end of the universe—that is, beyond an ocean of worlds as innumerable as particles of atoms constituting a Buddha-land—is this not a wonderful event? And let us remind you that this Bodhisattva is accompanied by his retinues as innumerable as the number of atoms constituting a Buddha-land, and again that these visitors are coming from all the ten quarters, accompanied not only by their innumerable retinues but surrounded by luminous clouds, shining banners, etc. Depict all this in your own minds, exercising all the power of imagination that you can command—is it not really a most miraculous sight altogether transcending human thought? All that the poor writer of the *Gaṇḍavyūha* can say is 'inconceivable' (*acintya*) and 'indescribable' (*anabhilāpya*). The miracles performed are not of such local or partial nature as we encounter in most religious literature. Miracles so called are ordinarily a man's walking on water, a stick changing into a tree, a blind man being enabled to see, and so on. Not only are all such petty miracles as are recorded in the history of religion quite insignificant in scale and of no value when compared with those of the *Gaṇḍavyūha*, but they are fundamentally different from the latter; for the *Gaṇḍavyūha* miracles are possible only when the whole scheme of the universe as we conceive it is altered from its very basis.

2. We are impressed now with the spiritual powers of the Buddha who can achieve all these wonders by merely entering into a certain Samādhi. What are these powers? They are defined thus: (1) the sustaining and inspiring power (*adhiṣṭhāna*)[1] which is given to the Bodhisattva to

[1] This is an important conception in Mahāyāna Buddhism. For explanation see my *Studies in the Laṅkāvatāra Sūtra*, pp. 202 ff.

achieve the aim of his life; (2) the power of working miracles (*vikurvita*); (3) the power of ruling (*anubhāva*); (4) the power of the original vow (*pūrvapraṇidhāna*); (5) the power of goodness practised in his former lives (*pūrvasukṛitakuśalamūla*); (6) the power of receiving all good friends (*kalyāṇamitraparigraha*); (7) the power of pure faith and knowledge (*śraddhāyajñānaviśuddhi*); (8) the power of attaining a highly illuminating faith (*udārādhimuktyavabhāsapratilambha*); (9) the power of purifying the thought of the Bodhisattva (*bodhisattvādhyāśayapariśuddhi*); and (10) the power of earnestly walking towards all-knowledge and original vows (*adhyāśayasarvajñatāpraṇidhānaprasthāna*).

3. The fact that the transformation of the entire city of Jetavana was due to the miraculous power of the Samādhi attained by the Buddha makes one inquire into the nature of the Samādhi. According to the *Gaṇḍavyūha*, the miracle was effected by the strength of a great compassionate heart (*mahākaruṇā*) which constitutes the very essence of the Samādhi; for compassion is its body (*śarira*), its source (*mukha*), its leader (*pūrvaṅgama*), and the means of expanding itself all over the universe. Without this great heart of love and compassion, the Buddha's Samādhi, however exalted it may be in every other way, will be of no avail in the enactment of the great spiritual drama so wonderfully described here. This is indeed what characteristically distinguishes the Mahāyāna from all that has preceded it in the history of Buddhism. Owing to its self-expanding and self-creating power, a great loving heart transforms this earthly world into one of splendour and mutual fusion, and this is where the Buddha is always abiding.

4. The *Gaṇḍavyūha* is in a sense the history of the inner religious consciousness of Samantabhadra the Bodhisattva, whose wisdom-eye (*jñānacakṣus*), life of devotion (*caryā*), and original vows (*praṇidhāna*) make up its contents. Thus all the Bodhisattvas taking part in the establishment of the Dharmadhātu are born (*abhiniryāta*) of the life and vows of Samantabhadra. And Sudhana's chief object of pilgrimage which is told in such detail in the *Gaṇḍavyūha* was nothing

else but the identifying of himself with Samantabhadra the Bodhisattva. When after visiting more than fifty teachers of all sorts he came to Samantabhadra, he was thoroughly instructed by the Bodhisattva as regards his life of devotion, his knowledge, his vows, his miraculous powers, etc.; and when Sudhana realized what all these Buddhist disciplines meant he found himself in complete identity not only with Samantabhadra, but with all the Buddhas. His body filled the universe to its ends, and his life of devotion (*caryā*), his enlightenment (*sambodhi*), his transformation-bodies (*vikurvita*), his revolution of the Dharma-wheel, his eloquence, his voice, his faith, his abode, his love and compassion, and his emancipation and mastery over the world were exactly those of Samantabhadra and all the Buddhas.

What most concerns us here is the idea of the vow (*praṇidhāna*) which is made by a Bodhisattva at the beginning of his career and which controls all his later life. His vows are concerned with enlightening, or emancipating, or saving all his fellow-beings, which include not only sentient beings but the non-sentient. The reason he gives up everything that is ordinarily regarded as belonging to oneself is not to gain a word or a phrase of truth for himself—there is in fact no such thing as truth abstractly conceived, nor is there anything that is to be adhered to as ego-substance, in the great ocean of Reality; what he wants to accomplish by his life of self-sacrifice is to lead all beings to final emancipation, to a state of happiness which is not of this world, to make the light of knowledge illuminate the whole universe, and to see all the Buddhas praised and adored by all beings. This is what mainly constitutes a life of devotion as practised by Samantabhadra the Bodhisattva.

5. When I say that the Mahāyāna or Bodhisattva-ideal is contrasted with the Hīnayāna or Arhat-ideal in the former's being practical and intimately connected with our everyday earthly life, some may doubt this, seeing what a mysterious world the Dharmadhātu is where all kinds of apparent impossibilities are taking place as if they were the

most ordinary things, such as carrying a bucket of water, or kindling a bundle of faggots. The Dharmadhātu which is the world of the *Gaṇḍavyūha* is assuredly a transcendental one standing in no connection with the hard facts of this life. But the objector must remember that the point from which we are to survey the world according to the *Gaṇḍavyūha* is not that of a mind immersed in the mire of individualization. In order to see life and the world in their proper bearing, the Mahāyāna expects us first to clear off all the obstacles that rise from our obstinacy in taking the world of relativity as the ultimate limit of reality. When the veil is lifted, the obstacles are swept away, and the self-nature of things presents itself in the aspect of Suchness; and it is then that the Mahāyāna is ready to take up the so-called real problems of life and solve them in accordance with the truth, i.e. *yathābhūtam*. Contradiction is so deep-seated in life that it can never be eradicated until life is surveyed from a point higher than itself. When this is done, the world of the *Gaṇḍavyūha* ceased to be a mystery, a realm devoid of form and corporeality, for it now overlaps this earthly world; no, it becomes that 'Thou art it', and there is a perfect fusion of the two. The Dharmadhātu is the Lokadhātu, and its inhabitants—that is, all the Bodhisattvas, including the Buddhas—are ourselves, and their doings are our doings. They looked so full of mystery, they were miracles, so long as they were observed from this earthly end, where we imagined that there was really something at the other end; but as soon as the dividing-wall constructed by our imagination is removed, Samantabhadra's arms raised to save sentient beings become our own, which are now engaged in passing the salt to a friend at the table, and Maitreya's opening the Vairochana Tower for Sudhana is our ushering a caller into the parlour for a friendly chat. No more sitting on the summit of reality (*bhūtakoṭi*), in the tranquillity of absolute oneness, do we review a world of turmoil; but rather we see both the Bodhisattvas and the Buddhas shining in the sweat of their foreheads, in the tears shed for the mother who lost a child in the fury of passions burning against injustice in its multifarious forms—in short, in their never-ending fight against all that goes under the name of evil. This again reminds us of P'ang's reputed verse:

> How wondrously supernatural!
> And how miraculous this!
> I draw water, I carry fuel!

Lin-chi's sermon on Mañjuśrī, Samantabhadra and Avalokiteśvara may be considered also in this connection. 'There are,' he says, 'some student-monks who look for Mañjuśrī at Wu-tai Shan,[1] but they have already taken the wrong road. There is no Mañjuśrī at Wu-tai Shan. Do you wish to know where he is? There is something this very moment at work in you, showing no tendency to waver, betraying no disposition to doubt—this is your living Mañjuśrī. The light of non-discrimination which flashes through every thought of yours—this is your Samantabhadra who remains true all the time. Every thought of yours which, knowing of itself how to break off the bondage, is emancipated at every moment—this is entering into the Samādhi of Avalokiteśvara. Each of them functions in harmonious mutuality and simultaneously, so that one is three, three is one. When this is understood, you are able to read the sūtras.'

Commenting on Lin-chi's view of 'No Mañjuśrī at Wu-tai Shan', a Zen master has this verse:

> Whenever there is a mountain well shaded in verdure,
> There is a holy ground for your spiritual exercises;
> What then is the use of climbing up, supported by the
>   mountain staff,
> Mañjuśrī to worship on the Ch'ing-ling Peak?
> Even when the golden-haired lion reveals itself in the
>   clouds,
> Indeed, rightly viewed, this is no auspicious sign.

[1] The Wu-tai is the sacred abode of Mañjuśrī in China while the E-mei is consecrated to Samantabhadra and the P'u-t'o-lo to Avalokiteśvara.

3

Reference was made to the sense of mystery which envelops the whole text of the *Gaṇḍavyūha* as one of its striking characteristics. I want now to fathom this and point out where it originates—that is, what may be termed its fundamental spiritual insight. For the *Gaṇḍavyūha* has its own intuition of the world and the mind, from which so many miracles, mysteries, or inconceivabilities succeed one after another in a most wonderful manner—which to many may appear to be altogether too fantastic, too far beyond the bounds of common sense. But when we grasp the central fact of the spiritual experience gone through by the Bodhisattvas as narrated in the sūtra, all the rest of the scenes depicted here will suggest perfect naturalness, and there will be no more irrationalities in them. The main thing, therefore, for us to do if we desire to understand the *Gaṇḍavyūha*, is to take hold of its fundamental insight.

The fundamental insight of the *Gaṇḍavyūha* is known as Interpenetration. It is, philosophically speaking, a thought somewhat similar to the Hegelian conception of concrete-universals. Each individual reality, besides being itself, reflects in it something of the universal, and at the same time it is itself because of other individuals. A system of perfect relationship exists among individual existences and also between individuals and universals, between particular objects and general ideas. This perfect network of mutual relations has received at the hand of the Mahāyāna philosopher the technical name of Interpenetration.

When the Empress Tsê-t'ien of T'ang felt it difficult to grasp the meaning of Interpenetration, Fa-tsang, the great master of the Avataṁsaka school of Buddhism illustrated it in the following way. He had first a candle lighted, and then had mirrors placed encircling it on all sides. The central light reflected itself in every one of the mirrors, and every one of these reflected lights was reflected again in every mirror, so that there was a perfect interplay of lights, that is, of concrete-universals. This is said to have enlightened the mind of the Empress. It is necessary to have this kind of philosophy for the understanding of the *Gaṇḍavyūha* or the *Avataṁsaka.* The following extracts from the text before us will help us to have a glimpse into its deep intuition.

After describing the transformations that took place in Jetavana when the Buddha entered into a Samādhi known as Siṁhavijṛimbhita, the *Gaṇḍavyūha* goes on to say: 'All this is due to the Buddha's miraculous (*acintya*) deeds of goodness, to his miraculous work of purity, to his miraculously mighty power; all this is because he has the miraculous power of transforming his one body and making it pervade the entire universe; it is because he has the miraculous power of making all the Buddhas, all the Buddha-lands with their splendours, enter into his own body; it is because he has the miraculous power of manifesting all the images of the Dharmadhātu within one single particle of dust; it is because he has the miraculous power of revealing all the Buddhas of the past with their successive doings within a single pore of his skin; it is because he has the miraculous power of illuminating the entire universe with each one of the rays which emanate from his body; it is because he has the miraculous power of evolving clouds of transformation from a single pore of his skin and making them fill up all the Buddha-lands; it is because he has the miraculous power of revealing in a single pore of his skin the whole history of all the worlds in the ten quarters from their first appearance until their final destruction. It is for these reasons that in this grove of Jetavana are revealed all the purities and splendours of the Buddha-lands.'

When all the Bodhisattvas with an inconceivable number of followers come from the ten quarters of the world and begin to get settled around the Buddha, the *Gaṇḍavyūha* explains for its readers who these Bodhisattvas are miraculously assembling here, accompanied generally by luminous clouds, and gives among others the following characterization of the Bodhisattvas:

'All these Bodhisattvas from the ten quarters of the world

together with their retinues are born of the life and vows of Samantabhadra the Bodhisattva. By means of their pure wisdom-eye they see all the Buddhas of the past, present, and future, and also hear the ocean of the sūtras and the revolving of the Dharma-wheel by all the Buddhas. They are all masters of the excellent Pāramitās; they approach and serve all the Tathāgatas who are performing miracles every minute; they are also able to expand their own bodies to the ends of the universe; they bring forth by means of their body of light all the religious assemblies conducted by the Buddhas; they reveal in each particle of dust all the worlds, singly and generally, with their different conditions and multitudes; and in these different worlds they choose the most opportune season to discipline all beings and to bring them to maturity; emitting a deep, full sound from every pore of the skin, which reverberates throughout the universe, they discourse on the teachings of all the Buddhas.'

All such statements may sound too figurative, too fantastic to be seriously considered by the so-called rationally minded. From the realistic or rationalistic point of view, which upholds objective validity and sense-measurement as the sole standard of truth, the *Gaṇḍavyūha* fares rather ill. But we must remember that there is another point of view, especially in matters spiritual, which pays no attention to the rationalistic interpretation of our inner experiences. The human body, ordinarily or from the sense-point of view, occupies a limited area of space which can be measured, and continues to live also during a measurable period of time. And against this body there is the whole expanse of the universe, including all the mountains and oceans on earth and also all the starry heavens. How can this body of ours be made to take in the entire objectivity? How can our insignificant, ignominious 'hair-hole' or 'pore of the skin' (*romakūpa*) be turned into a holy stage where all the Tathāgatas of the past, present, and future can congregate for their spiritual discourses? Obviously, this is an utter impossibility or the height of absurdity. But the strange fact is that when a door opens and a light shines from an unknown source into the dark chamber of consciousness, all time- and space-limitations dissolve away, and we make a Siṁhanāda (lion-roar), 'Before Abraham was I am,' or 'I alone am the honoured one above and below all the heavens.' The *Gaṇḍavyūha* is written always from this exalted point of view. If science surveys the objective world and philosophy unravels intricacies of logic, Buddhism dives into the very abyss of being, and tells us in the directest possible manner all it sees under the surface.

When we speak, as we sometimes do, of the philosophical background of the *Gaṇḍavyūha* or the Hegelian idea of concrete-universals, the reader may think that Buddhism is a system of philosophy, and the sūtras are attempts to expound it in their characteristic manner. If we have made him take their attitude towards the Mahāyāna, we must withdraw everything that was said in this connection and start afresh in our study of the sūtras. Whatever misunderstandings or misinterpretations Zen has incurred from its outside critics, its chief merit consists in clearing our consciousness of all the rubbish it has gathered in the way of philosophical explanations of existence. By its disclaiming the letter which is so apt to thwart the progress of the spirit, Zen has kept its central thought unspoiled. That is to say, it has succeeded in steadily upholding the value of experience and intuition in the understanding of Reality. The method of Zen differs from that of the *Gaṇḍavyūha*, but as both agree in spirit, the one will prove complementary to the other when we endeavour to study Buddhism comprehensively as it has developed in the Far East. The sūtras and Zen are not antagonistic, nor are they contradictory. What the sūtras express through the psychology and tradition of their compilers, Zen treats after its own fashion as conditioned by the intellectual equipment and psychological and racial peculiarities of its masters. Read the following Zen sermon[1] and compare it with the *Gaṇḍavyūha*:

[1] Given by Hsiao-ch'un of Ling-ch'üan temple, perhaps of the eleventh century. *Hsü Chuan-têng Lu*, XX.

'Here is a man who, even from the very beginning of things, has had no dwelling, nothing to depend on; above, not a fraction of tile is over his head; below, not an inch of earth supports his feet. Tell me where he gets his body at rest and his life established for the twelve periods of the day. When you understand, he is known to be gone to India in the morning and to be back here in the evening.'

4

Having acquainted ourselves with the general atmosphere in which the *Gaṇḍavyūha* moves, let us now proceed to see what are the constituents of the audience—that is, what are the particular characteristics of Bodhisattvahood as distinguished from those of Śrāvakahood. In other words, the question is concerned with the differentia of Mahāyāna Buddhism. When we know how the Bodhisattva is qualified in the *Gaṇḍavyūha*, we know also how Bodhisattvahood differentiates itself from Śrāvakahood and what are the Mahāyāna thoughts as they are presented in this sūtra against those of the Hīnayāna. For the opening chapter of the *Gaṇḍavyūha* emphatically sets up the Bodhisattvas against the Śrāvakas, giving reasons why the latter are unable to participate like the Bodhisattvas in the development of the grand spiritual life.

The Bodhisattvas numbering five hundred are attending the assembly which takes place under the supervision of the Buddha in Jetavana. The same number of the Śrāvakas are also found among the audience. Of the Śrāvakas such names are mentioned as Maudgalyayana, Mahākāśyapa, Revata, Subhūti, Aniruddha, Nandika, Kapphiṇa, Kātyāyana, Pūrṇa, Maitrāyaṇīputra, etc., while Samantabhadra and Mañjuśrī stand out prominently as the two leaders of the five hundred Bodhisattvas. The Bodhisattvas are all said to have 'issued from the life and vows of Samantabhadra', and qualified in the following way: (1) they are unattached in their conduct because they are able to expand themselves in all the Buddha-lands; (2) they manifest innumerable bodies because they can go over wherever there are Buddhas; (3) they are in possession of an unimpeded and unspoiled eyesight because they can perceive the miraculous transformations of all the Buddhas; (4) they are able to visit anywhere without being bound to any one locality because they never neglect appearing in all places where the Buddhas attain to their enlightenment; (5) they are in possession of a limitless light because they can illumine the ocean of all the Buddha-truths with the light of their knowledge; (6) they have an inexhaustible power of eloquence through eternity because their speech has no taint; (7) they abide in the highest wisdom which knows no limits like space because their conduct is pure and free from taints; (8) they have no fixed abode because they reveal themselves personally in accordance with the thoughts and desires of all beings; (9) they are free from obscurities because they know that there are really no beings, no soul-substances in the world of beings; and finally (10) they are in possession of transcendental knowledge which is as vast as space because they illumine all the Dharmadhātus with their nets of light.

In another place where the Bodhisattvas visiting Jetavana from the ten quarters of the universe to contribute their share in the grand demonstration of the Buddha's spiritual powers are characterized, we find among other things the following statements: 'All the Bodhisattvas know that all beings are like Māyā, that all the Buddhas are like shadows, that all existence with its rise and fall is like a dream, that all forms of karma are like images in a mirror, that the rising of all things is like a *fata morgana*, that all the worlds are mere transformations; further, the Bodhisattvas are all endowed with the ten powers, knowledge, dignity, and faith of the Tathāgata, which enable them to roar like lions; they have deeply delved into the ocean of inexhaustible eloquence, they have acquired the knowledge of how to explain the truths for all beings; they are complete masters of their conduct so that they move about in the world as freely as in space; they are in possession of all the miraculous powers belonging to a Bodhisattva; their strength and energy will crush the army of Māra; their knowledge-power penetrates into the past, present, and future; knowing that all things are like space, they practise non-resistance, and are not attached to them; though they work indefatigably for others, they know that when things are observed from the point of view of all-knowledge, nobody knows whence they come; though they recognize an objective world, they know that its existence is something unobtainable; they enter into all the worlds by means of incorruptible knowledge; in all the worlds they reveal themselves with the utmost freedom; they are born in all the worlds, take all form; they transform a small area into an extended tract of land, and the latter again into a small area; all the Buddhas are revealed in one single moment of their thought; the powers of all the Buddhas are added on to them; they survey the entire universe in one glance and are not at all confused; they are able to visit all the worlds in one moment.'

Against this characterization of the Bodhisattvas, what have we for that of the five hundred Śrāvakas? According to the *Gaṇḍavyūha*, 'They are enlightened in the self-nature of truth and reason, they have an insight into the limit of reality, they have entered into the essence of things, they are out of the ocean of becoming, they abide where the Buddha-merit is stored, they are released from the bondage of the Knots and Passions, they dwell in the house of non-attachment, they stay in the serenity of space, they have their desires, errors, and doubts wiped off by the Buddha, and they are rightly and faithfully devoted to the Buddha-ocean.'

When Śrāvakahood is compared with Bodhisattvahood as they are here particularized, we at once perceive how cold, aloof, and philosophical the one is, in great contrast to the spiritual activities and miraculous movements of the other. The Bodhisattva is always kept busy doing something for others, sometimes spreading himself all over the universe, sometimes appearing in one or another path of existence, sometimes destroying the army of evil ones, sometimes paying reverence and making offerings to the Buddhas of the past, present, and future. And in these movements he is perfectly at home, he goes on everywhere with the utmost ease and spontaneity as nothing impedes his manœuvring as a world-saviour. The Śrāvaka is, on the other hand, an intellectual recluse, his insight is altogether philosophical and has no religious fervour accompanying it; he is satisfied with what he has attained by himself, and has no desire stirred within himself to let others share also in his spiritual or rather metaphysical realization. To him the entire world of inconceivabilities is a closed book, and this world of inconceivabilities is the very place where all the Bodhisattvas belong and find the reason of their existence. However penetrating and perspicuous may be the intellect of the Srāvaka, there is still a world altogether beyond his grasp.

This world, to use the *Gaṇḍavyūha* terminology, is where we find the Buddha's transformations (*vikurvita*), orderly arrangements (*vyūha*), superhuman virility (*vṛiṣabha*), playful activities (*vikrīḍita*), miracles (*pratihārya*), sovereignty (*adhipateyata*), wonderful performances (*caritavikurvita*), supreme power (*prabhāva*), sustaining power (*adhiṣṭhāna*), and land of purity (*kṣetrapariśuddhi*). And again here is where the Bodhisattvas have their realms, their assemblies, their entrances, their comings-together, their visits, their transformations, their miracles, their groups, their quarters, their fine array of lion-seats, their palatial residences, their resting abodes, their transports in Samādhi, their survey of the worlds, their energetic concentrations, their heroisms, their offerings to the Tathāgatas, their certifications, their maturities, their energies, their Dharmakāyas of purity, their knowledge-bodies of perfection, their vow-bodies in various manifestations, their material bodies in their perfected form, the fulfilment and purification of all their forms, the array of their boundless light-images, the spreading out of their great nets of lights, and the bringing forth of their transformation-clouds, the expansion of their bodies all over the ten quarters, the perfection of all their transformation-deeds, etc.

5

What are the causes and conditions that have come to differentiate Bodhisattvahood so much from Śrāvaka-hood?

The *Gaṇḍavyūha* does not forget to point out what causes are contributive to this remarkable differentiation, to tell what are the conditions that make the Śrāvakas altogether blind to the various manifestations and transformations going on in a most wonderful way at the assembly of the Bodhisattvas in Jetavana. The *Gaṇḍavyūha* gives the following reasons:

Because the stock of merit is not the same (1); because the Śrāvakas have not seen, and disciplined themselves in, the virtues of the Buddha (2); because they have not approved the notion that the universe is filled with Buddha-lands in all the ten quarters where there is a fine array of all Buddhas (3); because they have not given praise to the various wonderful manifestations put forward by the Buddhas (4); because they have not awakened the desire after supreme enlightenment attainable in the midst of transmigration (5); because they have not induced others to cherish the desire after supreme enlightenment (6); because they have not been able to continue the Tathāgata-family (7); because they have not taken all beings under their protection (8); because they have not advised others to practise the Pāramitās of the Bodhisattva (9); because while yet in the transmigration of birth and death they have not persuaded others to seek for the most exalted wisdom-eye (10).

Further, because the Śrāvakas have not disciplined themselves in all the stock of merit from which issues all-knowledge (11); because they have not perfected all the stock of merit which makes the appearance of the Buddha possible (12); because they have not added to the enhancement of the Buddha-land by seeking for the knowledge of transformation (13); because they have not entered into the realm which is surveyed by the Bodhisattva-eye (14); because they have not sought the stock of merit which produces an incomparable insight going beyond this world (15); because they have not made any of the vows constituting Bodhisattvahood (16); because they have not conformed themselves to all that is the product of the Tathāgata's sustaining power (17); because they have not realized that all things are like Māyā and the Bodhisattvas are like a dream (18); because they have not attained the most exhilarating excitements (*prativega-vivardhana*) of the Bodhisattva (19); in short, because they have not realized all these spiritual states belonging to the wisdom-eye of Samantabhadra to which the Śrāvakas and Pratyekabuddhas are strangers (20).

So, concludes the *Gaṇḍavyūha*, all these great Śrāvakas such as Śāriputra, etc., have no stock of merit, no wisdom-eye, no Samādhi, no emancipation, no power of transformation, no sovereignty, no energy, no mastery, no abode, no realm, which enable them to get into the assemblage of the Bodhisattvas and participate in the performance of the great spiritual drama that is going on in Jetavana. As they have sought their deliverance according to the vehicle and way of Śrāvakahood, what they have accomplished does not go beyond Śrāvakahood. They have indeed gained the knowledge whereby the truth is made manifest, they are abiding in the limit of reality (*bhūtakoṭi*), they are enjoying the serenity of the ultimate (*atyantaśānti*); but they have no great compassionate all-embracing heart for all beings, for they are too intently occupied with their own doings (*ātmakārya*) and have no mind to accumulate the Bodhisattva-knowledge and to discipline themselves in it. They have their own realization and emancipation, but they have no desire, make no vows to make others also find their resting abode in it. They do not thus understand what is really meant by the inconceivable power of the Tathāgata.

To sum up: the Śrāvakas are yet under the covering of too great a karma-hindrance; they are unable to cherish such great vows as are made by the Bodhisattvas for the spiritual welfare of all beings; their insight is not clear and penetrating enough to see into all the secrets of life; they have not yet opened what is designated as the wisdom-eye (*jñānacakṣus*) in the *Gaṇḍavyūha*, wherewith a Bodhisattva takes in at a glance all the wonders and inconceivabilities of the spiritual realm to its deepest abyss. How superficial, compared to this, is the philosophical insight of the Śrāvakas!

6

The *Gaṇḍavyūha* gives us several parables to tell more graphically the conditions of Śrāvakahood under which its followers are still labouring. Let me quote one or two.

Along the river Gangā there are millions of millions of hungry ghosts (*preta*) all naked and tormented with hunger and thirst; they feel as if their bodies were burning; and their lives are threatened every minute by birds and beasts of prey. Thirst impels them to seek for water, but they cannot find it anywhere even though they are right close to the river. Some see the river, but for them there is no water, only the dried-up bed. Why? Because their karma-hindrance lies too heavy on them. In the same way, these great learned philosophical Śrāvakas, even though they are in the midst of the large assembly of the Bodhisattvas, are not capable of recognizing the grand miracles of the Tathāgata. For they have relinquished all-knowledge (*sarvajñatā*) owing to the ignorance-cataract covering their eyes; for they have never planted their stock of merit in the soil of all-knowledge.

In the Himālaya mountains many kinds of medicinal herbs are found, and they are distinguished by an experienced doctor each according to its specific qualities. But because they have no eye for them all these are not recognized by the hunters, nor by the herdsmen, who may frequent these regions. In the same way, the Bodhisattvas who have entered into a realm of transcendental knowledge and gained a spiritual power over form are able to see the Tathāgatas and their grand display of miracles. But the Śrāvakas, in the midst of these wonderful events, cannot see them, because they are satisfied only with their own deeds (*svakārya*), and not at all concerned with the spiritual welfare of others.

To give another parable: here is a man in a large congregation of people. He happens to fall asleep, and in a dream he is suddenly transported to the summit of Mount Sumeru where Śakrendra has his magnificent palatial residence. There are a large number of mansions, pavilions, gardens, lakes, etc., each in its full splendour. There are also celestial beings incalculable in number, the grounds are strewn with heavenly flowers, the trees are decorated with beautiful robes, and the flowers are in full bloom. Most exquisite music is placed among the trees, and the branches and leaves emit of their own accord pleasing sounds, and these go on in harmonious concert with the melodious singing of the celestial damsels. The dancers, innumerable and attired in resplendent garments, are enjoying themselves on the terrace. The man is now no more a bystander at these scenes, for he is one of the participants himself apparelled in heavenly fashion, and going around among the inhabitants of Sudarśana as if he has belonged to them from the beginning.

These phenomena, however, have never come to be noticed by any other mortals who are congregated here, for what is perceived by the man is a vision only given to him. In a similar manner, the Bodhisattvas are able to see all the wonderful sights in the world taking place under the direction of the Buddha's power. For they have been accumulating their stock of merit for ever so many kalpas, making vows based on all-knowledge which knows no bounds in time and space. For, again, they have studied all the virtues of the Buddhas, disciplining themselves in the way of Bodhisattvahood, and then perfecting themselves for the attainment of all-knowledge. In short, they have fulfilled all the vows of Samantabhadra and lived his life of devotion, whereas the Śrāvakas have none of the pure insight belonging to the Bodhisattvas.

7

From these quotations and delineations, we have now, I hope, a general background of the *Gaṇḍavyūha* more or less clearly outlined, and from them also we learn the following ideas which are really the contents of at least the opening chapter of the sūtra, while they also give us a further glimpse into the essence of the Mahāyāna teaching generally.

1. There is a world which is not of this world, though inseparable from it.

2. The world where we ordinarily move is characterized with limitations of all sorts. Each individual reality holds itself against others, which is indeed its self-nature (*svabhāva*). But in the world of the *Gaṇḍavyūha* known as the Dharmadhātu, individual realities are enfolded in one great Reality, and this great Reality is found participated in by each individual one. Not only this, but each individual existence contains in itself all other individual existences as such. Thus there is a universal interpenetration, so called, in the Dharmadhātu.

3. These supernatural phenomena cannot take place in a world where darkness and obduracy prevail, because then a penetration would be impossible. If a penetration should take place in these conditions it would mean the general breaking-down of all individual realities, which is a chaos.

4. Therefore, the Dharmadhātu is a world of lights not accompanied by any form of shade. The essential nature of

light is to intermingle without interfering or obstructing or destroying one another. One single light reflects in itself all other lights generally and individually.

5. This is not a philosophical interpretation of existence reached by cold logical reasoning, nor is it a symbolical representation of the imagination. It is a world of real spiritual experience.

6. Spiritual experience is like sense-experience. It is direct, and tells us directly all that it has experienced without resorting to symbolism or ratiocination. The *Gaṇḍavyūha* is to be understood in this manner—that is, as a document recording one's actual spiritual life.

7. This realm of spirit belongs to the Bodhisattva and not to the Śrāvaka. The latter serenely abides in a world of intellectual intuition and monotony, supremely above the endlessly intermingling world of particulars and multiplicities. The Bodhisattva has a loving heart, and his is a life of devotion and self-sacrifice given up to a world of individualities.

8. A society of spiritual beings is approachable only by means of a great loving heart (*mahākaruṇā*), a great friendly spirit (*mahāmaitrī*), morality (*śīla*), great vows (*praṇidhāna*), miraculous powers (*abhijñā*), purposelessness (*anabhisaṁskāra*), perfect disinterestedness (*anāyūha*), skilful means born of transcendental wisdom (*prajñopāya*), and transformations (*nirmāṇa*).[1]

9. As these attributes are lacking in Śrāvakahood, its devotees are not allowed to join the congregation of Buddhas and Bodhisattvas. Even when they are in it they are incapable of appreciating all that goes on in such assemblages. The Mahāyāna is more than mere Emptiness, a great social spirit is moving behind it.

10. Lastly, we must remember that there is a sustaining power (*adhiṣṭhāna*) behind all these spiritual phenomena that are going on in Jetavana, and also behind all those transformation-Bodhisattvas who have gathered around the Buddha. This power comes from the Buddha himself. He is

[1] From Maitreya's instructions given to Sudhana. MMG, pp. 1414–5.

the great centre and source of illumination. He is the sun whose light reaches the darkest corners of the universe and yet leaves no shadow anywhere. The Buddha of the *Gaṇḍavyūha* is, therefore, called Mahāvairochana-Buddha, the Buddha of Great Illumination.

8

In conclusion, let me quote the verse uttered by one of the Bodhisattvas[1] in praise of the virtues of the Buddha, by which we can see in what relationship he generally stands to his devotees in the *Gaṇḍavyūha*:

'1. The great Muni, the best of the Śākya, is furnished with all the perfect virtues; and those who see him are purified in mind and turn towards the Mahāyāna.

'2. That the Tathāgatas appear in the world is to benefit all beings; out of a great compassionate heart they revolve the wheel of the Dharma.

'3. The Buddhas have gone through many a heart-rending experience for ages, for the sake of sentient beings; and how can all the world requite them for what it owes them?

'4. Rather suffer terribly in the evil paths of existence for ever so many kalpas, than seek emancipation somewhere else by abandoning the Buddha.

'5. Rather suffer all the pain that may befall all beings, than find comfort where there are no Buddhas to see.

'6. Rather abide in the evil paths of existence if the Buddhas can all the time be heard, than be born in the pleasant paths and never have the chance to hear them.

'7. Rather be born in the hells, however long one has to stay in each one of them, than be delivered therefrom by cutting oneself away from the Buddhas.

[1] Dharmadhātu-tala-bheda-jñāna-abhijñā-rāja is his name; he comes from the upper part of the world to take part in the Jetavana assembly. MMG, p. 86.

'8. Why? Because even though one may stay long in the evil paths, one's wisdom will ever be growing if only the Buddha is to be seen.

'9. When the Buddha, the Lord of the world, is to be seen somewhere, all pain will be eradicated; and one will enter into a realm of great wisdom which belongs to the Tathāgatas.

'10. When the Buddha, the peerless one, is to be seen somewhere, all the hindrances will be cleared away, and infinite bliss will be gained and the way of enlightenment perfected.

'11. When the Buddhas are seen, they will cut asunder all the doubts cherished by all beings, and give satisfaction to each according to his aspirations worldly and super-worldly.'

The above is given to illustrate the attitude which is generally assumed towards the Buddha by the Bodhisattvas who come to the community from every possible quarter of the world. To show how this conception of the Buddha changes in Zen, I quote a few of the answers given by the masters to the question: 'What, or Who, is the Buddha?' As will readily be observed, he is here no more a transcendental being enveloped in heavenly rays of light, he is an old gentleman like ourselves, walking among us, talking with us, quite an accessible familiar being. Whatever light he emits is to be discovered by us, for it is not already there as something to be perceived. The Chinese imagination does not soar so high, so brilliantly, so dazzlingly. All those resplendent scenes depicted in the first part of this Essay are folded up, leaving us once more on the grey earth. Superficially there is a serious gap between Zen and *Gaṇḍavyūha* as far as the Buddha and his supernatural functions and surroundings are considered. But when we go deeper down into the essence of the matter, we will recognize that there is much of 'Interpenetration' in Zen, which is intelligible only in the light of the *Gaṇḍavyūha*.

• • • • •

Huai-hai (720–814) of Pai-chang Shan[1] was asked by a monk, 'Who is the Buddha?'

Hai: 'Who are you?'

Monk: 'I am "so and so".'

Hai: 'Do you know this "so and so"?'

Monk: 'Most distinctly here.'

Hai now raised his *hossu* and said, 'Do you see?'

Monk: 'Yes.'

Hai then shut himself up and did not speak any further. But where was the monk's question answered? Did he find the Buddha?

Ling-hsün of Fu-jung Shan,[2] who was a disciple of Chih-chang, once asked the master, 'Who is the Buddha?'

Chang answered, 'Would you believe if I told you?'

Hsün: 'When Master truthfully tells me, why should I not believe him?'

Chang: 'You are he.'

Hsün: 'How should I hold to the view?'

Chang: 'Even when one particle of dust gets settled in your eye, all kinds of visions are sure to upset you.'

Later on, Fa-yen remarked, 'If Kuei-tsung (meaning Chih-chang) failed to put in his last words, he would no more be Kuei-tsung.'

A monk asked Hung of Tai-lung,[3] 'Who is the Buddha?'

Hung: 'You are he.'

Monk: 'How do I understand it?'

Hung: 'Do you wish to put a handle to your begging-bowl?'

The monk called Hui-chao asked Fa-yen, 'Who is the Buddha?'

Yen replied, 'You are Hui-chao.'

On this Hsüeh-tou, the compiler of the *Pi-yen-chi*, has this verse:

[1] *Chuan*, VI.

[2] *Chuan*, XI.

[3] 'Zen Materials Classified', Fas. II.

The spring breeze is gently rising over the Chang district,
The partridge is softly singing among the bushes laden with blossoms.
The carp leaping up the turbulent cataract trebly broken turns into a dragon,
And what a fool is he who still at night seeks for it in the mill-pond!

Ma-tsu's[1] answer was more abstract and philosophical when Tai-mei asked, 'What is the Buddha?' for it was 'What is Mind, that is Buddha.' But later on Ma-tsu changed his favourite answer to, 'Not Mind, not Buddha.' When this was reported to Tai-mei, the latter strongly asserted himself, saying, 'Whatever the old master may tell you now, I state, as ever, "What is Mind, that is Buddha".'

When this answer was given by Nêng of Yün-chü to a monk, the latter said: 'I fail to understand. May I ask you to help me out in some way?' The master replied: 'To help you out we call him Buddha. By throwing your light inwardly, see by yourself what is this body of yours, this mind of yours.'

The constant advice given by the Zen master to his monks is not to cling to the latter. The letter is what is known technically as Upāya or 'some means to help one out in the understanding of Zen truth'. Hence the following 'Mondo'[2] between Wên of Chên-ching and a monk. When the latter asked, 'Who is the Buddha?' the master laughed most heartily.

Monk: 'I do not see why my question makes you laugh.'

Master: 'I laugh at your attempt to get into the meaning by merely following the letter.'

Monk: 'Inadvertently I have lost the bargain.'

The master then called out, 'No need of your making bows now!'

[1] *Chuan*, VII.

[2] *Wên-ta*, 'questions and answers'.

The monk now went back to the company, whereupon the master remarked again, 'Your understanding as ever follows the letter.'

It was for this reason that when asked, 'Who is the Buddha?' some masters answered, 'The mouth is the gate of woes.'

As there will be no end if I go on like this, quoting the masters as recorded in the history of Zen, I will give here only a few more examples and show how many aspects have been pointed out by them in their understanding of what or who the Buddha is. All the answers do not necessarily point to one aspect of Buddhahood; for they are conditioned by the circumstances in which the question was evoked.

Shou-ch'u of Tung-shan answered, 'Three *chin* of sesame.'

Wên-yen of Yün-mên: 'A dirt-wiping stick.'

Wu-yeh of Fên-chou: 'No idle thinking.'

Hsing-nien of Shou-shan: 'A new bride rides on a donkey, and her mother-in-law holds the rein.'

I of Pa-chiao: 'The mountains are blue and the waters green.'

Tao-ch'üan of Kuei-tsung[1]: 'When snow melts away, the spring will come by itself.'

Shu of Pao-fu: 'Nothing can portray him truthfully.'

Tuan of Têng-hui: 'The clay-moulded and gold-gilt.'

Nêng of Tao-wu: 'One who is never angry however insulted.'

Fa-yen of Wu-tsu Shan: 'One with the bare chest and naked feet.'

Ts'ung-shên of Chao-chou was once asked the question, 'Who is the Buddha?' He replied, 'The one in the shrine.'

The monk said, 'In the shrine sits a clay-moulded statue.'

'That's it.'

'Who is the Buddha?'

'The one in the shrine.'

[1] 928–985. *Chuan*, XXIV.

Another time Chao-chou was asked by another monk, 'Who is the Buddha before us?'

The master again said, 'The one in the shrine.'

'That Buddha has a form. Who is the Buddha?'

'Mind is he.'

'Mind is still subject to measurement. Who is the Buddha?'

'No-mind[1] is he.'

'Is it permissible for one to make a discrimination between mind and no-mind?'

The master said, 'You have already made a discrimination, and what more do you want me to say about it?'

So much for citations. For we have now enough to see what was going on in the minds of the masters when they gave these answers each according to his light and circumstances. We can say that the Chinese practical genius has brought the Buddha down again on earth so that he can work among us with his back bare and his forehead streaked with sweat and covered with mud. Compared with the exalted figure at Jetavana surrounded and adored by the Bodhisattvas from the ten quarters of the world, what a caricature this old donkey-leading woman-Buddha of Shou-shan, or that robust sinewy bare-footed runner of Chih-mên![2] But in this we see the spirit of the *Gaṇḍavyūha* perfectly acclimatized in the Far Eastern soil.

[1] *Wu-hsin*, 'mindlessness' or 'the unconscious'.

[2] Chih-mên Kuan-tso answered, when asked 'Who is the Buddha?', 'After wearing out his sandals, he runs bare-footed.'

III. THE BODHISATTVA'S ABODE

I

Ts'ung-yüeh, abbot of Tou-tsu,[1] used to ask the following three questions to see how deeply his disciples' insight went into the truth of Zen Buddhism: '(1) The reason why you all go about on pilgrimage from one master to another is to have an insight into the nature of your own being; where then is your self-nature this very moment? (2) When you realize your self-nature, you are free from the bonds of birth and death; how are you free then at the moment of your death? (3) When you are free from birth and death, you know whither you depart; whither are you bound then at the moment of a general dissolution of the four elements?'

'What am I?' 'Where am I?' 'Whence do I come?' 'Whither do I go?' All these are one and the same question differently stated. When any one of them is understood, all the rest solve themselves. 'What am I?' is an inquiry into the self-nature (*svabhāva*) of Reality, the foundation of all things subjective and objective. When this is clearly grasped, we know where we are, that is to say, we know in what relationship we stand to our surroundings as they expand in space and continue in time. When this is definitely fixed, the after-death question will no more trouble us, because life and death are correlative terms, and intelligible only when they are so regarded. In fact, all these interrogatives, 'What?' 'Where?' 'How?' 'Whither?' 'Whence?' have their meaning as long as they are applied to our relative life on earth. But the moment we abandon this life as controlled by time, space, and causality, we abandon the interrogatives as not at all relevant. For an insight into the nature of Reality reveals life in an entirely different aspect where

[1] 1044–1091. *Hsü Chuan-têng Lu*, XXII.

no such inquiries belonging to a world of relativity are needed. For this reason, Yüeh's triple question can be considered essentially simple and reducible in this case to the question, 'Where is your self-nature?' (i.e. 'Where is your abode?')—the abode from which all your activities rise. And this abode is the abode of Bodhisattvahood, the subject I wish here to treat, mainly by passages from the *Gaṇḍavyūha*.

Psychologically, the answer to 'Where?' indicates one's fundamental mental attitude towards the objective world generally, and in Zen the question usually takes the form 'Where do you come from?', by which the Zen master wishes to see where his monks find their spiritual refuge located. The whole training of Zen Buddhism, it may be said, consists in this location, or searching, or digging-down. Enlightenment, therefore, is no more than coming in touch with the rockbed of one's own being, if there is really such. The form which the question 'Where?' takes in Zen Buddhism is thus, 'Where do you come from?' This is quite a conventional question, but those who know knew what a tremendous question this is. The question may also be, 'Whither do you go?' 'Whence?' and 'Whither?'—those who can adequately answer these are really the enlightened.

The venerable Ch'ên,[1] also known as Mu-chou, where he used to reside, often asked his monks, 'Where do you come from?' or 'Where did you spend your last season?' One monk said, 'When you have your own regular residence, I will tell you where I come from.' The venerable master sarcastically remarked, 'The fox does not belong to the lion-family; a lamp does not shine like the sun or the moon.'

When this question was put to a monk who had newly arrived at his monastery, the latter opened his eyes widely and gazed at the master without saying a word. Remarked the master, 'O you who run after the horse!'

A third one answered, 'O master, I come from the west of the river.' Said the master, 'How many sandals did you wear out [to make such a stupid answer]?'

[1] A senior contemporary of Lin-chi (867). *Chuan-têng Lu*, XII.

A fourth was told by the master, 'You tell a lie,'[1] when he said that he came from Yang-shan, a noted master of the day.

When Ling-shu Ju-min[2] was asked by a monk, 'Where is your native place?' the master said, 'The sun rises in the east, the moon goes down in the west.'

Tai-sui Fa-chên[2] asked a monk, 'Where do you go?'

The monk replied, 'I wish to pay homage to Samantabhadra.'

The master raised his *hossu*,[3] saying, 'Mañjuśrī, as well as Samantabhadra, is residing here in this.'

The monk drew in the air a circle which he threw behind him, and then bowed respectfully to the master.

Thereupon the master said, 'O attendant, get a cup of tea for this monk.'

At another time a monk who was asked the same question answered, 'I am going to have my hut in the western mountain.'

The master queried, 'When I call out to you facing the eastern mountain, can you come down to me?'

The monk replied, 'How can that be possible?'

The master told him that he was not yet ready to take up his residence [as if he were a finished master].

When Ling-hsün of Fu-chou was about to leave his master Kuei-tsung,[4] the latter said, 'Where do you go?'

Hsün: 'I am going to return to Ling-chung.'

Tsung: 'You have been here with me for some time; when you are ready to depart, come up once more to see me, for I want to tell you what Buddhism is.'

Hsün put on his travelling-suit and appeared before the master, who said, 'Come up nearer.' Hsün stepped forward, whereupon Tsung remarked, 'The cold season is here, and you will take good care of yourself while travelling.'

[1] Literally, 'You do not observe the five precepts.'

[2] Both Ju-min and Fa-chên were disciples of Tai-an of Fu-chou, who died in 833. *Chuan-têng Lu*, XI.

[3] *Fu-tzu.*

[4] Kuei-tsung probably flourished late in the eighth and early in the ninth century.

Lin-chi's[1] answer to Huang-po, his master, is one of the most noted answers given to the question, 'Where do you go?' He said, 'If not to the south of the river, it will be to the north.'

It is thus natural that the question 'Where?' is sometimes expressed in terms relating to the master's own residence. In this case the questioner is generally the monk wanting to know what are the characteristic sights (*ching*) of the monastery where the master resides. The Chinese character *ching* means, besides, 'sights' or 'views', 'ground', 'territory', 'boundary', or 'realm', and is generally used as equivalent to the Sanskrit *gocara* or *viṣaya*. *Viṣaya* is 'sphere', 'dominion', 'district', 'range', 'abode', while *gocara* is 'pasture ground for cattle', 'field for action', 'dwelling-place', 'abode'. When it acquires a subjective sense, as it does in Buddhist literature, it is a general characteristic psychic or spiritual attitude a person assumes towards all stimuli. But, strictly speaking, Zen Buddhists do not regard *gocara* or *ching* as a mere attitude or tendency of mind but as something more fundamental constituting the very ground of one's being, that is to say, a field where a person in the profoundest sense lives and moves and has his reason of existence. This field is essentially determined by the depth and clarity of one's spiritual intuitions. 'What are the sights (*ching*) of your monastery?' means, therefore, 'What is your understanding of the ultimate truth of Buddhism?' or 'What is the ruling principle of your life, whereby you are what you are?' While thus the questions, 'Whence?' 'Where?' or 'Whither?' are asked of a monk who comes to a master to be enlightened, the questions as to the residence, abode, site, or sights are asked of a master who feels no more need now of going on pilgrimage for his final place of rest. These two sets of questions are, therefore, practically the same.

Lin, of Ts'ang-chi,[2] answered when asked about the sights of Ts'ang-ch'i, 'Eastward flows the mountain stream as you see it before yourself.'

[1] Died 867. *Chuan-têng Lu*, XII.
[2] Disciple of Yün-mên (died 949). *Chuan*, XXIII.

Ming, of Hsiang-t'an,[1] answered, 'The mountain here belongs to the Tai-yüeh range and the stream runs into the Lake Hsiao-hsiang.'

T'ai-ch'in,[2] of Ch'ing-liang, gave this while residing at Shang-lin, 'You cannot paint it however much you try.'

Ch'ing-hsi,[3] of Yün-chü, was not apparently inclined to give any positive answer about the sights of his monastery, for his counter-question was, 'What do you mean by "sights" (*ching*)?' When the monk further asked, 'Who is the man living here?' the master was not at all communicative, and simply made this remark, 'What did I say to you just now?'

All these sayings concern the abode of Bodhisattvahood. The way the master expresses himself is characteristic of Zen Buddhism, and it may be difficult for general readers to find the connection between these statements as above cited and the following descriptions of the abode of the Bodhisattva as quoted from the *Gaṇḍavyūha*. To help them understand this, let me first quote some passages from other Mahāyāna texts with which we are already familiar.

2

In many Mahāyāna sūtras, reference is quite frequently made to 'the raising of thought unattached to anything'. One of the most famous of such phrases occurs in the *Vajracchedikā*, which is said to have awakened the mind of Hui-nêng, the Sixth Patriarch of Zen Buddhism in China, to a state of enlightenment, and which has ever since been utilized by Zen masters for the exposition of their teaching. The phrase runs in Chinese, *Ying wu so chu êrh shêng ch'i hsin*, the original Sanskrit of which is, *Na kvacit pratiṣṭhitaṁ cittam utpādayitavyam.*[4] Freely translated, it is, 'Let your

[1] Disciple of Yün-mên (died 949). *Chuan*, XXIII.
[2] A disciple of Fa-yen (died 958). *Chuan*, XXV.
[3] Another disciple of Fa-yen. *Chuan*, XXV.
[4] Max Müller, p. 27.

PLATE IX
THE SOLITARY ANGLER

By Ma Yüan (Southern Sung)

This Chinese artist of the twelfth century was noted for painting just "one corner" and leaving the rest to the imagination of the reviewer. In this particular respect he was a typical Oriental, perhaps more Japanese than Chinese, and more Zen than Shingon or Jodo.

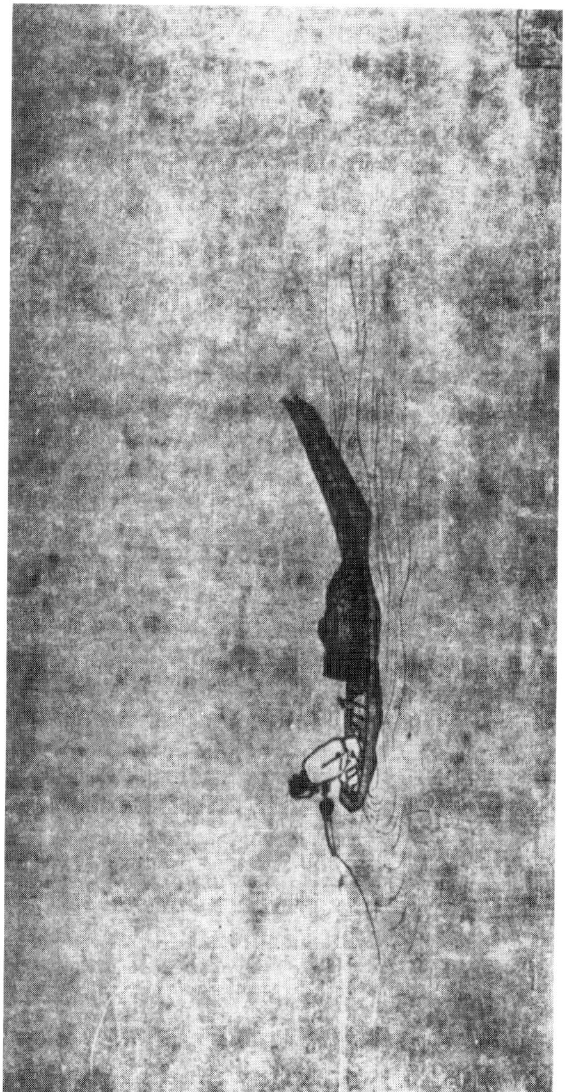

PLATE X

THE "PA-PA" BIRD

Ascribed to MU-CH'I

Is the Pa-pa a kind of crow? It perches on an old pine tree symbolic of unbending strength. It seems to be looking down on something. The life of the universe pulsates through him while quietness rules the enveloping nature. Here truly asserts the ancient spirit of solitude. This is when God has not yet given his fiat to the darkness of the unborn earth. To understand the working of the spirit in this—is not it the end of the Zen discipline?

mind (or thought) take its rise without fixing it anywhere.' *Citta* is generally rendered as 'thought', but more frequently it is 'mind' or 'heart'. The Chinese character *hsin* has a much wider connotation than 'thought' or 'mind', for it also means the 'centre or reason of being' and is one of the most significant and comprehensive terms in Chinese philosophy as well as in conventional everyday Chinese. In this case, 'to set up one's mind without fixing it anywhere' means 'to be perfect master of oneself'. When we are dependent on anything, we cannot be perfectly free; and it is then that the idea of an ego-soul or of a creator known as God is generally found to be taking hold of us. For this reason, we cannot act without attaching ourselves to something—a state of dependence and slavery. To the question, 'Where are you?' we have to say, 'I am tied to a pole'; and to the question, 'What are the sights or limits (*ching*) of your monastery?' 'I move within the circle whose radius is the full length of the rope which is attached to the pole.' As long as this rope is not cut off, we cannot be free agents. The rope has its length which is measurable, and the circle described by it has its calculable limits. We are puppets dancing on somebody else's string. But a circle whose circumference knows no limits, because of its having no central pole and its string, must be said to be a very large one indeed, and this is where a Zen master locates his residence. The circle, the field (*ching* or *gocara*), whose range is infinity, and therefore whose centre is nowhere fixed, is thus the fit site for the Bodhisattva to have his abode.

In the *Aṣṭasāhasrikā-Prajñāpāramitā*[1] we have: 'The Tathāgata's thought is nowhere fixed, it is not fixed on things conditioned, nor it is fixed on things unconditioned; and it is therefore never put out of fixation.'[2] By 'thought not being fixed' is meant psychologically that consciousness rises from an unconscious source, because, according to Buddhism, there is no such psychological or metaphysical

[1] Mitra, p. 37.

[2] *Apratiṣṭitamāmaso hi tathāgato 'rhan samyaksaṁbuddaḥ. Sa naiva saṁskṛite dhātau sthito nāpy asuṁskṛite dhātau sthito na ca tato vyutthitaḥ.*

entity as that which is known as the ego-soul, and which is generally regarded as making up the basis of an individual being, and which is therefore the point of fixation for all its mental activities. But as this point of fixation is to be wiped off in order to reach the state of Buddhahood, the Mahāyāna sūtras, especially the *Prajñāpāramitās*, lay the entire stress of their teaching upon the doctrine of Emptiness. For it is by means of this alone that one can be cut off from a fixation and free for ever from the shackles of transmigration.

Buddhism being a practical spiritual training, whatever statements it makes are direct expressions of experience, and no interposition of intellectual or metaphysical interpretation is permitted here. It may sound quaint and unfamiliar to say that thought or mind is to be set up without any point of fixation behind it, like a cloud which floats away in the sky with no screws or nails attached to it. But when the sense is grasped the idea of no-fixation is altogether to the point. It is generally better to leave the original expressions as they are, and let the reader experience them within himself. Their conversion into modern terminology may frequently be very desirable, but the intelligibility thus gained is generally the result of abstraction or intellectualization. This gain naturally means the loss of concrete visualization, a loss which may well outweigh the gain.

In the *Vimalakīrti* also, we have such phrases as 'Bodhi has no abode, therefore it is not to be attained'; or 'Depending on a source which has no abode, all things are established'; and in the *Śurāngama*: 'Such Bodhisattvas make all the Buddha-lands their abode, but they are not attached to this abode, which is neither attainable nor visible.' Expressions of this sort are encountered everywhere in the Mahāyāna texts.

The *Prajñāpāramitā Sūtras*, again, which are disposed to be negative in their statements, give among others the following: 'The truth as given out by the Tathāgata is unattainable, it knows no obstruction, its non-obstructibility resembles space as no traces (*pada*) are left; it is above all forms of contrast, it allows no opposition, it goes beyond birth and death, it has no passageway whereby one may approach it. This truth is realizable by one who follows the Tathāgata as he is in his Suchness (*tathatā*). For this Suchness is something uniform, something beyond going and coming, something eternally abiding (*sthititā*), above change and separateness and discrimination (*nirvikalpā*), absolutely one, betraying no traces of conscious striving, etc.'[1] As the truth (*dharma*) of the Tathāgata cannot be defined in any positive way, the *Prajñāpāramitā* has a series of negations. The only affirmative way is to designate it *tathatā*, 'state of being so', or 'suchness', or 'so-ness'. To those who know, the term is expressive and satisfying, but from the logical point of view it may mean nothing, it may be said to be devoid of content. This is inevitable; terms of intuition are always so, and all the truths belonging to the religious consciousness, however intellectual they may appear, after all belong to this class of terminology. 'What am I?' 'Where am I?' or 'Whither am I bound'—the questions are raised by the intellect, but the solution is not at all logical. If it is not a series of negations it is simply enigmatical, defying the ordinary way of understanding. In this respect the Zen sayings are the worst. Note the following, which will conclude this part of an introductory to the *Gaṇḍavyūha* description of the abode of Bodhisattvahood.

San-shêng, a disciple of Lin-chi,[2] once sent a monk-messenger Hsiu to Ching-ch'ên of Chang-sha who succeeded Nan-ch'üan[3] as a master of Zen, and made him ask Ching-ch'ên this question, 'Where has Nan-ch'üan, your late master, gone after his death?'

Ch'ên replied, 'When Shih-tou[4] was still a boy-novitiate, he personally attended on the Sixth Patriarch.'

This is simply stating an historical fact. Shih-tou was still a young boy while the Sixth Patriarch, Hui-nêng,[5] was

[1] Abridged, *Aṣṭasāhasrikā-prajñāpāramitā*, Chapter XXVI, on 'Tathatā'.
[2] Died 867. [3] 748–834. [4] 700–790. [5] 673–713.

yet alive; he was only thirteen years old when Hui-nêng died. Later, he studied Zen under Hsing-szŭ[1] and became one of the great teachers of the day. But what has this simple historical statement about an event probably a hundred years past to do with the whereabouts of Nan-ch'üan who is dead? In one sense, the question seems to concern too serious a matter to be treated so lightly, so enigmatically if you like. In what relationship, you may protest, does the passing of my master stand to my boy-attendant's going out on an errand, for instance, to buy some stationery?

Hsiu, the monk-messenger from San-shêng, was not to be easily sent off; he evidently wished to get everything Ch'ên had. Hence the second shot: 'I do not ask you about the novitiate life of Shih-tou, but where has Nan-ch'üan gone after his death?'

'As to that,' replied Ch'ên, 'it makes one think.'

Hsiu said, 'You are like an old stately pine-tree standing against the cold winter sky, but there is nothing of a bamboo-shoot about you, which shoots straight up through the rocks.'

Ching-ch'ên remained silent.

The monk Hsiu said, 'I thank you for your kind reply.'

The master still remained silent.

Hsiu reported the interview to San-shêng, who remarked: 'If this is the case, Ching-ch'ên must be said to have gone seven steps further ahead of Lin-chi. But wait, I will see myself how deep his understanding really goes.'

The following day San-shêng called on Ching-ch'ên and said: 'I was told of your interview yesterday with the monk Hsiu regarding Nan-ch'üan's after-death life. Your reply was indeed the most remarkable and illuminating of all I know in the history of Zen.'

To this the master Ch'ên's response was another silence.

There is a Japanese popular song which may be quoted in this connection:

[1] Died 740.

Is he come? Is he come?
To the shore I go to meet him.
But on the shore there's nothing but the breeze
That sings among the pine-trees.

The following Chinese poem is taken from *Selections from T'ang Poetry*, which may also throw some light on Chin-ch'ên's understanding of Zen:

Under the pine-tree I ask the attendant-boy
  [where the master is].
Says he, He's gone out hunting for herbs.
No doubt he is in the mountain somewhere,
But the fog is too deep; how I long to locate him!

When the intellect fails to give an accurate analytical account of the truth, our resource is the imagination, which goes deeper into the constitution of Reality. Reality evidently refuses to expose itself before the intellect, for it is something that can never be exhausted. Unknowability here is not to be referred to the domain of logic, but somewhere else where visions are created. Intellectually more or less hazy, but fundamentally quite satisfying is this realm of inconceivabilities. The intellect struggles to penetrate this density of the mystic fog or to locate the wherefore of the capricious breeze, but the riddle remains for ever unsolved.

Having viewed the principle of life that regulates the activities of Bodhisattvahood as it is asserted by the Zen master and also as it is conceived by compilers of the *Prajñāpāramitā Sūtras*, etc., let us proceed to see how it is described in the *Gaṇḍavyūha*. The Zen master does not use abstract terms such as the principle of life; he always makes use of events of daily life and the concrete objects with which he is surrounded and with which his monks are quite familiar. When he asks them whence they come or whither they go, he can tell at once by the answer he gets where their abode is, that is, what is that which prompts them to a definite set of actions. This method of training may be considered too difficult for ordinary minds to grasp what is really behind it.

Nor may the doctrine of no-fixation be easy to take hold of for those who are not used to this way of expressing their spiritual conditions. To have their minds set to working without anything behind them, without anything holding them to a definite intelligible centre, may sound like jargon. When we state that the abode of the Bodhisattva is really no abode, that he is fixed where he is not fixed, that he wanders or floats like a cloud in the sky without anything at its back, the statements may seem to have no meaning whatever. But this is the way the Mahāyāna Buddhists have been trained in their religious life, to which no stereotyped rules of syllogism can be applied.

We are now perhaps ready to see what we can gather from the *Gaṇḍavyūha* on this subject: 'Where is the abode of the Bodhisattva?' This it has been from the first our intention to find out, especially in contrast to the Zen way of handling the same idea. In the *Gaṇḍavyūha* the question 'Where?' stands out before us in the form of the Tower known as Vairochana-vyūha-alaṅkāra-garbha—that is, the 'tower which holds within itself an array of brilliantly shining ornaments'. Sudhana, the young pilgrim, stands before it and describes it as he looks at it, knowing that it is the site of residence for the Bodhisattva Maitreya. The description is not of an objective sort, it is based on the reflections of the young aspirant after Bodhisattvahood, reflections taken from all his past experiences and whatever instructions he has gained in his long pilgrimage. When the Vairochana Tower is thus described as the Vihārā (abode or retreat) of Maitreya, the attributes enumerated here apply not only to Maitreya himself but to all the Bodhisattvas of the past, present, and future, including all the Zen masters also who have really attained spiritual enlightenment. In short, the Tower is the abode of all the spiritual leaders who have followed the steps of the Buddha.

All that is said here is not Sudhana's own idea as to where the Bodhisattva should have his spiritual residence; it is in fact the Mahāyāna ideal.

3

'This Tower[1] is the abode where they are delighted to live who understand the meaning of Emptiness, Formlessness, and Will-lessness; who understand that all things are beyond discrimination, that the Dharmadhātu is devoid of separateness, that a world of beings is not attainable, that all things are unborn.

'This is the abode where they are delighted to live who are not attached to any world, who regard all the habitable worlds as no home to live in, who have no desire for any habitation, refuge, devotion, who have shaken off all thoughts of evil passions.

'This is the abode where they are delighted to live who understand that all things are without self-nature; who no more discriminate things in any form whatever; who are free from ideas and thoughts; who are neither attached to nor detached from ideas.

'This is the abode where they are delighted to live who have entered into the depths of Prajñā-pāramitā; who know how to penetrate into the Dharmadhātu which looks out in all directions; who have quieted all the fires of evil passions; who have destroyed by means of their superior knowledge all the wrong views, desires, and self-conceit; who live a playful life issuing from all the Dhyānas, Emancipations, Samādhis, Samāpattis, Miraculous Powers, and Knowledges; who produce all the Bodhisattvas' realm of Samādhis; who approach the footsteps of all the Buddhas.

'This is the abode ot all those who make one kalpa (eon)

[1] These quotations are based mainly on the palm-leaf MS. kept by the Royal Asiatic Society, London. Folio 247b et seq., corresponding to MMG, p. 1264 ff.

enter into all kalpas and all kalpas into one kalpa; who make one kshetra (land) enter into all kshetras and all kshetras into one kshetra, and yet each without destroying its individuality; who make one dharma (thing) enter into all dharmas and all dharmas into one dharma, and yet each without being annihilated; who make one sattva (being) enter into all sattvas and all sattvas into one sattva, and yet each retaining its individuality; who understand that there is no duality between one Buddha and all Buddhas and between all Buddhas and one Buddha; who make all things enter into one thought-moment (*kṣaṇa*); who go to all lands by the raising of one thought; who manifest themselves wherever there are beings; who are always mindful of benefiting and gladdening the entire world; who keep themselves under perfect control.

'This is the abode of all those who, though they themselves have already attained emancipation, manifest themselves into this world for the sake of maturing all beings; who, while not attached to this earthly habitation, go about everywhere in the world in order to do homage to all the Tathāgatas; who, while not moving away from their own abode, go about everywhere in order to accept all the orderly disposition of things in all the Buddha-lands; who, while following the footsteps of all the Tathāgatas, do not become attached to the idea of a Buddha; who, while depending upon good friends, do not become attached to the thought of a good friend; who, while living among the evil ones, are yet free from the enjoyment of desires and pleasures; who, while entering into all kinds of thoughts, are yet in their minds free from them; who, while endowed with the body after the manner of the world, yet have no dualistic individualistic thoughts; who, while endowed with the body belonging to the Lokadhātu, are not separated from the Dharmadhātu; who while desiring to live through all the time that is yet to come, are free from the thought of duration; who manifest themselves in all the worlds without moving a hair's breath from the place where they are.

'This is the abode of all those who preach the Dharma which rarely falls in one's way; who enjoy the Dharma which is difficult to understand, deep in meaning, non-dualistic, formless, having nothing in opposition, beyond obtainability; who abide in good-will and compassion all-embracing; who are not immersed in the realm of all the Śrāvakas and Pratyekabuddhas; who have gone beyond the realm of all evil beings; who are not soiled by any worldly conditions; who are abiding where all the Bodhisattvas are, where all the Pāramitā-virtues are amassed, where all the Buddhas are enjoying their comfortable habitations.

'This is the abode of all those who have severed themselves from all form and gone beyond the order of all the Śrāvakas; who are enjoying themselves where all things are unborn, and yet do not stay in the unbornness of things; who live among impurities, not penetrating into the absolute truth which is detached from greed, though they are in no way attached to objects of greed; who enjoy practising compassion with a heart unattached to the defilement of morbidity; who dwell in the world where the chain or origination prevails, but absolutely free from being infatuated with things of the world; who practise the four Dhyānas but are not born according to the bliss they bring about; who practise the four immeasurables but are not born in the world of form because of their wish to mature all beings; who practise the four formless Samāpattis but are not born in the world of no-form because of their wish to embrace all beings with a great loving heart; who practise tranquillization (*śamatha*) and contemplation (*vipaśya*), but for the sake of maturing all beings do not themselves realize knowledge and emancipation; who practise great indifference but are not indifferent to affairs of the world; who enjoy Emptiness but do not give themselves up to wrong views of mere nothingness; who, putting themselves in the realm of formlessness, are ever bent on instructing beings attached to form; who have no vows for their own sake but do not cut themselves off from the vows belonging to the Bodhisattva; who are masters of all karma- and passion-hindrances and yet show themselves for the sake of maturing all beings, as if subject to karma- and passion-hindrances; who thoroughly know what is meant by birth and death and yet show themselves as if subject to birth and transformation and death; who are themselves beyond all the paths of existence, but for the sake of disciplining all beings show themselves entering into the various paths; who practise compassion but are not given up to petty kindnesses; who practise loving-kindness but are not given up to attachments; who are joyous in heart but ever grieved over the sight of suffering beings; who practise indifference but never cease benefiting others; who are disciplined in the nine successive Samāpattis, but are not horror-stricken with the idea of being born in the world of desire; who are detached from all efforts but do not live in the realization of the limit of reality (*bhūtakoṭi*); who are living in the triple emancipation but do not come in contact with the emancipation of Śrāvakahood; who view the world from the viewpoint of the four noble truths but do not live in the realization of the fruit of Arhatship; who perceive the deep significance of the doctrine of origination but do not take to absolute annihilation; who discipline themselves according to the eight noble paths but do not seek for an absolute deliverance; who have gone beyond the state of commonalty but do not fall into the state of Śrāvaka-hood and Pratyekabuddhahood; who know well what is the destiny of the five grasping Skandhas but do not look for the absolute annihilation of the Skandhas; who have gone beyond the path of the four Māras[1] but do not make distinction between them; who go beyond the six Āyatanas but do not desire their absolute annihilation; who enjoy Suchness but do not remain in the limit of reality; who appear as if teaching all the vehicles (*yāna*) but by no means forsake the Mahāyāna. This is indeed the abode of beings endowed with such virtues.'

[1] The four Māras (evil ones) are: Skandha (aggregates), Kleśa (passion), Devaputra (son of a god), and Mṛtyu (death).

4

Sudhana the youth then uttered the following gāthās:

'Here is the venerable compassionate Maitreya endowed with a great loving heart and undefiled knowledge and intent on benefiting the world. He who abides in the stage of Abhisheka is the best son of all the Victorious Ones; he is absorbed in the contemplation of the Buddha-realm.

'This is the abode of all the sons of enlightenment, whose renown is far-reaching, who are established in the realm of supreme knowledge and emancipation, who walk around in the Dharmadhātu, unattached and companionless.

'This is the abode of those who have grown powerful in self-control, charity, morality, patience, and strenuousness; who are thoroughly equipped with the supernatural powers gained by means of Dhyāna; who are established in the transcendental wisdom and power of the vows; who are in possession of the Pāramitā virtues of the Mahāyāna.

'This is the abode of those whose intelligence knows no attachment; whose heart is broad, expansive, and unfettered as the sky expands; who know all that is moving in time and all that exists and becomes.

'This is the abode of those wise men endowed with transcendental wisdom, who enter into the reason of all things as unborn, examine into the original essence of things as by nature like space, which like a bird in the sky neither works nor is dependent on anything else.

'This is the abode of those who understand that greed, anger, and folly have no self-nature, and that the rise of falsehood is caused by imagination, and yet who do not discriminate as to detaching themselves from greed, anger, and folly, and who have thus reached a state of peace and quietude.

'This is the abode of those who are skilful in the use of transcendental wisdom, knowing what is meant by the triple emancipation, the doctrine of the twofold truth, the eightfold noble path, the Skandhas, Dhātus, Āyatanas, and the chain of origination, and yet not falling into the way of disquietude.

'This is the abode of those who have acquired perfect peace as they see into the realm of knowledge which is free from obstruction and in which all the Buddha-lands and beings with their imaginations and discriminations are quiescent, observing that all things have no self-nature.

'This is the abode of those who go about everywhere in the Dharmadhātu, unattached, depending on nothing, with no habitation, burden-free, like the wind blowing in the air, leaving no track of their wanderings.

'This is the abode of those who are renowned on account of their love and compassion, for when they see those suffering beings in the evil paths of existence they would descend into the midst of the sufferers and experience their sharp pain on themselves, shedding their light of sympathy on all unfortunate ones.

'This is the abode of those who are like the leader of a caravan; for they, observing how a company of wanderers is out of the track, destitute, and lost like men born blind in the wrong narrow path of transmigration, lead them to the highway of emancipation.

'This is the abode of those who are brave and unconquerable in rescuing and giving a friendly consolation to all those beings who are seen entrapped in the net of birth, old age, and grief and death—the threatening fate that befalls the Skandhas.

'This is the abode of those who, seeing people struggle under the bonds of the passions, give them, like the great kind physician, the wonderful medicine of immortal knowledge, and release them by means of great expanding love.

'This is the abode of those who, like the boatman, carry people on the boat of the immaculate Dharma across the ocean of birth and death where they are seen suffering all forms of grief and pain.

'This is the abode of those who, like the fisherman, lift all beings from the ocean of becoming and carry them over the waves of evil passions where they are seen drowning themselves, and who will arouse in them the desire for all-knowledge which is pure and free from sensualities.

'This is the abode of those who have reached where great vows are made and things are always viewed with love, and who, like the young king of Garuda, looking upon all beings immersed in the ocean of becoming, lift them up.

'This is the abode of those who are illuminators of the world, going about like the sun and the moon in the sky of the Dharmadhātu, and pouring the light of knowledge and the halo of vows into the homes of all beings.

'This is the abode of those who, being devoted to the salvation of the world, do not relax their efforts for nayutas of kalpas to bring one being to maturity, and would do so with the entire world as with one being.

'This is the abode of those whose determination is as hard as Vajra; for in order to benefit beings in one country they put forward their untiring efforts until the end of time, and would do so also for all beings in all the ten quarters.

'This is the abode of those whose intelligence is as deep as the ocean; for they never feel exhausted in their minds even when nayutas of kalpas expire before they can preach all the truth-clouds as declared by the Buddhas in the ten quarters, not to speak of their making an assembly at one sitting, unbewildered, imbibe all the truth.

'This is the abode of those who wander about, unattached, visiting an indescribable ocean of countries, entering into the ocean-like assemblies of the Buddhas, and making an ocean of offerings to all the Buddhas.

'This is the abode of those who have practised all kinds of virtue by entering into the ocean of deeds from the midst of eternity, by persistently arousing the ocean of vows, and, in order to benefit all beings, by going about in the world for ever so many kalpas.

'This is the abode of those who are endowed with an eyesight that knows no obstructions; for they can penetratingly see into all the innumerable countries at the end of a hair, into all the limitless lands where are the Buddhas, beings, and kalpas, thus with nothing left to them which cannot clearly be perceived by them.

'This is the abode of those who come forth from the meritorious Pāramitās as they are able to perceive the great ocean of kalpas in one moment of thought, together with the appearance in it of all Buddhas, all worlds, and all beings, with a transcendental intelligence which defies every hindrance standing in its way.

'This is the abode of those who are altogether free from obstruction in any form, being able to arouse an innumerable number of vows which are equal in measure to the number of atoms to which all the worlds may be crushed, or to the number of drops to which the water of the great oceans may be analysed.

'This is the abode of those Buddha-sons who, establishing and practising the various phases of Praṇidhānas (vows), Dhāraṇis, Samādhis, and also of Dhyānas, and of Vimokshas (emancipations), make them established also in every one of limitless kalpas.

'Here abide all classes of those Buddha-sons who enjoy planning and establishing varieties of treatises, stories, dogmas, discourses, and also the useful arts and places of enjoyment belonging to the world.

'Here abide those who practise in a Māyā-like way deeds of unobstructed emancipation by means of miraculous powers, by contriving means of salvation based on transcendental wisdom, by appearing everywhere in the various paths of existence in the ten quarters of the world.

'Here abide those Bodhisattvas who, ever since their first awakening of the desire for enlightenment, have perfected all the deeds of the Dharma full of merit, and reveal themselves mysteriously all over the Dharmadhātu in their innumerable bodies of transformation.

'This is the abode of those who are hard to approach because of their supernatural wisdom which grasps the Buddha-knowledge in one moment of thought and accom-

PLATE XI

HOTEI (PU-TAI) AND TWO FIGHTING COCKS

By Musashi Miyamoto

It was not a rare combination in the feudal days of Japan—to be a swordsman and an artist. The rarer thing was to be perfect in both. As fencer, Musashi was interested in the fighting cocks and as Zen student in the character of Hotei. In Japan Hotei is associated with the god of wealth and happiness. His bag symbolises the inexhaustible resources of treasure and his fullness of features spiritual contentedness. But in China, as is suggested by the "Dancing Pu-tai," his legendary character is preserved. Musashi's Hotei depicts his transcendentalism. He quietly reviews all forms of contention that are going on in the outside world. Does the fencer discover the secret way of attack by observing the fight of two spirited cocks? Does the philosopher contemplate the teaching of Sunyata by which there is no killing, no killer, no killed? A certain atmosphere of detachment pervades the entire picture.

PLATE XII, SUMMER MOUNTAINS,

Ascribed to KAO JAN-HUI

PLATE XIII, LANDSCAPE,

By MA YUAN

PLATE XIV, LANDSCAPE WITH A COW,

By SOTAN OGURI

plishes illimitable karma all of which issues from their wisdom, while the wisdom of worldly thought ends nowhere but in complete madness.

'This is the abode, the immaculate shelter, of those who, being the owners of unimpeded intelligence, walk about in utmost freedom through the Dharmadhātu, and whose minds go even beyond the limits of intelligibility.

'This is the abode of those peerless ones who walk about everywhere and enjoy staying everywhere without ever leaving a track behind, as their knowledge rests on absolute oneness.

'This is the abode of those spotless ones who, seeing into the original nature of all things as quiet and homeless as the sky, live in a realm which may be likened unto the vastness of space.

'Here abide those compassionate ones whose loving hearts and intelligence, being deeply stirred as they observe all beings groaning with grief and pain, are ever contriving for the welfare of the world.

'Here abide those who make themselves visible like the sun and the moon everywhere where there are beings, and deliver them from the snare of transmigration by means of Samādhi and emancipation.

'Here abide those Buddha-sons, who, following the footsteps of the Buddhas, manifest themselves in all countries through endless kalpas.

'Here abide all the Buddha-sons who, in conformity with the dispositions of all beings, are seen manifesting themselves in their transformation-bodies like clouds universally in all the ten quarters.

'Here abide those great beings who have entered the realm of all the Buddhas, and are never tired of enjoying it and walking in it for nayutas of kalpas.

'Here abide those who, knowing well what characterizes each one of the innumerable indescribable Samādhis, manifest the Buddha-realm as they enter into it.

'Here abide those who hold in one thought-moment all the kalpas, countries, and Buddha-names, and whose all-comprehending intelligence can in one moment take in all kalpas beyond calculation.

'Here abide those who perceive in one thought all immeasurable kalpas, and who, while conforming themselves to the worldly way of thinking, are free from ideas and discriminations.

'Here abide those who have trained themselves in Samādhis perceiving in one thought-moment all the past, present, and future, while themselves living in emancipation.

'Here abide those who, sitting cross-legged and without moving away from their seats, are able to manifest themselves simultaneously in all the paths of existence in all the lands.

'Here abide those great bulls who drink from the Dharma-ocean of all the Buddhas and crossing over the water of knowledge attain to all the virtues that are perfect and indestructible.

'Here abide those who know with an unimpeded mind the number of all the lands, kalpas, Dharmas, and Buddha-names.

'Here abide the Buddha-sons who are familiar with the number of all the lands of the past, present, and future, and even also instantaneously think of their birth and disappearance.

'Here abide those who, disciplining themselves in the life of the Bodhisattva, are thoroughly conversant with the life and the vows of all the Buddhas, as well as the various dispositions of all beings.

'In one particle of dust is seen the entire ocean of lands, beings, and kalpas, numbering as many as all the particles of dust that are in existence, and this fusion takes place with no obstruction whatever.

'So with all the dust-particles, all the lands, beings, and kalpas which are also seen here in fusion with all their multifariousness of appearances.

'Here in this abode the Bodhisattvas reflect, in accordance with the truth of no-birth, on the self-nature of all things, on all the lands, on the divisions of time, on kalpas, and on the enlightened ones, who are detached from the idea that there is such a thing as self-nature.

'While abiding here they also perceive that the principle of sameness prevails in all beings, in all things, in all the Buddhas, in all the lands, and in all the vows.

'Sitting firmly here, they are engaged in disciplining all beings, in paying homage to all the Buddhas, reflecting on the nature of things.

'For nayutas of kalpas they have been working for the perfection of the vows, knowledge, condition, mentality, conduct, the extent of which is indeed beyond description, beyond estimation.

'Before an immense amount of works accomplished by those irreproachable beings who are in enjoyment of their life of non-obstruction here, I bow and pay them my homage.

'O noble Maitreya, thou art the eldest son of the Buddha, thou livest a life of non-obstruction, thy immaculate knowledge goes beyond form; thinking of this I prostrate myself before thee.'

5

Sudhana now asks the Bodhisattva Maitreya to open the Tower and allow him to enter. The Bodhisattva approaches and snaps his fingers, and lo! the doors open. How gladly Sudhana enters, when they close by themselves as mysteriously as they had opened before!

What a sight is now revealed before him!

The Tower is as wide and spacious as the sky itself. The ground is paved with asamkhyeyas[1] of precious stones of all kinds, and there are within the Tower asamkhyeyas of palaces, porches, windows, staircases, railings, and passages, all of which are made of the seven kinds of precious gems.

[1] Literally, innumerable.

There are again banners, canopies, strings, nets, and hangings of various shapes, also made of precious stones—asamkhyeyas in number. Asamkhyeyas of bells tinkle in the breeze, asamkhyeyas of flowers are showered, asamkhyeyas of wreaths are swinging, asamkhyeyas of incense-burners stand everywhere, asamkhyeyas of golden flakes are scattered, asamkhyeyas of mirrors are shining, asamkhyeyas of lamps are burning, asamkhyeyas of robes are spread, asamkhyeyas of gem-thrones covered with asamkhyeyas of tapestries are arranged in rows.

There are also asamkhyeyas of figures of various sorts, made of pure Jambūnada gold or of precious stones—figures of young maidens, of Bodhisattvas, etc.

Asamkhyeyas of beautiful birds are singing melodiously, asamkhyeyas of lotus-flowers in several colours are in full bloom, asamkhyeyas of trees are planted in regular rows, asamkhyeyas of great mani-jewels are emitting their exquisite rays of light—and all these asamkhyeyas of beautifully set-up decorations of precious stones fill the spacious Tower as far as it extends.

And within this Tower, spacious and exquisitely ornamented, there are also hundreds of thousands of asamkhyeyas of towers, each one of which is as exquisitely ornamented as the main Tower itself and as spacious as the sky. And all these towers beyond calculation in number stand not at all in one another's way; each preserves its individual existence in perfect harmony with all the rest; there is nothing here that bars one tower being fused with others individually and collectively; there is a state of perfect intermingling and yet of perfect orderliness. Sudhana the young pilgrim sees himself in all the towers as well as in each single tower, where all is contained in one and each contains all.

Finding himself in this wonderful sight and with his mind wandering from one mystery to another, his joy knows no bounds. He is free from all individualistic ideas, from all the hindrances, from all the bewilderments; for he is now in the midst of an emancipation which goes beyond all limitations.

Sustained by the power of the Bodhisattva Maitreya, Sudhana finds himself in each one of these towers simultaneously where he perceives an endless series of wonderful events taking place in regard to the Bodhisattva's life. That is to say, he sees how the Bodhisattva Maitreya first comes to rouse his devotional heart towards the realization of supreme enlightenment; he sees what is his name, who are his family and his friends, what good stock of merit he plants, what is his age, what Buddha-land he is engaged in arraying, what discipline he undergoes, what vows he makes, what assemblies of Buddhas and Bodhisattvas he attends, and for how many kalpas he personally serves Buddhas and pays them homage—all these things in the life of the Bodhisattva Maitreya, Sudhana sees.

Sudhana sees how the Bodhisattva Maitreya for the first time attains the Samādhi called Maitra (compassion) and how after that the Bodhisattva comes to be known as Maitreya. He sees again by the Bodhisattva Maitreya what deeds are performed, what Pāramitās perfected, what Kshāntis gained, what stages of Bodhisattvahood attained, what Buddha-land put in order, what Buddhist doctrines maintained. He sees again how Maitreya realizes the truth that all things are unborn, and when, where, and under what Tathāgata he is assured of supreme enlightenment.

Sudhana sees that in a certain tower the Bodhisattva is requested by a ruler of the world to lead all beings to the practice of the ten deeds of morality, that he is asked by a world-protector to benefit and gladden all beings, that he is asked by Śakra to subjugate the pleasure-hunting instincts of all beings, by Brahma to praise the immeasurable merits of Dhyāna, by the god Yāma to praise the immeasurable merits of thoughtfulness, by the god of Tushita to eulogize the virtues of the Bodhisattva who becomes a Buddha in his next birth, by the god Nirmita to manifest himself in his transformation-bodies for the sake of the heavenly beings, by the god Vaśavartin to preach Buddhism to his followers.

Sudhana sees that, becoming the king of evil ones, the Bodhisattva demonstrates the evanescence of all things, that for the sake of Asura he dives into the depths of the ocean of knowledge, and, seeing that all things are like a vision, teaches Asura and his army to put away all their pride, arrogance, and intoxication. Sudhana sees the realm of the dead displayed where the Bodhisattva radiating a great light is engaged in delivering all beings from the pain of the hells; he sees the Bodhisattva in the world of the hungry ghosts where he gives away all kinds of food and drink to relieve the inhabitants of their intense sufferings; he sees the Bodhisattva in the kingdom of beasts where he disciplines the creatures by varieties of means. He sees the Bodhisattva preaching the Dharma to the groups of beings in the heavens of the world-protector, the Tushita, the Yāma, the Nirmita, the Vaśarvartin, and the Brahma Indra; to the groups of the Nāgas, the Yakshas and Rakshas, the Gandharvas, the Asuras, the Garuḍas, the Kinnaras, the Mahoragas, the Manushyas, and the Amanushyas. He sees the Bodhisattva preaching the Dharma to the groups of the Śrāvakas, Pratyekabuddhas, and of the Bodhisattvas from the first stage to the last. He sees the Bodhisattva eulogizing the merits of Bodhisattvahood in all stages, the fulfilment of all the Pāramitā virtues, the realization of all the Kshāntis, the attainment of all the great Samādhis, the deepness of the emancipation, the realm of the mysterious powers accruing from the Dhyanas and Samādhis, the Bodhisattva's life and deeds of devotion, and his vows. He also sees the Bodhisattva Maitreya, together with other Bodhisattvas of the same society, praising worldly business and all forms of craftsmanship which would increase the happiness of all beings. He sees the Bodhisattva Maitreya together with other Bodhisattvas who are to be Buddhas in another birth praising the Abhisheka (baptism) of all the Buddhas. He also sees the Bodhisattva Maitreya untiringly engaged in the performance of the various acts of devotion, in the practice of the Dhyānas and the four immeasurables, the Kṛitsuāyatanas, and the emancipations, in the displaying of the various mystic powers by the means gained in the Samādhis.

Sudhana sees the Bodhisattva Maitreya together with other Bodhisattvas enter into a Samādhi and issue from every single pore of their skin multitudes of transformation-bodies: clouds of heavenly beings, clouds of the Nāgas, Yakshas, Gandharvas, Asuras, Garuḍas, Kinnaras, Mahoragas, Śakras, Brahmas, Lokapālas, great sovereigns, minor lords, royal princes, state ministers, court dignitaries, wealthy householders, and lay-disciples, clouds of Śrāvakas, Pratyekabuddhas, Bodhisattvas, and Tathāgatas, and clouds of all beings.

Sudhana now hears all the teachings and doctrines of the Buddha melodiously issuing from every single pore of the skin of all the Bodhisattvas—such teachings as concern the merits of the Bodhicitta, charity, morality, patience, strenuousness, meditation, transcendental knowledge, the four forms of acceptance, the immeasurables, tranquillization (*samādhi*), concentration (*samāpatti*), miraculous powers, sciences (*vidyā*), Dhāraṇis, intellectual perspicuity (*pratibhāna*), truths (*satya*), knowledges, Śamatha, Vipaśya, emancipations, chain of origination, refuges (*pratiśaraṇa*), utterances (*udhāna*), subjects of memory, attendance (*upasthāna*), right efforts, miracles, roots of strength (*indṛiyas*), powers, the seven factors of enlightenment, the eightfold path of righteousness, the vehicle of Śrāvakahood, the vehicle of Pratyekabuddhahood, the vehicle of Bodhisattvahood, the stages of Bodhisattvahood, Kshāntis, deeds of devotion, and vows.

Sudhana sees the Buddhas surrounded each by his assemblies; he sees their various places of birth, their families, their forms, ages, kalpas, countries, names, discourses on the Dharma, ways of benefiting all beings, periods of continuation, etc., which vary according to different Buddhas.

Sudhana sees one especially high, spacious, and most exquisitely decorated tower, incomparably beautiful, among all the towers that are to be seen inside the Vairochana Tower. In this peerless tower, he sees all the tri-chiliocosm at one glance, containing hundreds of kotis of Tushita heavens. And in each one of these worlds he sees the Bodhisattva Maitreya's descent on earth and his birth, and Śakra, Brahma, and other celestral beings paying respect to the Bodhisattva, his walking seven steps, his surveying of the ten quarters, his lion-roar, his child-life in the court, the royal pavilion, and the pleasure ground, his renunciation for the sake of all-knowledge, his ascetic life, his accepting the milk, his visit to the ground of spiritual discipline, his subjugation of the army of the Evil One, his attainment of supreme enlightenment under the Bodhi-tree, Brahma's request to revolve the Dharma-wheel, the Buddha's ascent to the heavens to discourse on the Dharma; while his kalpa, his duration of life, his assemblies, the arraying of his country, the purification of lands, deeds of discipline, vows, the maturing of beings, the distribution of the ashes, the maintenance of the Dharma are seen to differ according to different Buddhas.

At this moment Sudhana finds himself to be with all those Buddhas who are performing the various works of Buddhahood among various assemblies. He is deeply impressed with these scenes which are never to be forgotten.

Then he hears all the bells large and small, all the jewel-nets, all the musical instruments in all the towers preaching varieties of teachings in perfect melody and harmony beyond human conception. One voice is heard to be the teaching about the Bodhisattva's rousing the desire for enlightenment, another to be the teaching about the practice of the Pāramitās, another to be concerned with various vows, the states of Bodhisattvahood, the paying homage and making offerings to the Buddhas, the arraying of the Buddha-lands, the differences of discourses to be given by different Buddhas—all these teachings in the form of heavenly music are heard proclaimed in their fulness.

Sudhana hears a voice, which says that certain Bodhisattvas are discoursing on such doctrines at such places, rousing the desire for enlightenment under the guidance of such good friends, listening to such Buddha's sermons in such assemblies of Bodhisattvas, in such kalpas, in such countries.

Sudhana hears another voice, saying that these Bodhisattvas on account of these merits awaken such desire, make such vows, plant a great stock of merit, and, after continuing deeds of Bodhisattvahood for a certain number of kalpas, attain supreme enlightenment, assume such names, live so long, complete the arraying of such countries, fulfil such vows, teach such beings, such Śrāvakas, and such Bodhisattvas, and after Nirvāṇa see the Dharma continuing to thrive for the benefit and happiness of all beings.

Sudhana hears another voice, saying that certain Bodhisattvas are at such places, practising the six Pāramitās; that certain other Bodhisattvas at other places abandon the throne and all their precious possessions, even their own limbs, heads, and entire bodies ungrudgingly for the sake of the Dharma; that still other Bodhisattvas in other places, in order to guard the Dharma of all the Tathāgatas against corruption, become great teachers of the Dharma, strenuously engaged in its propagation and transmission, in erecting the Buddhist stupas and shrines, in producing Buddhist figures, and also in giving people what pleases them.

Sudhana hears another voice, saying that such Tathāgatas are in such places and in such kalpas and, after attaining supreme enlightenment, are living in such countries, in such assemblies, living so long, preaching such doctrines, fulfilling such vows, and teaching such innumerable beings.

Listening to these exquisitely melodious voices beyond human conception, Sudhana the young pilgrim is exceedingly gladdened in his heart. He attains innumerable Dhāraṇis, eloquences, deeds of devotion, vows, Pāramitās, miraculous powers, knowledges, sciences, emancipations, and Samādhis.

Sudhana sees again in all the mirrors figures and images of all sorts beyond calculation. That is, he sees representations of all the spiritual assemblages conducted by Buddhas, by Bodhisattvas, by Śrāvakas, by Pratyekabuddhas; he sees representations of lands of defilement, of lands of purity, of worlds with no Buddhas in them, of worlds large, middling, and small, of worlds with nets of Indra, of worlds irregularly shaped, of worlds even-surfaced, of worlds where there are the hells, the hungry ghosts, and all sorts of beasts, of worlds inhabited by celestial and human beings.

And in these worlds there are asamkhyeyas of Bodhisattvas walking, sitting, engaged in all kinds of work, doing charitable deeds out of a great compassionate heart, writing various treatises whereby to benefit the world, receiving them from the master, holding them for the future generations, copying them, reciting them, asking questions, answering them, or practising confession three times a day and dedicating the merit to the attainment of enlightenment, or raising bows for the sake of all beings.

Sudhana sees all the pillars emitting all kinds of mani-jewel light: blue, yellow, red, white, crystal-coloured, water-coloured, rainbow-coloured, coloured like purified gold, and in all colours of light.

Sudhana sees figures of young maidens in Jambūnada gold and other figures made of precious stones. Some hold in their hands clouds of flowers, some clouds of draperies, banners, streamers, canopies, wreaths; some others hold incense of various kinds, precious nets of mani-jewels; some wear gold chains, necklaces of precious gems; some have on their arms varieties of ornaments; some are decorated with mani-gem crowns. Bending their bodies, they all gaze intently at the Buddhas.

Sudhana sees the scented water possessing eightfold merit issuing from the necklaces of pearl, long rays of bright light streaming from necklaces of lapis lazuli; he sees banners, nets, streamers, and canopies, all of which are made of various kinds of precious stones, most pleasing to the eye.

Sudhana sees the ponds planted with all kinds of lotus such as the Utpala, the Kumuda, the Puṇḍarīka, the Padma, each one of which bears innumerable flowers varying in magnitude; and within every flower are seen beautifully arrayed multitudes of figures, all with the body bent and hands folded in a most reverential attitude: men, women, young boys, young girls, Śakras, Brahmas, Lokapālas, Devas, Nāgas, Yakshas, Gandarvas, Asuras, Garuḍas, Kinnaras, Mahoragas, Śrāvakas, Pratyekabuddhas, and Bodhisattvas.

Sudhana sees the Tathāgatas, sitting cross-legged, who are fully arrayed with the thirty-two marks of great manhood.

Sudhana sees the ground perfectly paved with lapis lazuli, where at every step there are representations of wonderful things and personages, such as Buddha-lands, Bodhisattvas, Tathāgatas, and towers in full array.

Sudhana sees in the jewel-made trees, branches, leaves, flowers, and fruits, the wonderful bust-representations of Buddhas, Bodhisattvas, Devas, Nāgas, Yakshas, Lokapālas, Cakravartins, kings of lesser importance, royal princes, state ministers, head-officers, and of the four classes of Buddhists. Some of those representations are seen carrying flower-wreaths in their hands, some jewel-wreaths, some all kinds of ornamental articles. They are all in a most reverential attitude with the body bent forward and with the hands folded, intensely gazing at the Buddhas. Some praise the Buddhas, while others are in deep meditation. Their bodies in full array emit varieties of lights in different colours: gold, silver, coral, Tūshara, Indra-blue, Vairochana-jewel, Campaka, etc.

Sudhana sees in those crescent-representations in the towers asamkhyeyas of suns, moons, stars, constellations, and luminosities of all kinds, which illumine all the ten quarters.

Sudhana sees all the towers surrounded on all sides with walls which are ornamented at every step with all sorts of precious stones, and in each one of these stones the Bodhisattva Maitreya is seen reflected as he practised in his past lives deeds of Bodhisattvahood. He is seen giving away his own head, eyes, limbs, lips, teeth, tongue, bones, marrow, etc. He is also seen giving away all his belongings such as wives, mistresses, maids, servants, towns, palaces, villages, countries, and even his own throne, to whomsoever needed them. He liberates those who are kept in prison, he releases those who are in bondage, he heals those who are afflicted with diseases, he leads back to the right path those who have gone astray. Becoming a boatman he helps people to cross the sea; becoming a charioteer he rescues people from disasters; becoming a great sage he discourses on various teachings; becoming a great sovereign he practises on himself the ten deeds of goodness and induces people to do the same; becoming a physician he heals all sorts of disease. To the parents he is a filial son, to friends a faithful companion. He becomes a Śrāvaka, a Pratyekabuddha, a Bodhisattva, a Tathāgata, thereby disciplining, educating, and teaching all beings. He becomes announcer of the Dharma in order to serve the cause of Buddhism by accepting, holding and reading it, by reflecting on it in the proper way, by erecting Caityas for the Buddhas, by making their images, by paying them homage not only by himself but making others do the same, by making them offerings, incense, and flowers, by repeating all these deeds of religious devotion without interruption.

Further, the Bodhisattva Maitreya is seen to be sitting on a lion-throne giving to all beings sermons on the Dharma, instructing them in the ten deeds of goodness, in the threefold refuge, in the five precepts, and the eightfold Poshadha; and further, he teaches people to lead the life of a recluse, to listen to the Dharma, to accept and hold it, and to reflect on it in the right away. The Bodhisattva appears again represented as practising the six Pāramitās and all other deeds of devotion for ever so many innumerable asamkhyeyas of kalpas; and all those good friends whom the Bodhisattva served in his past lives are seen as fully arrayed with multitudes of virtues. The Bodhisattva Maitreya is again seen himself as befriended by all the good friends.

Then those good friends said: 'O Sudhana, thou art welcome! As thou seest all these wonderful things belonging to Bodhisattvahood, thou mayest not be fatigued!'

6

After this, the sūtra continues to explain how it came to pass that Sudhana the young pilgrim was permitted by the Bodhisattva Maitreya to be the witness of all these wonderful sights.

That Sudhana the young pilgrim should see all these and many other innumerable wonderful transformations in full array and beyond human conception, which were going on in each one of the towers, was because he had gained a power of memory which never allowed anything to slip off the mind, because he had gained a pure eye to survey all the ten quarters, because he had gained a knowledge which sees unobstructedly, because he had gained the Bodhisattva-knowledge, his sustaining power, and perfect mastery over things, because he had gained the far-reaching knowledge which belongs to those Bodhisattvas who have already entered on the first stage.

It is like the way of one who sees in his sleep all manner of things such as towns, villages, hamlets, mansions, parks, mountains, woods, rivers, lakes, dresses, provisions, and everything that is needed for a comfortable living. He may also see his own parents, brothers, relatives, great oceans, Mount Sumeru, all the celestial palaces, Jambudvīpa, etc.; he may also see his own body stretched out in size over hundreds of yojanas and the house wherein he lives and the garments which he wears and other things correspondingly grown up in magnitude. While his experience may have lasted just one day or one night, he will imagine it to have been a period of incalculable length, and that for ever so long he had been the recipient of all kinds of enjoyment and pleasurable excitement. When he is awakened, he realizes that all that appeared to him was in a dream though everything is perfectly remembered by him.

Similarly, Sudhana has been the witness of all these wonders (*vikurvita*) because of the sustaining powers of the Bodhisattva Maitreya, because of his knowledge that the triple world is like a dream, because of his having put an end to the limited knowledge shared by all beings, because of his attainment of an extensive, unobstructed understanding, because of his abiding in the unexcelled thought and spiritual state of Bodhisattvahood, because of his inconceivable knowledge whereby he can conform himself to the understandings of all beings.

When a man is about to die, he sees all that is going to happen to him after his death according to the life he lived. If he had been a doer of evil deeds, he will have a vision of a hell, or the realm of the hungry ghosts, or that of the beasts where all forms of pain are being suffered. He may see the demons armed with terrible weapons maltreating all those who have fallen into their hands. He may hear the wailing voices of lamentation or screams of pain. He may see the stream of alkaline, the boiling cauldron, the razor-hill, the forest of thorns, the sword-leaved trees—all of which are meant to torment and harass the wicked. Whereas, those who had behaved properly may see the celestial palaces, celestial beings, celestial maidens, beautiful robes, exquisitely arrayed gardens and terraces, etc. Though they are not yet quite dead, they are able, because of their karma, to have such visions before them. Similarly, Sudhana has been able to see those wonderful scenes on account of his inconceivable Bodhisattva-karma.

Again, like a spirit-seized man who can answer any question asked of him, Sudhana has been able to see those wonders and answer whatever questions have been asked of him because of his being sustained by the knowledge of the Bodhisattva Maitreya.

Again, like a man who, imagining himself to be a Nāga under the spell of the Nāgas, has entered into their palaces, and, spending a short time there, thinks he has passed many a year with them, Sudhana, because of his abiding in the knowledge belonging to Bodhisattvahood and also because of his being sustained by the power of the Bodhisattva Maitreya, has been able to see events of many a kalpa in the twinkling of an eye.

Again, like the Brahma palace called Vyūhagarbha surpassing anything of this world, where all the chiliocosm is seen comprehended and yet with all things in perfect order, all things in the Vairocana Tower were seen by Sudhana distributed in perfect scale so that all the differences did not at all interfere with one another.

Again, like a Bhikshu abiding in a Samāpatti called Kṛitsnāyatana, who, whether walking or sitting or standing or lying, sees all the world presented in the light of the Dhyāna in which he is, Sudhana too saw in a clear light all the wonderful scenes in the Tower.

Again, it is like a man's seeing the city of Gandharvas in the sky, which is in full array with all kinds of ornamentation, without intermingling, without obstructing one another.

Again, it is like the Yakshas' abodes and the human worlds occupying the same space, and yet distinctly separate from one another so that one can see either of them according to one's karma.

Again, it is like the great ocean where one can see reflected everything that is in the chiliocosm.

Again, it is like the magician who because of his knowledge of the art can create all manner of things and make them do the same work.

Similarly, Sudhana, because of the sustaining power of the Bodhisattva Maitreya, because of his inconceivable power of Māyā-knowledge, has been enabled to see all the wonderful transformations in the Tower.

7

At that time the Bodhisattva Maitreya, suspending his miraculous power, entered into the Tower, and snapping his fingers said this to Sudhana the young pilgrim:

'O son of a good family, arise! Such is the nature of all things appearing as they do in the accumulation and combination of conditions; such is the self-nature of things, which is not complete in itself, being like a dream, a vision, a reflection.'

At that time Sudhana, hearing the sound of the fingers snapped rose from the Samādhi. Maitreya continued: 'Seest thou now the wondrous transformations of the Bodhisattva, the outflowings of his power, the propagation of his vows and wisdom, the joy of his final beatitude, his deeds of devotion, the immeasurable array of the Buddha-land, the unsurpassable vows of the Tathāgata, the inconceivable way of emancipation belonging to Bodhisativahood, the pleasures of the Samādhi enjoyed by the Bodhisattva—these things seest thou and understandingly followest thou?'

Said Sudhana: 'Yes, I do, O Venerable Sir, by the wondrous sustaining power of the good friend. But pray tell me, what is this emancipation?'

Maitreya: 'This is known as the Vyūhagarbha in which the knowledge of all the triple chiliocosm is contained, retained, and never put out of memory. O son of a good family, in this emancipation there are more emancipations than can be described and enumerated, which can be attained only by the one-birth Bodhisattva.'

Sudhana: 'O Venerable Sir, pray tell me whither does all this go?'

Maitreya: 'Where it comes from.'

Sudhana: 'Whence comes it?'

Maitreya: 'It comes from the knowledge and the sustaining power of the Bodhisattva. It goes nowhere, it passes away nowhere, there is no accumulation, no increase, no standing-still, no attachment, no dependence on the earth or in the sky.

'O son of a good family, it is like the Nāga-king's pouring forth the rain: it does not issue from his body, nor does it from his mind, nor is there any accumulation within him, but it comes from the mind-power of the Nāga—this showering over the entire world. It goes beyond human comprehensibility.

'O son of a good family, it is the same with the arraying

of things thou hast seen. It comes neither from within, nor from without, yet it is before thee, coming out of the wondrous power of the Bodhisattva, because of the merit of goodness thou hast accomplished.

'O son of a good family, it is like the art of a magician, whose magical creations do not come from anywhere, nor do they pass away anywhere, yet they are seen as existing before people because of the spell of the mantram.

'Similarly, O son of a good family, the wonderful arraying of things thou hast seen comes from nowhere, passes away nowhere, stays nowhere accumulated, and it is there just because the Bodhisattva is to learn of his inconceivable Māyā-knowledge, because of the all-sustaining and all-ruling power of the Bodhisattva's vows and knowledge.'

Sudhana: 'O Venerable Sir, pray tell me whence thou comest.'

Maitreya: 'The Bodhisattva comes as neither coming nor going; the Bodhisattva comes as neither moving nor staying, as neither dead nor born, as neither staying nor passing away, as neither departing nor rising, as neither hoping nor getting attached, as neither doing nor reaping the reward, as neither being born nor gone to annihilation, as neither eternal nor bound for death.

'And yet, O son of a good family, it is in this way that the Bodhisattva comes: he comes where an all-embracing love abides, because he desires to discipline all beings; he comes where there is a great compassionate heart, because he desires to protect all beings against sufferings; he comes where there are deeds of morality, because he desires to be born wherever he can be agreeable; he comes wherever there are great vows to fulfil because of the power of the original vows; he comes out of the miraculous powers because wherever he is sought after he manifests himself to please people; he comes where there is effortlessness because he is never away from the footsteps of all the Buddhas; he comes where there is neither giving nor taking because in his movements mental and physical there is no trace of striving;

he comes out of the skilful means born of transcendental knowledge because he is ever in conformity with the mentalities of all beings; he comes where transformations are manifested because all that appears is like a reflection, like a transformed body.

'This being the case, O son of a good family, yet thou askest whence I come. As to that, I am here from my native country, Maladi. My object is to teach the Dharma to a young man called Gopālaka and all the other people living in my district each according to his or her fitness. It is also to get their parents, relatives, Brahmans, and others into the way of the Mahāyāna. . . .'

8

We are now in the position to ascertain where the Bodhisattva Maitreya, representing the entire family of Bodhisattvas, keeps his final abode and also what kind of abode this is. We notice the following points:

Since the Indian imagination is very much richer and more creative than the Chinese, the description of the Vairochana-alaṅkāra-vyūha-garbha, which is the abode of Bodhisattvahood, may appear at first sight quite different from the simple and direct way in which the Chinese Zen master expresses himself. When the latter is asked where his abode is, he does not waste many words in describing it, he is not at all prolix, as we have already seen elsewhere. This is what most specifically characterizes Zen, while the *Gaṇḍavyūha* goes far beyond Zen; for it is not satisfied with merely pointing at the Tower, or entering into it with the snapping of the fingers, or exclaiming with a Japanese *haiku* poet:

Oh! This is Yoshino!
What more can I say?
The mountain decked with cherry-blossoms!

Every kind of imagery is resorted to in order to bring home to the reader's imagination the real nature of the Tower. This verbosity, however, helps him, in a way better than the Zen master, we might say, to get acquainted with the object of his curiosity, for we find this:

1. That Maitreya's Tower is no other than the Dharmadhātu itself;

2. That the Dharmadhātu is from one point of view different from the Lokadhātu which is this world of relativity and individuality, while from another point of view the Dharmadhātu is the Lokadhātu;

3. That the Dharmadhātu is not a vacuum filled with empty abstractions, but is brimful of concrete individual realities, as we can see from the use of the words *vyūha* and *alaṅkāra*;

4. That in the multiplicity of objects filling up the Dharmadhatu, however, there is perfect orderliness;

5. That this orderliness is described as: *Asya kūtāgāra-vyūha anyonyā saṁbhinnā anyonyā maitrībhūtā anyonyā saṅkīrṇāḥ pratibhāsayogena 'bhāsam agamannekasminnārambaṇe yathā caikasminnārambaṇe tathā 'śeṣasarvārambaṇeṣu*;[1]

6. That in the Dharmadhātu, therefore, there is an interfusion of all individual objects, each of which, however, retaining all its individuality there is in it;

7. That there is not only a universal interfusion of things in such a way that in one object all the rest of the objects are reflected, but there is a reflection in each one of them of one personality known as Sudhana;

8. That the Dharmadhātu is, therefore, generally characterized as *anāvaraṇa*, 'unobstructed', meaning that there is here a state of interpenetration of all objects in spite of their divisibility and mutual resistance;

[1] The Royal Asiatic Society MS., folio 270a. Freely rendered: 'The objects are arrayed in such a way that their mutual separateness no more exists, as they are all fused, but each object thereby never losing its individuality, for the image of the Maitreya-devotee is reflected in each one of the objects, and this not only in specific quarters but everywhere all over the Tower, so that there is a thoroughgoing mutual inter-reflection of images.' (MMG, p. 1376.)

9. That the Dharmadhātu is a world of radiance where not only each object of Alaṅkāra shines in its own light variously coloured, but it does not refuse to take in or reflect the light of others as they are;

10. That all these wonderful phenomena, and indeed the Dharmadhātu itself, take their rise through the sustaining power of the Bodhisattva which is symbolized in the *Gaṇḍavyūha* by the 'snapping of fingers';

11. That the sustaining power, Adhishṭhāna, while not expressly defined, is composed of the Bodhisattva's Praṇidhāna (vow) and Jñāna (knowledge);

12. That when this Dharmadhātu, where such an exquisitely beautiful and altogether inconceivable spectacle takes place, is psychologically described, the *Gaṇḍavyūha* has this: *Abhisyanditakāyacittaḥ sarvasaṃjñāgatavidhūtamānasaḥ sarvāvaraṇavivarjitacittaḥ sarvamohavigataḥ.*[1] And it was in this state of mind that Sudhana could remember all he saw and all he heard, that he could survey the world with a vision which knew no obstructions in whichever directions it moved, and that he could circulate in the Dharmadhātu with his body, nothing checking its perfectly free movements.

(Compare this with the instruction of Dōgen and his teacher Ju-ching. When Dōgen, who is founder of the Japanese Sōtō School of Zen, was studying Zen in China under Ju-ching early in the thirteenth century, the master used to tell him, 'Mind and body dropped-off; dropped-off mind and body!' Dōgen repeats the idea in one of his sermons: 'Dropped off! Dropped off! This state must once be experienced by you all; it is like piling [fruit] into a basket without a bottom, it is like pouring [water] into a bowl with a pierced hole; however much you may pile or pour you cannot fill it up. When this is realized, we say that the pail bottom is broken through. As long as there is

[1] R.A.S. MS., folio 270a; MMG, p. 1376. 'Sudhana the young pilgrim felt as if both his body and mind completely melted away; he saw that all thoughts departed away from his consciousness; in his mind there were no impediments, and all intoxications vanished.'

a trace of consciousness which makes you say, "I have this understanding, or that realization," you are still playing with unrealities.')

9

The Tower described in these terms, one may suspect, is a symbolical creation issuing from some abstract philosophical conceptions. Indeed, this wonderfully mysterious spectacle was once the object of metaphysical speculation on the part of some brilliantly-gifted Chinese intellects, and from them started what is now known as the Hua-yên School (*Avataṁsaka*) of Buddhism. But I gravely doubt whether this philosophical systematization did such good as was expected to the proper understanding of the *Gaṇḍavyūha*; that is to say, whether the truest and deepest significance of the Vairochana Tower has gained by being so analysed and rendered more or less comprehensible by the intellect. By this I do not mean that those great Chinese minds did something altogether unnecessary for the advancement of human culture. But I mean this, that the outcome of their systematization of the *Gaṇḍavyūha* has been a pushing of its spiritual value behind the screen of intelligibility, and consequently that the general reader now comes to discover its original message in the conceptualism of speculative analysis itself. If this had really been the case throughout the history of the *Gaṇḍavyūha* it would have been a most unfortunate state of affairs. In order, however, to see how the Chinese intellects of the first order endeavoured to grasp the wonders of the Vairochaṇa Tower, let me refer to the so-called doctrine of the fourfold Dharmadhātu advanced by Têng-kuan, and also to the theory of Identity by Fa-tsang.

The idea of the fourfold Dharmadhātu did not entirely originate with Têng-kuan, who is said to have lived over one hundred years (738–839). The idea was more or less definitely foreshadowed by his predecessors such as Fa-tsang

(643–712), Chi-yen (602–668), and Tu-shun (557–640), but it was by the final formulation of Têng-kuan that the philosophy of the *Gaṇḍavyūha* came to be identified with the doctrine of the fourfold Dharmadhātu. According to this, there are four ways of viewing the Dharmadhātu: (1) the Dharmadhātu as a world of individual objects, in which case the term *dhātu* is taken to mean 'something separated'; (2) the Dharmadhātu as a manifestation of one spirit (*ekacitta*) or one elementary substance (*ekadhātu*); (3) the Dharmadhātu as a world where all its particular existences (*vastu*) are identifiable with one underlying spirit; and (4) the Dharmadhātu as a world where each one of its particular objects is identifiable with every other particular object, with whatever lines of separation there may be between them all removed.

Of these four views of the Dharmadhātu, the last is what is most characteristic of the teaching of the *Gaṇḍavyūha* as distinguished from other schools of Buddhism. According to Fa-tsung, in the following infinite series

$$a_1, a_2, a_3, a_4, a_5, a_6, a_7, a_8, a_9, a_{10} \ldots\ldots\ldots$$

each term may be considered related to the others in two ways, existentially and functionally, or statically and dynamically. From the existential point of view, the relation is known to be *hsiang-chi*, that is, identical, thus:

$$a_1 = a_2, a_3, a_4, a_5, a_6, a_7, a_8, a_9, a_{10} \ldots\ldots\ldots$$
$$a_2 = a_1, a_3, a_4, a_5, a_6, a_7, a_8, a_9, a_{10} \ldots\ldots\ldots$$
$$a_3 = a_1, a_2, a_4, a_5, a_6, a_7, a_8, a_9, a_{10} \ldots\ldots\ldots$$

and so on. For the relation of each term to the whole series is such that a_1 is a_1 because of the series, while the series itself gains its meaning because of a_1. The relation is reversible and one can say that

$$a_2, a_3, a_4, a_5, a_6, a_7, a_8, a_9, a_{10} \ldots\ldots\ldots = a_1$$
$$a_1, a_3, a_4, a_5, a_6, a_7, a_8, a_9, a_{10} \ldots\ldots\ldots = a_2$$
$$a_1, a_2, a_4, a_5, a_6, a_7, a_8, a_9, a_{10} \ldots\ldots\ldots = a_3$$

and so on. As long as an infinite series cannot be complete without its individual terms, and the latter without the whole series in which they are what they are, says Fa-tsang, the theory of existential statical identity must hold good.

The series can be viewed also as functionally or dynamically related. In the series

$$a_1, a_2, a_3, a_4, a_5, a_6, a_7, a_8, a_9, a_{10} \ldots\ldots\ldots$$

each term as contributing to the general make-up of the series is functioning in its own way to make the latter possible. Even with one term dropped out of the series, the series will cease to be itself—that is, it will no more function as such. This being the case, there is a state of perfect inter-penetration (*hsiang-ju*) throughout the series. When a_1 is picked up independent of the series, it has no meaning, hence no existence, because a_1 is a_1 in the series. Thus, a_1 is at once a_1 and $a_2, a_3, a_4, a_5 \ldots\ldots$ When $a_1 = a_1$, a_1 is 'exhaustible'; when $a_2, a_3, a_4, a_5 \ldots\ldots = a_1$, a_1 is 'inexhaustible',[1] to use *Gaṇḍavyūha* terminology. In the same manner each term: $a_2, a_3, a_4, a_5, \ldots\ldots$ is at once 'exhaustible' and 'inexhaustible'. So, we have the following formulas:

$$a_1 = a_1;$$
$$a_1 = a_2, a_3, a_4, a_5, a_6, a_7, a_8, a_9, a_{10}, \ldots\ldots$$
$$a_2 = a_2;$$
$$a_2 = a_1, a_3, a_4, a_5, a_6, a_7, a_8, a_9, a_{10}, \ldots\ldots$$
$$a_3 = a_3;$$
$$a_3 = a_1, a_2, a_4, a_5, a_6, a_7, a_8, a_9, a_{10}, \ldots\ldots$$

....

....

There is another way of looking at the whole series of $a_1, a_2, a_3, a_4, a_5, a_6, a_7, a_8, a_9, a_{10}, \ldots\ldots$, whereby each term is to be regarded as embracing in itself the entirety of

[1] *Kṣaya* and *akṣaya*.

the series, and not, as in the first case, as an independent and separable unit entering into the system. Then, let each term be picked up, and the whole series comes along with it. When an image is reflected in the mirror, there is a state of identity between mirror and image, for outside the mirror there will be no reflection and without the reflection the mirror is non-existent. A mirror is distinguishable only when there are some images to bring forth its existence, and the same can be affirmed of the images that come to reflect themselves on the mirror. The one without the other will mean the non-existence of both. From this point of view, the relations between each term of the series and the series itself may be formulated thus in triplicity:

$$a_1 = a_1;$$
$$a_1 = a_1, a_2, a_3, a_4, a_5, a_6, a_7, a_8, a_9, a_{10} \ldots\ldots;$$
$$a_1, a_2, a_3, a_4, a_5, a_6, a_7, a_8, a_9, a_{10} \ldots\ldots = a_1.$$
$$a_2 = a_2;$$
$$a_2 = a_1, a_2, a_3, a_4, a_5, a_6, a_7, a_8, a_9, a_{10} \ldots\ldots;$$
$$a_1, a_2, a_3, a_4, a_5, a_6, a_7, a_8, a_9, a_{10} \ldots\ldots = a_2.$$
$$a_3 = a_3;$$
$$a_3 = a_1, a_2, a_3, a_4, a_5, a_6, a_7, a_8, a_9, a_{10} \ldots\ldots;$$
$$a_1, a_2, a_3, a_4, a_5, a_6, a_7, a_8, a_9, a_{10} \ldots\ldots = a_3.$$
$$a_4 = a_4;$$
$$a_4 = a_1, a_2, a_3, a_4, a_5, a_6, a_7, a_8, a_9, a_{10} \ldots\ldots;$$
$$a_1, a_2, a_3, a_4, a_5, a_6, a_7, a_8, a_9, a_{10} \ldots\ldots = a_4.$$

and so on, *ad infinitum*. In this case, the distinction between existential identity and functional interpenetration may not be so noticeable as in the first case where each unit was considered individually separable. If any such distinction is to be applied to the present case, it will be for the reason of conceptual exactitude. Interpenetration implies the functioning of each unit upon the others individually and as a whole, while identity is a static conception. Whatever this is, the practical outcome of these considerations amounts to the same, that is, that all things in fine array embellishing the whole universe are in a state of perfect mutual fusion in every possible manner one can conceive of.

When we speak of identity, interpenetration, or unobstructedness as the fundamental philosophical conception of the *Avataṁsaka*, we must not, however, forget that this conception by no means ignores the reality of individual existences. For unobstructedness is only possible when there are individual existences; for interpenetration is to be regarded as characteristic only of a world of particulars; for when there are no particulars, no individual existences, identity is an empty notion. The Dharmadhātu must be a realm of Vyūhas and Alaṅkāras. We must not forget that while

$$a_1 = a_1, a_2, a_3, a_4, a_5, a_6, a_7, a_8, a_9, a_{10} \ldots\ldots,$$

and

$$a_1, a_2, a_3, a_4, a_5, a_6, a_7, a_8, a_9, a_{10} \ldots\ldots = a_1;$$

it is also absolutely true that

$$a_1 = a_1;$$

and that

$$a_1 = a_1$$

because

$$a_1 = a_1, a_2, a_3, a_4, a_5, a_6, a_7, a_8, a_9, a_{10} \ldots\ldots,$$

and

$$a_1, a_2, a_3, a_4, a_5, a_6, a_7, a_8, a_9, a_{10} \ldots\ldots = a_1.$$

Since interpenetration or unobstructedness is not uniformity or an undifferentiated state of existence, the awakening of the Bodhicitta is made possible in each sentient being, and this awakening in turn causes a response in the realm (*kṣetra*) of all the Buddhas. A Shin Buddhist expresses this idea by saying that each time there is a new convert to the Pure land teaching there opens a fresh Lotus-flower in the pond of the country of Amitābha.

The doctrine of interpenetration may also be expressed in the terminology of causal relativity. But in this case the term must be understood in a much higher or deeper sense, for the *Avataṁsaka* world is not that of forms and appearances which are governed by such laws as mechanical causation, or teleological biological causation, or statical mutuality. The Dharmadhātu, which is the world of *Avataṁsaka*, is the one which reveals itself to our spiritual insight—an insight attainable only by transcending the dualism of being (*asti*) and non-being (*nāsti*). The Dharmadhātu is, therefore, realizable only when all the traces of causation (*hetupratyaya*) are wiped off from our vision. Interpenetration is then directly perceived without any medium of concepts, which is to say, not as the result of intellectualization.

It is also in this sense that this world constructed by the notions belonging to the category of causation is declared by Mahāyāna Buddhists to be empty (*śūnya*), not born (*anutpāda*), and without self-nature (*asvabhāva*). This declaration is not a logical inference, but the intuition of the Mahāyānist genius. When it is interpreted as relativity or as connected with the idea of causal relation, the spirit of the statement is altogether lost, and Mahāyāna Buddhism turns into a system of philosophy, which, however, has been the attempt on the part of some European Buddhist scholars. This Emptiness of all things (*sarvadharmasya śūnyatā*), enveloping, as it were, all the worlds with their multitudinous objects, is what makes possible the *Avataṁsaka* intuition of interpenetration and unobstructedness. Emptiness is a Mahāyāna perception of Reality itself. When it is conceptually reconstructed, the significance of the perception is completely struck out. Those who make a trial of such reconstruction are doing so against the spirit of the Mahāyāna. And for these reasons I recommend the study of the sutras themselves and not that of the śāstras or philosophical treatises of Mahāyāna Buddhism—that is, if students really wish to grasp the spirit, or share in the experience, of the Mahāyāna.

Whatever intellectual analysis was given by Fa-tsang, one of the finest philosophical minds of China, to the state of affairs in the Vairochana Tower as presented to the spiritual eye of Sudhana the young Buddhist pilgrim, the fact itself has nothing to do with the analysis. The analysis may satisfy the intellect, but the intellect is not all of our being. We with Fa-tsang and Sudhana must once be in the Tower itself and be a witness to all the Vyūhālaṅkāras shining by themselves and reflecting one another unobstructedly. In matters religious, life and experience count far more than analysis. Therefore, the Tower with all its Vyūhas[1] must come out of one's own life.

10

To a certain extent, let us hope, we have succeeded in delineating the inner nature and constitution of the Vairochana Tower both in terms of experience and from the point of view of intellectual clarification. After 'What' comes 'Whence' and 'Whither'. Without these, indeed, our inquiry into life will not be a complete one. Sudhana, therefore, naturally asks, after seeing all the wonders of the Tower, whence it comes and whither it passes. The Bodhisattva Maitreya answers that it comes from the Jñāna (knowledge) and the Adhishṭhāna (sustaining power) of the Bodhisattva. What is this Jñāna? What is this Adhishṭhāna?

[1] *Vyūha*, as explained elsewhere, means 'dispositions', or 'arranging in order', and in Buddhist literature it is often used in the sense of 'embellishment' or 'ornamentation'. But here it is equivalent to 'multiplicity of existences'. The Tower with its Vyūhas is, therefore, this universe extending before us with all its particular objects; and Dharmadhātu = Lokadhātu, Lokadhātu = Dharmadhātu.

Jñāna is a difficult term to translate, for 'knowledge' or 'intellection' does not cover its entire sense. It is something more fundamental. It is man's innate urge to discriminate, his constitutional inclination to dualism whereby subject and object, seer and the seen, are separated; it is that which makes a world of multiplicities possible. When, therefore, it is said that all the Vyūhas come forth from the midst of Jñāna, it has no other meaning than this, that the world evolves itself from the very constitution of our mind, that it is the content of our consciousness, that it is there simultaneously with the awakening of a mind which discriminates, that it comes and departs as mysteriously as our consciousness does. It is not proper in fact to ask whence is the world, or whither. The question itself issues from the very source of all mysteries and inconceivabilities, and to ask it is to defeat its own end. Its answer is possible only when we stand away from the conditions in which we are. That is to say, the question is answered only when it is no more asked. It is like fire's asking: 'What am I?' 'Whence do I come?' 'Whither do I go?' 'Why do I burn?' As long as fire is fire and keeps on burning these questions are unanswerable, because fire is to burn, just to burn, and not to reflect on itself; because the moment it reflects it is no more fire; because to know itself is to cease to be itself. Fire cannot transcend its own conditions, and its asking questions concerning itself is transcending them, which is to deny itself. The answer is possible when it contradicts itself. While standing still, we cannot leap. This contradiction is in the very essence of all intellectual questions as to the origin and the destiny of life. Hence Maitreya's statement: *na kvacid gato, nānugato, na rāśībhūto, na saṁcayabhūto, na kūṭastho, na bhāvastho, na deśastho, na pradeśasthaḥ.*[1] These negations, one may think, lead us nowhere, and naturally so, because the real answer lies where the question has not yet been asked.

Our next dealing will be with Adhishṭhāna. What does

[1] MMG, p. 1413. 'The Tower comes from nowhere, passes away nowhere; is neither a mass nor a collection; is neither static nor becoming; it is not to be located, nor is it to be located in a definite quarter.'

this mean? This is generally translated in Chinese as *shên-li* or *wei-li*, or *chia-chih-li*. It is 'power', 'will-power', 'spiritual power' belonging to a great personality, human or divine. As long as we remain on the plane of Jñāna, the world does not seem to be very real, as its Māyā-like existence in which it presents itself to Jñāna is too vapoury; but when we come to the Adhishṭhāna aspect of Bodhisattvahood, we feel as if we have taken hold of something solid and altogether sustaining. This is where life really begins to have its meaning. To live ceases to be the mere blind assertion of a primordial urge, for Adhishṭhāna is another name for Praṇidhāna, or it is that spiritual power emanating from the Praṇidhāna which constitutes with Jñāna the essence of Bodhisattvahood. Adhishṭhāna is not mere power which likes to assert itself against others. Behind it there is always a Buddha or Bodhisattva, who is endowed with a spiritual insight looking into the nature of things and at the same time with the will to sustain it. The will to sustain means the love and desire to save the world from its delusions and entanglements. Praṇidhāna is this will, love, and desire, called 'inexhaustible' (*akṣaya*).

Jñāna and Praṇidhāna are what constitutes Bodhisattvahood or Buddhahood, which is the same thing. By means of Jñāna we climb, as it were, and reach the summit of the thirty-three heavens; and sitting quietly we watch the underworld and its doings as if they were clouds moving underneath the feet; they are the whirling masses of commotion, but they do not touch one who is above them. The world of Jñāna is transparent, luminous, and eternally serene. But the Bodhisattva would not remain in this state of eternal contemplation above the world of particulars and hence of struggles and sufferings; for his heart aches at the sight. He is now determined to descend into the midst of the tempestuous masses of existence. His vows (*praṇidhāna*) are made, his power (*adhiṣṭhāna*) is added to all who look towards him, and every attempt (*upāya*) is made to lift up all those who are groping in the darkness and reduced to a state of utter subjugation. Praṇidhāna as an aspect of

Adhishṭhāna is thus the descending ladder, or the connecting link between Bodhisattva and Sarvasattva (all beings). From this grows what is technically known as Nirmāṇakāya, or the transformation-body, and in many Mahāyāna texts as Vikurvita or Vyūhavikurvita, an array of wonders.

II

That the Bodhisattva with all his penetrating and illuminating insight into the self-nature of things which is no self-nature should become himself entangled in the ever-ravelling intricacies of a world of particulars is a mystery of mysteries, and yet here opens the gate of inconceivable emancipation (*acintya-vimokṣa*) for him who is the embodiment of Jñāna and Praṇidhāna. And in this way we have to understand the contradiction between Maitreya's coming from nowhere and his being born in the province of Maladi.

This contradiction must have struck the reader as quite inexplicable, though contradictions are generally of this nature; but in this case of Maitreya the contradiction comes too soon and in a glaring manner. At one moment, he says, he has no abode, and before we have hardly risen from this startling exclamation we are told that his native country (*jamnabhūmi*) is Maladi and that his mission is to teach Gopālaka, son of a wealthy household, in Buddhism. Is this not too sudden a descent from the Tushita heaven upon earthly business? Ordinarily, quite so. But when we realize what enters into the constitution of Bodhisattvahood we shall not think so. For he is born in Maladi as if born nowhere, as if coming nowhence. He is born, and yet unborn is he; he is before us, and yet he has not come from anywhere. He is with Sudhana in the Vairochana Tower as we are told in the *Gaṇḍavyūha*, but he has never left his abode in the Tushita heaven. So, says a Zen master, 'The Bodhisattva's assemblage listening to the discourse of the Buddha at the Mount of Holy Vulture has never been dispersed; it is still going on, and the discourse is still reverberating

PLATE XV

HAN-SHAN AND SHIH-TE

By Mincho

Han-shan (Kanzan) and Shih-tê (Jittoku) are two inseparable characters in the history of Zen Buddhism, forming one of the most favourite subjects of Sumiye painting by Zen artists. Han-shan was a poet-recluse of the T'ang dynasty. His features looked worn-out, and his body was covered with clothes all in tatters. He wore a head-gear made of birch-bark and his feet carried a pair of sabots too large for them. He frequently visited the Kuo-ch'ing monastery at T'ien-tai, where he was fed with whatever remnants there were from the monks' table. He would walk quietly up and down through the corridors, occasionally talking aloud to himself or to the air. When he was driven out, he would clap his hands and laughing loudly leave the monastery.

One day Han-shan and Shih-tê were talking together by the fireplace, when a high government officer called Lü-chi came in. As soon as he saw them he saluted them in a most reverential manner. This astounded the monks who exclaimed: "How is it that a great person like yourself should pay such respect to these crazy beggars?" Han-shan took Lü-chi's hand and said, "That talkative fellow Fêng-kan is to be blamed for all this!" Later the couple hid themselves in a crevice of rock and never came out.

Shih-tê literally means "picked up." He was an orphan, and as nobody knew what his family was, he came to be known as "the Picked-up" among the monks at the Kuo-ch'ing monastery, T'ien-tai. While working in the Buddha-hall, he was one day found sitting facing the Buddha and sharing his offerings. Another day he was heard saying to the statue of Kaundinya, "O you Śrāvaka, seeker of a small fruit!"

While Shih-tê was sweeping the monastery court, the master asked, "You are known here as 'the Picked-up' because Fêng-kan came back with you, saying you were picked up on his way home. But, really, what is you family name? and where do you come from?" Thus asked, Shih-tê threw up the broom and stood with his hands crossed before his chest. The master did not know what to make of it. Han-shan happened to pass by. Striking his own breast, he cried, "Oh! Oh!" Shih-tê said, "What is the matter with you, O Brother?" Han-shan remarked, "Don't you know the saying, 'When a next-door neighbour is in mourning, we all share the sorrow'?" They then both danced, and went away crying and laughing.

(*The Chuan-têng Lu*, XXVII.)

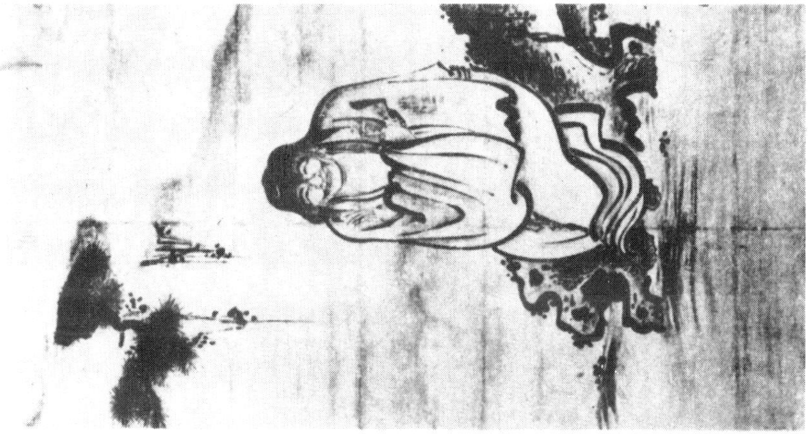

PLATE XVI

HAN-SHAN AND SHIH-TE

By Indra

This is another picture of the two Zen lunatics by Indra whose works, I believe, are already known to our readers. (See *Zen Essays*, II.) Han-shan left a number of poems one of which runs thus:

"I think of the past twenty years,
When I used to walk home quietly
  from the Kuo-ch'ing;
All the people living in the Kuo-
  ch'ing monastery—
They say, 'Han-shan is an idiot.'
'Am I really an idiot?' I reflect.
But my reflections fail to solve the
  question:
For I myself do not know who the
  self is,
And how can others know who I am?
I just hang down my head—no more
  asking is needed;
For of what service can the asking be?
Let them come then and jeer at me all
  they like,
I know most distinctly what they mean;
But I am not to respond to their sneer,
For that suits my life admirably."

in the Mount.' This—what seems to be 'too sudden a descent'—is in fact a prearranged order in the Bodhisattva's life of devotion (*bodhisattvacaryā*).

Where then is his real native country?[1]

'1. Wherever there is the awakening of the Bodhicitta there is the Bodhisattva's native land, because it belongs to the Bodhisattva-family.

'2. Wherever there is deep-heartedness, there is the Bodhisattva's native land, because it is where the family of good friends rises.

'3. Wherever there is the experience of the Bhūmis, there is the Bodhisattva's native land, because it is where all the Pāramitās grow.

'4. Wherever the great vows are made, there is the Bodhisattva's native land, because it is where deeds of devotion are carried on.

'5. Wherever there is a great all-embracing love, there is the Bodhisattva's native land, because it is where the four ways of acceptance develop.

'6. Wherever there is the right way of viewing things, there is the Bodhisattva's native land, because it is where transcendental knowledge takes its rise.

'7. Wherever the Mahāyāna thrives well, there is the Bodhisattva's native land because it is where all the skilful means unfold.

'8. Wherever there is the training of all beings, there is the Bodhisattva's native land because it is where all the Buddhas are born.

'9. Wherever there are means born of transcendental knowledge,[2] there is the Bodhisattva's native land, because

[1] R.A.S. MS., folio 276b, et. seq. Cf. MMG, p. 1415, et. seq.

[2] *Prajñā-upāya*. When Upāya is used in its technical sense in Buddhism, it is the expression of the Buddha's or Bodhisattva's love for all beings. When the Buddha sees all the sufferings that are going on in the world owing to ignorance and egotism, he desires to deliver it and consequently contrives every means to carry out his intense desire. This is his Upāya. But as his desire has nothing to do with egotism or the clinging to the individualistic conception of reality, his Upāya is said to be born of his transcendental knowledge. See infra where the philosophy of the Prajñāpāramitā is expounded.

it is where the recognition obtains that all things are unborn.

'10. Wherever there is the practising of all the Buddha-teachings, there is the Bodhisattva's native land, because it is where all the Buddhas of the past, present and future are born.'

Who then are his parents and relatives? What are his duties?

'Prajñā is his mother; Upāya (skilful means), his father; Dāna (charity), his wet nurse; Śīla (morality), his supporter; Kshānti (patience), his decoration; Vīrya (strenuousness), his nurse; Dhyāna, his cleaner; good friends, his instructors; all the factors of enlightenment, his companions; all the Bodhisattvas, his brothers; the Bodhicitta, his home; to conduct himself in accordance with the truth, his family manners; the Bhūmis, his residence; the Kshāntis, his family members; the vows, his family motto; to promote deeds of devotion, his family legacy; to make others accept the Mahāyāna, his family business; to be anointed after being bound for one more birth, his destiny as crown-prince in the kingdom of the Dharma; and to arrive at the full knowledge of Tathāgatahood forms the foundation of his pure family relationship.'[1]

What is that which makes up the definite basic mental attitude with which the Bodhisattva comes into our lives?

'The Bodhisattva does not detest anything in whatever world he may enter, for he knows (*parijñā*) that all things are like reflected images. He is not defiled in whatever path he may walk, for he knows that all is a transformation. He feels no fatigue whatever in his endeavour to mature all beings, for he knows that there is nothing to be designated as an ego-soul. He is never tired of receiving all beings, for he is essentially love and compassion. He has no fear in going through all kalpas, for he understands (*adhimukta*) that birth-and-death, for he understands that all the Skandhas are like a vision. He does not destroy any path of existence, for he knows that all the Dhātus and Āyatanas are the Dharma-

[1] Cf. MMG, p. 1417 f.

dhātu. He has no perverted view of the paths, for he knows that all thoughts are like a mirage. He is not defiled even when he is in the realm of evil beings, for he knows that all bodies are mere appearances. He is never enticed by any of the evil passions, for he has become a perfect master over things revealed. He goes anywhere with perfect freedom, for he had full control over all appearances.'[1]

12

In concluding this Essay on the abode of the Bodhisattva where lies the fountainhead of his life of devotion let me cite a few more examples of the Zen way of treating the subject and see how the Chinese mind differs from the Indian.

Hui-yün of Ch'êng-t'ien, who was a disciple of Chih-pên of Yün-kai,[2] probably of the late twelfth century, was asked by a monk, 'What are the sights of Ch'êng-t'ien?'

The master raised his *hossu*.

Monk: 'Who is the man enjoying the sights?'

The master tapped the chair with the *hossu*.

Monk: 'As regards the sights and the man I have now your kind instruction; please acquaint me with the ultimate truth of Zen.'

The master put back the *hossu* beside his chair.

When Ch'ing of Chih-ping[3] was asked by a monk, 'What are the sights of Chih-ping?' he said:

> 'Into the rock-cave
> As the night advances
> Shines the pale frosty moon;
> In my old worn-out grass-robe,
> Scantily wadded,
> I shiver with cold.'

[1] Cf. MMG, pp. 1419–20. [2] *Hsu-ch'uan*, XXV. [3] Loc. cit.

Monk: 'Who is the man enjoying the sights?'
Master:

> 'Carrying a cane he walks along the lonely mountain stream;
> With the bowl well cleansed, invited he goes out to the village to dine.'

Monk: 'As regards the sights and the man I have now your kind instruction; please let me be acquainted with the ultimate truth of Zen.'

Master: 'The wooden horse neighs against the breeze, and the mud-made bull walks over the waves.'

When Shou-ch'u[1] of Tung-shan came to Yün-mên,[2] the latter asked, 'Where do you come from?'

Ch'u: 'I come from Ts'o-tu.'

Master: 'Where did you pass your summer?'

Ch'u: 'At Pao-tzu, of Hu-nan.'

Master: 'When did you leave that place?'

Ch'u: 'August the twenty-fifth.'

Master: 'I spare you thirty blows.'

This must have puzzled the poor monk very much; his answers were all straightforward, and he thought there was nothing deserving 'thirty blows' which for some reason the master was lenient enough to spare him. He must have spent the night in great mental agony. He came up to the master again the following day and asked, 'Yesterday you were good enough to spare me thirty blows, but pray tell me where was my offence to deserve such punishment?'

Master: 'You stupid rice-bag! Is that the way you wander about through Chiang-hsi and Hu-nan?'

This apparently sarcastic remark caused a general upheaval in the spiritual constitution of Shou-ch'u, who now exclaimed to the following effect:

'After this, I will go out into the street crossings, and while myself not hoarding up one grain of rice, not planting one

[1] *Chuan-têng Lu*, XXIII. [2] Died 949.

stalk of herb, I will treat all the pilgrimaging monks who go about visiting one master after another for their spiritual edification, and I will make them take off their dirty grimy caps, I will make them cast their foul-smelling shirts. For they will thereby be set free with nothing obstructing their movements, with nothing bedimming their eyesight. Is this not a perfect joy?'

The master remarked sarcastically again, but in a different mood this time, I surmise: 'O you rice-bag! With a body hardly as large as a cocoa-nut, how widely you open your mouth!'

IV. THE DESIRE FOR ENLIGHTENMENT

AS DEFINED IN THE GAṆḌAVYŪHA SŪTRA

I

THAT the realization of supreme enlightenment (*anuttara-samyaksaṁbodhi*) is the end of the Buddhist life, Mahāyāna and Hīnayāna, is a well-known fact to all Buddhist students; for what constitutes Buddhahood is the enlightenment itself, which the Buddha attained under the Bodhi-tree by the River Nairañjanā about twenty-five centuries ago. All the teachings of Buddhism which are taught in the East at present uniformly find their source of inspiration in this truth which is at once historical and metaphysical. If not for this enlightenment there would be no Buddhas, no Buddhism, no Śrāvakas, no Pratyekabuddhas, no Arhats, no Bodhisattvas. Enlightenment is the basis of all Buddhist philosophy as well as all Buddhist activity, moral and spiritual.

The early Buddhists sought enlightenment for their own sakes, for their own spiritual welfare, and evidently had no thought for others and for the world at large. Even when they thought of them, they required of each individual Buddhist to make his own effort for salvation—that is, for enlightenment; because, according to them, ignorance which prevents them from getting enlightened and karma which keeps them bound to transmigration are based on the notion of individual realities.

It was otherwise with the Mahāyānists. Their wish for enlightenment was first of all for the sake of the world. Just because they desired the enlightenment and emancipation of all the world they strove first to enlighten themselves, to emancipate themselves, to make themselves free from the bondage of all the karma- and the knowledge-hindrances. Being thus prepared they could go out into the world and proclaim the Buddha-dharmas to their fellow-beings.

For this reason the Mahāyānists put great stress upon the significance of a compassionate heart (*mahākaruṇā*). Whatever Mahāyāna texts we may turn over, we never fail to notice terms belonging to the category of love (*karuṇā*) and compassion (*anukampana*) which are directed towards all beings (*sarvasattva* or *jagat*) in such a way as to give them refuge (*paritrāṇa*), protection (*saṁgraha*), inspiration (*paricodana*), maturity (*paripāka*), discipline (*vinaya*) purification (*pariśuddhi*), etc.

The idea of the Bodhisattva, a being (*sattva*) who seeks enlightenment (*bodhi*), as I said elsewhere, thus came to take root in Buddhism, and a sort of secular Buddhism came to replace the old school of ascetic and exclusive monasticism. The householder was made more of than the homeless mendicant, the teaching of the Buddha was to be practised outside a community of the *élite*, and this democratic social tendency brought about many great changes in Buddhist thought. One of them was to analyse in a practical way the process of enlightenment.

The doctors of the Hīnayāna busied themselves with many subtle problems regarding the world of form (*rūpaloka*), the doctrine of the non-existence of a soul-substance (*anātmya*), the personality of the Buddha, the analysis of the mind, etc. They tended to be too metaphysical, too scholastic, too rationalistic, with the result that practical questions concerning the attainment of enlightenment and its effective application in the realm of our daily lives were neglected. The Mahāyānists' chief concern was with life itself.

When the actual process of enlightenment was examined, the Mahāyāna found that it consisted of two definite steps. In the beginning it was necessary to create for the sake of others an urgent longing for enlightenment, and then the attainment of the final goal itself would be possible. The longing was just as important and full of meaning as the attainment itself, for the latter was impossible without the former; indeed the latter determined the former in every way; that is, the time, strength, efficacy, etc., of enlightenment entirely depended upon the quality of the initiative will-power raised for the attainment of the final object. The motive determined the course, character, and power of the conduct. The desire for enlightenment intensely stirred meant, indeed, that the greater and more difficult part of the work was already achieved. In one sense, to begin was fulfilment.

However this is, the Mahāyānists are fully conscious of the value of the initial cherishing of the desire for the realization of enlightenment. While there still remain much in the spiritual exercises which follow the first awakening, the course the Bodhisattva has now to take is fully and clearly defined. The task is arduous, no doubt, but he is no more in the darkness of doubt and ignorance. Therefore, in the Mahāyāna texts this first stirring of the desire for enlightenment is considered a great event in the life of a Buddhist, and receives special mention in them.

The idea of the Bodhisattva as a being who on the one hand seeks after enlightenment and, on the other, out of his compassionate heart intensely desires to lead the whole universe to the enjoyment of spiritual welfare has been persistently alive among all the Mahāyāna followers. '*Jyō gu bo dai, ge ke shu jō*'[1] has thus come to be the normative principle of the Buddhist life in the Far East. In all the Zen monasteries the following 'Four Great Vows' are heard chanted on every occasion, after a service, after a lecture, after a meal, and after the sūtra-reading:

'All beings, however limitless, I vow to carry across;
My evil passions, however inexhaustible, I vow to destroy;
The Dharma teachings, however innumerable, I vow to study;
The Buddha-way, however peerless, I vow to attain.'

[1] '*Chang Ch'iu p'u ti, hsia hua chuang chêng.*' Literally, 'Above, [I] seek for Bodhi (enlightenment); below, [I] convert all beings (*sarvasattva*).'

It is not known exactly when these 'vows' came to be formulated and incorporated into the life of the Zen monk; but there is no doubt that the spirit pervading them is the spirit of the Mahāyāna and as such that of Zen, and that ever since the introduction of Buddhism into China and Japan the principle of the 'Vows' has influenced the cultural life of the East in all its branches.

In the *Gaṇḍavyūha*, these two aspects of the Buddhist life are described, first, as raising the desire for supreme enlightenment, and, secondly, practising the life of the Bodhisattva—that is, the Bodhisattva Samantabhadra. Sudhana the young pilgrim had his first awakening of the desire (*cittotpāda*) under the direction of Mañjuśrī, and his later pilgrimage consisted wholly in inquiries into living the life of enlightenment (*bodhicaryā*). So says Mañjuśrī to his disciple when he sends Sudhana off on his long, arduous 'Pilgrim's Progress': 'Well done, well done, indeed, O son of a good family! Having awakened the desire for supreme enlightenment,[1] thou now wishest to seek for the life of the Bodhisattva. O son of a good family, it is a rare thing to see beings whose desire is raised to supreme enlightenment; but it is a still rarer thing to see beings who, having awakened the desire for supreme enlightenment, proceed to seek for the life of the Bodhisattva. Therefore, O son of a good family, if thou wishest to attain the knowledge which is possessed by the All-knowing One, be ever assiduous to get associated with good friends (*kalyāṇamitra*) . . .'

In the *Prajñāpāramitā*, the second aspect of the Buddhist life after the awakening of the desire for enlightenment consists in practising Prajñāpāramitā. In the *Gaṇḍavyūha* this practice is deeply associated with the life of the Bodhisattva known as Samantabhadra, and the Bodhicaryā, the life of enlightenment, is identified with the Bhadracaryā, the life of Bhadra, that is, Samantabhadra. Samantabhadra thus stands contrasted to Mañjuśrī in the *Gaṇḍavyūha*; the idea of personality we may say has entered here. In the

[1] *Annuttarāyai samyaksaṁbodhaye cittam utpādya.* Idzumi, p. 154.

Prajñāpāramitā Sūtras Prajñā remains impersonal throughout. One of the sūtras[1] gives the following:

'There are only a few people in this world who can clearly perceive what the Buddha, Dharma, and Samgha are and faithfully follow them. . . . Fewer are those who can raise their minds to supreme enlightenment.[2] . . . Fewer still are those who practise Prajñāpāramitā. . . . Fewer and fewer still are those who, most steadfastly practising Prajñāpāramitā and finally reaching the stage of No-turning-back, abide in the state of Bodhisattvahood. . . .'

The usual Sanskrit phrase for 'the desire for enlightenment' is *bodhicittotpāda*, which is the abbreviation of *anuttarāyāṁ samyaksaṁbodhau cittam utpādam*—that is, 'to have a mind raised to supreme enlightenment'. To translate the phrase by 'to awaken the idea of enlightenment' would be incorrect and misleading, as will be explained later. For it is equivalent to *anuttarāṁ samyaksaṁbodhim ākāṅkṣamāṇa*, 'longing for supreme enlightenment',[3] or to *anuttarāyāṁ samyaksaṁbodhau praṇidhānaṁ parigṛihya*, 'cherishing an intense desire for supreme enlightenment'.[4] In the *Gaṇḍavyūka* we have such expressions as these, which convey the same idea: *vipula-kṛipa-karaṇa-mānasa, paryeṣase 'nuttamāṁ bodhim*, 'raising a far-reaching compassion, thou seekest for supreme enlightenment';[5] *ye bodhiprārthayante*, 'those who desire enlightenment'.[6]

Anuttarāyāṁ samyaksaṁbodhau cittam utpādam, the abbreviated form of which, as already referred to, is *bodhicittotpādam*, is also equivalent to *anuttarāyāṁ samyaksaṁbodhau praṇidadhanti.*[7] *Praṇidadhāti* means 'to give one's entire

[1] The *Aṣṭasāhasrikā*, edited by Rājendralāla Mitra, p. 60 ff.

[2] Tebhyo 'pyalpebhyo 'lpatarakās te ye 'nuttarāyāṁ samyaksaṁbodhau cittānyutpādayanti.

[3] *Saddharma-puṇḍarīka*, edited by Kern and Nanjo, p. 414.

[4] Op. cit., p. 43.

[5] Idzumi, p. 152.

[6] Op. cit., p. 154.

[7] This expression is used by Maitreya when he praises Sudhana's determination to pursue the course of Bodhisattvahood. *Durlabhāḥ kulaputrās te sattvaḥ sarvaloke ye 'nuttarāyāṁ samyaksaṁbodhau praṇidadhanti.* Idzumi MS., p. 1321.

attention to something', that is, 'to resolve firmly to accomplish the work'. The Bodhisattva's Praṇidhāna is his intense determination to carry out his plan of universal salvation. Of course, it is necessary here to have an adequate knowledge or a full intellectual grasp of the work he intends to accomplish, but a Praṇidhāna is far more than this, it is the will to do. Mere intellectuality has no backing of the will-power; mere idealism can never be an efficient executive agency. The Cittotpāda is a form of Praṇidhāna. 'To conceive an idea' or 'to awaken a thought' is one thing, and to carry it out in action is quite another, especially when it is carried out with intensity and fervency.

For *anuttarāyāṁ samyaksaṁbodhau cittam utpādam*, the Chinese translators generally have a phrase which literally means 'to raise supreme-enlightenment-mind'. This is, however, not an exact translation. The original literal sense is 'to have a mind raised to enlightenment' and not 'to raise enlightenment-mind'. If the latter, we may think that there is a special mental quality to be called 'enlightenment-mind', and that by means of this faculty one's mind opens up to enlightenment, or that this mind itself is enlightenment. But the sense is really 'cherishing the desire for enlightenment'. It is a sort of conversion, the turning towards enlightenment of the mind which was formerly engaged in something worldly, or the awakening of a new spiritual aspiration which has been dormant, or a new orientation of one's mental activities in the way hitherto undreamed of, or the finding of a new centre of energy which opens up an entirely fresh spiritual vista. We can say that here a glimpse of enlightenment has been caught which helps one to determine one's future course of conduct, and that here a Bodhisattva enters upon the stage of aspiration.

There is another misunderstanding as regards the abbreviated form of *anuttarāyāṁ samyaksaṁbodhau cittam utpādam*, by which I mean the usual interpretation by scholars of the compound *bodhicittotpāda* in Sanskrit. When this is carelessly taken, as is frequently done, it may seem to mean 'to awaken the thought of enlightenment'. But this is wrong, because the compound simply means 'to cherish the desire for enlightenment', that is, 'to cherish a spiritual aspiration for the attainment of supreme enlightenment'. *Citta* here is not 'thought', but 'desire', and *bodhicittotpādam* is after all the shortening of *anuttarāyāṁ samyaksaṁbodhau*[1] *cittam utpādam.*

'To awaken or raise the thought of enlightenment' means, if it means anything definite, to have the conception of enlightenment, or to find out what enlightenment means. But *citta* as we have it suggests no such intellectual content, for it is used in its conative sense. *Cittotpāda* is a volitional movement definitely made towards the realization of enlightenment. Where the intellect is concerned, the Mahāyānists use such words as *jñāna, mati, buddhi, vijñāna,* etc. *Citta,* or *cittāśya,* or *adhyāśaya,* on the other hand, has generally a conative force, and the Chinese translators have very properly adopted *hsin* for it. Whether *citta* is derived from the root *ci,* 'to collect', or *cit,* 'to perceive', the Mahāyāna usage is decidedly not intellectual, but affective and volitional. The Citta is a disposition, predilection or characteristic attitude of mind.

The Bodhicittotpāda is, therefore, a new spiritual excitement which shifts one's centre of energy. It is the becoming conscious of a new religious aspiration which brings about a cataclysm in one's mental organization. A man who has been a stranger to the religious life now cherishes an intense desire for enlightenment, or all-knowledge (*sarvajñatā*), and the whole course of his future life is thereby determined—this is the Bodhicittotpāda.

By way of a note I wish to add the following. Since the *Outlines of Mahāyāna Buddhism* was published in 1907, my views of the Mahāyāna have changed in some details, and there are many points in it upon which I would now express

[1] The locative is not always adhered to. Sometimes it is in the dative, for instance, *anuttarāyai samyaksaṁbodhaye cittam utpādya* (Idzumi copy of *Gaṇḍavyūha,* p. 154). Further, the form *bodha* alone is frequently used for *sambodhi* and in the dative. Examples: *Bodhāya cittam utpadyate* (Rahder—*Daśabhūmika,* p. 11, R); *bodhāya cittam utpādya* (*Aṣṭasāhasrikā,* pp. 62, 63, 71, 93, etc.); *bodhāya cittam utpadyate* (*Gaṇḍavyūha,* p. 169, etc.).

myself differently, especially in connection with the explanation of some Sanskrit terms. For instance, in treating of the Bodhicitta, I defined it to be 'intelligence-heart', adding that theoretically the Bodhi or Bodhicitta is in every sentient being and constitutes its essential nature, only it is in most cases found enveloped in ignorance and egotism. Thus the Bodhicitta is understood to be a form of the Tathāgatagarbha or Ālayavijñāna. In some respects, this way of interpreting the Citta is not incorrect, seeing that supreme enlightenment is the perfection of the Citta, that is, that the Citta when fully developed leads up to enlightenment. But now I find that it is not legitimate from the historical point of view to consider Bodhicitta in the same manner as we do such compounds as *ātmagrahacitta*, *ātmaparanānātvacitta*, *bodhimārgavipravāsacitta*, etc. For, as I propose in this article, *bodhicitta* is the abbreviation of *anuttarāyāṃ samyaksaṁbodhau cittam utpādam*, and is synonymously used with *sarvajñatācitta*, so *bodhicittotpāda* = *sarvajñatācittotpāda*.[1] Bodhi is what makes up the essence of Buddhahood, so is Sarvajñatā, all-knowledge. It is true that later this historical connection between the compound *bodhicitta* and the phrase *anuttarāyāṁ samyaksaṁbodhau cittam utpādam* was altogether forgotten so that the Bodhicitta came to be treated as having an independent technical value. This was natural, and it is not necessarily incorrect so to treat the

[1] In the *Gaṇḍavyūha* where Maitreya describes the desire for enlightenment as one of the most wonderful things a Buddhist can experience in his spiritual career, the compound *bodhicitta* frequently changes into *sarvajñatā*, p. 1332 et passim. In the Chinese translations, *fa p'u t'i hsin* seems to be used both for *bodhicitta* and *sarvajñatācitta*. *Fa p'u t'i hsin* is misleading, as I said before, although we have in the sūtras, e.g. in the *Aṣṭasāhasrikā* (p. 61), such phrases as *bodhicittam utpādyanti* or *bodhicittam upavṛinhayanti*. That the latter means 'to raise or to strengthen the desire for enlightenment' is evident from the context, and the compound is used no doubt to avoid the repetition of the longer phrase. While this is so in the *Prajñāpāramitā*, the *Gaṇḍavyūha*, etc., the later writers of the Buddhist texts have come to treat the desire for enlightenment as if it were a specific faculty of the mind whereby we can testify to the truth of enlightenment. As was said above, this is not altogether wrong, only that it ignores the historical significance of the term. As to rendering it by 'the thought of enlightenment', the original sense is here altogether missed.

compound. But it will be well to remember what I have explained here.

In the *Tathāgata-guhyaka* or the *Guhyasamāja Tantra*, I find the Bodhicitta described in a more abstract and highly technical manner. The text must date much later than the *Gaṇḍavyūha*. It is mixed with a great deal of Tantrism, which must be regarded as a degeneration of pure Mahāyāna Buddhism. The treatment of the Bodhicitta deviates from that in the *Gaṇḍavyūha* as we shall see further on. Below are the definitions of the Citta as given by the different Buddhas who constitute the great mystic Vajra assemblage:

Vairochana: 'To perceive a being as devoid of efficiency in itself, is said not to perceive it; if a being is perceived as not a being, it is said to be unattainable.'[1]

Another statement by Vairochana: 'The Bodhicitta is free from all becoming, is neither attached to nor detached from the Skandhas, Dhātus, and Āyatanas; seeing into the egolessness and sameness of all things, it is my own Mind from the first unborn, and of the nature of Śūnyatā.'

Akshobhya: '[The Bodhicitta sees that] these existences are unborn, that they are neither individual objects nor that which constitutes their being; the Citta is like the sky and has no ego-substance; and this is where the principle of enlightenment is firmly established.'

Ratnaketu: '[The Bodhicitta sees that] all individual objects are unborn, they are devoid of forms of individuality, they are born of the egolessness of things; and this is where the principle of enlightenment is firmly established.'

Amitāyus: 'Individual objects being unborn, there is neither becoming nor perceiving; as the term sky is used [though it has no reality], so is the Citta said to be something existent.'

Amoghasiddhi: 'Individual objects are by nature illuminating, they are as pure as the sky; when there is no [something to be designated] as enlightenment or realization, there is the principle of enlightenment firmly established.'

[1] This verse requires a full explanation as it is too abstractedly and technically expressed.

PLATE XVII

THE DANCING PU-TEI

By Liang Kai

Who Pu-tei (Hotei) was, has already been told in the Second Series of my *Zen Essays*. He was another Zen lunatic, affording a favourite subject of painting for the Zen artist. Here he is shown as going around dancing with his staff over the shoulder and his inevitable bag on his back. His looks are ugly as tradition has them, and his dress is mere shreds. But how happy he appears! The master remarks that such an attitude as this is a great concern for all Zen students through ages to come. Has he really gone crazy? Or are we ourselves not quite in the middle way?

PLATE XVIII

BODHIDHARMA CROSSING THE OCEAN ON A REED-LEAF

Ascribed to INDRA

One tradition makes Bodhidharma, after his nine years' meditation at Shiao-lin monastery, cross the ocean to return to his own country or somewhere else. This must have been a fine subject for Zen artists, for they could thus depict his mysterious personality with appropriate settings. Nothing perhaps could bring out his character more appropriately than to represent him on a reed-leaf floating on a broad expanse of waters. This was the way the Zen artists tried to symbolise the teaching of Zen after their own light. In the Bodhidharma sitting stolidly for nine years, Zen is absolutely immovable, and in the Bodhidharma giving himself up to the utmost capriciousness of the waves and yet remaining perfect master of his destiny in this world of vicissitudes, Zen has its thoroughgoing intellectual penetration. There is no desperateness here of a drowning man who will seize at a straw, nor is there the irrationality of walking over the waves. The reed-leaf is an insignificant piece of a plant, it grows near the shore, Bodhidharma picks it, and trusting himself to its carrying power he sails out on it into the boundless ocean of transmigration. The artist with only a few strokes of the brush finishes the picture of a Zen monk's attitude towards life.

2

To cherish the desire for enlightenment is no ordinary event in the life of the Mahāyāna Buddhist, for this is the definite step he takes towards the goal as distinguished from the life of the so-called Hīnayāna follower. Enlightenment is not a mere personal affair which does not concern the community at large; its background is laid in the universe itself. When I am enlightened, the whole Dharmadhātu is enlightened; in fact the reason of my enlightenment is the reason of the Dharmadhātu, the two are most intimately bound up with each other. Therefore, that I have been able to conceive a great longing for enlightenment means that the entire world wishes to be liberated from ignorance and evil passions. This is the meaning of the following statement made by Sāgaramegha, one of the teachers whom Sudhana visited in his long spiritual pilgrimage: 'It is indeed well for you that you have already awakened the desire for enlightenment; this is an impossibility for those who have not accumulated enough stock of merit in their past lives.' 'A stock of merit' so called has value only when it concerns the welfare of the world generally. Unless a man is able to survey the entire field of relationships in which he stands—that is, unless his spiritual outlook extends to its furthest end—his '*merit*' (*kuśala*) is not real 'merit', and no accumulation of such will result in the awakening of the desire for enlightenment. Hence the utmost importance of this awakening.

Sāgaramegha continues to praise Sudhana's cherishing the desire which is only possible to those who have the following qualities:

1. That their meritorious deeds are of universal character and illuminating;
2. That their attainment of the Samādhi is full of the light of knowledge which is derived from walking the path of righteousness;
3. That they are able to produce the great ocean of merit;

4. That they are never tired of amassing all kinds of purities;

5. That they are ever ready to associate with good friends and attend upon them with reverence;

6. That they are not accumulators of wealth and never hesitate to give up their lives for a good cause;

7. That they are free from the spirit of arrogance and like the great earth treat others impartially;

8. That their hearts being filled with love and compassion they are always thinking of the welfare of others;

9. That they are always friendly disposed towards all beings in the various paths of existence;

10. That they are ever desirous of being admitted into the community of Buddhas.

Sāgaramegha now concludes that only to those souls who are endowed with these aspirations, affections, and dispositions is vouchsafed the privilege of cherishing the desire for enlightenment. For this desire for enlightenment is really aroused from:

1. A great loving heart (*mahākaruṇācitta*) which is desirous of protecting all beings;

2. A great compassionate heart (*mahāmaitrīcitta*) which ever wishes for the welfare of all beings;

3. The desire to make others happy (*sukhacitta*), which comes from seeing them suffer all forms of pain;

4. The desire to benefit others (*hitācitta*), and to deliver them from evils and wrong deeds;

5. A sympathetic heart (*dayācitta*) which desires to protect all beings from tormenting thoughts;

6. An unimpeded heart (*asaṁgacitta*) which wishes to see all the impediments removed for others;

7. A large heart (*vipulacitta*) which fills the whole universe;

8. An endless heart (*anantacitta*) which is like space;

9. A spotless heart (*vimalacitta*) which sees all the Buddhas;

10. A pure heart (*viśuddhacitta*) which is in conformity with the wisdom of the past, present, and future;

11. A wisdom-heart (*jñānacitta*) by which one can enter the great ocean of all-knowledge.

The further quotations from the *Daśabhūmika*[1] will throw more light on the preliminary steps leading to the desire for enlightenment, on the reasons why enlightenment is desired, on the constituent elements of enlightenment, and on the effect of enlightenment. Both the *Daśabhūmika* and the *Gaṇḍavyūha* belong in the Chinese Tripitaka to the Mahāyāna collection known as the *Kegon-gyō*.[2]

What are the preliminary conditions that lead to the cherishing of the desire for supreme enlightenment? They are:

1. The stock of merit (*kuśalamūla*) is well filled;
2. Deeds of goodness (*caraṇa*) are well practised;
3. The necessary moral provisions (*sambhāra*) are well stored up;
4. The Buddhas have been respectfully served (*paryupāsita*);
5. Works of purity (*śukladharma*) are well accomplished;
6. There are good friends (*kalyāṇamitra*) kindly disposed;
7. The heart is thoroughly cleansed (*viśuddhāśaya*);
8. Broad-mindedness (*vipulādhyāśaya*) is firmly secured;
9. A deep sincere faith (*adhimukti*) is established;

[1] Rahder Edition, p. 11, R.

[2] The Sanskrit title of the *Kegon-gyō* is *Avataṁsaka*, as we gather from the *Mahāvyutpatti* and also from the *Chih-yüan Lu*, a catalogue of the Chinese Tripitaka compiled in A.D. 1285–1287, but it is *Gaṇḍavyūha* according to Fa-tsang's commentary on the sixty-fascicle *Kegon-gyō*. *Avataṁsaka* means 'a garland', and *gaṇḍa* is 'a flower of ordinary kind', and *vyūha* 'an orderly arrangement' or 'array'. From this, *Kegon* more exactly corresponds to *Gaṇḍavyūha* than to *Avataṁsaka*. *Ke* (*hua*) is a flower, and *gon* (*yen*) or *shōgon* (*chüang-yen*) in Chinese is equivalent to *vyūha*. When the contents of the Chinese *Kegon*, either of sixty or eighty fascicles, are examined, we find that there were in the beginning many independent sūtras which were later compiled into one encyclopaedic collection, as the subject-matters treated in them are all classifiable under one head, and they came to be known as the *Avataṁsaka* or *Kegon*. It will be better to restrict the use of *Avataṁsaka* to the whole collection of the *Kegon* and *Gaṇḍavyūha* to the Sanskrit text as an independent one, though it constitutes the last chapter of the sixty- and eighty-fascicle *Kegon*. The forty-fascicle *Kegon* corresponds to the *Gaṇḍavyūha*. See also p. 73 et seq. of this book.

10. There is the presence of a compassionate heart (*karuṇā*).

According to the *Daśabhūmika*, these ten things are needed for the awakening of the desire for enlightenment. To have this desire is in itself a great Buddhist experience, which does not take place without some spiritual preparation. It sprouts from a seed deeply laid in the ground and well nourished. One of the ideas requiring special notice in the enumeration here cited is the reference to good friends. Their goodwill and assistance are powerful instruments in the cultivation of the Buddhist aspiration. The *Gaṇḍavyūha* is emphatic in this respect.

All the sūtras belonging to Kegon literature have a deliberate penchant for decimal enumeration, and even when there is apparently no intrinsic need for filling up the required formula the author or compiler scrupulously proceeds to count up a complete series of ten. Thus in the above recapitulation ideas belonging to one category are divided into so many heads, evidently for no other purpose than to keep up the form. 'Stock of merit', 'deeds of goodness', 'moral provision', and 'work of purity' may be gathered up under the one head of moral conduct. If this is possible, the conditions necessary for awakening the desire for enlightenment may be summarized thus: (1) moral conduct, (2) the friendly disposition of the Buddhas and good friends, and (3) a heart pure, true, loving and all-embracing. When these three conditions are perfectly fulfilled, the Bodhicitta is said to raise its head and to be ready for further evolution.

The question next is, Why is the desire for supreme enlightenment so necessary in the life of a devout Mahāyānist? Or simply, What has the Buddhist enlightenment to do with our life? The *Daśabhūmika*[1] gives the following reasons:

1. For the realization of Buddha-knowledge (*jñāna*);
2. For the attainment of the ten powers (*daśabala*);

[1] Rahder, p. 11, S.

3. For the attainment of great fearlessness (*mahāvaiśā-radya*);

4. For the attainment of the truth of sameness which constitutes Buddhahood (*samatabuddhadharma*);

5. For protecting and securing the whole world (*sarva-jagatparitrāṇa*);

6. For the purification of a pitying and compassionate heart (*kṛipākaruṇā*);

7. For the attainment of a knowledge which leaves nothing unknown (*aśeṣajñāna*) in the ten quarters of the world;

8. For the purification of all the Buddha-lands so that a state of non-attachment (*asaṁga*) will prevail;

9. For the perception of the past, present, and future in one moment (*kṣaṇabodha*);

10. For the revolving of the great wheel of the Dharma (*dharmacakrapravarta*) in the spirit of fearlessness.

From this, we can partly see what are the elements of supreme enlightenment, for the reasons given for its realization are already found involved in it as its own constituents. Then what are these constituents? They are:

1. The knowledge which belongs to Buddhahood, and which see into everything that is in space and time—the knowledge which goes beyond the realm of relativity and individuation because it penetrates into every corner of the universe and surveys eternity at one glance;

2. The will-power that knocks down every possible obstruction lying athwart its way when it wishes to reach its ultimate end, which is the deliverance of the whole world from the bondage of birth-and-death;

3. An all-embracing love or compassion which, in combination with knowledge and will-power, never ceases from devising all means to promote the spiritual welfare of every sentient being.

In order to clarify further the nature of enlightenment as conceived by the Mahāyānists, the following is taken again from the *Daśabhūmika*,[1] according to which the desire for enlightenment comprises in it the following elements:

1. A great compassionate heart which is the chief factor of the desire;

2. Knowledge born of transcendental wisdom which is the ruling element;

3. Skilful means which works as a protecting agent;

4. The deepest heart which gives it a support.

And, further, the Bodhicitta is:

5. Of the same measure with the Tathāgata-power;

6. Endowed with the power to discern the power and intelligence of all beings (*sattvabalabuddhi*);

7. Directed towards the knowledge of non-obstruction (*asambhinnajñāna*);

8. In conformity with spontaneous knowledge (*svayambhūjñāna*);

9. Capable of instructing all beings in the truths of Buddhism according to knowledge born of transcendental wisdom;

10. Extending to the limits of the Dharmadhātu which is as wide as space itself.

In these qualifications too one can see what is meant by cherishing the desire for enlightenment. The cherishing of the desire at once stamps a man as a Bodhisattva and thus distinguishes him from the other followers of Buddhism; for he holds a great compassionate heart for all beings, and also has perspicuity of spiritual insight which sees into the nature of existence, and further the power of controlling love with wisdom and tempering wisdom with love so that he is able to adapt himself to the ever-changing conditions of existence.

Since the desire for enlightenment is composed of all these attributes as here described, the Bodhisattva is capable of producing the following results at the moment this desire asserts itself in the depths of his being.[2]

[1] Ibid, p. 11, T.
[2] Ibid, pp. 11–12, U.

1. He passes beyond the stage of an ordinary being;
2. He enters into the rank of Bodhisattvahood;
3. He is born in the family of Tathāgatas;
4. He is irreproachable and faultless in his family honour;
5. He stands away from all worldly courses;
6. He enters into a supra-worldly life;
7. He is established in things belonging to Bodhisattvahood;
8. He abides in the abode of the Bodhisattva;
9. He is impartially ushered into the Tathāgata-groups of the past, present, and future;
10. He is ultimately destined for supreme enlightenment.

When he thus takes his abode in these things, he is said to have gained the first stage of a Bodhisattva known as Joy (*pramuditā*), because he is now immovable in his faith.

These passages from the *Daśabhūmika* defining the source, nature, scope and outcome of the Bodhicitta or the desire for enlightenment are explicit enough. We can realize of what a weighty significance this aspiration is for the Mahāyānists. It is almost like the realization itself. When it is sufficiently strongly awakened, the Buddhist's course afterwards determines itself. If the Bodhicittotpāda or Bodhicitta were no more than mere thinking of enlightenment even as something of the utmost importance in the life of a Buddhist, the Citta as 'thought' could by no means achieve so much as is described above. The Citta is not an idea, is not mere thinking, it is an intense desire or aspiration which causes an entire rearrangement or reconstruction of all the former experiences made by the Buddhist. The Citta is the reason of one's being, it is the original will that constitutes the foundation of one's personality. Otherwise, the meaning of the forceful manner in which the editor of the *Gaṇḍavyhūya* endeavours to describe the nature of the Bodhicitta becomes incomprehensible, as will be seen in the following pages.

3

When the young Buddhist pilgrim Sudhana calls upon the Bodhisattva Maitreya for instruction, the latter first praises Sudhana for his strong determination to search for the final truth of Buddhism; and before he opens his magnificent Vairochana Tower for the young man's observation and contemplation, he eulogizes the virtues of the Bodhicitta, urged by which indeed the young pilgrim has until now visited one teacher after another until he comes to Maitreya. If not for this ardent desire for enlightenment, Sudhana would never have undertaken his arduous task of pilgrimaging among the seers and philosophers, the wise men and women, who probably represent to a certain extent historical personages of the day. The *Gaṇḍavyūha* is indeed the record of those intellectual and spiritual struggles which take place around the question, 'What is the life of a Bodhisattva?', that is to say, 'What is the meaning of human life?' The awakening of the Bodhicitta is the key to this eternal riddle, hence Maitreya's most extended and exhaustive characterization of the Bodhicitta, 'the desire for enlightenment'.

'Well done,' said Maitreya to Sudhana, 'well done, O son of a good family! Already you have awakened the desire for supreme enlightenment, in order to benefit the world, to lead it to happiness, to rescue all beings from sufferings, and to acquire all the truths of Buddhism. O son of a good family, you have many advantages, you enjoy the life of a human being, you live in the world of living beings, you live at the time when a Tathāgata has appeared, you have interviewed the good friend Mañjuśrī. You are indeed a good vessel of truth, you are well nourished with stocks of merit, well supported by works of purity, you are already well cleansed in the understanding, great in intuition, you are already well protected by all the Buddhas, well guarded by good friends, for the reason that you have already sincerely awakened the desire for supreme enlightenment

[I will tell you what the Bodhicitta means to us followers of the Mahāyāna.]'[1]

The Bodhicitta[1] [that is, the desire for enlightenment] is like a seed because from it grows all the truths of Buddhism. It is like a farm because here are produced all things of purity for the world.

The Bodhicitta is like the earth because all the worlds are supported by it. It is like water because all the dirt of the passions is thereby cleansed. It is like the wind because it blows all over the world with nothing obstructing its course. It is like fire because it consumes all the fuel of bad logic.

The Bodhicitta is like the sun because it leaves nothing unenlightened on earth. It is like the moon because it fills to perfection all things of purity. It is like a lamp because it brings things out in the light. It is like an eye because it perceives where the road is even and where it is uneven.

The Bodhicitta is like a highway because it leads one to the city of knowledge. It is like a sacred ford because it keeps away all that is not proper. It is like a carriage because it carries all the Bodhisattvas. It is like a door because it opens to all the doings of the Bodhisattva.

The Bodhicitta is like a mansion because it is the retreat where Samādhi and meditation are practised. It is like a park because it is where the enjoyment of truth (*dharmarati*) is experienced. It is like a dwelling-house because it is where all the world is comfortably sheltered. It is like a refuge because it gives a salutary abode to all beings. It is like an asylum because it is where all the Bodhisattvas walk.

The Bodhicitta is like a father because it protects all the Bodhisattvas. It is like a mother because it brings up all the Bodhisattvas. It is like a nurse because it takes care of all

[1] What follows is based chiefly on the Chinese translations although the original Sanskrit MSS. have been constantly made use of in connection with the Chinese. The English rendering is not literal, the idea being to show the reader what signification the Bodhicitta has in the teaching of Mahāyāna Buddhism.

the Bodhisattvas. It is like a good friend because it gives good advice to all the Bodhisattvas. It is like a king because it overpowers the minds of all the Śrāvakas and the Pratyekabuddhas. It is like a great sovereign because it fulfils all the excellent vows.

The Bodhicitta is like a great ocean because it harbours all the gems of virtues. It is like Mount Sumeru because it towers impartially above all things. It is like Mount Cakravada because it supports all the world. It is like Mount Himālaya because it produces all sorts of knowledge-herbs. It is like Mount Gandhamādana because it harbours all kinds of virtue-fragrance. It is like space because it infinitely spreads out the merit of goodness.

The Bodhicitta is like a lotus-flower because it is never spoiled by things of this world. It is like an elephant because it is obedient. It is like a well-bred horse because it is free from evil nature. It is like a charioteer because it keeps watch over all the truths of the Mahāyāna.

The Bodhicitta is like a medicine because it heals all diseases of the passions. It is like a chasm because it submerges all that is evil. It is like a vajra because it penetrates into everything.

The Bodhicitta is like a box of incense because it contains the fragrance of virtue. It is like a great flower because it delights those who catch the sight of it. It is like sandalwood because it cools off the heat of greed. It is like Kalāpa because its fragrance penetrates through all the Dharmadhātu. The Bodhicitta is like Sudarśana which is the king of medicine because it destroys all the diseases arising from the passions (*kleśa*). It is like a salve called Vigama because it draws out all the arrows of the passions (*anuśaya*).

The Bodhicitta is like Indra because it is the overlord of all the gods. It is like Vaiśravana because it destroys all the pain of poverty. It is like Śrī because it is embellished with all the virtues.

The Bodhicitta is like an ornament because all the Bodhisattvas are decorated with it. It is like the kalpa-consuming fire because it burns up all corruptions. It is like a great medicinal herb known as Anirvṛittamūla because it brings up all the truths of Buddhism.

The Bodhicitta is like a Nāga-gem because it nullifies the poison of all the passions. It is like a transparent water-gem because it purifies the turbidness of all the passions. It is like a Cintamāṇi (wish-gem) because it supplies all the wealth one desires. It is like a magic jar because it fulfils every desire. It is like a wish-granting-tree because from it are showered all the virtue-ornaments.

The Bodhicitta is like a robe made of goose-feathers because it is never stained by the dirt of birth-and-death. It is like pure Karpāsa thread because it remains from the first brilliantly luminous.

The Bodhicitta is like a plough because it clears the mind-field of all beings. It is like the iron arrows of Nārāyana because it strikes down the view of an ego-soul. It is like an arrow because it pierces the target of pain. It is like a spear because it vanquishes the enemy known as passion. It is like a coat of mail because it protects the mind that conforms to rationality. It is like a scimitar because it cuts off the heads of the passions. It is like a sword-blade because it cuts through the armour of pride, conceit, and arrogance. It is like a razor because it cuts the passions (*anuśaya*).[1] It is like the banner of a brave fighter because it bears down the banner of Māra. It is like a sharp cutter because it rends asunder the tree of ignorance. It is like an axe because it chops the wood of sufferings. It is like a weapon because it protects one from violence.

The Bodhicitta is like a hand because it guards the body of the Pāramitās. It is like a foot because it gives a support to virtue and knowledge.

The Bodhicitta is like a surgical instrument because it removes the sheath and film of ignorance. It is like a pair of tweezers because it picks out the splinter of the ego-soul. It like a bedstead because it gives rest to the vexations of the passions (*anuśaya*).

[1] The Anuśaya means 'what sleeps along with' and is the Kleśa.

The Bodhicitta is like a good friend because it loosens all the bondage of birth-and-death. It is like being in possession of wealth because it wards off poverty. It is like a great teacher because it points out the way to the devotional life of the Bodhisattva. It is like a depository of treasure because it contains an imperishable mind of merit. It is like a fountain because from it issues an inexhaustible supply of knowledge.

The Bodhicitta is like a mirror because it reveals all the images of truth. It is like a lotus-flower because it is stainless. It is like a great river because in it flow the Pāramitās as well as the rules of acceptance. It is like the Lord of Serpents because it showers clouds of good truths. It is like the giver of life because it supports the great compassionate heart of the Bodhisattva.

The Bodhicitta is like nectar because it makes one abide in the realm of immortality. It is like an all-trapping net because it gathers and draws up every tractable being.

The Bodhicitta is like a basket of sandal-wood because it contains all the fragrance of virtue. It is like medicinal Agada because it preserves one's perfect health. It is like an antidotal medicine because it counteracts the poison of sensuous pleasures. It is like a magical charm because it wipes out the poisonous effect of irrationality.

The Bodhicitta is like a whirlwind because it sweeps away every obstruction and opposition before it. It is like an isle of treasure because it produces the treasure of every factor of enlightenment. It is like a good family because from it issues every work of purity. It is like a dwelling-house because it is where everything virtuous has its refuge. It is like a city because it is where all the Bodhisattvas like merchants carry on their business.

The Bodhicitta is like quicksilver because it clears up all the hindrances of karma and the passions. It is like a honey preparation because it completes the provisions for the attainment of all-knowledge.

The Bodhicitta is like the highway because it leads all the Bodhisattvas to the city of all-knowledge. It is like a repository because it holds all the works of purity. It is like a shower because it washes away the dust of the passions. It is like a shelter because it provides all the Bodhisattvas with the instructions they need for their settlement. It is like the loadstone because it refuses to attract the fruit of emancipation attained by the Śrāvakas. It is like lapis lazuli because it is by nature stainless. It is like a sapphire because it far surpasses all the knowledge that is realized by the Śrāvakas and Pratyekabuddhas as well as by people of the world.

The Bodhicitta is like a kettle-drum because it awakens all beings from their sleep in the passions. It is like pure water because it is essentially limpid and stainless. It is like Jambūnada gold because it outshines all the stocks of merit obtainable in this world of created things. It is like the great prince of mountains, because it towers above all the world.

The Bodhicitta is like a shelter because it never refuses anyone that may come. It is like a real substance because there is in it nothing that is unreal. It is like a wish-fulfilling gem because it satisfies every heart.

The Bodhicitta is like a sacrificial utensil because by it all the world is gratified. It is like an enlightened one because there is nothing in worldly-mindedness that is comparable to it. It is like a rope because it lifts up all the truths of Buddhism.

The Bodhicitta is like a good binder because it holds the life and the vows of the Bodhisattva. It is like a protector because it protects the entire world. It is like a watchman because it holds back all that is bad. It is like Indra's net because it subdues the passions which resemble the Asuras. It is like Varuṇa's chain because it draws and controls. It is like Indra's fire because it consumes all the habit-energy, passions (*anuśaya*), and impure desires (*kleśa*). It is like a Caitya because it is respected by all the world, by human beings, and by Asuras.

'O son of a good family,' the Bodhisattva Maitreya then concluded, 'the Bodhicitta is attended with such and other innumerable excellent merits. Briefly, let it be known that the merits of the Bodhicitta are as numerous as the truths of Buddhism and the merits of Buddhahood. For what reason? Because it is from the Bodhicitta that the devotional life of the Bodhisattva starts its first step, and that all the Tathāgatas of the past, present, and future make their appearance in the world. Therefore, son of a good family, when the desire for supreme enlightenment is aroused, innumerable merits are produced along with it, and also the deepest consciousness of all-knowledge evolves from it.'

4

[Further said the Bodhisattva Maitreya to Sudhana:]

It is like possessing the mystic herb of fearlessness which dispels the five forms of fear: for the owner of the herb fire loses the power to burn, poison the power to kill, the sword the power to injure, water the power to drown, and smoke the power to suffocate. In like manner, when the Bodhisattva obtains the Bodhicitta-herb of all-knowledge, the fire of greed cannot burn him, the poison of anger cannot kill him, the sword of the passions cannot hurt him, the ocean of becoming cannot drown him, and the smoke of various philosophies cannot suffocate him.

Like a man who has the mystic herb of liberation whereby all calamities are warded off, the Bodhisattva, when he is the owner of the Bodhicitta-herb of knowledge, is kept forever out of the reach of birth-and-death.

Like man who has Maghi-herb which keeps away all poisonous snakes on account of the fragrance it emits, the Bodhisattva who is in possession of the Bodhicitta keeps away all the poisonous snakes of the passions by means of the fragrance issuing from the Citta.

Like a man who, being the possessor of the charm known as Invincible, is never vanquished by his enemy, the Bodhisattva becomes unconquerable by the antagonistic army of the Evil One when he is the possessor of the invincible Bodhicitta-charm of all-knowledge.

PLATE XIX

THE THREE LAUGHING ONES BY THE HU-CH'I

By Motonobu Kano

Hui-yüan (A.D. 371–454) was a great Buddhist student. Renouncing all worldly relations he retired to Lu-shan and passed a solitary life for over thirty years. When he saw off his visitors, he never went out beyond the mountain stream called Hu (=tiger). One day T'ao Yüanming, the great poet of the Six Dynasties, and Lin Ching-hsiu the Taoist called on Hui-yüan. They became so interested in their talk that Yüan forgot all about the bridge and walked beyond it, when a tiger all of a sudden roared aloud. They looked at one another, and, giving a hearty laugh, parted. Later, people erected a pavilion here called "San-hsiao T'ing" dedicated to the Three Laughing Ones.

建仁清拙題
宿客無因嫁禍胎
周家若是龍門女
歲寒深守下山來
一寸霜姿手自栽

PLATE XX

TSAI-SUNG TAO-CHE (THE PINE-PLANTER)

Ascribed to LIANG KAI

According to a legend, Hung-jên, the fifth Patriarch, was a pine-planter in his former life. When he for the first time saw Tao-hsin, the fourth Patriarch, he was told that he was too old a man to take up the study of Zen and advised to be born again, for Tao-hsin would still be waiting for him. Tsai-sung on his way home observed a young woman of the Shou family washing cloths in the stream. He asked her if he would be allowed to lodge himself in her for another birth. She agreed on condition that her family had no objection. When a child was born to her, they did not consider it a good omen and threw it into a river. But on the following morning it was found going up the stream with its body fresh and clean. The boy grew up and disciplined himself under the guidance of Tao-hsin to become a great master of Zen.

The fifth Patriarch here is represented in his former existence as an old pine-planter. The most interesting part in this legend in connection with the general history of Zen in China is that Hung-jên, like his successor Hui-nêng, was also an active participant in the practical business of life. He was no idle dreamer on abstract ideas; he was a manual worker and thoroughly democratic in his way of thinking and feeling.

Like a man who, by virtue of possessing the charm known as Vigama, makes every arrow against him fall on the ground, the Bodhisattva who is in possession of the Vigama-remedy of the Bodhicitta makes fall every arrow of greed, anger, and folly, and also that of false speculation, which may be directed against him.

Like a man who being in possession of the great charm called Sudarśana wards off every sort of disease, the Bodhisattva who has the great Sudarśana-charm of the Bodhicitta becomes free from the disease of the knowledge as well as the disease of passions.

There is a great medicinal tree called Santāna, the bark of which has a great healing quality for all kinds of sores, and yet the tree always retains its complete form because as soon as the bark is peeled off, new bark grows. In like manner, from the Bodhicitta cherished by the Bodhisattva there grows the tree of all-knowledge, and those who see it and believe it have their passion and karma sores completely healed, and yet the tree of all-knowledge shows no signs from the first of growing the less effective.

There is a great medicinal tree known as Anirvṛittamūla, by virtue of which all the trees in Jambūdvīpa gain the strength to grow. In like manner, the Anirvṛittamūla tree of Bodhicitta being cherished by the Bodhisattva has the power to keep all the learners, the Arhats, the Pratyekabuddhas, and the Bodhisattvas strong in all things good.

There is a medicinal plant known as Ratilambhya, which being rubbed on the body will make the mind as well as the body strong and healthy. In like manner, when the Bodhisattva takes hold of the Ratilambhya plant of Bodhicitta he grows strong and healthy in his mind and body.

There is a medicinal plant known as Good Memory. When this is given, the memory is improved. In like manner, when the good-memory plant of Bodhicitta is administered the Bodhisattva retains in his mind every good truth of Buddhism.

There is a medicinal plant known as Great-Lotus-Flower

which gives one a kalpa-long life. In like manner, when the Great-Lotus-Flower medicine of Bodhicitta is given to the Bodhisattva, his life will be prolonged as he wishes, even for a countless number of kalpas.

There is a medicinal plant known as Invisible which makes one invisible both to human beings and to non-human beings. In like manner, when the Invisible medicinal plant of Bodhicitta is taken, the Bodhisattva in whatever condition he may wander becomes invisible to all evil ones.

There is a gem, king of gems, in the great ocean, which is known as All-gem-treasure-collection (*sarvamaṇiratnasamuccayam*). When this is present, even the world-end fire which may destroy all the other worlds cannot consume even a drop of water in this ocean. In like manner, when the Bodhicitta is cherished in the heart of the Bodhisattva, which is to him the gem-king, Sarvamaṇiratnasamuccaya, not one jot of the great vows directed towards all-knowledge will ever disappear from him. Let, however, his aspiration after all-knowledge (*sarvajñatācittotpāda*)[1] be reduced to nothing, and all his stock of merit will vanish.

There is a gem known as all-illumination-mass (*sarvaprabhāsasamuccaya*), prince of all gems, which outshines, when it is worn as a necklace, all other ornamental jewelries. In like manner, the Sarva-prabhāsa-samuccaya gem of the Bodhicitta cherished by the Bodhisattva, which he wears as his spiritual necklace, outshines all the ornaments decorating the minds of the Śrāvakas and the Pratyekabuddhas.

There is a great gem which, when thrown into murky water, makes it thoroughly transparent. The Bodhicitta cherished by the Bodhisattva is like this water-purifying gem, for thereby all the filth of the passion-water is thoroughly purified.

There is a gem which preserves its owner from being drowned in the ocean even when he is thrown into it. The Bodhisattva's aspiration after all-knowledge is like this

[1] It is to be noted that the Sanskrit copies have 'aspiration after all-knowledge' and not 'aspiration after enlightenment'. How did *sarvajñatā* come to replace *bodhi*?

water-gem; when he has this he is saved from being drowned in the ocean of transmigration.

When a fisherman carrying a Serpent-gem with him goes down underneath the waves, all the gates to the Serpent palace will be opened to him, and he will not be hurt by dwellers of the ocean. In like manner when the Bodhisattva is provided with his aspiration after all-knowledge which is his spiritual Serpent-gem, he is able to enter unhurt into all the abodes in the world of desire.

As the crown of gem worn by Śakra outshines all other crowns on the heads of the lesser gods, so the Bodhisattva's crown of gem which he wears in the shape of the aspiration after all-knowledge on his forehead of the great vows, shines all over the triple world.

As when a man obtains a great Cintamaṇi-gem, every possibility of poverty is warded off, so the Bodhisattva when he cherishes the aspiration after all-knowledge comparable to the great gem of Cintamaṇi will be saved from the threats of life.

There is a sun-reflecting gem which when held against the sun will produce fire. The Bodhisattva's aspiration after all-knowledge resembles this sun-reflecting gem, for when it is held against the sun of Prajñā it will produce the fire of Prajñā.

There is a moon-reflecting gem, which when held against the light of the moon will produce water. The Bodhisattva's aspiration after all-knowledge resembles this moon-reflecting gem, for when it is held against the moonlight of the stock of merit, it will produce the water of vows and of the stock of merit.

There is a Cintamaṇi-gem decorating the head of the King Mahānāga, which keeps away all the threats of his enemies. The Bodhicitta issuing from the great compassionate heart of the Bodhisattva is like this Cintamaṇi-gem which decorates his head, and will distance all the ills that may rise from the evil paths of existence.

There is a great gem-king known as World-embellishing-receptacle which remains ever perfect however much it may fulfil every wish entertained by all beings. In like manner, the great gem-treasure of the Bodhicitta which is possessed by the Bodhisattva grants him every wish he may have, remaining all the time complete in every way.

A great gem is in the possession of the supreme ruler of the world, which dispels darkness wherever it is, radiating its rays in every direction. In like manner, the great royal gem-treasure of the Citta roused for all-knowledge dispels all the darkness of ignorance which hovers over every path of existence, as it releases the great light of knowledge in the world of desire.

There is a great blue Indra-gem-treasure which turns everything it touches into its own colour. In like manner, the great Indra-blue gem of the Citta roused for all knowledge reflects itself on all beings and turns all the stock of merit over to them, making them take up the Indra-gem colour of the Citta itself.

A cat's-eye-gem may be left among filth for hundreds of thousands of years and yet it will be found altogether free from contamination. In like manner, the gem-treasure of the Bodhicitta is not tainted by the faults of the world of desire however long it may remain buried in it, for the Citta-gem is purity itself.

Like a gem called Pure-light, whose brilliancy outshines all other gems, the Bodhicitta-treasure outshines all the virtues belonging to the simple-minded, to the learners, to the Pratyekabuddhas.

There is one great gem-treasure known as Consecrated-to-fire-god whose brilliancy disperses every possible speck of darkness. In like manner, the great gem-treasure of the Bodhicitta is equal in its brilliancy to the Consecrated-to-fire-god, and, accompanied by reflection, disperses every speck of darkness caused by ignorance.

There is a precious gem in the great ocean, invaluable in price; it falls into the hand of a merchant and when it is brought to the store all the gems there, hundreds of thousands of them, turn into a worthless dark mass of stones. In like manner, the great gem-treasure of the Bodhicitta, while abiding in the great ocean of birth-and-death, embarks on the boat of vows, and when the Bodhisattva thus equipped, deep and constant in faith, enters the city of emancipation, all the virtues of Śrāvakahood and Pratyekabuddhahood sink into utter insignificance.

There is a great gem-treasure called Supreme Sovereign which is kept in Jambūdvīpa 40,000 yojanas away from the sun and the moon, and yet on which are reflected all the illuminations and decorations ornamenting the palatial mansions in the sun and the moon. In like manner, the Supreme Sovereign-gem of the Bodhicitta while aroused in the midst of transmigration is filled with virtues of purity and reflects in it all the illuminations and decorations ornamenting the realm of Buddhahood which extends as infinitely as the Dharmadhātu or space and where the supreme knowledge of the Tathāgata shines like the sun and the moon.

The value of this Supreme Sovereign gem-treasure is such that no collection of worldly treasures—gold, silver, corn, precious stone, flower, fragrance, garland, dress, etc.—can ever surpass it as far as the light of the moon and the sun reaches. In like manner, the value of the Supreme Sovereign gem of the Bodhicitta can never be surpassed, so long as the supreme intelligence of the all-knowing one continues to illuminate the past, present, and future, by reason of the merits, conditioned or unconditioned, which belong to the gods, men, Śrāvakas, and Pratyekabuddhas.

There is a great gem-treasure called Ocean-array-womb in which all the magnificent views of the ocean are reflected. In like manner, the great gem-treasure, Ocean-array-womb, of the Bodhicitta reflects in it all the magnificent views of the ocean of supreme intelligence which is the realm of the all-knowing one.

As there is nothing comparable in value to celestial Jambūnada gold, except the great gem-treasure-king of mind, so is there nothing comparable (in spiritual value) to the Jambūnada gold of the Bodhicitta, except the king-mind of supreme intelligence belonging to the all-knowing one.

As one who has mastered the art of controlling the dragon can go freely and fearlessly among dragons and serpents, so does one who has the Bodhicitta go freely and fearlessly among dragons and serpents of the passions, because he has gained the complete mastery of the Bodhicitta—as of the dragon-taming art.

As an armour-clad warrior is undefeatable by the enemy, so is the Bodhicitta undefeatable by the enemy-passions, because he is protected by the armour of the Bodhicitta.

When one pinch of the powder of celestial sandal-wood is burned, its scent is diffused over the whole chiliocosm, and it is worth far more than all the treasures that can fill the triple chiliocosm. In like manner, the celestial sandal-wood of the Bodhicitta, even one jot of its deep faith, is enough to diffuse itself over the whole Dharmadhātu with its fragrant scent unsurpassed by the spiritual attainments of all the learners and Pratyekabuddhas.

There is a sandal-wood treasure known as white sandal-wood which, when applied to the body, allays all forms of fever and gives coolness to all asylum. In like manner, the white sandal-wood of the Bodhicitta cools off the fever of the passions, speculations, greed, anger, and folly, and gives happiness to the asylum of supreme knowledge.

As Mount Sumeru, king of all the mountains, transforms all that approaches it into its own sun-colour, so does the Bodhicitta transform every Bodhisattva who approached it into the colour of all-knowledge.

As there are no trees growing in Jambūdvīpa whose flowers can compete in fragrance with that emitted by the bark of a Kovidāra tree called Pāriyātraka, so are there no stocks of good, no unconditional minds, no moralities, no Samādhis, no transcendental knowledges, no emancipations, no knowledges, no philosophical views belonging to the Śrāvakas and Pratyekabuddhas, which can excel in fragrance that which issues from the seed of the Bodhicitta, from the trees of vows, from the back of virtue and knowledge belonging to the Bodhisattvas.

While the calyx of Pāriyātraka, a Kovidāra tree, is not

yet fully opened, it is known that it is the depository of many hundreds of thousands of flowers. In like manner, while the calyx of the Pāriyātraka tree of the Bodhicitta containing a stock of merit has not yet opened itself in full bloom, it is understood that it is the depository where flowers of enlightenment countless in number are stored whether they belong to the gods or men.

The fragrance of the Pāriyātraka flowers is such that a garment held in them for one day partakes of it so strongly as to surpass the fragrant odour of a garment soaked for hundreds of thousands of days in the flowers of the Campaka or the Vārshia or the Sumana tree. In like manner, the fragrance of the virtue and knowledge of the Bodhisattva penetrates, even when his Bodhicitta is kept alive only through one life of his, every corner in the ten quarters where the Buddha's footprints are discoverable. This fragrance is not to be found in all the good unconditioned work and knowledge attainable by the Śrāvakas and Pratyekabuddhas, however long, say, for hundreds of thousands of kalpas, one many remain soaked in them.

There is a tree called Nāḍikerī growing in an island in the midst of the ocean, and everything belonging to it from its roots to its flowers, fruits, etc. is constantly giving nourishment to people, and nothing in it is ever exhausted. In like manner, the Bodhicitta, since its first awakening to a great compassionate heart and vow till the attainment of enlightenment whereby the right Dharma remains established, never ceases from giving nourishment to the world.

There is a magical solution known as Hāṭakaprabhāsa one *pala* of which transforms one thousand *pala* of copper into genuine gold, while one thousand *pala* of copper is incapable of causing any change in the magic solution. In like manner, one *pala* solution of the Bodhicitta which is devoted to the attainment of all-knowledge by means of a stock of merit, is able to transform all copper-coloured things such as karma- and passion-hindrance into the golden colour of all-knowledge; although it is impossible for passion-hindrance to transform the Bodhicitta to its own colour.

As a fire starts in a small way but blazes brighter as it takes hold of more material to burn, so does the Bodhicitta fire. It may start small, but as it seizes upon more material to burn, the flame of knowledge blazes the stronger.

As from one lamp hundreds of thousands of kotis of lamps are lighted and yet the original lamp is not at all extinguished, nor diminished, on account of all those lamps, so is the lamp of the Bodhicitta never extinguished, nor diminished on account of all the Bodhicitta-lamps which are lighted from the original Citta-lamp kept by all the Tathāgatas of the past, present, and future.

When a lamp is brought into a dark house, the darkness that has prevailed there for hundreds of thousands of years is dispersed and replaced by the light. In like manner, when the lamp of the Bodhicitta is brought into the dark inner chamber of all beings where the darkness of passion-hindrances has accumulated for hundreds of thousands of indescribable kalpas, the chamber is at once brightened by the light of knowledge.

5

[The Bodhisattva Maitreya is far from being satisfied with these endless varieties of metaphors whereby he attempts to impress us with the utmost importance of the awakening of Bodhicitta; for he would still untiringly pursue the course first started until he seems to have exhausted his power of imagination if such a thing were possible with a Bodhisattva. He continues:]

As the brightness of a lamp-light is proportional to the size of its wick, keeping up its luminosity as long as there is a supply of oil, so does the lamp of the Bodhicitta keep up its brightness which shines over the entire Dharmadhātu as long as it is well provided with the wick of the great vows, and accomplishes, as long as there is the oil of a compassionate heart, all kinds of Buddhist works, by disciplining beings and purifying the Buddha-lands.

As the celestial crown worn by the sovereign ruler of all the gods, which is made of the finest Jambūnada gold, surpasses any of the crowns on the heads of the gods belonging to the world of desire, so does the Bodhicitta-crown worn by the Bodhisattva and made of great vows surpass those crowns on the heads of the ignorant, the learners, the non-learners, the Pratyekabuddhas.

When the lion, king of the wild beasts, roars, the cubs feel invigorated and are thereby nourished, while all other animals, frightened, run away. In like manner when the Tathāgata, the lion of mankind, utters the roar of all-knowledge approving of the Bodhicitta, all the Bodhisattvas who are sons of the Buddha-lion, are nourished in the Buddha-truths, while those who are devoted to their [inferior] attainments run away.

When a lute strung with the lion's sinews is played, all the other lute-strings are rent asunder. In like manner, when the Tathāgata-lion with the body of the Pāramitās plays his music with sinew-strings of the Bodhicitta, all the chords of desire, all the strings of pleasure are rent asunder; all the virtues and stores of the Śrāvakas and Pratyekabuddhas are done away with.

When one drop of the lion's milk is added to the ocean of milk obtained from cows, buffalo-cows, etc., it passes through them and is not at all hindered. In like manner, when one drop of the milk of the Bodhicitta issuing from the Tathāgata, who is the lion of mankind, is added into the great ocean of the karma- and passion-milk which has been accumulated for hundreds of thousands of kalpas, it penetrates into the ocean and destroys it all; it never stays in the emancipation belonging to all the Śrāvakas and Pratyekabuddhas, nor does it pay any attention to it.

Even before a Kalaviṅka chick comes out of its egg-shell, its excellent power of singing cannot be compared to the whole flock of the Himālaya birds whose power of singing has reached its maturity. In like manner, when the Bodhisattva-Kaḷaviṅka begins his work while in the midst of transmigration, he cannot be held back, if he is endowed with the power of a great compassionate heart and of the Bodhicitta, by all the attainments of the Śrāvakas and Pratyekabuddhas.

When Garuḍa, great king of the feathered race, is first born, his power of flying is marked with energy and his eyesight with penetration, so that no other birds with the body fully developed are able to surpass him. In like manner when the Bodhisattva first arouses the Bodhicitta as son of the noble family of the Tathāgata-Garuḍa, the power of his Citta is marked with energy, his great compassionate heart is stirred from the depths of his being, and his clear eyesight of knowledge penetrates far, with which all the attainments of the Śrāvakas and Pratyekabuddhas acquired for hundreds of thousands of kalpas cannot compare.

When a sharp spear is in the hand of a brave warrior, there is no coat of mail solid enough to stand its thrust. In like manner, the Bodhicitta-spear grasped in the resolute virile hand of the Bodhisattva pierces the armour of wrong views and passions (*anuśaya*).

When Mahānagna the athlete is enraged a growth appears on his forehead, and as long as it stays no one in Jambūdvīpa can treat him with indignity. In like manner, as long as the Bodhicitta-growth on the forehead of the Bodhisattva which has been actuated by a great compassionate and loving heart does not disappear, all the evil spirits and all the evil karmas that are overturning the world are unable to force him.

In learning archery, one who devotes himself to it staying in the house of his master far surpasses in skill, bearing, application, and strength all other disciples who are trained in the art. In like manner, the noble Bodhisattva who is training himself in the realization of all-knowledge far excels in his vows, knowledge, emancipation, deeds, and power all the learners and Pratyekabuddhas who have not yet aroused the Bodhicitta.

In mastering archery the first thing is to learn how firmly to fix the footing—this being precursory to the full knowledge of the art. In like manner, when the Bodhisattva is disciplining himself in the realization of all-knowledge, the first thing needed is to make himself firmly stand on the Bodhicitta, for this is the precursory step towards the mastery of all the truths of the Buddha.

In mastering all the arts of the magician, the first step is to learn attentively by heart all the mantric formulas, for then one is able to perform all sorts of magical works. In like manner when the Bodhisattva wishes to attain the life and wonderful activities of the Buddhas and Bodhisattvas the first thing he does is to wake the Bodhicitta and cherish the vows of the Bodhisattva, for he is thereby able to start in the life that belongs to all the Buddhas and Bodhisattvas.

Things created by magical art are really formless but seen as having form. In like manner, the Bodhicitta is characterized as having no form, yet the Dharmadhātu is seen as spreading itself fully arrayed in all sorts of virtues because of the Bodhisattva's mind being awakened by all-knowledge.

As soon as a cat is seen approaching, all the rats run away and hide themselves in a hole. In like manner as soon as the Bodhisattva surveys the world with the Bodhicitta aroused in the depths of his being, all the karma and passions run away and hide themselves in a hole.

When a man is arrayed with genuine Jambūnada gold ornaments, all other adornments grow pale. In like manner, when the Bodhisattva puts on the ornaments of genuine Bodhicitta-gold from Jambūnada, all the moral decorations of the Śrāvakas and Pratyekabuddhas grow pale.

As even a very small quantity of the loadstone will split asunder a solid chain of iron, so will even a small amount of the Bodhicitta aroused in the depths of one's being split asunder the solid iron chains of wrong views, deeds, ignorance, and desire.

Where there is a particle of the loadstone, all the iron that comes near it is dispersed, does not stay, does not remain fastened together. In like manner, wherever the Bodhicitta-loadstone directs its footsteps either towards karma or towards the passions, or towards the emancipation of the Śrāvakas and Pratyekabuddhas, the karma, the passions, and the emancipation being thus approached flee away, do not stay, do not remain united.

A fisherman who is well acquainted with the inhabitants of the ocean feels no peril of death under the waves even when he enters bodily into the jaws of Makara. In like manner, when the Bodhisattva has his Citta moved in the depths of his being he is free in the midst of transmigration from the hindrance of karma and passions; even when he has entered into the intellectual realization and spiritual attainment of the Śrāvakas and Pratyekabuddhas, he is not detained by them.

As a person who takes a cup of nectar cannot be hurt by any poison, so is the Bodhisattva who has the Citta roused to all-knowledge never hurt by Śrāvakahood, nor does he tarry there, because of his great compassionate heart and vows.

When a person applies Añjana to his eyelashes, he cannot be seen by people even though he may be walking among them. In like manner when the Bodhisattva has his Citta roused to all-knowledge he will not be seen by evil spirits even though he is walking among them, for he is protected by his transcendental knowledge and vows.

When a man puts himself under the protection of a powerful ruler, he will not be threatened by any ordinary people. In like manner, when the Bodhisattva is protected by the great Dharma-king of the Bodhicitta, he will not be terrified by any sort of hindrance or difficulty.

As a man living in the mountains is protected by earth on all sides, he is free from the threat of fire. In like manner, the Bodhisattva who lives besieged by the stock of merit issuing from the Bodhicitta will never be threatened by the emancipation-fire of the Śrāvakas and Pratyekabuddhas.

As a person under the protection of a brave warrior is not

terrified by an enemy, so is the Bodhisattva under the protection of the brave warrior known as the Bodhicitta never terrified by the enemy of evil deeds.

When Śakra, chief of the gods, takes hold of his weapon, Vajra, the whole army of the Asura is demolished. In like manner, when the Bodhisattva firmly holds on his Bodhicitta stirred in the depths of his being, the whole army of Māra and Asura composed of false teachers is demolished.

As a person taking the medicine called Rasāyana prolongs his life and never becomes weak, so the Bodhisattva who is well provided with the Rasāyana of the Bodhicitta never feels exhausted even though he may go through many a birth transmigrating for innumerable kalpas, nor is he ever contaminated by the defilements due to transmigration.

When preparing an elixir, the first thing is to keep it in perfect condition and never have it come in contact with impurities. In like manner, the first thing the Bodhisattva has to prepare for his life of devotion and great vows is to have the Bodhicitta awakened in him, which will never get contaminated.

When a person wishes to accomplish any work the first thing he has to look after is his own life. In like manner, when the Bodhisattva undertakes to practise all the truths belonging to the Buddha, the first thing he has to look after is his Bodhicitta.

When a person loses his own life, he is no more able to accomplish any work for his parents and relatives. In like manner, when the Bodhisattva is cut away from his Bodhicitta he is dead to the merit of all-knowledge and incapable of attaining the Buddha-knowledge for the sake of all being.

As a great ocean cannot be spoiled by any poison, so the Bodhisattva whose Citta is like the ocean can never be spoiled by karma, passions, and the Citta cherished by the Śrāvaka and Pratyekabuddha.

As the sun-light can never be overshadowed by the stars, so can the sun-light of the Bodhicitta never be outdone by the stars of the unconditioned merit belonging to the Śrāvakas and Pratyekabuddhas.

As soon as a regal prince is born, he is revered and never slighted by any of the elders and ministers, because he belongs to the noble ruling family. In like manner, as soon as the Bodhicitta is for the first time aroused, the Bodhisattva is destined to be born in the family of the Tathāgata, lord of the Dharma, and he is sure not to be slighted even by those Pratyekabuddhas and Śrāvakas who have been disciplining themselves for a long time in deeds of moral purity, for the Bodhicitta is born of the ruling family of great compassion.

However yet young the royal prince is, he is highly respected by the elders and ministers, although the prince himself treats them not without due estimation. In like manner, however long the Pratyekabuddhas and Śrāvakas may have disciplined themselves in deeds of purity, they are to bow down before the Bodhisattva whose Citta has begun to assert itself, even though the Bodhisattva himself is not to treat the Pratyekabuddhas without due consideration.

While the royal prince is not yet fully developed as ruler he is not without royal dignity and distinction, and because of his noble birth is not treated as of the same rank as the ministers. In like manner, the Bodhisattva whose Citta has for the first time been aroused to all-knowledge is still bound up with karma, passions, and attachments, but he is not without dignity and distinction of the enlightened and is not to be regarded as of the same rank as the Śrāvakas and Pratyekabuddhas, for he is of the noble family of all the Buddhas.

To the dim-eyed and falsely-minded a pure gem-eye appears as devoid of purity. In like manner, the Bodhicitta-gem essentially spotless appears impure to those who are ignorant and destitute of faith, as they are like dim-eyed and falsely-minded ones.

When people take hold of, or see, or touch, or stay with a medicinal herb bearing a magical charm in it, they are cured of diseases. In like manner, in the magical pill of the

PLATE XXI

THE SIXTH PATRIARCH AS A BAMBOO-CUTTER

By Liang Kai

The sixth Patriarch is here represented as a bamboo cutter. The remarkable fact about Hui-nêng while he was studying Zen under the fifth Patriarch was that he did not get any special literary or intellectual training as preliminary to the mastering of Zen, but that he was left to his own devices to find the way to the truth while being engaged in various practical affairs, chiefly manual, of the monastery. Evidently, Zen was to be extracted from life itself as it is lived by every one of us and not as it is abstractedly discussed by the scholar. The development of Zen along this line in China and Japan is what really distinguishes it from Indian Buddhism as well as from the other schools of Buddhism. When Buddhism was first introduced to China, the criticism it underwent in the hands of the thoughtful Chinese was that it neglected the social and economic significance of life, and that its philosophy was too abtruse and high-flown and not at all practical. To acclimatise itself in China, there was no other way for Buddhism but to become practical, to be always in close contact with life, especially with its manual and physical aspects. The use of the muscles in religion is something not to be despised. When it is not intimately related to them, it loses its touch with realities. But at the same time religion is to preserve its high thinking and contemplation. In Zen these two compartments of life are harmoniously fused. The bamboo-cutting, straw-twining, pine-planting, or soil-tilling loses in Zen the sordidness or ignobleness which is generally regarded as attached to all forms of manual labour. On the other hand, the moon-gazing, sutra-reading, or quiet contemplation as we see in these pictures is no idling away of time, but the reading into the deeper meaning of life. Fantasies and realities in Zen go happily hand in hand.

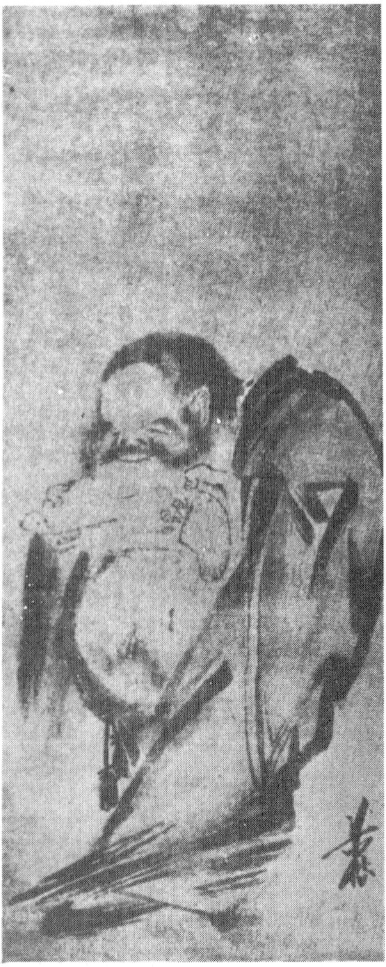

PLATE XXII

HSIEN-TZU AND CHU-T'OU

By LIANG KAI

Some critics are very sceptical about these being from Liang-kai's brush. They do probably not quite attain the standard we generally set up for the artist.

Theer was a Zen master of Sung known as Chu-t'ou whose regular name was Chih Mêng, hsien, (in the *Orthodox Lineage of the Sakya Teaching*, IV). I do not know how he came to be so called; *chu-t'ou* means the "boar-headed." Did his head look like that of a boar? If Chu-t'ou means no more than this, the picture has no bearing here. It is likely that by Chu-t'ou, "the boar-headed," is meant Wên-shu Szu-yêh who before his conversion earned his livelihood by butchery. One day when he was about to kill a swine, he sounded the source of his being, and exclaimed:

"Yesterday the heart of a Yaksha,
This morning the face of a Bodhisattva;
Between the Bodhisattva and the Yaksha
There is not a hairbreadth difference."

When he came to see his master Tao of Wên-shu, the latter asked: "What did you see to make you shave your head and go on a Zen pilgrimage when you were about to butcher a pig?" Yêh without saying a word stood up as if ready to sharpen the knife. (*The Hsü Chuan-têng Lu*, XXXI.)

Some one came to a butcher and asked for a fine piece of meat. The butcher held up his knife and said, "Sir, what is here that is not fine?"

In one of the *Prajñâpâramitâ* supposed to have been delivered by Mañjusri, we have this: "The yogin of pure morality is not destined for the Land of Bliss; the precept-violating Bhikshu does not fall into hell." Butchering and meat-eating are against the rules of good behaviour among the Buddhists, and here we see Zen masters ostentatiously committing deeds of violence or preaching a most unconventional and therefore highly disturbing sermon. How do we account for this?

Bodhicitta all the stock of merit ever accumulated is held together with transcendental knowledge and means, and it supplies the body to the vows and knowledge belonging to the Bodhisattva; when this Bodhicitta-herb is heard, or seen, or remembered, or lived together by sentient beings, it cures them of the diseases of evil passions.

As a man clad in goose-feathers is not soiled by dirt, so the Bodhisattva clad in the goose-feathers of the Bodhicitta is not soiled by the dirt of transmigration and evil passions.

That a wooden puppet holds itself together, is not disjointed, and accomplishes much work, is due to the screws. In like manner, that the Bodhisattva is competent to accomplish works of Bodhisattvahood is due to his cherishing the Bodhicitta, which is the screw holding together the body of all-knowledge and vows, and just because of this he is not disjointed.

If not for screws a machine with all its parts would never be equal to its work. In like manner, if the Bodhisattva did not have the Bodhicitta stirred in the depths of his being, he would never be equal to the task of perfecting the truths of the Buddha and also of preparing the factors of enlightenment.

There is an incense-wood called Hastigarbha which is in the possession of a sovereign ruler of the world; and when this is burned its fragrance will raise all his four armies up to the sky. In like manner, when the incense-wood of the Bodhicitta is burned, the Bodhisattva with his stock of merit is enabled to escape the bondage of the triple world and have the unconditioned knowledge of all the Tathāgatas extend to the limits of the firmament.

Vajra does not come from any other mine than the one where Vajra or gold is found. In like manner, the Vajra-like Bodhicitta does not come from any other stock-of-merit-mine than the Vajra-mine of great compassion, where the Bodhisattva is engaged in saving the world, or the gold-mine of transcendental knowledge which is the efficient agency of Buddhahood.

There is a tree called Rootless; where its roots are can

never be ascertained, and yet all the branches, leaves, fruit, and flowers are seen growing luxuriantly. In like manner, where the roots of the Bodhicitta-tree are, nobody can ascertain, and yet all the flowers of merit, knowledge, and supernatural power are in full bloom, and the Bodhisattva's great compassionate heart is seen covering the entire world like a network.

Vajra is not to be kept in a broken imperfect vessel, but in a solid perfect bright vessel. In like manner, the Bodhicitta-Vajra is not to be kept in the vessel of beings fit for little faith, poor morality, defaced, inert, obscured, trampled down; nor is it to be kept in any vessel which is meant for a mind ruined and agitated because of lack of intelligence; it is to be kept only in a vessel fit for harbouring the Bodhisattva-mind.

As Vajra pierces through every precious stone, so does the Bodhicitta pierce through even Dharma-treasure.

As Vajra crushes every rocky mountain, so does the Bodhicitta-Vajra crush every rocky mountain of false views.

However broken, Vajra surpasses all other precious stones and is superior to all gold ornamentations. In like manner, however imperfect and undeveloped in spirit, the Bodhicitta-Vajra is superior to the gold ornaments of merit belonging to the Śrāvakas and Pratyekabuddhas.

However broken, Vajra is able to put an end to all poverty. In like manner, the Bodhicitta-Vajra is able to put an end to every poverty due to transmigration.

However small a piece of Vajra, it is characterized with the power of breaking every stone precious or base. In like manner, however small and humble its undertaking may be, the Bodhicitta piece of Vajra is characterized with the power of destroying ignorance.

As Vajra is not in the hand of an ordinary person, so is the Bodhicitta-Vajra not in the possession of the gods and men whose stock of merit is inferior and whose deeper mind is ordinary.

A person who is not well acquainted with the value of jewellery fails to recognize the virtue of the Vajra-gem; nor does he know how to make use of its unsurpassable virtue. In like manner, a person who belongs to the weak-minded does not know the value of the Bodhicitta-Vajra and of great transcendental knowledge-Vajra; nor does he appreciate its unsurpassed virtue.

As Vajra can never be made to wear out, so can the Bodhicitta-Vajra which is the cause and reality of all-knowledge never be made to wear out.

As the Vajra-hammer cannot be carried even by the most powerful man except by the supernatural strength of Nārāyana, so can the great Vajra-hammer of the Bodhicitta never be borne by the Śrāvakas and Pratyekabuddhas however strong they may be, except by the Nārāyana strength of those great Bodhisattvas who are supported by the cause and power of all-knowledge, who have devoted their stock of merit to all-knowledge, and who have acquired the power of great manifestation.

While no instruments can break up Vajra, Vajra is able to destroy anything and everything, itself remaining perfect. In like manner, while no vows and knowledge of the Śrāvakas and Pratyekabuddhas can keep up for an infinite number of kalpas the work of salvation, or the disciplining and maturing of all beings in this world of ills, the Bodhisattva never feels exhausted in this work, nor is he ever beaten back, for he had taken hold of the great Vajra-hammer of the Citta.

As no other grounds than the Vajra ground can bear the weight of Vajra, so it is only on the solid ground of the Bodhicitta which is cherished in the depths of the Bodhisattva's own being and not by the Śrāvakas and Pratyekabuddhas, that the Vajra of emancipation, vow, and preparation belonging to Bodhisattvahood can be borne.

Water kept in a Vajra vessel solid and unbroken will never leak in the great ocean. In like manner, the Bodhisattva's stock of merit set up and turned over in the Bodhicitta solid and unbroken will never be destroyed in the various paths of existence where all beings rise.

The great earth supported by the Vajra-stratum will

never be torn asunder or sink down. In like manner, the Bodhisattva's vows supported by the solid Vajra-stratum of the Bodhicitta will never be torn asunder or sink down on account of its being in the triple world.

As Vajra can never be soiled by water, so can the Bodhicitta-Vajra never be soiled by the water of karma and passions, nor can it suffer any change by associating with karma.

As Vajra can never be burned or scorched by any fire, so can the Bodhicitta-Vajra never be burned by the fire of suffering due to transmigration, nor can it be scorched by the heat issuing from the fire of the passions.

There cannot be any other seat in this great triple chiliocosm than the Vajra-seat, which is fit to be the seat of the Tathāgata, Arhat, Fully-enlightened One when he, subduing Māra the Evil One, attains all-knowledge on the throne of enlightenment. In like manner, it is no other minds than the solid Vajra heart of vow and knowledge born of the Bodhicitta that the Bodhisattva, by means of supreme enlightenment, practices deeds of vow, fulfils the Pāramitā, ascends the grades of acceptance, attains the stages of Bodhisattvahood, turns over his stock of merit, receives the prediction, arranges all the means and preparations relating to Bodhisattvahood, and furnishes the power of a great stock of merit.

'Thus,' concludes Maitreya, 'innumerable and indescribably excellent are the virtues arising from the Bodhicitta as cherished by the Bodhisattva; and indeed if any one should raise the desire for the supreme enlightenment he is sure to be furnished with these virtues. O son of a good family, you have gained a very good opportunity, you have already gained these wonderful virtues by raising your heart toward the supreme enlightenment in order to practise the Bodhisattva's life of devotion. As regards your question, "How should one discipline oneself in the Bodhisattva's life of devotion? How should one practise it?" you enter into this magnificent and splendidly ornamented tower of

Vairochana-garbha, and, thoroughly looking around, understand how one is to be disciplined in the Bodhisattva's life of devotion, and, having been disciplined in it, to have all these innumerable virtues perfected.'

6

Evidently Maitreya exhausted his power of speech in order to extol the importance of the Bodhicitta in the career of a Bodhisattva, for without this being duly impressed on the mind of the young Buddhist pilgrim Sudhana, he could not have been led into the interior of the Tower of Vairochana. The Tower harbours all the secrets that belong to the spiritual life of the highest Buddhist. If the novice were not quite fully prepared for the initiation, the secrets would have no signification whatever. They may even be grossly misunderstood, and the result will be calamitous indeed. For this reason Maitreya left not a stone unturned to show Sudhana what the Bodhicitta really meant. The following points may be gathered concerning the Bodhicitta:

1. The Bodhicitta rises from a great compassionate heart, without which there will be no Buddhism. This emphasis on Mahākaruṇā is characteristic of the Mahāyāna. We can say that the whole panorama of its teachings revolves on this pivot. The philosophy of Interpenetration so pictorially depicted in the *Gaṇḍavyūha* is in fact no more than the outburst of this life-energy. As long as we tarry on the plane of intellection, such Buddhist doctrines as Emptiness (*śūnyatā*), Egolessness (*anātmya*) etc., may sound so abstract and devoid of spiritual force as not to excite anyone to fanatic enthusiasm. The main point is to remember that all the Buddhist teachings are the outcome of a warm heart cherished towards all sentient beings and not of a cold intellect which tries to unveil the secrets of existence by logic. That is to say, Buddhism is personal experience and not impersonal philosophy.

2. The raising of the Bodhicitta is not an event of one day, for it requires a long preparation, not of one life but of many lives. The Citta will remain dormant in those souls where there is no stock of merit ever accumulated. Moral merit must be stored up in order to germinate later into the great overshadowing tree of the Bodhicitta. The doctrine of karma may not be a very scientific statement of facts, but all Buddhists, Mahāyāna and Hīnayāna, believe in its working in the moral realm of our lives. Broadly stated, as long as we are all historical beings we cannot escape the karma that preceded us, whatever this may mean. Wherever there is the notion of time, there is a continuity of karma. When this is admitted, the Bodhicitta could not grow from the soil where no nourishing stock of goodness had ever been secured.

3. If the Bodhicitta comes out of a stock of merit, it cannot fail to be productive of all the good things that belong to the Buddhas and Bodhisattvas and other great beings. At the same time it must also be the great crusher of evils, for nothing can withstand the terrible blow inflicted by the thunderbolt of the Citta-Indra.

4. The intrinsic nobility of the Bodhicitta can never be defamed even when it is found among defilements of every description, whether they belong to knowledge or deeds or passions. The great ocean of transmigration drowns every body that goes into it. Especially the philosophers, who are satisfied with interpretations and not with facts themselves, are utterly unable to extricate themselves from the bondage of birth and death, because they never cut asunder the invisible tie of karma and knowledge that securely keeps them down to the earth of dualities because of their intellectualism. Therefore, the awakening of the Bodhicitta which takes place in the depths of one's being is a great religious event.

5. For this reason again the Bodhicitta is beyond the assault of Māra the Evil One, who represents the principle of dualism in Buddhism. It is he who is always looking for his chance to throw himself against the solid stronghold of Prajñā and Karuṇā. Before the awakening of the Bodhicitta

the soul is inclined towards the dualism of being and non-being, and is thus necessarily outside the pale of the sustaining power of all the Buddhas, Bodhisattvas, and good friends. The awakening, however, marks a decisive turning-away from the old line of thought. The Bodhisattva has now an open highway before him, which is well guarded by the moral influence of all his good protectors. He walks on straightway, his footsteps are firm, and the Evil One has no chance to tempt him away from his steady progress towards perfect enlightenment.

6. The Bodhicitta means, as was explained in the beginning of this article, the awakening of the desire for supreme enlightenment which was attained by the Buddha, enabling him to become the leader of the religious movement known as Buddhism. Supreme enlightenment is no other than all-knowledge, *sarvajñatā*, to which reference is constantly made in all the Mahāyāna texts. All-knowledge is what constitutes the essence of Buddhahood. It does not mean that the Buddha knows every individual thing, but that he has grasped the fundamental principle of existence and that he has penetrated deep down into the centre of his own being. When the Bodhicitta is aroused, the Bodhisattva's hold on all-knowledge is definite and firm.

7. The rise of the Bodhicitta marks the beginning of the career of a Bodhisattva. Before this, the idea of a Bodhisattva was no more than an abstraction. We are perhaps all Bodhisattvas, but the notion has not been brought home to our consciousness, the image has not been vivid enough to make us feel and live the fact. The Citta is aroused and the fact becomes a personal event. The Bodhisattva is now quivering with life. The Bodhisattva and the Bodhicitta are inseparable; where the one is there the other is. The Citta indeed is the key that opens all the secret doors of Buddhism.

8. The Bodhicitta is the first stage of the Bodhisattva's life of devotion and vow. The chief object of Sudhana's quest as far as the *Gaṇḍavyūha* is concerned consists in finding out what is the Bodhisattva's life of devotion and vow. It was

through Maitreya that the young Buddhist pilgrim came to realize within himself all that he had been searching for among the various teachers, philosophers, gods, etc. The final confirmation comes from Samantabhadra, but without Maitreya's instruction in the Bodhicitta and his admission into the Tower of Vairochana, Sudhana could not expect to start really on his career of Bodhisattvahood. The life of devotion and vows which stamps a Buddhist as Mahāyānist and not as Hīnayānist is impossible without first arousing the Bodhicitta.

9. The *Gaṇḍavyūha* describes the Bodhisattva as one who never becomes tired of living a life of devotion in order to benefit all beings spiritually as well as materially. His life lasts till the end of the world spatially and temporarily. If he cannot finish his work in one life or in many lives, he is ready to be reborn a countless number of times when time itself comes to an end. Nor is his field of action confined to this world of ours. As there are innumerable worlds filling up an infinite expanse of space, he will manifest himself there, until he can reach every being that has any value at all to be delivered from ignorance and egotism. Not to know what exhaustion means characterizes Bodhisattvahood born of the Bodhicitta.

10. Lastly, the notion of Bodhicitta is one of those marks which label the Mahāyāna as distinct from the Hīnayāna. The exclusiveness of the monastic organization is a death to Buddhism. As long as this system rules, Buddhism limits its usefulness to a specific group of ascetics. Nor is this the last word one can say about the Hīnayāna; the weightiest objection is that it stops the growth of the spiritual germ nursed in the depths of every sentient being, which consists in the arousing of the Bodhicitta. The Citta has its desire never to be nipped by the cold frost of intellectual enlightenment. This desire is too deep-seated, and the enlightenment itself must yield to its dictates. The Bodhisattva's untiring activities are the outcome of this desire, and this is what keeps the spirit of the Mahāyāna very much alive in the Far East in spite of its worn-out institutionalism.

In short, the Bodhicitta is more than love, it contains something of a philosophical insight. It is a concrete unified embodiment of Prajñā and Karuṇā. In the Citta they really begin to work. What this means will become clearer when we come to the exposition of the *Prajñāpāramitā*. The latter makes no explicit references to the Bodhicitta, but the study or practice of the deep Prajñāpāramitā is really the awakening of the Citta and the beginning of the Bodhisattva's life of devotion and vows (*praṇidhānacaryā*). If the Mahāyāna has anything to contribute to the deepening of the religious consciousness, it is no other than our realization of the Citta as Prajñā and Karuṇā.

7

As I started this paper with an introductory quotation from the *Daśabhūmika*, it may not be out of place to conclude it with another quotation from the same sūtra, which, as was stated before, belongs to the same *Avataṁsaka* group of Mahāyāna literature as the *Gaṇḍavyūha* itself. The following[1] is from the final gāthās attached to the tenth stage of Bodhisattvahood known as Dharmameghā (law-cloud), in which Vajragarbha, the leading Bodhisattva of the *Daśabhūmika* assembly, tells all the other Bodhisattvas gathered in the heavenly palace called Paranirmita-vaśavartin, about the desire for enlightenment:

'Listen to the most distinguished, most excellent deeds
of the Bodhisattvas,
Who enjoy peace and self-control, and whose hearts
are quiet and tamed,
Who are like the passage in the sky, who resemble the
air,
Who are free from crudities and defilements, abiding
in the knowledge of the path.

[1] 'The Gāthā Portion of the *Daśabhūmika*', Final Gāthās, 1–14. *The Eastern Buddhist*, VI–1, 1932.

'They have accumulated hundreds of thousands of stocks of merit for kotis of kalpas,
They have paid homage to hundreds of thousands of the Buddhas and great Rishis,
They have also paid homage to an unlimited number of the Arhats and Pratyekabuddhas,
And in order to benefit all the world the Bodhicitta is produced [in them].

'[In the Bodhisattvas] who have disciplined themselves in moral austerities, who have perfected the virtue of patience,
Who are shy [of evil-doings] but active in blissful deeds, who have merit and knowledge ever increasing,
Who are broad in intellectual understanding with a heart filled with Buddha-knowledge,
[In them] the Bodhicitta is produced which is equal to [the owner of] the ten powers.

'Homage has been offered to all the Buddhas of the past, present and future,
All the lands have been purified extending as far as space extends,
And seeing that all things partake of the nature of sameness,
The Bodhicitta is produced [in the Bodhisattvas] in order to liberate the entire world.

'[In the Bodhisattvas] who are the owners of joy and good understanding, who are delighted in practising charity,
Who are ever striving to benefit the whole world,
Who find pleasure in the virtues of the Buddha, who are strenuous in guarding beings [from evils],
[In them] the Bodhicitta is produced in order to accomplish works of beneficence for the triple world.

'[In the Bodhisattvas] who have ceased from evil doings, ever strenuous in pure morality,
Who are delighted in disciplining themselves in austerities, with all their senses under perfect control,

Who take refuge in the Buddha and who are wholeheartedly devoted to deeds of enlightenment,
[In them] the Bodhicitta is produced in order to carry out works of beneficence for the triple world.

'[In the Bodhisattvas] who are sympathetic for all that is good and share in the delights of patience,
Who understand the taste of meritorious deeds and are averse to arrogant spirit,
Who are fixed in religious thought, and in disposition gentle and happy,
[In them] the Bodhicitta is produced so that the whole world may be regulated beneficially.

'The Bodhisattva-lions carry out their deeds of purity, courageously enduring hardships,
Nobly rising for the interest of all beings,
They continually achieve what is meritorious, subduing the army of the passions:
In such minds the Bodhicitta is instantly produced.

'Their minds are in the state of perfect tranquillity, they have dispelled the darkness of ignorance,
Their minds are drained of intoxication, they have forsaken paths of defilement,
They are happy with the pleasure of tranquillity, released from the bondage of transmigration:
In such minds the Bodhicitta is instantly produced.

'Their thoughts are as pure as the sky, they know what is meant by transcendental and relative knowledge.
They have subdued Māra the Evil One, they have ejected the threatening passions,
They have taken refuge in the words of the Buddha, they have attained to the meaning of Suchness:
In such minds the Bodhicitta is instantly produced.

'In order to bring about the weal of the triple world, they stand firmly in knowledge,
In order to remove the wrappage of contention, they are furnished with knowledge and power;

They praise the virtues of the Sugata, and are delighted with his mind:
In such minds the Bodhicitta is instantly produced.

'They desire the happiness of the triple world, fulfilling the requirements of the Bodhi,
Determined in their minds to carry out their plans, the Bodhisattvas will practise deeds however difficult,
Striving for ever to do what is good:
In such minds the Bodhicitta is instantly produced.

'Desirous of the virtues of one who has the ten powers, delighted with deeds of enlightenment,
They are victorious over the ocean veiled with contention, they have severed the bonds of self-conceit,
Following the way of goodness, they are desirous of attaining to the meaning of the Dharma:
In such minds the Bodhicitta is instantly produced.

'Let them practise such deeds of enlightenment full of merits as are recounted here,
Let them attain the wonderful powers, who are in possession of the Buddha-words and vows,
Let them attain the Bodhicitta, who are cleansed in the triple virtue,
Let them be the Bodhisattvas who are cleansed in the triple refuge.'

V. THE SIGNIFICANCE OF THE PRAJÑĀ-PĀRAMITĀ-HṚIDAYA SŪTRA IN ZEN BUDDHISM

I

THE *Prajñā-pāramitā-hṛidaya Sūtra* is a very short text on the Prajñāpāramitā. It consists of two hundred and sixty-two Chinese characters in Hsüan-chuang's translation, which is the one most commonly used by the Japanese Buddhists, Shingon, Tendai, and Zen.[1] The object of this Essay is to examine in what sense the *Hṛidaya Sūtra* occupies a significant position, as it does in the teaching of Zen Buddhism. To do this, it is desirable to have a good knowledge of the text itself. Being short, a translation of the whole Sanskrit sūtra is given on the next page.

F. Max Müller edited and published in 1884 the Sanskrit text of the *Prajñā-pāramitā-hṛidaya Sūtra* from the ancient palm-leaves preserved in Japan.[2] But the following is based on Hsüan-chuang's Chinese-Sanskrit text with a few alterations, which were adopted on the strength of the Chinese versions. Hsüan-chuang rendered the *Hṛidaya* into Chinese in A.D. 649, which is incorporated in the Taishō edition of the Buddhist Tripitaka as No. 251, with an Imperial preface of the Ming dynasty. But this translation does not seem to have been done from his own Sanskrit text, No. 256, for they disagree, though slightly.

[1] It is known in Japan as *Hannya Shingyō* or simply as *Shingyō*. At a Zen monastery it is recited on all occasions. There are many commentaries on it, and Zen masters frequently give a course of lectures on them.

[2] The MS. has been kept since A.D. 609 at Hōryūji, Yamato, which is one of the oldest Buddhist temples in Japan. It has a considerable archæological interest as it supplies us with 'the earliest specimen of a Sanskrit alphabet used for literary purposes'. The MS. is said to have been brought to China by Bodhidharma from India, and then to Japan.

Translation of the *Prajñā-pāramitā-hṛidaya Sūtra*

When (1)[1] the Bodhisattva Avalokiteśvara was engaged in the practice of the deep Prajñāpāramitā, he perceived: there are the five Skandhas (2); and these he saw in their self-nature to be empty (3).

'O Śāriputra, form is here emptiness (4), emptiness is form; form is no other than emptiness, emptiness is no other than form; what is form that is emptiness, what is emptiness that is form. The same can be said of sensation, thought, confection, and consciousness.

'O Śāriputra, all things are here characterized with emptiness: they are not born, they are not annihilated; they are not tainted, they are not immaculate; they do not increase, they do not decrease. Therefore, O Śāriputra, in emptiness there is no form, no sensation, no thought, no confection, no consciousness; no eye (5), ear, nose, tongue, body, mind; no form (6), sound, odour, taste, touch, objects; no Dhātu of vision (7), till we come to (8) no Dhātu of consciousness; there is no knowledge, no ignorance (9), no extinction of knowledge, no extinction of ignorance, till we come to there is no old age and death, no extinction of old age and death; there is no suffering (10), accumulation, annihilation, path; there is no knowledge, no attainment, [and] no realization,[2] because there is no attainment. In the mind of the Bodhisattva who dwells depending on the Prajñāpāramitā there are no obstacles;[3] and because there are no obstacles in his mind, he has no fear, and, going beyond the perverted views, reaches final Nirvāṇa. All the Buddhas of the past, present, and future, depending on the Prajñāpāramitā, attain to the highest perfect enlightenment.

[1] See following Notes.

[2] *Nābhisamayaḥ* is missing in the Chinese translations as well as in the Hōryūji MS.

[3] For *varaṇa* all the Chinese have 'obstacle', and this is in full accord with the teaching of the *Prajñāpāramitā*. Max Müller's rendering, 'envelop', is not good.

'Therefore, one ought to know that the Prajñāpāramitā is the great Mantram, the Mantram of great wisdom, the highest Mantram, the peerless Mantram, which is capable of allaying all pain; it is truth because it is not falsehood: this is the Mantram proclaimed in the *Prajñāpāramitā*. It runs "*Gate, gate, pāragate, pārasaṁgate, bodhi, svāhā!*" ("O Bodhi, gone, gone, gone to the other shore, landed at the other shore, Svāhā!")'

NOTES

1. There are two texts with the title of the *Hṛidaya*: the one is known as the Shorter and the other the Larger. The translation above, of the shorter sūtra, is in general use in Japan and China.

The opening passage in the larger text in Sanskrit and Tibetan which is missing in the shorter one is as follows: [The Tibetan has this additional passage: 'Adoration to the Prajñāpāramitā, which is beyond words, thought, and praise, whose self-nature is, like unto space, neither created nor destroyed, which is a state of wisdom and morality evident to our inner consciousness, and which is the mother of all Excellent Ones of the past, present, and future.'] 'Thus have I heard. At one time the World-honoured One dwelt at Rājagṛiha, on the Mount of Vulture, together with a large number of Bhikshus and a large number of Bodhisattvas. At that time the World-honoured One was absorbed in a Samādhi (Meditation) known as Deep Enlightenment. And at the same moment the Great Bodhisattva Āryāvalokiteśvara was practising himself in the deep Prajñāpāramitā.'

The concluding passage, which is also missing in the shorter text, runs as follows:

'O Śāriputra, thus should the Bodhisattva practise himself in the deep Prajñāpāramitā. At that moment, the World-honoured One rose from the Samādhi and gave approval to the great Bodhisattva Āryāvalokiteśvara, saying: Well done, well done, noble son! so it is! so should the practice of the deep Prajñāpāramitā be carried on. As it has been preached by you, it is applauded by Tathāgatas and Arhats. Thus spoke the World-honoured One with joyful heart. The venerable Śāriputra and the Great Bodhisattva Āryāvalokiteśvara together with the whole assemblage, and the world of Gods, Men, Asuras and Gandharvas all praised the speech of the World-honoured One.'

2. From the modern scientific point of view, the conception of Skandha seems to be too vague and indefinite. But we must remember that the Buddhist principle of analysis is not derived from mere scientific interest; it aims at saving us from the idea of an ultimate individual reality which is imagined to exist as such for all the time to come. For when this idea is adhered to as final, the error of attachment is committed, and it is this attachment that for ever enslaves us to the tyranny of external things. The five Skandhas ('aggregates' or 'elements') are form (*rūpam*), sensation or sense-perception (*vedanā*), thought (*saṁjñā*), confection or conformation (*saṁskāra*), and consciousness (*vijñāna*). The first Skandha is the material world or the materiality of things, while the remaining four Skandhas belong to the mind. *Vedanā* is what we get through our senses; *saṁjñā* corresponds to thought in its broadest sense, or that which mind elaborates; *saṁskāra* is a very difficult term and there is no exact English equivalent; it means something that gives form, formative principle; *vijñāna* is consciousness or mentation. There are forms of mentation distinguishable as seeing, hearing, smelling, tasting, touching, and thinking.

3. Hsüan-chuang's translation has this added: 'He was delivered from all suffering and misery.'

4. 'Empty' (*śūnya*) or 'emptiness' (*śūnyatā*) is one of the most important notions in Mahāyāna philosophy and at the same time the most puzzling for non-Buddhist readers to comprehend. Emptiness does not mean 'relativity', or 'phenomenality', or 'nothingness', but rather means the Absolute, or something of transcendental nature, although this rendering is also misleading as we shall see later. When Buddhists declare all things to be empty, they are not advocating a nihilistic view; on the contrary an ultimate reality is hinted at, which cannot be subsumed under the categories of logic. With them, to proclaim the conditionality of things is to point to the existence of something altogether unconditioned and transcendent of all determination. Śūnyatā may thus often be most appropriately rendered by the Absolute. When the sūtra says that the five Skandhas have the character of emptiness, or that in emptiness there is neither creation nor destruction, neither defilement nor immaculacy, etc., the sense is: no limiting qualities are to be attributed to the Absolute; while it is immanent in all concrete and particular objects, it is itself not at all definable. Universal negation, therefore, in the philosophy of Prajñā is an inevitable outcome.

5. No eye, no ear, etc., refer to the six senses. In Buddhist

philosophy, mind (*manovijñāna*) is the special sense-organ for the apprehension of *dharma* or objects of thought.

6. No form, no sound, etc., are the six qualities of the external world, which become objects of the six senses.

7. 'Dhātu of vision, etc.', refer to the eighteen Dhātus or elements of existence, which include the six senses (*indṛiya*), the six qualities (*visaya*), and the six consciousnesses (*vijñāna*).

8. 'Till we come to' (*yāvat* in Sanskrit, and *nai chih* in Chinese) is quite frequently met with in Buddhist literature to avoid repetition of well-known subjects. These classifications may seem somewhat confusing and overlapping.

9. 'There is no knowledge, no ignorance, etc.' is the wholesale denial of the Twelvefold Chain of Causation (*pratītyasamutpāda*), which consists of ignorance (*avidyā*), deeds (*saṁskāra*), consciousness (*vijñāna*), name and form (*nāmarūpa*), six sense-organs (*saḍāyatana*), contact (*sparśa*), sense-perception (*vedanā*), desire (*tṛiṣṇa*), attachment (*upādāna*), being (*bhava*), birth (*jāti*), and old age and death (*jarāmaraṇa*). This Chain of Twelve has been a subject of much discussion among Buddhist scholars.

10. The allusion is of course to the Fourfold Noble Truth (*satya*): 1. Life is suffering (*duḥkha*); 2. Because of the accumulation (*samudaya*) of evil karma; 3. The cause of suffering can be annihilated (*nirodha*); 4. And for this there is the path (*mārga*).

2

As the title indicates, the *Prajñā-pāramitā-hṛidaya Sūtra* is supposed to give the gist or kernel or heart (*hṛidaya*) of the *Prajñāpāramitā*. The question, then, is: Does it really give the essence of this great Buddhist work? Or, does it contain something foreign? If it contains something foreign or something more than the *Prajñāpāramitā* itself, we must try to account for it, that is, we must see if this extraneous matter also really belongs to the sūtra proper, justifying its claim for giving us the kernel of that huge mass of literature. Let us examine the *Hṛidaya Sūtra* as we have it here.

In the first place, as far as we can ascertain, the Bodhisattva Avalokiteśvara does not appear in any of the

Prajñāpāramitā Sūtras, of which there are several compilations such as the *Śatasāhasrikā*, the *Pañcaviṁśatisāhasrikā*, the *Aṣṭasāhasrikā*, the *Saptaśatikā*, etc. in Sanskrit, and the *Mahāprajñāpāramitā* in six hundred fascicles in Chinese, and the corresponding works in Tibetan. This being so, we can say that the *Hṛidaya* is a later production, and that there is an admixture of foreign elements. This, however, is not the essential point I would discuss in this Essay. There is another point in the *Hṛidaya*, apart from its reference to Avalokiteśvara, that makes us suspect its later compilation. By this I mean the Prajñāpāramitā's being identified with the Mantram which forms the conclusion of Avalokiteśvara's discourse on Śūnyatā (emptiness). The Prajñāpāramitā literature is singularly free from the intrusion of magical formulas known as Vidyā, or Mantram, or Dharāṇi. It is true that the Prajñāpāramitā itself is regarded as a great wondrous Vidyā in the text, but no special independent Mantrams are given, which is actually the case with the *Hṛidaya Sūtra*. For in this latter there is a Mantram to be specifically known as 'Prajñāpāramitā', consisting of these phrases: '*Gate, gate, pāragate, pārasaṁgate, bodhi, svāhā.*' This insertion is quite a departure and requires special attention.

Keeping these two points in mind—the appearance of Avalokiteśvara and the insertion of the Mantram—let us proceed to analyse the contents of the *Hṛidaya* text itself.

What superficially strikes us most while perusing the text is that it is almost nothing else but a series of negations, and that what is known as Emptiness is pure negativism which ultimately reduces all things into nothingness. The conclusion will then be that the Prajñāpāramitā or rather its practice consists in negating all things. The five Skandhas are negated; the eighteen Dhātus are negated; the eighteen Ayatanas are negated; the twelvefold Chain of Origination is negated; the fourfold Noble Truth is negated. And at the end of all these negations, there is neither knowledge nor attainment of any sort. Attainment (*prāpti* or *labdhi*) means to be conscious of and be attached to an understanding which is the result of relative reasoning. As there is no attainment of this nature, the mind is entirely free from all obstructions, that is, errors and confusions which arise from intellectualization, and also from the obstructions that are rooted in our conative and affective consciousness, such as fears and worries, joys and sorrows, abandonments and infatuations. When this is realized, Nirvāṇa is reached. Nirvāṇa and enlightenment (*saṁbodhi*) are one. Thus from the Prajñāpāramitā arise all the Buddhas of the past, present, and future. The Prajñāpāramitā is the mother of Buddhahood and Bodhisattvahood, which is reiterated throughout the Prajñāpāramitā literature.

So far, we can say that the *Hṛidaya* is in perfect concordance with the spirit of the *Prajñāpāramitā*. Beginning with negations it winds up with an affirmation called in Buddhist terminology 'Enlightenment'. The idea of Emptiness may startle the uninitiated, because they are generally apt to regard it as an utter annihilation, especially when the *Hṛidaya* appears to be no more than a string of denials. But since this *via negativa* leads us finally to something definite, although this latter is far from being definite in its ordinary sense, the *Hṛidaya* is not after all a gospel of nihilism. The Prajñāpāramitā which achieves this wonder, that is, the deducing, or conjuring of an affirmation from those invincible negations, may rightly be designated a great incomparable Mantram. The *Hṛidaya*, ordinarily speaking, must end with this statement; Avalokiteśvara's discourse addressed to Śāriputra has found its natural conclusion; and there is no need of going further on and declaring most dramatically that the Mantram is '*Gate, gate*, etc.'.

To state that the Prajñāpāramitā is a great Mantram is intelligible, but to say that this great Prajñāpāramitā Mantram is '*Gate, gate*, etc.' does not seem to give any sense. What has been so far clear and rational goes at once through a miraculous transformation. The *Hṛidaya Sūtra* is turned into a text of mystic formula, a book of incantation. This is apparently a degradation or a degeneration. What is the meaning of this abrupt transformation? Why this nonsense, so to speak?

The so-called Prajñāpāramitā Mantram, when translated, means: 'O Wisdom, gone, gone, gone to the other shore, landed at the other shore! Svāhā!' *Svāhā* is a term of blessing, and is invariably found at the conclusion of a Mantram or Dhāraṇī. What has this ejaculation to do with the disciplining oneself in the deep Prajñāpāramitā? A Mantram or Dhāraṇī is generally supposed, when uttered, to effect wonders. In the present case, the wondrous effect producible by the utterance of '*Gate!*' must be the realization of Enlightenment. Can we say, then, that the end of the Buddhist discipline can be attained by means of mere mystic phrase? As far as the *Hṛidaya* is concerned, this is evidently the conclusion, for no other inference is here possible. How can one identify the Prajñāpāramitā with the Mantram '*Gate!*'?

We can see how easy and natural it was for followers of the Shingon (Mantram Sect) to adopt the *Hṛidaya* for one of their text-books. But how did the Zen come to recite it for its daily service? The idea of Mantram is so foreign to its followers. The transition from the philosophy of Śūnyatā and Saṁbodhi to a religion of incantation cannot easily be conceived.

Another thing which makes this presence of a Mantram in the *Hṛidaya* more mystifying is that the concluding Mantram is always recited untranslated as if the very sound of the Sanskrit-Chinese transliteration were a miracle-working agency. Mantrams of all kinds are never translated into Chinese. This is in a way quite natural. If phrases are unintelligible any way, and this unintelligibility is what is aimed at by them, the more unintelligible they are, being left in the original, the more effective will be the miraculous power hidden in them. But why is this unintelligibility needed in Zen? Unintelligibility is not unattainability, which the *Prajñāpāramitā* makes so much of.

No doubt, in its development in China Zen has incorporated much of the Shingon usage, and we find in its ritualism many Mantrams and Dhāraṇīs which properly belong to the Shingon. For this reason, I think that the production of the *Hṛidaya* was in a much later period than the entire body of Prajñāpāramitā literature itself. However this may be, what is the signification of the '*Gate!*' Mantram in the *Hṛidaya Sūtra* as one of the most important texts in the teaching of Zen? If the Mantram occupied an indifferent position in the sūtra, although it is difficult in such a short work as this to find room for anything of secondary importance, the question as to the meaning of the Mantram might not be a very weighty one. But even a superficial reader will at once recognize the very prominent position filled by the Mantram in the evolution of the doctrine of Prajñāpāramitā. In fact, the whole sūtra seems to have been written for the sake of the Mantram and for nothing else. If so, all the more what is the meaning of the Mantram apart from its literary sense? Why does it form the climax of the whole series of negations in the *Hṛidaya*?

To my mind, the solution of this mystery gives the key to the understanding not only of the whole philosophy of the Prajñāpāramitā, but of its most essential relationship to the teaching of Zen. This is why I have said so much about the interposition of the Mantram in the *Hṛidaya*.

Before the Mantram '*Gate!*' yields up its secret in connection with the doctrine of Emptiness and Enlightenment, it may not be inopportune to see what are the essential teachings of the *Prajñāpāramitā Sūtras*. This knowledge will make the valuation of the *Hṛidaya* much easier, especially in its vital connection with the experience of Zen.[1]

From what I am going to remark about the *Prajñāpāramitā Sūtras* in the succeeding pages, we can see that the teaching of the *Hṛidaya* agrees in one sense, and disagrees in another, with that of the principal sūtras. The agreement takes place

[1] The main teachings of the *Prajñāpāramitā* are given below in a separate *Essay*, entitled 'The Philosophy and Religion of the *Prajñāpāramitā*'. See p. 234 ff.

in the sense that both make Prajñā the main source of Buddhist enlightenment, while the disagreement is that the *Hṛidaya* puts its entire emphasis on the Mantram '*Gate!*' This is the phase completely absent in the principal sūtras of the Prajñāpāramitā class. In the *Hṛidaya*, the disciplining oneself in the Prajñāpāramitā is identified with the recitation of the Mantram.

Not the recitation of the Mantram, according to Hsüan-chuang's own account, but the recitation of the whole *Hṛidaya* was recommended by Avalokiteśvara, who appeared to him in a vision when he was on his way to India. He was told to recite the sūtra whenever he met difficulties and hardships while travelling through the wildernesses covered with icy snows, swept over by suffocating winds, and frequented by ferocious beasts. The Bodhisattva, who was then manifested in the form of a sick monk, recited the sūtra for the benefit of the great pilgrim-priest of China. He followed this advice faithfully, and was thus finally enabled to reach in safety the land of his heart. The sūtra was at that time referred to as containing the quintessence of the Buddha-mind.[1]

The story is interesting, but the recitation is concerned here with the avoidance of physical troubles and not with the opening of the mind to supreme enlightenment. As to the identification of the Prajñāpāramitā with the Mantram as clearing one's mind of all its obstructions and agitations, there is no reference here. The meaning of this is to be found somewhere else.

When the Mantram is repeated without thinking of the result that may come out of it, and in the way the *Prajñāpāramitā* advises those who would take up the study of the Prajñā, is it possible that in some miraculous way the spiritual eye is opened and sees into the secrets of the Prajñā? When a Zen master was asked about the number

[1] From Tzŭ-ên's preface to the *Hṛidaya*. Taishō, No. 256.

of monks in his monastery, he answered, 'Ahead, three and three; behind, three and three.' To the ordinary mind such an answer does not give any idea as to what the master had in his mind at the time. Perhaps the '*Gate!*' Mantram has something of this in it, and only those who have been initiated into it can understand it; and when this mystery in the answer is understood, the question itself becomes clear, and all that is contained in the Prajñā is laid bare before the eye. That may be so; then why this particular '*Gate!*' Mantram and not any other? The Mantram, senseless enough in one sense, is not altogether unintelligible as far as its literary meaning is concerned. Its senselessness comes out when it is considered in relation to the whole content of the *Hṛidaya* as it is already known to us. Our question here will be: What inherent relationship is there between this statement or rather exclamation, 'Gone, gone to the other shore, O Bodhi!' and the general teaching of the *Hṛidaya*?

3

To my mind, the solution of all the difficulties encountered in a thorough understanding of the *Hṛidaya Sūtra* is reached in the following way.

When the Prajñāpāramitā teaching came to be thoroughly identified with the Buddhist experience, the *Hṛidaya* was produced as giving in a most epitomized form the essentials of the Prajñāpāramitā and at the same time as indicating the psychological process of the Yogin who disciplines himself in the deep Prajñāpāramitā. When the sūtra took the other course of development, it expanded to a most diffusive, verbose, grandiose literature known in Chinese as the *Mahāprajñāpāramitā Sūtra*, the first 400 fascicles of which roughly correspond to the Sanskrit *Śatasāhasrikā-prajñāpāramitā*, that is, the one of 100,000 verses. Which was earlier, contraction or expansion,[1] we cannot tell. But the contraction did not mean mere condensing; it turned the text at the same time into a psychological document of the Prajñā experience. This was a remarkable transformation, seeing that the addition of the '*Gate!*' Mantram changed the whole aspect of the epitome. Without the Mantram the epitomization remains a simple fact, means nothing, and the weighty importance of the literature as it now stands is all lost.

While I have not been able to find exactly when the *Hṛidaya* came to be used as a Zen text in China, the masters must have been keen-sighted enough early in the history of Zen to see something more in it than a mere attempt at condensation. As far as the latter went, the *Vajracchedikā*

[1] This requires an explanation. Most scholars agree at present that the earliest *Prajñāpāramitā* was something like the *Aṣṭasāhasrikā* in Sanskrit and the *Tao-hing Prajñāpāramitā* or Kumārajīva's *Smaller Prajñāpāramitā* in Chinese. With this as the original text, the literature developed into the *Śatasāhasrikā*, the *Mahāprajñāpāramitā* of Hsüan-chuang, etc. While this expansion was going on at one end, contraction must have also taken place at the other. Chronology is difficult to settle as regards the Buddhist texts, as most other Indian works; but, as I said before, the addition of the '*Gate!*' Mantram seems to suggest the *Hṛidaya* being later, although we do not know exactly when this Mantram also came to be affixed to the Chinese *Mahāprajñāpāramitā*.

answered the purpose as it did even prior to the time of Hui-nêng. When Hsüan-chuang told his story of wonders achieved by the recitation of the *Hṛidaya,* the Zen masters took to it, and at the same time saw something more in it. This 'something more' might have escaped scholars of the Vijñaptimātra philosophy, but not the Zen masters who put experience before philosophy, and who were keenly alive to the psychological value of all Buddhist literature. They understood the meaning of the Mantram in a way very different from that of the Shingon followers.

It is a noteworthy fact that the '*Gate!*' Mantram is also found at the end of the Chinese version by Hsüan-chuang of the *Mahāprajñāpāramitā.* It seemed to have been added in the Yüan period, for the Yüan edition of the text contains it. Was the idea of affixing the Mantram possibly derived from the *Hṛidaya* when it began to circulate extensively among the Buddhists? The Prajñāpāramitā is said in the *Aṣṭasāhasrikā* to be a great, immeasurable, unfathomable, incomparable, and most supreme magical formula (*vidyā*); if so, it is easy to take the '*Gate!*' as such in view of the *Hṛidaya's* extolling of the Mantram in such glowing terms.

To come back to the main subject, the disciplining oneself in the deep Prajñāpāramitā is the koan exercise, to which the first Essay in the Second Series of my Zen Essays has been devoted. Avalokiteśvara is the Zen student, and the Buddha in the *Hṛidaya* tells us how Avalokiteśvara studied the Prajñā. For the Prajñā is the koan given to him for solution, as the means of realizing supreme enlightenment. His course of realization is along the *via negativa.* He is told to negate everything which he can intellectually comprehend as an object of thought. This is the way with Zen. It starts intellectually. Ignorance which has possessed the mind from the beginningless past is to be dispelled, this being the first step towards enlightenment. And ignorance means not seeing the truth (*dharma*) as it really is, *yathābhūtam.* The *Hṛidaya* thus gives us a series of negations, even knowledge being denied; for as long as there is the consciousness of having attained something, this is a real obstacle in the way to supreme enlightenment. Becoming master of oneself and all things means having the way to move thoroughly cleansed of all obstacles that may thwart the free, self-governing course of the Prajñā. Negation is this cleansing, this purgation. In the koan exercise, the cleansing is also the preliminary procedure.

Negation, as we know, is a mere means whereby we reach somewhere. In the *Prajñāpāramitā* also it is meant to lead us to the goal of its discipline. Zen from the very beginning gives us a koan which defies intellectual interpretation, and thus without explicitly telling us to walk the path of negation it makes us do so. The *Hṛidaya*, which belongs to the Prajñā literature, follows the general course, and is filled with No's. But where do we land after abandoning every intellectual, conceptual treasure? Is it mere nothingness, mere vacuity of space, mere emptiness which is supposed to be the sense of Śūnyatā? If it were so, we are still in the realm of concepts. 'Nothingness' is still one of our thought-objects. This must also be abandoned, being one of the 'perverted thoughts and illusive dreams'.

In Shin Buddhism the abandoning of 'self-power' means being born in the land of Amitābha. The negation is at once an affirmation. Shin avoids being intellectual. Its negativism is not so frightening or despairing as that of the Prajñāpāramitā. Even here, however, a state of mind which knows 'no fears', 'no obstacles' is held up as the goal. What is this goal? What is this supreme enlightenment? Where is it? When is it reached?

It is reached when Avalokiteśvara exclaimed, '*Gate*, *gate*, *pāragate*, *pārasaṁgate!*' For this is the ejaculation which came out of his inner being when he went through the entire course of negations. He as Yogin of the Prajñāpāramitā could not eternally be going round and round in a circle of negations. Once he came to an end, exhausted and in despair, there was no hope before him, and he knew what he had left behind. But there was still something that urged him to go ahead. Utterly exhausted intellectually and emotionally, he made a final leap. The last tie which held him to the world of relativity and 'self-power' completely snapped. He found himself on the other shore. Overwhelmed with his feelings, he could only keep uttering the '*Gate!*' The '*Gate!*' then became his Mantram, the '*Gate!*' became the Mantram of the Prajñāpāramitā. With this ejaculation everything was cleared up, and Avalokiteśvara's discipline in the Prajñā was brought to a finish.

This, I conclude, is the meaning of the *Hṛidaya*. By thus interpreting the text we can understand why the '*Gate!*' is the conclusion, and why this conclusion expresses in a most conclusive manner the content of the *Hṛidaya*. The Mantram taken in itself conveys no meaning, and its vital relation to the *Prajñāpāramitā* is unintelligible. The *Hṛidaya* must not be approached by an intellectual passageway, though it superficially suggests that. It must be approached along the line of religious experience, that is, by the line we have taken hold of in the study of the koan exercise. The meaning of the Mantram thus yields up its secrets, and as the result the *Hṛidaya* becomes a wholly comprehensible document of great religious value.

If the *Hṛidaya* were a product of the Chinese genius, the Mantram would not have taken the shape of '*Gate!*' As we have already seen on various occasions, the Mantram of the Zen masters has assumed quite different colourings. But, psychologically speaking, the spiritual process experienced by the Chinese as well as the Indians was exactly the same —this could not, indeed, be otherwise. When a Chinese was asked who the Buddha was, he answered, 'It is like a pail full of water which is broken through the bottom.' This sounds like a Dhāraṇī, judged by the ordinary standard of logic. To compare the Buddha to a pail of water may seem desecrating, but from the Zen point of view the pail must be broken through the bottom and all the water be completely poured out, with no moon reflecting herself in it. The Buddha then reveals himself with his thirty-two marks of excellence. The *Hṛidaya* is not so concrete as this, but its depiction of the Zen experience is illuminating enough.

In the '*Gate!*' the *Hṛidaya* negations have reached the

great affirmation designated as Suchness (*tathatā*) in all the Mahāyāna texts. The negations were all meant to lead Yogins of the Prajñā to this catastrophe. Hsüan-chuang's recitation which did not go beyond a form of incantation now comes to be laden with religious values of great moment. By dint of the concluding Mantram, supreme enlightenment, more or less intellectually understood by scholars, becomes a great fact of spiritual experience. The position which the *Hṛidaya* has in the teaching of Zen is here appraised in its true dimension.

What still remains to be explained is the circumstance how this special Mantram came to be uttered in this connection. This requires more space than is available here; all that I can say is that the idea of 'the other shore' is peculiarly Indian and that it appears early in the religious literature of India. To give one instance from early Buddhist literature, we have this in the *Dhammapāda*:

> *Appakā te manussem ye janā pāragāmino,*
> *Athāyam itarā pajā tīram evānudhāvati.*[1]

In one sense Tathāgata is Pāragata, one who has gone to the other shore. But the idea of *tathā* has grown more predominant in Buddhist philosophy than that of *pāram*, and the Pāragata has been replaced by the Tathāgata. The trace of Pāram-idea is left in the Pāramitā, which means those virtues which lead the Yogins to the other side of enlightenment. *Pāramitā* is generally translated 'arriving at the other shore', which practically means the same fact as *pāragata*, 'gone to the other shore', the difference between the two expressions is that of direction. From this end it is 'gone', from the other 'arrived'; it depends where we take our stand. In the *Prajñāpāramitā*, it is most appropriate to describe the course of Avalokiteśvara as having 'landed on the other shore' (*pārasaṁgate*).

While Tung-shan Liang-chih[2] was still a boy a Vinaya

[1] 85. 'There are few people who reach the other shore; others are running wild on this shore.'

[2] A.D. 807–869. *The Chuan-têng Lu*, XV.

teacher made him study the *Hṛidaya Sūtra*, and tried to explain the sentence, 'There is no eye, no nose, . . .' But Liang-chih surveyed his teacher scrutinizingly with his eye, and then touched his own body with his hand, and finally said: 'You have a pair of eyes, a pair of ears, and the other sense-organs, and I am also provided with them. Why does the Buddha tell us that there are no such things?' The Vinaya teacher was surprised at his question and told him: 'I am not capable of being your teacher. You be ordained by a Zen master, for you will some day be a great teacher of the Mahāyāna.'

When a young inquiring mind like Liang-chih's stumbles over the negativism of the *Prajñāpāramitā*, it is promising. If it goes on inquiring, it will surely come to an explosion some day. But after the explosion it is advisable to walk back the *via negativa* and see what there is in the way of confirming the experience. What a man has not been able to grasp in the beginning will be seen charged with meaning. The doctrine of Śūnyatā is no more pure negativism. As I shall explain in what follows, it is simply seeing things *yathābhūtam*, taking them in their aspect of Tathatā (suchness). It does not deny the world of multiplicities; mountains are there, the cherries are in full bloom, the moon shines most brightly in the autumnal night; but at the same time they are more than particularities, they appeal to us with a deeper meaning, they are understood in relation to what they are not. Herein lies the purport of the *Hṛidaya Sūtra*.

Tung-shan's poem, which was composed when he saw his reflection in the stream which he was crossing at the time, may give us some glimpse into his inner experience of the Prajñāpāramitā:

> Beware of seeking [the Truth] by others,
> Further and further he retreats from you;
> Alone I go now all by myself,
> And I meet him everywhere I turn.
> He is no other than myself,
> And yet I am not he.
> When thus understood,
> I am face to face with Tathatā.

VI. THE PHILOSOPHY AND RELIGION OF THE PRAJÑĀPĀRAMITĀ

Preliminary

THE *Prajñāpāramitā*[1] is one of the oldest Buddhist canonical books translated into Chinese. The first *Prajñāpāramitā*, known as the *Tao-hsing* ('The Practising of the Way'), appeared in A.D. 172. *The Sūtra of Forty-two Chapters* is supposed to have been translated by the first Indian missionaries who came to China in A.D. 69, but we are not quite sure of its historical authenticity. An Shih-kao, who came from Parthia to China in A.D. 148, worked for twenty-two years on converting the Buddhist texts into Chinese, but they were all Hīnayāna. This being the case, the *Tao-hsing Prajñāpāramitā*, which was translated by Lokaraksha of Yüeh-chih (then known as the kingdom of Kuṣana), must be said to be really the first Mahāyāna text of all the Buddhist sūtras ever introduced into China. It is wonderful to notice that the Buddhist teaching which declares all things 'empty' and as having 'no self-nature' was the first really important work to be propagated among a people who are deeply imbued with the pragmatic, utilitarian spirit. Decidedly, the followers of 'Emptiness' did not think this kind of missionary activity to be a work of 'empty' significance.

In the third century A.D. two sūtras belonging to the Prajñāpāramitā were translated into Chinese, and in the fourth century still another appeared. Kumārajīva's were finished early in the fifth century. It was in the latter half of the seventh century that Hsüan-chuang completed his grand translation of the *Mahāprajñāpāramitā* in six hundred fascicles. This is an encyclopedic compilation including most sūtras

[1] Italiziced when it means the sūtra.

PLATE XXIII

HSIEN-TZU THE SHRIMP-CATCHER

By Mu-ch'i

Mu-ch'i is very much admired in Japan; his paintings have a certain quality deeply appealing to the Zen consciousness of the Japanese, while the artist himself was not so much taken notice of by his contemporary compatriots. The present picture is no doubt one of his masterpieces, in which the artist attempts to express, to the limits of the material means allowed to him, the spirit of a Zen devotee, whose life, not different from that of an ordinary man of the world, is engaged in earning a livelihood by catching the river fish.

Hsien-tzü, after reading into the secrets of his being under Tung-shan Liang-chieh, lived by the River Min. He possessed nothing except things necessary for his bare living. He had no fixed residence and was generally found sleeping in a shrine among the paper coins offered to the god by the villagers. Since his daily occupation consisted in fishing for shrimps, he was known among them as Hsien-tzü the shrimp-man.

Ching of Hua-yen heard of this strange character and wishing to test his Zen understanding concealed himself one evening among the papers in the shrine before the fishing monk returned. At midnight, he seized the old fisher-resident as he came back, and abruptly asked, "What was the idea of the First Patriarch's visit to this country?" The fisher-monk had no hesitation in answering this: "The wine-stand in front of the god." (*The Chaun-têng Lu*, XVII.) Here remarks Kuang-wên of Ling-ch'üan:

> "If not for this 'Wine-stand in front of the god,'
> His life is after all one of a ghostly spirit."

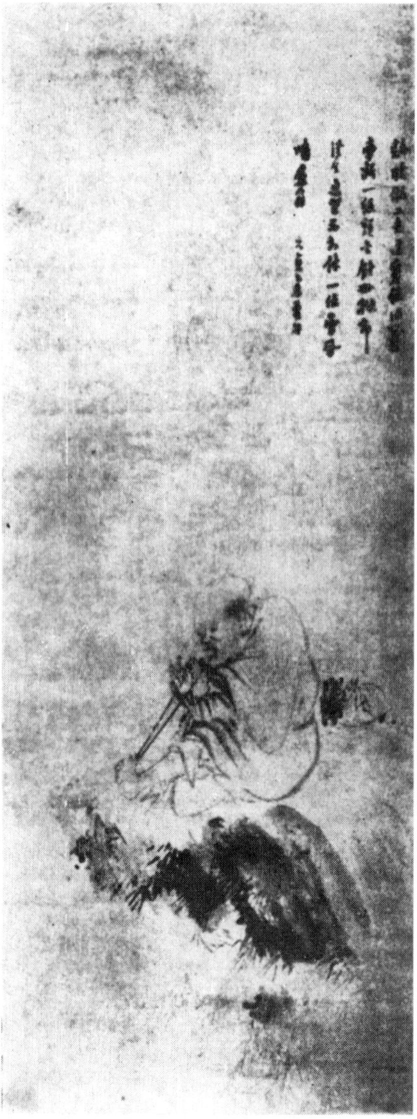

PLATE XXIV

IN THE MORNING SUN

By Mu-ch'i

This generally goes together with the following "Facing the Moon." It is said that this is to illustrate the artist's own life. As every Zen monk does in China as well as in Japan, he awakes early in the morning. All his morning service is accomplished even before the sun is up. When it is finally out and warm enough, the monk basks himself in it and here is engaged in making straw ropes which are needed for various purposes in the monastery. The evening comes, the moon is fine, bright enough to read the large scripts. Nothing is more soul-inspiring for a Buddhist monk in the mountain monastery than to pass his time in the quiet moonlight by reading the sutra and thereby testifying to his experience.

pertaining to the Prajñāpāramitā group of the Mahāyāna sūtras.

In Sanskrit the largest collection consists of 125,000 slokas or stanzas of thirty-two syllables. The four shorter ones contain 100,000, 25,000, 10,000, and 8,000 slokas respectively. The shortest one was published in 1888 by the Indian pundit Rājendralāla Mitra, and the 100,000 one was edited by Pratāpacandra Ghosha in 1902, but as far as I know a complete edition of it has not yet seen the light. The oldest of these various *Prajñāpāramitā* compilations seems to have been the shortest of them, the 8,000-sloka one known as *Aṣṭasāhasrikā*. The longer ones are all later amplifications. The *Aṣṭasāhasrikā* corresponds to Lokaraksha's *Tao-hsing*, Kumārajīva's *Shorter Prajñāpāramitā* known as *Hsiao-p'in*, Hsüan-chuang's *Mahāprajñāpāramitā*, Fas. 538–555, and Shih-hu's *Fo-mu Prajñāpāramitā*.[1] As all the essential ideas, philosophically and religiously considered, of the *Prajñāpāramitā* are contained in it, my thesis will be mainly based on this sūtra in Sanskrit and its corresponding Chinese versions, though occasional quotations are taken from the other *Prajñāpāramitās*. Readers interested in the *Prajñāpāramitā* literature may consult Dr. Tokumyō Matsumoto's brochure on *Die Prajñāpāramitā-literatur*.[2]

But as the Sanskrit *Aṣṭasāhasrikā* as well as the several Chinese *Prajñāpāramitās* here mentioned are not easily accessible to the reader, the *Vajracchedikā* or 'Diamond Cutter' in English translations by Max Müller and William Gemmel may be recommended for his persual. The chief defect, however, with the Diamond Cutter is that it emphasizes the Śūnyatā aspect of the Prajñāpāramitā teaching too strongly, giving to the general reader the

[1] These different versions of the *Prajñāpāramitā* are in this article abbreviated as follows: *Aṣṭa* for *Aṣṭasāhasrikā*, *Hsiao-p'in* or Kumārajīva for Kumārajīva's *Shorter Prajñāpāramitā*, *Mahā* or Hsüan-chuang for Hsüan-chuang's *Mahāprajñāpāramitā*, *Fo-mu* for Shih-hu's translation, *Tao-hsing* for Lokaraksha's. The Kōkyō-shoin edition of the Tripitaka popularly known as 'Shuku-satsu' (*so-shua*) which means 'in smaller print' is used throughout this article.

[2] Verlag W. Kohlhammer, Stuttgart, 1932.

impression that this is the Alpha and Omega of the Mahāyāna. Dr. Max Walleser of Heidelberg translated into German some chapters of *Aṣṭasāhasrikā*.[1]

The object of this Essay is to state that the teaching of the *Prajñāpāramitā* consists in defining the essence of Bodhisattvahood. This is what is known in all the Mahāyāna texts as Bodhisattvacaryā. *Caryā* means 'life', and the Bodhisattvacaryā is what distinguishes the Bodhisattva as such from other beings; in Mahāyāna Buddhism especially from the Śrāvaka and the Pratyekabuddha. The *Prajñāpāramitā* finds this life in the understanding of Prajñā with all its implications, intellectual, moral, and spiritual. In the following pages, therefore, we shall see first what is meant by Prajñā and then proceed to discover its practical contents. When this is done, the essence of Bodhisattvahood will naturally come to light. That Zen is most intimately connected historically and doctrinally with the Prajñā teaching is, I believe, already well known to the reader.

Prajñā will then be described from the various points of view in which it is generally observed in the *Prajñāpāramitā Sūtras*.

I

The Philosophy of the Prajñāpāramitā

1. *Prajñā as the Directing Principle*

Prajñā is one of the six virtues of perfection (*pāramitā*) especially designed for the Mahāyāna Buddhists or Bodhisattvas. When they are satisfactorily disciplined in each of these six virtues they are assured of finally attaining enlightenment. But the sūtras of the Prajñāpāramitā group regard the Prajñā as the directing principle of the other five virtues; for without the Prajñā the other Pāramitās are

[1] *Prajñāpāramitā, die Vollkommenheit der Erkenntnis*, published by Vandenhoeck und Ruprecht, Göttingen, 1914.

unable to know by themselves where they are bound, or what they are meant for. They are, when left alone, lost like a company of blind men in the wilderness. They cannot enter into the final abode of Reality. They are without any eye, they cannot recognize all-knowledge, and all their efforts are in vain without the leadership of the Prajñā. The Prajñā is the eye that surveys with perfect clearness the entire field of the Buddhist life and determines where and how the Bodhisattva's steps are to be guided. The five Pāramitās—charity, morality, humanity (or patience), strenuousness, and meditation—are called Pāramitās[1] because of the Prajñā which is their eye.[2]

Again, the Prajñā is like the earth which makes possible the growth of vegetation. All the other conditions may be there for a seed to grow, but without the earth it will never grow. So without the Prajñā the other Pāramitās will altogether lose their potentiality; there will be no life in them.[3] Again, it is by virtue of the Prajñā that all the other Pāramitās are guarded, taken hold of, gathered together, and systematically practised. As all the sixty-two heretical views issue from the notion that there is a real individual substance (*satkāyadṛiṣṭi*), so all the five Pāramitās issue from the Prajñā. As all the bodily organs enjoy their vitality when 'life' continues, so all the five Pāramitās are very much alive when the Prajñā embraces them under her protective wings.[4]

2. *The Prajñā Compared to the Bird's Wings and the Jar*

The Bodhisattvas are like those heavenly birds whose wings may stretch out to the extent of one yojana, or even to five yojana. When they are not fully developed they cannot fly. They may wish to fly from their heavenly abodes down

[1] *Pāram* = the other shore, *ita* = reached.
[2] *Aṣṭa*, pp. 172–3. [3] Ibid, p. 81. [4] Ibid, pp. 431–2.

to this world, or they may change their minds in the meanwhile and want to go back to the heavens. In the first case can they come on earth without hurting themselves? In the second case can they fly back safely to their home? No, they can do neither, but they are doomed to self-destruction, because they are still fledgelings, they are not yet qualified for such flights. In like manner, the Bodhisattva may have the desire already fully awakened for enlightenment, he may have accumulated all kinds of virtues in the form of charity, morality, strenuousness, and tranquillization; and yet if he has not Prajñā and its Upāya (skilful means) all his desires and efforts will come to naught, and he will fall back to the state of Śrāvakahood and Pratyekabuddhahood.[1]

Again, the Bodhisattva without the Prajñā may be likened to an earthenware jar which has not been perfectly baked. A man may use such a jar half-baked for carrying water from the well or the river, but he will certainly find it broken before he reaches home. Why? Because the jar had been taken out of the kiln before it was fully baked and dry. In a similar manner, the Bodhisattva may have faith in the enlightenment, and the desire for it, and also patience, joy, understanding, reverence, diligence, pure thought, etc.; but if he has not Prajñā and its Upāya (skilful means) wherewith he is properly guarded in the course of his Bodhisattva-life, he will surely retrogress and, falling back to the state of Śrāvakahood and Pratyekabuddhahood, will not be able to attain Sarvajñatā.[2]

By these appraisals of the Prajñā the sūtra strongly impresses us with the extraordinary importance of this Pāramitā virtue. Before the development of this idea, the six Pāramitās were treated as equally significant in the life of the Bodhisattva. The rise of the Mahāyāna has altered this relative position. The Prajñā is now singled out and

[1] *Fo-mu*, 43b–44a.

[2] Ibid., 40a. *Sarvajñatā* = all knowledge. When the Prajñā is perfected, this is attained. 'All-knowledge' belongs to Buddhahood, it is what constitutes the essential nature of the Buddha. 'All-knowledge' and 'Enlightenment' (*saṁbodhi*) are interchangeable terms in the *Prajñāpāramitā Sūtras*, and also in the *Gaṇḍavyūha*.

given the highest prominence. Without this the rest of the Pāramitās are like a boat which has lost her compass and her captain. This is a remarkable phase in the evolution of Buddhist thought. When we know that Buddhism derives its vitality from the doctrine of Enlightenment, the all-importance of the Prajñā is inevitably asserted. But it is possible that the author of the *Prajñāpāramitā* had some apprehension about his teaching being immediately and unreservedly accepted by the Buddhists. For this reason I believe the sūtra makes so many references to not being frightened or depressed over the theory of Prajñāpāramitā. The sūtra says that it is of rare occurrence indeed for one to listen to the doctrine of Prajñā in his life and yet not to become frightened about it. To embrace it and not to waver in following its dictates requires the accumulation of merit for many lives.

3. *The Prajñā as Mother of Buddhas and Bodhisattvas*

That the Prajñā is the directing principle of the Pāramitās comes from the fact that it is conceived by the Mahāyānists to constitute all-knowledge (*sarvajñatā*), that is, the perfect knowledge which is in the possession of the all-knowing one. Therefore the Prajñā is an all-illuminating light which demands our respect. It stands above all the contaminating influence of worldly objects. It eradicates all the darkness there is in this world of dualities, thus giving peace and comfort to all beings. It supplies a light to the blind who can thereby walk safely through the dark night of ignorance. It leads those who have gone astray to the right path. It reveals to us the truth of all things, which is all-knowledge (*sarvajñatā*). It is the refuge of all beings, it bestows on them perfect fearlessness, it is the five-eyed one who illuminates the entire world. It is the truth that is above birth and death, above all doings and hankerings. It is Emptiness itself. It is the treasure house of all truth (*dharmakośa*). It is the mother of all the Buddhas and Bodhisattvas.[1]

Since Prajñā is the mother and progenitor (*janayitrī*) of all the Buddhas and Bodhisattvas, they are always quite anxious over her health and well-being and prosperity. The sūtra says:[2] 'It is like a woman who has a large number of children. If she should be ill, all her sons and daughters would see to it that she soon recovers her health. For the one thought they have is that she is their mother who has brought them up with care and love, that everything they claim now to be their own is her gift of wisdom and tenderness. She cannot be neglected, she must be well looked after, and all medical care must be given her so that she will be well again, free from suffering and annoyance of all kinds. Thus she will be cherished by all her children.' In the same manner, the Buddhas and Bodhisattvas are deeply concerned with the well-being of the Prajñā as their own mother, they make use of every contrivance to guard her from the interferences of evil spirits and to help her to be firmly established in the world. Hence their missionary activities of seeing the *Prajñapāramitā* copied, studied, recited, memorized, meditated upon, and preached until the end of time.

4. *Prajñā = Saṁbodhi = Sarvajñatā*

The Prajñā was said in the beginning to be the means of attaining enlightenment, the highest end of the Buddhist discipline. But it has now come to be identified with the end itself—Prajñā is enlightenment (*saṁbodhi*); for in the Buddhist experience the working of the Prajñā in its original purity is possible only when there is enlightenment. When it is conceived as possessing an end which lies outside, it is not yet itself, it is not in its pure state; it comes back to itself only when it is identified with enlightenment. As

[1] *Aṣṭa*, pp. 170–1, 253, 272, 396–7, etc.

[2] Ibid., p. 253. Chapter XII, 'Viewing the World'.

long as enlightenment is considered something to be sought after by means of Prajñā, not only is enlightenment far away from you but Prajñā fails to function in its native activity. Prajñā to be Prajñā must be identified with enlightenment. We can say, therefore, that Prajñā finds itself, recognizes its own undisguised, unspoiled figure in enlightenment. When the practice of the Prajñāpāramitā is to be brought to its judicious culmination, the identification of Prajñā and enlightenment must be achieved, must become fact.

Conceptually, Prajñā makes its first movements towards the apprehension of what it supposes its object. When it is actually taken hold of, however, the seizer and the seized become one; dualism ceases and there is a state of perfect identity which is known as enlightenment, and also all-knowledge (*sarvajñatā*). This experience may be described in this way too: Prajñā first divides or contradicts itself in order to see itself, starting a state of duality such as means and end, subject and object, this and that, the seer and the seen. When the work of seeing itself is accomplished, in Prajñā there is no more duality. Prajñā is seen in enlightenment, and enlightenment in Prajñā. It sees everywhere its own names, only differently spelt; Prajñā is one name, enlightenment is another, Nirvāṇa is a third, and so on. That is to say, all these names are only conceptual, they are discriminated as such for the convenience of our intellection. What really and truly is, is the identity of these names, and nothing more.

Prajñā is then Saṁbodhi (enlightenment), Prajñā is Sarvajñatā (all-knowledge), Prajñā is Nirvāṇa, Prajñā is Tathatā (suchness), Prajñā is Citta (mind), Prajñā is Buddhatā (Buddhahood); Prajñā taken in itself then is pre-eminently the Unattainable (*anupalabdha*) and the Unthinkable (*acintya*). And this Unattainable and Unthinkable is the basis of all realities and thoughts. Quite naturally, therefore, the writers of the *Prajñāpāramitā Sūtras* extol the Prajñā as a worker of miracles, almost personifying Prajñāpāramitā as an object of worship and finally urging its devotees to pay the highest homage even to all the texts containing the teaching of the Prajñāpāramitā as if the texts themselves were active living embodiments of the agency that achieves wonders. Not only their study (*paryavāpti*), recitation (*vācana*), memorizing (*dhāraṇa*), and copying (*lekhana*) are recommended, but the reverence (*satkāra*) and worship (*gurakāra*) of them are encouraged, by means of offerings (*pūjā*) of flowers, wreaths, incense, ointment, lamps, flags, banners, canopies, and robes. As to the spiritual merit that accrues from believing (*abhiśraddhā*) and trusting (*adhimukti*) with the utmost sincerity (*adhyāśayata*) in the Prajñāpāramitā, no one can begin to estimate it accurately. The devotional side of the Prajñāpāramitā is curiously blended with its most high-soaring metaphysics.

The subject of the *Prajñāpāramitā Sūtras* is, however, properly speaking, the Bodhisattva-life which consists in the practice of the Prajñā whereby one comes to the realization of supreme enlightenment. The question how to practise the Prajñā is constantly raised and answered—this indeed being the most absorbing topic of all the *Prajñāpāramitā Sūtras*. When it is successfully carried out the Buddhist discipline comes to an end. But as was said before, the practising of the Prajñā is not something heterogeneous in nature with what makes up enlightenment itself. Enlightenment grows out of this practising as the flower grows out of the plant; there is a continuity of life between the two terms, and continuity is no less than a form of identity. Thus, the following logic holds good: the Prajñā takes form in its being practised, and this practising is the content of enlightenment; therefore, the Prajñā is enlightenment. Prajñā = Saṁbodhi may be ascertained also from the practical side of the question. As these terms are constantly used interchangeably in all the *Prajñāpāramitā Sūtras*, what characterizes the one is equally applicable to the other. In fact the trinity Prajñā = Saṁbodhi = Sarvajñatā is the thread linking the various chains of teaching in them. You pick up one of the links and the rest follow. But if we wish to make a differentiation here we can define Prajñā as an epistemological instrument with which Sarvajñatā is attained, while Saṁbodhi (enlightenment) is more or less psychological in the sense that it connotes a state of spiritual awakening. Prajñā is shared by all beings without distinction, although it may not be found in them functioning in its absolute purity. In the Buddha Prajñā is Sarvajñatā because he is in the state of perfect enlightenment.

Enlightenment is described in the *Mahāprajñāpāramitā* in the following terms:[1] 'By enlightenment (*bodhi*) is meant emptiness (*śūnyatā*), suchness (*tathatā*), reality-limit (*bhūtakoṭi*), spiritual realm (*dharmadhātu*), and essence (*dharmatā*). These are, however, names, words, provisional connotations. Enlightenment itself is the highest truth and ultimate reality; it is the norm not subject to change; it is indestructible, beyond discrimination; it is the true, pure, and all-pervading knowledge possessed by all the Buddhas; it is the most fundamental perfection whereby the Buddhas gain an insight into the nature of all realities, of all forms; it is beyond every mode of expression, beyond all thought-constructions created by the mind.'

When the Bodhi, enlightenment, is thus described with further identifications the result may appear somewhat confusing, and further remarks will be made on these later on. As far as the characterization itself is concerned, it is bodily transferable to Prajñā, and we can say this: that the Prajñā is seeing into the essence of things as they are (*yathābhūtam*); that the Prajñā is seeing things as in their nature empty; that the thus seeing things is to reach the limit of reality, i.e. to pass beyond the realm of the human understanding; that, therefore, the Prajñā is grasping the ungraspable, attaining the unattainable, comprehending the incomprehensible; that when this intellectual description of the working of the Prajñā is translated into psychological terms, it is not becoming attached to anything whether it is an idea or a feeling.

We read in the 'Devaparavarta' of the *Aṣṭasāhasrikā-prajñāpāramitā*: 'Those who have first taken up the practice

[1] Fas. 526, Division III, Chapter 26 (4), 'On Skilful Means', 29a.

of the Prajñā should practise all the six Pāramitās in such a way as to turn all the merit thereby gained to the realization of enlightenment. To do this, however, they should never cling (*parāmṛikśa*) to enlightenment as the goal of their exercises nor to the five Skandhas as irreducible individual realities. For all-knowledge (*sarvajñatā*) is something beyond grasp (*aparāmṛiṣṭā*).'[1]

'Beyond grasp' means 'not being attached'. The Unattainable and the Unthinkable being the nature of the Prajñā, the Bodhisattva who has regained its original function will naturally have no attachment even to Prajñā, Sarvajñatā, or Saṁbodhi. This is an important phase in the life of the Bodhisattva, to which I may later have occasions to make further reference.

5. *Prajñā as Seeing Things Yathābhūtam*

Because of this virtue of non-attachment we can say that Prajñā is able to see the world as it is, to see things in their aspect of suchness (*yathābhūtatā*). This is the most characteristic function of the Prajñā, which is gained by the Bodhisattva when he realizes that he comes, such as he is, from the Prajñā itself, and, therefore, that the latter is the begetter of him as well as of all the Buddhas. Once his eyes are open to this truth, he surveys the world and all its multiplicities in the state they truly are. That is to say, as far as our senses go, the world is seen to be all the time changing, undergoing various forms of combination and decomposition. But the Bodhisattva whose Prajñā is fully awakened perceives that the five Skandhas which make up this world, in spite of their superficial transformations, are in their self-nature (*svabhāva*) never destroyed, show no signs of destruction, are never subject to vicissitudes, to birth and death, to taking forms, to cherishing desires or passions.

The *Prajñāpāramitā* being at once a philosophy and a

[1] Ibid., p. 292.

religion, its teaching is always a mixture of ontology and psychology. In fact, it is not concerned with being as such, but with its human implications. To know the world is to know the human spirit and its workings. There are no metaphysical questions which are not at the same time questions of salvation and enlightenment. Therefore, when the Bodhisattva perceives the world as *yathābhūtam*, he also perceives human minds as they are; he is thus prepared to work out his skilful means (*upāya*). So, says the sūtra, the Bodhisattva perceives by means of his Prajñā-eye the minds of all sentient beings, and he knows how inexhaustibly varied they are in character, in function, in response, in moral value, in spirituality, and so on. Yet his perception *yathābhūtam* penetrates through these superficialities and recognizes that whether their minds are pure or impure, collected or scattered, greedy or not-greedy, they are all devoid of self-substance, of attachment, of discrimination. This is known as seeing all beings in their aspect of suchness, where pluralities in all forms vanish, revealing themselves such as they are in the light of the Prajñā.[1]

It is evident therefore that the seeing things *yathābhūtam* in the *Prajñāpāramitā* means to see them through the veil of multiplicity which obscures our sight, and to grasp them with Prajñā in their state of suchness. Suchness (*tathatā*) is an uncouth term, but in Buddhist phraseology one of the most expressive terms. To understand exactly what it means is to understand the whole system of Buddhist thought. Suchness is not to be confounded with the sameness or oneness of things. When 'the vanishing of pluralities' is talked of, one may imagine that they are ignored or annihilated in order to reveal their aspect of oneness. But what the Prajñā devotees mean is that they are understood in their true relations, not only to one another but to that which makes up their reason of being.

There is a section[2] in the *Prajñāpāramitā* devoted to the discussion of Subhūti's being an Anujāta of the Tathāgata.

[1] *Fo-mu*, 35b; *Aṣṭa*, p. 259 ff.
[2] *Aṣṭa*, Chap. XVI, 'On Tathatā'.

Anujāta means 'to be born after' or 'to be born in accordance with'. That Subhūti who is the expounder of the philosophy of the Prajñāpāramitā is born after the Tathāgata, i.e. his younger brother, or, better, that he is born in accordance with what makes the Tathāgata such as he is, is one of the most significant statements in the *Prajñāpāramitā*, especially when this is considered in relation to the teaching of Suchness.

Tathāgata, which is generally regarded as another title of the Buddha, literally means either 'one who has thus come' or 'one who is thus gone'. What is important here is the meaning of *tathā* rather than *āgata* or *gata*; and apparently the author of the *Prajñāpāramitā* places great stress on *tathā* as the key to the understanding of the doctrine of Tathatā or Yathābhūtatā (suchness). When he refers to the suchness of Tathāgatahood (*tathāgata-tathatā*), he means the reason, or cause, or ground principle that makes possible the appearance of the Tathāgata on earth. Therefore, Subhūti's being born after (*anujata*) the suchness of Tathāgatahood means that Subhūti and Tathāgata come from the same cosmic womb, which is called, in the *Laṅkāvatāra* and other Buddhist texts, *tathāgatagarbha* or the 'Womb of Tathāgatahood'. With this preliminary explanation the following passage on Anujāta and Tathatā will become more intelligible.

'When it is said that Subhūti is born after the Tathāgata, it means this: that the suchness of the Tathāgata is the suchness of Subhūti, that there is no difference between the two suchnesses, for suchness is one in all sentient beings and here is no dualism, no separation, no twofoldness; that in all suchness there is neither coming nor going as they have never been born; that they have no abiding place where they can be located as particularities; that they are non-doing, by which it is meant that they are not to be perceived as functioning in a certain definite manner so as to reveal their specific characteristics which are their limitations; and yet that they are not to be taken as remaining for ever quiescent and doing nothing; that they retain their suchness in all places, at all times, under all circumstances, in all causal combinations; that in them there is neither past nor present nor future though sentient beings themselves are reckoned as coming into existence, abiding, and passing away; they are not subject to discrimination, do not take particular forms, are beyond attainability; and finally that in spite of all these qualifications they appear as realities, capable of being named and defined and discriminated, though when they are thus treated they are no more of suchness. For these reasons Subhūti's suchness is the Tathāgata's suchness, and the Tathāgata's suchness is the suchness of all beings, and between these no division is conceivable. One uniform suchness prevails here, but as soon as this definite statement is made of suchness, suchness ceases to be suchness. It is the most elusive thought, yet without this thought there are no Tathāgatas, no Subhūtis, no Buddhas, no Arhats, no sentient beings. To understand this is the Tathāgata; no other beings can grasp this truth. Subhūti, since he understands, can expound the deep mysteries of the Prajñāpāramitā, and for this reason he is the Anujāta of the Tathāgata.'

Further, we read in Chapter XVII, 'On the Special Features of the Avinivarta Stage of Bodhisattvahood': 'There are varieties of spiritual stages in the Buddhist life, but they are all one as regards their aspect of suchness, and no discrimination is to be made among them. For it is through this oneness of suchness that the Bodhisattva can enter into the Dharmatā (briefly, Truth). Thus entering into the Dharmatā, he does not therein cherish any discrimination. Even when he listens to other teachings he refrains from criticizing them, for he knows how to get into the Dharmatā through various avenues of approach. Even when he listens to all forms of verbal and conceptual argumentations, he entertains no doubts as to the absolute validity of suchness which he embraces within himself.'

One of the functions of the Prajñā is then seen as perceiving things *yathābhūtam* or in their aspect of suchness (*tathatā*). In this suchness, all beings are found to be free from defilement, and therefore to be one with the Buddhas who may in this especial respect be called Tathāgatas. As they are thus all one, they are brothers (*anujāta*) to one another, including Buddhas and Bodhisattvas. The motherly womb from which all these brothers issue is truly known as 'Tathāgata-garbha'. The motherhood of the Prajñā becomes more convincing than ever, and the meaning of the reverence paid to the Prajñāpāramitā more natural.

6. *Prajñā and Śūnyatā*

The *Prajñāpāramitā* is generally regarded as exclusively teaching the philosophy of Emptiness (*śūnyatā*). Most people, including scholars of Buddhism, subscribe to this view, but as to what is really meant by Emptiness they do not seem to have a very clear conception. Since the study of the Prajñāpāramitā means viewing all things in their aspect of suchness or emptiness, let me make a few remarks here about the doctrine of Emptiness.

In Hsüan-chuang's version of the *Mahāprajñāpāramitā*, eighteen[1] forms of emptiness are enumerated, and they are explained in detail in Nāgārjuna's commentary on the sūtra. This enumeration is in fact concerned with so many ways of definitely arriving at the idea of emptiness. The eighteen ways of describing it are: (1) Adhyātmā-śūnyatā, emptiness of the inner things, (2) Bahirdhā-śūnyatā, emptiness of the outer things, (3) Adhyātmā-bahirdhā-śūnyatā, emptiness of the inner-and-outer things, (4) Śūnyatā-śūnyatā, emptiness of emptiness, (5) Mahā-śūnyatā, great emptiness, (6) Paramārtha-śūnyatā, emptiness of the ultimate truth, (7) Saṁskṛita-śūnyatā, emptiness of things created, (8) Asaṁskṛita-śūnyatā, emptiness of things uncreated, (9) Atyanta-śūnyatā, ultimate emptiness, (10) Anavarāgra-śūnyatā, emptiness of limitlessness, (11) Anavakāra-śūnyatā, empti-

[1] Twenty in the *Śatasāhasrikā*, but no such reckoning in the *Aṣṭasāhasrikā*.

PLATE XXV

FACING THE MOON

Ascribed to Mu-ch'i

As far as our purpose of reproducing the ancient masters is concerned, it does not really matter whether the picture here is the work of Mu-ch'i or not. Let us observe the way the monk gazes upon the scroll, he is evidently intensely interested in it, his reading must be deeply sinking into his mind. A poet remarks at the top: "Read on, read on, and when there is nothing more to read, there shines out the meaning of the whole scripture, and the moon too is forgotten."

PLATE XXVI

FACING THE MOON

Ascribed to PEI-CHIEN

The title is also "Facing the Moon." Pei-chien is a descendant of Tá-hui. Though he was not unknown as a Zen painter, it is doubtful whether this really comes from his brush. The picture, as was stated before, is illustrative of a phase of monkhood; an air of grave serenity envelops all his features and lines, he is no doubt intently gazing on eternity as he sits all alone in the soft and all-pervading moonlight.

ness of dispersion, (12) Prakṛita-śūnyatā, emptiness of primary nature, (13) Svalakṣaṇa-śūnyatā, emptiness of selfhood, (14) Sarvadharma-śūnyatā, emptiness of things, (15) Anupalambha-śūnyatā, emptiness of unattainability, (16) Abhāva-śūnyatā, emptiness of non-being, (17) Svabhāva-śūnyatā, emptiness of self-nature, and (18) Abhāva-svabhāva-śūnyatā, emptiness of the non-being of self-nature.

1. By 'the inner things' are meant the six consciousnesses (*vijñāna*). When they are said to be 'empty' is meant that all our psychological activities have no ego-soul behind them, as is commonly imagined by us. This is another way of upholding the doctrine of Anātman or Anatta.

2. 'The outer things' are objects of the six Vijñānas, and their emptiness means that there are no self-governing substances behind them. As there is no Ātman at the back of the psychological phenomena, so there is no Ātman at the back of the external world. This is technically known as the 'egolessness of things'. Primitive Buddhism taught the theory of Anātman in us, but it was by the Mahāyānists, it is said, that the theory was applied to external objects also.

3. We generally distinguish between the inner and the outer, but since there is no reality in this distinction it is here negated; the distinction is no more than a form of thought-construction, the relation can be reversed at any moment, there is no permanent stability here. Change the position, and what is inner is outer, and what is outer is inner. This relativity is called here emptiness.

4. When things outside and inside are all declared empty we are led to think that the idea of emptiness remains real or that this alone is something objectively attainable. The emptiness of emptiness is designed to destroy this attachment. To maintain the idea of emptiness means to leave a speck of dust when all has been swept clean.[1]

5. The 'great emptiness' means the unreality of space. Space was conceived in olden days to be something object-

[1] Cf. Jōshu's remark on nothingness. *Zen Essays*, Series I, p. 175.

tively real, but this is regarded by the Mahāyāna as empty. Things in space are subject to the laws of birth and death, that is, governed by causation, as this all Buddhists recognize; but space itself is thought by them to be eternally there. The Mahāyānists teach that this vast vacuity also has no objective reality that the idea of space or extension is mere fiction.

6. The 'ultimate truth' means the true being of all things, the state in which they truly are, apart from all form of subjectivity. This is something not subject to destruction, not to be held up as this or that, to which nothing can be affixed. Therefore, this ultimate truth is empty. If real, it is one of those objects that are conditioned and chained to the law of causation. Nirvāṇa is but another name. When Nirvāṇa has something attachable to it, it will no more be Nirvāṇa. It will be seen that 'emptiness' is here used in a somewhat different sense from number 3, when objects inner or outer are declared 'empty'.

7 and 8. These may be treated together. *Saṁskṛita* means things that have come to existence owing to conditions of causation. In this sense they are 'created'. *Asaṁskṛita* are things not subject to causation, such as space. To say that the Saṁskṛita are empty is another way of saying that the world external as well as internal is empty. Existence is sometimes divided into Saṁskṛita and Asaṁskṛita, sometimes into inner and outer, sometimes into the five Skandhas, etc., according to points of view necessitated by course of reasoning. All these distinctions are, however, only relative and have no corresponding objectivity, and are, therefore, all empty. The Asaṁskṛita exist because of their being contrasted to the Saṁskṛita. When the latter have no reality, the former are also no more. They both are mere names, and empty.

9. This emphasizes the idea of all 'things' being absolutely empty. 'Ultimate' means 'absolute'. The denial of objective reality to all things is here unconditionally upheld. The 'emptiness of emptiness' means practically the same thing. The room is swept clean by the aid of a broom;

but when the broom is retained it is not absolute emptiness. Nay, the broom, together with the sweeper, ought to be thrown aside in order to reach the idea of Atyanta-śūnyatā. As long as there is even one dharma left, a thing or a person or a thought, there is a point of attachment from which a world of pluralities, and, therefore, of woes and sorrows, can be fabricated. Emptiness beyond every possible qualification, beyond an infinite chain of dependence—this is Nirvāṇa.

10. When existence is said to be beginningless, people think that there is such a thing as beginninglessness, and cling to the idea. In order to do away with this attachment, its emptiness is pronounced. The human intellect oscillates between opposites. When the idea of a beginning is exploded, the idea of beginninglessness replaces it, while in truth these are merely relative. The great truth of Śūnyatā must be above those opposites, and yet not outside of them. Therefore, the *Prajñāpāramitā* takes pains to strike the middle way and yet not to stand by it; for when this is done it ceases to be the middle way. The theory of Emptiness is thus to be elucidated from every possible point of view.

11. There is nothing perfectly simple in this world. Everything is doomed to final decomposition. It seems to exist as a unit, to retain its form, to be itself, but there is nothing here that cannot be reduced to its component parts. It is sure to be dispersed. Things belonging to the world of thought may seem not to be subject to dissolution. But here change takes place in another form. Time works, no permanency prevails. The four Skandhas—Vedanā, Saṁjñā, Saṁskāra, and Vijñāna—are also meant for ultimate dispersion and annihilation. They are in any way empty.

12. Prakṛiti is what makes fire hot and water cold, it is the primary nature of each individual object. When it is declared to be empty, it means that there is no Ātman in it, which constitutes its primary nature, and that the very idea of primary nature is an empty one. That there is no individual selfhood at the back of what we consider a particular object has already been noted, because all things are

products of various causes and conditions, and there is nothing that can be called an independent, solitary, self-originating primary nature. All is ultimately empty, and if there is such a thing as primary nature, it cannot be otherwise than empty.

13. Lakshaṇa is the intelligible aspect of each individual object. In some cases Lakshaṇa is not distinguishable from primary nature, they are inseparably related. The nature of fire is intelligible through its heat, that of water through its coolness. The Buddhist monk finds his primary nature in his observance of the rules of morality, while the shaven head and patched garment are his characteristic appearance. The *Prajñāpāramitā* tells us that these outside, perceptible aspects of things are empty, because they are mere appearances resulting from various combinations of causes and conditions; being relative they have no reality. By the emptiness of self-aspect or self-character (*svalakṣaṇa*), therefore, is meant that each particular object has no permanent and irreducible characteristics to be known as its own.

14. The assertion that all things (*sarvadharma*) are empty is the most comprehensive one, for the term *dharma* denotes not only an object of sense but also an object of thought. When all these are declared empty, no further detailed commentaries are needed. But the *Prajñāpāramitā* evidently designs to leave no stone unturned in order to impress its students in a most thoroughgoing manner with the doctrine of Emptiness. According to Nāgārjuna, all dharmas are endowed with these characters: existentiality, intelligibility, perceptibility, objectivity, efficiency, causality, dependence, mutuality, duality, multiplicity, generality, individuality, etc. But all these characterizations have no permanence, no stability; they are all relative and phenomenal. The ignorant fail to see into the true nature of things, and become attached thereby to the idea of a reality which is eternal, blissful, self-governing, and devoid of defilements. To be wise simply means to be free from these false views, for there is nothing in them to be taken hold of as not empty.

15. This kind of emptiness is known as unattainable (*anupalambha*). It is not that the mind is incapable of laying its hand on it, but that there is really nothing to be objectively comprehensible. Emptiness suggests nothingness, but when it is qualified as unattainable, it ceases to be merely negative. It is unattainable just because it cannot be an object of relative thought cherished by the Vijñāna. When the latter is elevated to the higher plane of the Prajñā, the 'emptiness unattainable' is understood. The *Prajñāpāramitā* is afraid of frightening away its followers when it makes its bold assertion that all is empty, and therefore it proceeds to add that the absence of all these ideas born of relativity does not mean bald emptiness, but simply an emptiness unattainable.

With the wise this emptiness is a reality. When the lion roars, the other animals are terrified, imagining this roaring to be something altogether extraordinary, something in a most specific sense 'attained' by the king of beasts. But to the lion the roaring is nothing, nothing specifically acquired by or added to them. So with the wise, there is no 'emptiness' in them which is to be regarded as specifically attained as an object of thought. Their attainment is really no-attainment.

16, 17, and 18. These may be treated together. Existence is viewed here from the point of being (*astitva*) and non-being (*nāstitva*), and these two views, whether taken individually or relatively, are said to be empty. *Abhāva* is the negation of being, which is one sense of emptiness; *svabhāva* means 'to be by itself', but as there is no such being it is also empty. Is then the opposition of being and non-being real? No, it is also empty, because each term of the opposition is empty.

What 'emptiness' really means I believe has been made clear by these detailed explanations. Emptiness is not to be confounded with nothingness; nor is one to imagine that there is an object of thought to be designated as emptiness, for this idea goes directly contrary to the nature of emptiness itself. Nor is it to be defined as relativity, as is done by some scholars. It is true that the *Prajñāpāramitā* teaches that things exist mutually related as results of causal combinations and therefore they are empty. But for this reason we cannot state that relativity and emptiness are synonymous. In fact, it is one thing to say that things are relative, but quite another to say that they are empty. Emptiness is the result of an intuition and not the outcome of reasoning, though the use here of the particle of inference, 'therefore', gives this effect. The idea of Emptiness grows out of experience, and in order to give it a logical foundation the premise is found in relativity. But, speaking strictly logically, there is a gap between relativity and Emptiness. Relativity does not make us jump over the gap; as long as we stay with relativity we are within a circle; to realize that we are in a circle and that therefore we must get out of it in order to see its entire aspect presupposes our once having gone beyond it. The experience of Emptiness has been there all the time when we began to talk about relativity. From Emptiness we can pass to relativity, but not conversely. This analysis is important in the understanding of the *Prajñāpāramitā* philosophy. It is the Prajñā that sees into all the implications of Emptiness, and not the intellect or Vijñāna, and they are wise who have opened their Prajñā-eye to the truth of Emptiness. If the Mahāyāna system were built upon the idea of relativity, its message would never have called out such responses as we see in its history in India, China, and Japan. That the teaching of Emptiness has actually achieved wonders in the spiritual life of the Far-eastern peoples is the irrevocable proof of its deep insight into the abyss of human consciousness.

Emptiness, for these reasons, is called the unattainable (*anupalabdha*) or the unthinkable (*acintya*), showing that it is not a notion to be subsumed in any categories of logic. It is synonymous with suchness (*tathatā*). Tathatā or Śūnyatā is thus truly the object of study for the Bodhisattvas.

7. *Prajñā and Māyā*

One of the favourite analogies used by the Prajñā philosophers when they wish to impress us with the doctrine of Emptiness is that of Māyā, and they are frequently called by other teachers the Māyāvādins. What is the meaning of this Māyā simile? Let me quote a few passages and see what Māyā means.

'The Buddha asked Subhūti: O Subhūti, do you think Māyā to be different from Rūpam[1] and Rūpam from Māyā? Do you think, again, Māyā to be different from Vedanā, Saṁjñā, Saṁskāra and Vijñāna; and Vedanā, Saṁjñā, Saṁskāra and Vijñāna from Māyā?

'Subhūti said: No, Blessed One, they are not different. If Rūpam is different from Māyā, it is not Rūpam; if Māyā is different from Rūpam, it is not Māyā. Māyā is Rūpam and Rūpam is Māyā. The same can be said of Vedanā, Saṁjñā, Saṁskāra and Vijñāna.

'The Buddha: O Subhūti, do you think the five clinging Skandhas constitute Bodhisattvahood, or not?

'Subhūti: O Blessed One, they do.

'The Buddha: O Subhūti, and you should know that these five clinging Skandhas are no more than Māyā itself. Why? Because Rūpam is like Māyā, and Vedanā, Saṁjñā, Saṁskāra and Vijñāna are like Māyā; and these five Skandhas and six senses are what constitutes Bodhisattvahood and, therefore, the Bodhisattva too is like Māyā. Those who wish to discipline themselves in the Prajñāpāramitā should do so as if disciplining themselves in Māyā. . . . But those Bodhisattvas who have first started in their

[1] Rūpam (form), Vedanā (sensation), Saṁjñā (thought), Saṁskāra (conformation), and Vijñāna (consciousness)—these five are technically known by Buddhists as the Five Aggregates (*pañcaskandhāḥ*), that is, the five ultimate constituents of existence. Therefore, when reference is made to these Five Aggregates, we may regard them as meaning this world of matter and thought in its entirety. They are 'clinging' when we regard them as final realities, and are unable to extricate ourselves from their tyrannical hold on us.

disciplining exercises may be terribly frightened and led astray, if they are not properly guided by good spiritual teachers.'[1]

Such a discourse as this, indeed, if the hearer is not properly instructed by a great competent master of the Prajñāpāramitā, will lead us to the follies of libertinism. Listen further to this:

'The Buddha: It is like a magician (*māyākāra*) conjuring up by his magical art a large crowd of beings at a crossroad. As soon as they are seen to come into existence they vanish. O Subhūti, what do you think? Do they really come from some definite locality? Are they real realities? Do they really pass away somewhere? Are they really destroyed?

'Subhūti: O no, Blessed One.

'The Buddha: It is the same with the Bodhisattva. Although he leads innumerable sentient beings to Nirvāṇa, in reality there are no sentient beings to be led to Nirvāṇa. Those who are not frightened at all, even when listening to such discourses as this, are true Bodhisattvas well fortified in the Mahāyāna armour.'[2]

'Subhūti said to Pūrṇa: The Rūpam of the magical creation is neither in bondage nor released from it; so with his Vedanā, Saṁjñā, Saṁskāra, and Vijñāna—they are neither in bondage nor released from it. The same is to be said of the suchness of his Rūpam and the other four Skandhas. Nothing of him has ever been in bondage, and he is therefore never released from anything. Why? Because of non-actuality (*asadbhūtatvāt*), there is for him neither bondage nor emancipation; because of detachment (*viviktatvāt*), there is for him neither bondage nor emancipation; because of no-birth (*anutpannatvāt*), there is for him neither bondage nor emancipation. Those Bodhisattvas who realize this are really abiding in the Mahāyāna and are well furnished with the Mahāyāna armour.'[3]

'Then the Devaputras asked Subhūti: Are all beings like Māyā, or are they not?

[2] *Aṣṭa*, pp. 16–17 (Fo-mu, 3b). [2] Ibid., p. 21 (*Fo-mu*, 4a).
[3] Ibid., pp. 22–3 (*Fo-mu*, 4b).

'Subhūti said: O Devaputras, they are all like Māyā; again, they are like a dream (*svapna*). Why? Because no distinction is to be made between all beings and Māyā or a dream; there is indeed between them no dualistic contrast. Therefore, all beings are like Māyā and a dream. The four orders of Śrāvakahood as well as Pratyekabuddhahood; they are like Māyā and a dream; supreme enlightenment itself is like Māyā and a dream.

'The Devaputras: If this is so, is Nirvāṇa, too, Māyā and a dream?

'Subhūti: Nirvāṇa is indeed like Māyā and a dream, and how much more the rest of things!

'The Devaputras: Why so?

'Subhūti: Even when you declare that there is something superior to Nirvāṇa, I tell you that this something too is no more than Māyā and a dream; for there is between them no difference, no dualistic contrast to be made out.'[1]

From this point of view it is natural for followers of the Prajñāpāramitā to conclude that 'Buddha is mere name[2] (*nāmadheya-mātram*); Bodhisattva is mere name; Prajñāpāramitā is mere name; and these names have no real origination (*anabhinirvṛitta*)'.[3]

Names that have never known their real origination are like a void space (*ākāśa*) whose whence and whither are in no way indicable, and which is thus altogether beyond all forms of predicability. In other words, this void is Śūnyatā. 'The Buddha's teaching is in accordance with the nature of all beings, which is beyond attainability. This truth knows no hindrances anywhere. It is like a vacuity of space which is not hindered by anything, it refuses to take any predicates. As it is beyond all forms of dualism, in it there are no contrasts, no characterization is possible of it. As there is in it no opposition, it knows nothing that goes beyond it. As there is in it no origination, it leaves no traces behind it. As

[1] Ibid., p. 39 (*Fo-mu*, 6b).

[2] Name here means concept or thought-construction. Name-only, therefore, is the same as Prajñaptimātrā. This is where the teaching of Śūnyatā comes in contact with the idealism of the Yogācāra.

[3] Ibid., p. 25 (*Fo-mu*, 5*a*).

there is in it no birth-and-death, it is unborn. As there are in it no pathways to mark its transformation, it is pathless.'[1]

From these quotations one may feel like drawing the conclusion that the Dharma of the *Prajñāpāramitā* is after all quite a visionary, dreamy, ungraspable something almost equal to a non-enity. If to view all things in accordance with the Prajñāpāramitā is to view them in accordance with Sarvajñatā (all-knowledge) and if to view all things in accordance with Sarvajñatā is to view them in accordance with the nature of a void space (*ākāśa*), the teaching of the *Prajñāpāramitā* may be regarded after all as the teaching of nothingness, fairly termed as 'Māyāvada', the doctrine of the unrealness of all things.[2] No wonder, we may say, that the sūtra repeatedly warns its readers not to become alarmed, or terrified, or horrified out of their senses, when they listen to the philosophy of the deepest Prajñāpāramitā (*gambhīrā-prajñāpāramitā*).[3] Can we then for these reasons declare that the Prajñā is Māyā and a dream and a mere name and that the Mahāyāna is an edifice constructed on sand? Is it no more than a conceptual plaything consisting of bubbles and echoes? This has decidedly been the conclusion of some scholars, especially of the West. It is very difficult to rise above the notion of the unreality of things and to take them for what they are—that is, in their aspect of suchness. To understand the Māyā theory is to perceive the suchness of things.

The Indians are noted for being clever in magic, and it is natural for the Buddhist philosophers to illustrate the fleeting nature of all existence by means of magical creations. But we must not take their rhetoric in its literal sense. We must try to get at its true meaning. As has repeatedly been stated, the force of argument adopted in the *Prajñāpāramitā* is directed against the fundamental error we all have in regard to the world generally—that is, naïve realism. The

[1] Ibid., p. 306 (*Fo-mu*, 43a).

[2] Ibid., p. 302 (*Fo-mu*, 42b).

[3] This warning is given throughout all the sūtras on Prajñāpāramitā, and it is said that the true test of Bodhisattvahood consists in boldly accepting this doctrine and feeling really cheerful about it.

chief feature of this realism is to take the world as a reality eternally fixed and externally existing against what is conceived to be an inner world of thoughts, feelings, and sensations, while the latter is governed by an ego-soul individually isolated from others and warring against them. One of the best weapons for destroying the stronghold of naïve realism is to declare that all is Māyā and that there is no permanently fixed order in the world, that the dualistic conception of existence, inner and outer, being and non-being, etc., is visionary, and that to reach the real basis of existence it is necessary to awaken the Prajñā which takes hold of the unattainable. For it is only by means of the Prajñā that all kinds of clinging and attachment, whether intellectual or affectional, can be rightly corrected, and that the suchness of existence can be truthfully perceived and acted upon. The *Prajñāpāramitā* has always in view this pragmatic consideration of its philosophy in spite of its soaring flights of imagination and its ever-vanishing mysticism.

The Buddhist idea of having any system of philosophy at all is thereby to uproot the evil passions (*kleśa*) which clog the harmonious unobstructed activity of the Prajñā. The passions are always one-sided, and create all forms of clinging, and by means of these passions and clingings evil deeds are committed in three ways, by body, mouth, and mind, and these lead further on to endless repetitions of the same. So we are told that the pleasures and pains with which we are affected have no permanent nature as such; and likewise with objects of pleasure and pain, they are transitory and changeable like Māyā. They all have no substantial reality. They are mere appearances, and to be regarded as such and of no further value. As far as appearances go, they are there, and this fact will not be ignored; but as for clinging to them thus as finalities, the wise know much better, for their Prajñā-eye has penetrated into the rockbed itself of reality. According to Nāgārjuna,[1] the child sees the moon in the water, the desire is stirred in him to scoop it out, he

[1] His commentary on the *Prajñāpāramitā*, Fas. XXXII.

extends his arm into the water. Not, however, being able to take hold of it, he is very much grieved. A wise man now tells him that what he sees there in the water is not to be handled. In the same way, a world of appearances is not denied, only its seizability or attainability is denied. A world of pluralities is there before the wise as well as the ignorant; the difference between the two is that the former see it with a mind free from attachments while the latter have not yet gone far enough into the realm of Śūnyatā. The veil of Māyā is recognized as such by the Bodhisattvas, but those who are still in bondage take it for reality.

The Māyā teaching is, therefore, to be understood against the background of Śūnyatā or Tathatā. Without this, the Māyā remains forever as such, and the Buddhists will never be able to find their foothold, although this foothold ought not to be reckoned as belonging to the realm of discriminations. When this commentary is not given, the Māyā will entirely lose its significance in the teaching of the *Prajñāpāramitā*. The statement, 'even Nirvāṇa is Māyā and a dream', will be no more than gibberish. The Māyā is a pointer. Those who follow it intelligently will see behind the screen a world of inexpressible mysteries and 'unattainable' realities.

8. *Prajñā and Intuitions*

To understand the position of the Prajñāpāramitā as a philosophical teaching, it is necessary to ascertain where its foundation lies. When this is not properly done, the critic may take the shadow for the substance. Where, then, is the foundation of the Prajñāpāramitā? As the Mahāyānists take it, it is not based on logic as the latter is commonly interpreted; but it is based on intuitions. The Prajñāpāramitā is a system of intuitions. Its thorough understanding requires a leap from logic to the other shore. When one tries to unravel it without this experience, the system becomes all the more a mass of confusion or an unintelligible jargon. Most writers approach the Mahāyāna without this indispensable preliminary. They must discard conceptual arguments.

What is the meaning of this discarding in the doctrine of the Prajñāpāramitā?

According to the Mahāyānists, logic so called or our ordinary human way of thinking is the outgrowth of a dualistic interpretation of existence—*astitva* and *nāstitva*, being and non-being. This dualism goes on throughout our thinking. We can never get away from this so long as we stay with the conditions of thinking. The opposition of 'A' and 'not-A' is fundamental, is the warp and woof of human understanding. But, singularly, our heart or spirit never rests quietly so long as we do not transcend this apparently logically essential position. Ordinary logic is the most useful implement in our practical life, for without it we can never expect to rise above the animal plane of existence. It is due to our faculty of forming concepts that we can go, as it were, out of ourselves, out of our immediate experiences. It is the greatest weapon we have over our brother animals. Unfortunately, we have become so enamoured with our concept-forming power that we have gradually detached ourselves from the sources of our being—the sources that enabled us to construct ideas and carry out abstract reasoning. The result of this is that we have begun to feel somehow uneasy about ourselves. Even when we are convinced of the accuracy and perspicuity of our logic, we seem to cherish somewhere a sense of inner vacancy, we are not able to locate it in our logic, but the logic itself as a whole seems to lack a certain fundamental convincing power. In any event we are dissatisfied with ourselves and with the whole world so long as we cling to the dualism of *asti* and *nāsti*, 'A' and 'not-A'.

Perhaps our so-called logic is only the ultimate utilitarian instrument wherewith we handle things belonging to the superficialities of life. The spirit or that which occupies the deepest part of our being requires something thoroughly non-conceptual, i.e. something immediate and far more penetrating than mere intellection. The latter draws its materials from concepts. The spirit demands immediate perceptions. Evidently, what may be designated an inner or a higher perception, which expresses itself through the ordinary senses, but which is not bound by them, must be awakened, if the spirit is to be satisfied with itself.

The final goal of all the Buddhist disciplines is the awakening of this inner sense. So with the Prajñāpāramitā, the awakening is the one thing that is most needful here. All the teachings expounded in the sūtras, all the bold statements at which the student is warned not to become terrified, are the views extended before the awakened sense of the Bodhisattva. They are his intuitions, they are the dialectic of his immediate experiences, and not that of his concepts. This is the reason why the sūtra so repeatedly refers to seeing things *yathābhūtam*, i.e. as they are. It must be remembered that 'seeing' and not 'reasoning' or 'arguing' logically is here the topic. *Yathābhūtam* is the term applicable only to the act of seeing or viewing, and not to the process of inference.

The Mahāyānists uphold this new point of view acquired by the awakening of the inner sense which is the Prajñā or Sarvajñatā, and declare it to be something more fundamental than mere logic. However logically impossible or full of contradictions a statement which is made by the Prajñāpāramitā may be, it is utterly satisfying to the spirit, inasmuch as it is a statement made *yathābhūtam* in perfect accord with the inner sense, which functions in a realm beyond the dualism of *astitva* and *nāstitva*. Such statements are then said to be characterized with *yathābhūtatā*, or simply they are statements of Tathatā (suchness). That they are not at all logical does not mean that they are untrue. As far as truth is concerned, there is more of it in them. *Truth* means 'it is so'; *yathābhūtatā* means no less.

Statements of immediate perception in a realm beyond *astitva* and *nāstitva* cannot fail to be most frightening to those whose eyes have never been raised above the utilitarian dualism of the sense-world. To announce that all is Māyā, all is a dream, is surely horrifying. But let us here rise above the dualistic interpretation of existence, and we realize that what is is because of what is not, and that what is not is not because of what is. We cannot single out one thing and declare it to be final. But this is what we are practising in our daily life and in our ordinary logic. When the *Prajñā-pāramitā* says that all is Māyā, it simply describes what it sees *yathābhūtam* in this sense-world. Māyā, more exactly stated, is 'to exist as if not existing'.[1] This is not denying the world in a wholesale manner. Superficially, it is a denial, but at the same time it is asserting something behind. It is at once a negation and an affirmation. Logic cannot uphold this position, but the Prajñā intuition does. Students of the Mahāyāna sūtras are always advised to keep this in mind.

9. *The Prajñā as Unattainable, and Relativity*

This position of the Prajñāpāramitā attained by the awakening of the inner sense is called *anupalabdha*, 'unattainable'. Paradoxes are here unavoidable. The Hegelian dialectic may explain them as being also in accordance with the law of logic. But in the Prajñāpāramitā there is no need to go through the process of thesis, antithesis, and synthesis because there is no room in the Mahāyāna world of intuitions to admit such a roundabout process of moving from one idea to another. Once beyond a world dualistically constructed, the unattainable is the attainable, and the attainable is the unattainable. This may be called the transcendental viewpoint of the Prajñāpāramitā.

We can now see why those scholars are in the wrong who want to identify the doctrine of Emptiness (*śūnyatā*) with that of relativity. According to them, all things are empty because their existence is thoroughly conditioned by the principle of relativity, which is the same as saying that all things are bound up by the law of causation. If Buddhist philosophy is based on causation and karma, this means

[1] *Yathā na saṁvidyante tathā saṁvidyante. Aṣṭa*, p. 15.

relativity; and if all things are what they are because of the causal net pervading the entire range of existence, and if they are thus characterized as Emptiness, Emptiness is relativity. But this identification of Emptiness and relativity is untenable; the so-called identification is confusion. The scholars have not fully grasped the purpose of the Mahāyāna teaching; they are still holding to their former position, that is, the position we generally have prior to the awakening of the inner sense to which allusion has already been made.

To understand truthfully, *yathābhūtam*, what Emptiness is, the awakening (*saṁbodhi*) is indispensable. The awakening is the turning-up (*parāvṛitti*), so repeatedly mentioned in the Mahāyāna sutras such as the *Laṅkāvatāra*, etc. This turning-up or turning-back means reversing the order of one's mental outlook. What used to be dualistic is now to be seen from the 'wrong side' of it. The inside which was hitherto hidden out of sight now stands revealed in full view. Things are now surveyed from this newly discovered position. Naturally, one's view of the world must change; things seen from the outside cannot be the same as things seen from the inside. A tree was observed as expressed in colour and with its branches swaying in the wind; but now there is no more a tree distinct from its fellow-trees, from its surroundings; the leaves are no more green; there are no swaying branches; no flowers are in bloom; and all these have vanished; what has appeared to the senses and been constructed by thought is all gone. Here lies a new world. All that has been 'attainable' remains here; but this is changed—though not to a state of nothingness, for nothingness still savours of somethingness. Lacking in all forms of expression, the *Prajñāpāramitā* calls this 'the unattainable', 'the empty', 'the unobstructed', etc.

There is no room here for relativity to design its machinery. Relativity is one of the notions we have formed while observing existence from the point of *astitva* and *nāstitva*, where everything has its second, where every 'A' is accompanied by its 'not-A'. From this position it is impossible to penetrate into a realm of Emptiness; the position must once for all be quitted; as long as the philosopher clings to this, his relativity dogs his every step; he cannot draw anything else out of it; it never transforms itself into Emptiness. In order to get into the world of Emptiness, existence itself must be made to turn a somersault. One must once experience sitting at the centre of existence and viewing things from this hub. Let one remain at this side of dualism and the gap between relativity and Emptiness can never be bridged. Things of this world are relative because of their being empty by nature; and not conversely. Śūnyatā is realized only after the awakening of the inner sense, after the turning-over (*parāvṛitti*) in the Ālayavijñāna. It is only after this 'turning' which is also a leaping that we can make such statements as these: 'All is bound up in the chain of origination, and therefore all is empty', or 'All is Māyā, all is Śūnyatā'; or 'All is such as it is (*yathābhūtam*), and yet all is not'.

When the Buddhists refer to the chain of origination (*hetupratyaya* or *kāraṇasamutpāda*), in order to explain the making-up of a fleet or the production of a Buddha-image,[1] and say that nothing is produced without the combination of various causes and conditions, and further that they do not come from any definite quarters, nor do they disappear into any definite quarters, the idea may seem to point towards the identification of relativity and Emptiness. In one of the Chinese versions of the *Prajñāpāramitā Sūtra*, known as the *Tao-hsing Pan-jê*,[2] we have the following:[3]

'It is like those heavenly mansions which are inhabited by beings of the Akanishṭa Heaven. Their glowing beauty surpasses everything we on earth can think of. But they have been made by themselves; they have not been brought

[1] See *Zen Essays*, Series II, p. 318 ff.

[2] *Tao-hsing* is the title of the first chapter. This was translated by Lou-chio-sh'an (Lokarakṣa), of the Eastern Han dynasty (A.D. 25–220), and is the earliest *Prajñāpāramitā* done into the Chinese language. In the Kumārajīva and the Hsüan-chuang 'Tao-hsing' is 'Miao-hsing', and in the Sanskrit *Aṣṭasāhasrikā* 'Sarvākārajñatācaryā'.

[3] This part is missing in Kumārajīva, and also in Shih-hu.

over here from anywhere else, nor is there any creator who has created them out of nothing, nor is their whence and whither known to anybody. Their coming into existence is due to the law of causation; when those celestial beings were matured on account of their previous deeds to enjoy such radiantly shining celestial palaces, the latter came into existence. In like manner, when various causes and conditions are matured, sentient beings are able to see the Buddha-body. They first conceive the desire to see the Buddha; they then accumulate all kinds of merit by practising good deeds; they avoid being born in the eight undesirable habitations; being intelligent they have full faith in the Buddha. When these several conditions are fulfilled, they will interview the Buddha. As to the Buddha-body itself, it has no whence and whither; it knows no creator; there is no one who has brought it over here for the benefit of the devotees, it has no form; it is not attached to anything; like the palaces of the Akanishṭa, it just manifests itself there in order to make all sentient beings attain final emancipation. . . .'

The doctrine of causation (*kāraṇasamutpāda*) as upheld here is only applicable to a world of dualities and combinations. Where there are no such happenings, the doctrine at once loses its significance. As long as we are bound to a world of particulars we see causation and relativity everywhere, because this is the place for them to function. But since we are never satisfied with this state of affairs, not only spiritually but logically in the deeper sense of the word, we leap for life or death over the bottomless abyss gaping before us. The leap lands us in the realm of Emptiness, and we realize that it is after all this Emptiness that lies underneath the world of causes and conditions.

Emptiness is that which makes the work of causation possible, it is a form of canvas on which causation paints its most variegated pictures. Emptiness thus comes first though not in time, for time presupposes a chain of causation; the coming first means being fundamental. When causation or relativity is made at all thinkable, there is already in it

Emptiness. This distinction is most vital in all our religious experience and, I should think, also in all our clear philosophical thinking. The *Prajñāpāramitā* philosophers, therefore, insists that Emptiness is the most fundamental idea when their intuitions strive to express themselves through the medium of the intellect. It is not a negative notion but decidedly positive. It sounds negative only to those who have not gone to the other side of the screen. When penetration is imperfect the intellect becomes muddled, and wrong inferences are many.

Scholars unfortunately slur over the fact that in the *Prajñāpāramitā* and other Mahāyāna texts Śūnyatā (emptiness) and Tathatā or Yathābhūtatā (suchness) are synonymously used as expressing an identical thought. If Emptiness is a negative term and connotes nothing of affirmation, it can never be made to build up the grand edifice of the religion known as Mahāyāna Buddhism. It is really astonishing to see how prejudiced and superficial some of the critics are who fail to see the needs of the human sense for something really affirmative and therefore soul-supporting. The oriental mind, generally speaking, is more inner and intuitive, working outwardly, as it were, from the centre of its being. It may not be so logical and system-loving as the Western mind, and for this reason it is capable of more deeply grasping the fundamental facts of life. Those who start from a dualistically constructed world are unable to destroy this construction and to return to its source which really is no-source. Thesis (*astitva*) and antithesis (*nāstitva*) may be raised to a synthesis, but this after all remains an idea, a concept, and never becomes an experience; and, therefore, when they are asked 'Where does the One return?' they are at a loss where to find the way out.[1]

Intuition may be despised by the philosopher, but there are grades of intuition. The deepest are those experienced by religio-philosophical minds belonging to the order of the Prajñāpāramitā. But when their intuitions are translated into terms of relative knowledge, how insipid, negative, and

[1] See *Zen Essays*, Series I, p. 283.

nonsensical! The understanding of the Prajñāpāramitā becomes an impossibility. Hence its repeated warnings not to hide oneself under a cover, not to cherish a shadow of doubt, not to feel dejected or frightened or threatened.

10. *The Prajñā and Irrationalities*

Seeing thus where the Prajñāpāramitā stands, we can realize why it abounds with negative phrases and irrational assertions. Its intuitions could not be conveyed in any other way if they were to be expressed at all. In fact, we can say that all the deep soul-stirring truths are paradoxically stated, so much, indeed, that we are almost led to imagine that the authors are incorrigibly and deliberately enigmatic. The following quotations supply examples:

'Subhūti asked: How does the Bodhisattva come to the knowledge of the five Skandhas when he disciplines himself in the deep Prajñāpāramitā?

'Buddha said: He comes to the knowledge of the five Skandhas when he disciplines himself in the deep Prajñāpāramitā by perceiving *yathābhūtam* (1) what the characteristic marks (*lakṣaṇa*) of the Skandhas are, (2) whence they come and whither they go, and (3) what is meant by their suchness.

'(1) Rūpam (form) has no ultimate solidity; it is full of cracks and holes; it is like a bubble. Vedanā is like a boil; it is like an arrow, quickly rising and quickly disappearing; it is like a foam, deceiving and fleeting; it takes its rise when there is a triple combination of conditions. Saṁjñā is like a mirage, there are no real fountains in it; because of thirst of desire it rises, and expresses itself in words though there is nothing substantial in it. Saṁskāra is like a plantain tree; when each leaf is peeled off, nothing remains. Vijñāna is like a Māyā creation; it is there when causes and conditions are variously combined. It is a provisionary construction; the magically created soldiers are seen marching through the streets; though they look real they are in fact without substantiality.

'(2) As regards the whence and whither of the five Skandhas, the Bodhisattva knows *yathābhūtam* that they come from nowhere although they seem to manifest themselves actually before him; that they depart nowhere although they seem to disappear altogether out of sight, and yet that there is in the Skandhas a happening known as their rise or their disappearance.

'(3) Lastly, the Bodhisattva perceives *yathābhūtam* that there is what is to be known as the suchness of the five Skandhas, which is neither born nor dead, neither comes nor departs, is neither pure nor tainted, neither loses nor gains; which for ever remains in the state of suchness free from all falsehood, from all forms of change.'[1]

The position of the Prajñāpāramitā is not necessarily to deny the so-called phenomenal world; it gives the world its judicious claim as a stage of birth and death, of being and non-being. But at the same time it never forgets to assert that what we see here displayed or performed are passing shadows of something behind, and that when the latter is not finally grasped by our experience the meaning of the passing shadows will never be properly recognized and appraised. Therefore, the Mahāyānists are always meticulously careful about distinguishing between 'the attainable' and 'the unattainable', technically so called. 'The attainable' belongs to this world dualistically constructed and 'the unattainable' to a world beyond that. Wherever the contrast between *astitva* (being) and *nāstitva* (non-being) is possible, there is attainability, and, therefore, attachment which is the enemy of enlightenment and emancipation.

'The Buddha says to Subhūti: Wherever there is a form of duality, this is attainability; wherever there is no duality in whatever form, this is non-attainability. When the eye stands against form (*rūpam*), or the mind against ideas (*dharma*) there is a duality. When there is what is known as supreme enlightenment set against the Buddha who is regarded as having attained it, this is again a duality. Any

[1] Abstract from Hsüan-chuang's translation of the *Mahāprajñāpāramitā*, Fas. 532, Chapter 29 (1) 55 ff.

teaching that is based on dualism is incorrect, it belongs to a realm of the attainables.

'Let the duality of eye and form, ear and sound, mind and thought be altogether done away with; likewise with that of the enlightened and enlightenment, let us have nothing to do; and then there will be a state of non-duality, free from all false teachings and illegitimate speculations. The unattainable is thus attained.

'Subhūti asks: 'Is it the unattainable because of depending on the attainable? Or because of depending on the unattainable?

'The Buddha: It is the unattainable because of depending on neither the attainable nor the unattainable. It is termed "unattainable" when the attainable and the unattainable are regarded as one. The discipline of the Bodhisattva in the Prajñāpāramitā consists in realizing this oneness of the attainable and the unattainable. Let him be freed both from the idea of the attainable and that of the unattainable; he will then be free from all faulty entanglements.

'O Subhūti, you may ask: if the attainable and the unattainable are one, how does the Bodhisattva, who is defined as progressively going through from one stage to another, finally reach the enlightenment of the all-knowing one? O Subhūti, the Bodhisattva's life is a series of unattainables. He has nothing attained while going through the various stages of Bodhisattvahood; for in the Prajñāpāramitā there is nothing attainable, nor is there any in the enlightenment of the all-knowing one. When the Bodhisattva is disciplining himself in the Prajñāpāramitā, there is in his discipline nothing to be recognized as attained, and in this non-attainment there is also really nothing attained in any time and at any place.'[1]

This sounds nonsensical when we confine ourselves to the relativity aspect of existence, or to the discursive understanding of the human mind. But let us reverse the order of things; let us see the world of pluralities from the other side which reveals itself to the inner eye now opened by a process

[1] Ibid., Fas. 525, Chapter 26 (3) 23a.

known as Parāvṛitti and we shall realize that all these irrationalities are possible. Irrationalities are such because of our position. The question is whether we can abandon this position, whether we can adopt an altogether new one where things are surveyed from their aspect of suchness. As we have already seen, the acquirement of this is made possible by the supreme efforts we put forward when impelled by a certain inner urge. The new position is open only to our will-power and not to the intellect. Logic halts here; ideas are unable to array themselves in regular sequence of cognition and analysis. The intellect surrenders itself to the dictates of the will. The door is forced to open, and we see a realm of unattainables extending itself before the eye. It is in this realm that we attain an unattainability by not really attaining it. Critics may declare: 'By this we have not gained anything, for we stand where we were before the Parāvṛitti. If this is so, what is the use of exercising ourselves so much over the so-called situation? When we have a thing as if not having it, it is practically the same as not having it at all from the first.' The reasoning is sound as far as intellection is concerned. But we may remember that we have already gone over to the other side of intellection, and that whatever statements we make are made after the leap. There is the history of an experience intervening; this is a great event which creates an unsurpassable gap between philosophy and the teaching of the *Prajñāpāramitā*.

11. *The Unattainable and the Unattached*

'Unattainable' (*anupalabdha*), otherwise expressed, is 'not-seized' or 'unattached' (*apāramṛiṣṭa*). 'Unattainable' has still an intellectual ring, while 'unseizable' or 'unattached' belongs to the terminology of emotion. The assertion that 'All-knowledge is indeed unattached' (*apāramṛiṣṭa hi sarvajñatā*) is in fact one of the refrains we constantly come across in the *Prajñāpāramitā Sūtra*. In this we are made to be strongly convinced that the Mahāyāna text is a document describing the views of the other side of existence where the dualism of *astitva* and *nāstitva* ceases to hold good. In the following passages, *apāramṛiṣṭa* is replaced by *aśleṣa* and *asamga*, which denote the same idea; our author tries hard to impress us with the importance of this teaching of non-attachment.

'When the Bodhisattva attains enlightenment, he teaches all beings with the doctrine of non-attachment (*aśleṣa*). By non-attachment is meant not to be bound by Rūpam (*rūpasyā-saṁbandhā*), by Vedanā, Saṁjñā, Saṁskāra, and Vijñāna. When a person is not bound by them, he is unconcerned with their rise and disappearance. Being unattached to these happenings, he is neither in bondage nor emancipated.'[1]

'This teaching of the *Prajñāpāramitā* is difficult to understand, difficult to believe. Because form itself (*rūpam*) is neither bound nor emancipated. Why? Because form has no self-nature (*asvabhāva*). The same may be said of the rest of the Skandhas. There is no self-nature in any one of them, neither in the beginning, nor in the midway, nor at the end. As this having no self-nature is its self-nature, there is nothing bound, nothing emancipated. The Prajñāpāramitā is, therefore, difficult to grasp.'[2]

'But as soon as we cling to name (*nāma*) and appearance (*nimitta*), there is attachment (*saṁga*). Name and appearance are products of discrimination (*vikalpa*). Discrimination takes place when the Prajñāpāramitā is clung to as such. Discrimination, attachment, and the losing sight of the Prajñāpāramitā are synonymous and interchangeable in the lexicon of Mahāyāna Buddhism. Form is empty (*rūpam śūnyam*), but when it is so asserted, there is clinging (*saṁga*), and the clinging separates us from the Prajñāpāramitā.

'Here is a novitiate Bodhisattva who has awakened the desire for enlightenment; he has gone through with a disciplinary course in the life of Bodhisattvahood; and he may

[1] *Aṣṭa*, p. 294 (*Fo-mu*, 41a).
[2] Ibid., pp. 185–6; Hsüan-chuang, Fas. 545, Chapter 8, 19b.

have conceived the idea that he has thereby accumulated a certain amount of merit. But no sooner is this idea stirred in him than he commits a deed of clinging, he is no more in the Prajñāpāramitā. Wherever there is discrimination, this leads to clinging; or we may reverse it and state that wherever there is clinging there is discrimination. Enlightenment is attained only when there is no clinging, no conscious striving, no dualism of *astitva* and *nāstitva*; for enlightenment is non-attainment, and its self-nature consists in not having self-nature.'[1]

This being free from discrimination, from clinging or attachment, and having no self-nature is sometimes called a state of 'absolute purity' (*atyantaviśuddhi*). And it is said that because of this absolute purity the Prajñāpāramitā is unfathomably deep, glowingly brilliant, a perfect unit, unattainable, unseizable, unknowable, unborn, indestructible, abiding nowhere, etc.[2]

To illustrate further the philosophy of the unattainable or of absolute solitude as described in the *Prajñāpāramitā*, I quote another passage from the sūtra where a chapter is devoted to the treatment of Māyā.[3]

'Subhūti then said: How can the mind which is like Māyā attain supreme enlightenment?

'The Buddha: Do you see the mind which is like Māyā?

'Subhūti: No, I do not.

'Buddha: Do you see Māyā?

'Subhūti: No, I do not.

'Buddha: When you do not see Māyā, nor the mind which is like Māyā, do you think there is an existence (*dharma*)—other than the Māyā or the Māyā-like mind—which attains supreme enlightenment?

'Subhūti: No, I do not see any such existence (*dharma*). If there is any existence apart from the mind which is like Māyā, nothing can be predicated of it, for it is neither a being (*asti*) nor a non-being (*nāsti*). All is absolutely

[1] Ibid., p. 190 (*Fo-mu*, 25b).
[2] Ibid., p. 186 et seq. (*Fo-mu*, 25b).
[3] Ibid., Chapter XXVI, 'On the Simile of Māyā'.

solitary (*atyantaviviktā*), and in this absolute solitude there is nothing of which we can assert either as being or as not being; there is nothing in which discipline is possible, or of which attainment is to be avouched. For this reason, the Prajñāpāramitā is absolutely solitary. So is supreme enlightenment. Between these two absolutely solitary terms there cannot be any relationship; we cannot describe the one as the means of attaining the other, nor the other as something attainable. The Bodhisattva is spoken of as attaining supreme enlightenment because of the Prajñāpāramitā. But the Bodhisattva himself is also an absolutely solitary being (*dharma*), and we cannot make any assertion about his attaining anything, even enlightenment.

'Buddha: Well done, Subhūti. It is just as you state. Absolutely solitary are all things (*dharma*)—the Bodhisattva, the Prajñāpāramitā, and supreme enlightenment. And yet amidst those absolutely solitary dharmas the Bodhisattva is awakened to the true nature of the Prajñāpāramitā and attains the knowledge that the Prajñāpāramitā is absolutely solitary, and that what is known as Prajñāpāramitā is not Prajñāpāramitā. There is really the attainment by the Bodhisattva of supreme enlightenment, and yet in this attainment there is really nothing that can be held out as something attained, something seized; and all things (*dharma*) remain absolutely solitary as if nothing ever happened.'[1]

12. *Reality as Seen from the Other Side*

'Absolutely solitary' (*atyantaviviktā*), 'absolutely pure' (*atyantaviśuddhi*), 'unattainable' (*anupalabdha*), 'unattached' (*aśleṣa*, or *asaṁga*, or *aparāmṛiṣṭa*), 'neither bound nor emancipated' (*abaddhāmukta*), 'neither born nor extinguished' (*anutpādānirodha*), 'not abiding anywhere' (*asthita*), 'not depending on anything' (*anāśrāya*), 'not exhausted' (*akṣaya*), pathless' (*apatha*), 'trackless' (*apada*), etc.—all these belong

[1] *Aṣṭa*, p. 438 ff; *Fo-mu*, 61; *Māhā*, Fas. 553, 60a; Kumārajīva, 78b.

to the terminology to be met with in the *Prajñāpāramitā Sūtra*, and come from the realm of Emptiness. When we try to understand them from our ordinary logical point of view, which deals with the relativity aspect of existence, they do not seem to convey much sense; they are too negative or too obscure in meaning for us to locate the definite quarters where they intend to lead us. As soon, however, as we abandon our dualistically built up relativity standpoint, and enter into the inner life of things, we seem to understand those obscure terms; we even come to think that this inner world is only describable by means of this kind of mystical phraseology. The religious life is after all a life to live and experience and not a concept to think about, yet the human mind is so constructed that it cannot avoid giving expression to the life. The expressions in the *Prajñāpāramitā* are thus the more or less intellectual outpourings of the Mahāyāna genius.

To study or discipline oneself in the Prajñāpāramitā is, therefore, to approach this realm of absolute solitude or absolute emptiness. The Prajñā generally lies obscured in the deepest recesses of consciousness. Unless this is successfully awakened and made to see the other side of reality, which is to see reality *yathābhūtam*, there is no escape from the bondage of ignorance and suffering. This release is called attaining supreme enlightenment or all-knowledge (*sarvajñatā*).

The Prajñāpāramitā is the objective of all the Buddhist discipline. But when this is attained there is really nothing of which one can say that one has attained it. This is the meaning of such phrases: 'There is no perception of Suchness in Suchness'; 'Not by means of absolute solitude is absolute solitude realized'; 'There is something accomplished, and yet no discrimination (*avikalpa*) we have, because of the Prajñāpāramitā's being non-discriminative'; etc. Some may call these phrases mystical in the sense that they are irrational and beyond syllogistic reasoning. This may be right, for 'incomprehensible' (*acintya*) is one of the terms most frequently used in all Mahāyāna literature. But from the standpoint of the Prajñā philosophers they are far from talking irrationalities; they are simply giving expression to what they actually see with their own Prajñā-eye.

In the beginning, not being satisfied with themselves and their so-called objective world, they had everywhere searched for Reality in or with which they could peacefully live. The Parāvṛitti took place somewhere in their mind. The order of things is reversed. The universe (*sarvadharma*) is no more observed from the point of view with which they have hitherto been so deeply, so inextricably, involved. This is now completely abandoned. Things are seen, as it were, from the reverse side. A world of Rūpam, Vedanā, Saṁjñā, Saṁskāra, and Vijñāna is there as before, but it is seen lined with the silver lining of Tathatā (suchness) and no more indeed as an isolated event cut off from its roots. Without the roots, which are, however, no roots, we merely drifted like a dead leaf before the autumn wind, and the drifting had no meaning whatever, which was, to use Buddhist terminology, ignorance and transmigration and torture. The scene has changed, and to describe this change simply, and in a most unsophisticated manner, the *Prajñāpāramitā* writers now exhaust their literary power. The 'irrationalities' so called belong to the philosopher and logician, and not to the Prajñā-devotee.

Teachers of the Prajñāpāramitā have their foothold or dwelling (*sthāna*) always on the other side (*pāram*) of this world of relativity. They thus seem to be negating the latter, regarding it as Māyā, as a dream, as an echo, and so on. Even when reference is made to their own quarters of Śūnyatā, this Śūnyatā is also empty and has no fixed abode. Because theirs is an absolute Śūnyatā and allows nothing to oppose it, it is absolutely without predicates of any sort whatever. Suchness has thus come to be one of the most favourite terms they use to designate Śūnyatā. 'Absolute emptiness' or 'absolute solitude' is indeed difficult for dualistically-minded beings to comprehend. This is the reason why the *Prajñāpāramitā* repeatedly warns its readers not to become frightened or depressed when they hear of the doctrine of Emptiness; it must sound to them as trumpeting a universal annihilation. And those who would embrace the teaching at once without the least hesitation are praised as being those who have listened to it for many times in their past existences. The warning and the assurance prove that the Prajñā is something most extraordinary; and most extraordinary indeed it is, seeing that the ordinary order of things is completely reversed in the Prajñāpāramitā. Is it not shocking to know that the Mount Hiei which we people of Kyoto see every day in the north-eastern part of the city is no more a reality; more than that, all the heavens including all the luminaries whose lights are measured to reach this earth after millions of years are said to be mere bubbles in the ocean of eternal Emptiness? Who would not be terrified before this audacious proclamation? But this is the proclamation that rings through the *Prajñāpāramitā*. What a grand, thoroughly penetrating intuition it must be that would blow out this entire cosmos like a soap bubble into the immensity of absolute Emptiness (*atyanta-śūnyatā*)!

Emptiness is absolute when it stands alone, rejecting all predicability. As long as reference is made to inner or outer, created or uncreated, substance or appearance, Emptiness is not yet absolute, it remains still relative and predicated. All must be set aside, Emptiness must stand shorn of all its trappings when its true features will strike us with their primeval awfulness. Primeval awfulness I say because Emptiness itself is now vanished; it is as if this physical body were left in mid-air, with nothing covering its head, nothing supporting its feet. It is awful to imagine such a situation. But the *Prajñāpāramitā* unmistakably contrives to create it for us. No wonder it gives us warnings constantly on this point.

'All is empty' (*sarvaṁ śūnyam*)—by this one of the legs is broken off. 'Emptiness itself is empty' (*śūnyatāśūnyatā*)—by this the remaining one departs; and at the same time the entire earth vanishes from beneath one. I am like Hsiang-yen's man up in a tree,[1] and even the teeth are now

[1] *Zen Essays*, Series I, pp. 277–8.

letting go the hold. Out of this great negation there is the awakening of the Prajñā, and the great affirmation takes place, which is Sarvajñatā and Saṁbodhi, all-knowledge and enlightenment. Śūnyata seems to have changed into Tathatā, but in reality Śūnyatā is Tathatā, and Tathatā Śūnyatā. The solid earth has not vanished. Mount Hiei stands before one even more solemnly than before, and the starry heavens are an ever-inspiring wonder not only for the philosopher but for all of us. We now really know what is meant by seeing *yathābhūtam*. The world is revealed as thoroughly pure, detached, unattainable, free from an ego-thought, and therefore the home of peace and happiness. The Mahāyāna sūtras talk so much of embellishing[1] the world. When the Bodhisattva is awakened in Tathatā, he is the embellisher.

13. *The Prajñā as Handled by Zen Masters*

Does all this sound vague? The Prajñāpāramitā itself being a Māyā creation, we are deprived of every possible point of reference whereby to give an intellectual account of this existence. This may be the idea of our readers after perusing the above characterization of the Prajñā. But the Mahāyānist would say that he knows (*abhibudhyate*) that there is really the experience of the Prajñāpāramitā, and that this knowledge is the foundation stone of the spiritual structure called Buddhism. In the following quotations the reader will see how this Prajñāpāramitā dialectics is handled by Zen followers, and also how their method is distinguishable from that of their Indian predecessors as well as from that of modern philosophers and logicians.

Tai-hui[2] once quoted Yung-chia Hsüan-chiao:[3] 'How clearly it is seen! Yet nothing to see! Neither a person nor

[1] *Alaṁkāra*, or *vyūha*.

[2] Daiye in Japanese, 1089–1163. See *Zen Essays*, Series II, p. 25, and elsewhere.

[3] Yo-ka Gen-kaku in Japanese. Died 713. See also ibid., p. 61.

PLATE XXVII

SAMANTABHADRA AND THE TEN RĀKSHASĪS

By Tamechika Reizei

The artist is a Japanese painter of the nineteenth century, who belonged to the Yamatoye school of painting. His speciality was the court-life, and this fact is shown in his depicting the Rakshasīs as court-ladies who look more like admirers than the body-guards of the Bodhisattva. Feminity is characteristic of the picture. This was perhaps inevitable seeing that Samantabhadra was love (*karuna*) while Mañjusrī was wisdom.

PLATE XXVIII

KUAN-YIN CARRYING A FISH-BASKET

By An Unknown Japanese Artist

Kuan-yin in this form has been frequently made a subject of painting by artists both Japanese and Chinese. She is also known as Kuanyin of the Ma family, that is, *Ma-lang-fu kuan-yin*. The story runs as follows: It was in the era of Yüan-ha (A.D. 806–820) that Kuan-yin conceived the idea of propagating Buddhism among the people of Shênyü, and appeared to them in the form of a beautiful maiden. There were many young men who wished to court her favour. She said: "If you can recite by heart the *Kuan-yin Sütra* in one evening, I will be the wife of such a one." In the morning there was twenty young candidates who thoroughly mastered the sutra. She told them, however, that she could not be a wife to so many of them; they were thus requested to memorise the *Diamond Sutra* in one night. Ten passed the test. Her final proposal was to commit to memory all the seven volumes of the *Pundarika* within three days. Young Ma was the only person who successfully met the demand. She promised to be his wife. When all the necessary formalities to a marriage were gone through and all the relatives and friends of Ma were invited to attend the ceremony, the maiden took suddenly ill, faded, and decomposed even before the guests dispersed.

Later, an old monk called on the Ma family, and, visiting their burial ground, dug the earth with his staff where the late Buddhist maiden was buried. To their great surprise, her bones were found turned into gold. He then told them that "She was no ordinary mortal. It was due to the merciful means (*upâya*) of the Bodhisattva that she appeared among you in the form you saw. The idea is to make you think of the Dharma and refrain from committing evils." This said, he flew up in the air. In this story, we see the Bodhisattva's actual mixing with people and being engaged in such proletarian activities as buying fish in the market.

the Buddha! Great chiliocosms, as many as sands of the Gangā, are like bubbles in the ocean; all the sages and worthies of old are like the weeping flashes of lightning.'[1] Tai-hui then proceeded to quote another old Zen master who commented on Yung-chia: 'When there is nothing to see, what is it that he sees so clearly?' Finishing these quotations, Tai-hui asked: 'What do you say to this old master's comment? Is he really supplied with an eye [of wisdom]?'

It is characteristic of Zen masters to ask a question without apparently expecting an answer. In such cases asking is answering. The master's interrogative comment explains itself. The Prajñāpāramitā is here described in a form of self-examination.

Tai-hui on another occasion quoted Mu-chou.[2] Mu-chou once asked Shêng-chêng: 'Do you discourse on the philosophy of Vijñaptimātra?' Chêng: 'Not very much, master, but while young I studied it a little.' Mu-chou picked up a piece of sugared pastry, divided it into halves, and said: 'What do you say?' Chêng made no answer, whereupon Chou asked: 'Is this to be called sugared pastry? Or is it not to be so-called?' Chêng: 'There is no other way but to call it sugared pastry.' Mu-chou now called in a young attendant monk and asked him: 'What do you call this?' The young novice: 'Sugared pastry, master.' Chou: 'You too can discourse on the philosophy of Vijñaptimātra.'

On this Tai-hui commented: 'Shêng-chêng and the young novice, they can both discourse well on the philosophy of Vijñaptimātra; only neither knows the whence of the sugared pastry. As to the old master Mu-chou himself, he is indeed an adept in Zen, but in the philosophy of Vijñaptimātra or Cittamātra he has absolutely no understanding whatever.'[3]

. . . . .

[1] These are lines from Yung-chia's famous ode 'On Enlightenment'.

[2] Bokujū. See also *Zen Essays*, Series I, p. 22 et passim; Series II, p. 75 et passim.

[3] *Sayings of Tai-hui*, Fas. II.

Ch'u-shih Fan-ch'i[1] (1296–1370) was one of the great Zen masters in early Ming. In one of his sermons he quoted Yün-mên: 'Yün-mên one day produced his staff before an assembly of monks and said: Common people naïvely take it for a reality; the two Yānas analyse it and declare it to be non-existent; the Pratyekabuddhas declare it to be a Māyā-like existence; and the Bodhisattvas accept it as it is, declaring it empty. As regards Zen followers, when they see a staff, they simply call it a staff. If they want to walk they just walk; if they want to sit, they just sit; they should not in any circumstances be ruffled and distracted.'

'Miao-hsi (i.e. Tai-hui) commented on this: I am not like Yün-mên the old master who contrives to scrape out a cave prison in the vacuity of space. So saying, he brusquely held out his staff before the monks and continued: This staff is not to be classed as being, nor as non-being, nor as Māyā-like existence, nor as of empty suchness. He then held his staff up straight on the floor, and declared: Common people, Śrāvakas, Pratyekabuddhas, and Bodhisattvas—each according to his original nature makes use of it. But the thing is different with you who are Zen monks; for you this staff is the source of terrible annoyances. When you want to walk, you are unable to walk; when you want to sit, you are unable to sit [all on account of the staff]. Advance a step, and you are led astray; retrace a step, and your nose is hurt. I ask you, Is there any one who is not quite satisfied with me? Then, let him come out before me and have an interview with the staff. If there is none,

> 'In the year to come there will be more fresh shoots,
> Swaying distractedly in the spring breeze that blows
> ever gently.'

After these references to the old masters, Ch'u-shih airs his own remarks on the staff: 'It is improper to cherish for common people the notion of reality, for the Śrāvakas the notion of non-being, for the Pratyekabuddhas the notion of

[1] This and what follow are all quoted from *Biographies of the Famous Ming Masters*.

Māyā-like existence, and for the Bodhisattvas the notion of empty suchness. Not to be released? Yün-mên the old master was so absorbed in watching the foaming waves that he was not conscious of losing his own oars. The woeful outcome of it is still engaging the anxious attention of the entire world of monks. They are not yet freed from the staff. To be released? No! Better have them all interred in one common graveyard!'

In this Zen sermon the staff has taken the place of the Prajñāpāramitā, and as far as outside critics are concerned the masters seem to be making mountains of mole-hills. But this is the way of the Zen adept, who, taking hold of anything that comes by, is ready to demonstrate his view of emptiness or suchness. The matter seems to have no bearing on such weighty metaphysical subjects. Superficially, no. But even a particle of dust is not outside the mind, and when this is understood, Śūnyatā and its cognate ideas will all become comprehensible.

Another time Ch'u-shih referred to Chao-chou: 'An old lady sent a messenger to Chao-chou with some offerings and asked him to revolve the Great Tripitaka. Chao-chou came down from his seat and, after walking once round the chair said, I have finished the revolving of the Tripitaka. When this was transmitted to the old lady, she remarked: I asked him for the revolution of one complete Tripitaka, and he has finished only one half of it.

'Miao-hsi commented on this statement of the old lady: Some of the Zen followers remark, "What is the other half?"; others say, "Make another round"; or "Snap your fingers"; still others say, "Give a cough"; or "Utter a *kwatz*!" or "Clap the hands!" Those who make these remarks do not know what shame means. As regards "the other half" don't say "Make another round"! Even when hundreds of thousands of kotis of rounds are made, they are, from the point of view of the old lady, no more than a half Tripitaka. Even when Mount Sumeru is gone round for hundreds of thousands of kotis of times, they are, from the point of view of the old lady, no more than a half Tripitaka. Even when the great Zen masters of the whole empire walk round the mountain for hundreds of thousands of kotis of times, they are, from the point of view of the old lady, no more than a half Tripitaka. Even when all the mountains and rivers and the great earth and everything that makes up this universe of multiplicities, including every plant and every blade of grass, each endowed with a long broad tongue, unanimously revolve the Tripitaka from this day on to the end of time, they are, from the point of view of the old lady, no more than a half Tripitaka.

'Miao-hsi remained silent for a while and continued:

> 'The beautiful pair of ducks, embroidered in the finest style, is there for you to see as much as you like;
> But take care not to deliver up the gold needle that did the work!'

After these references Ch'u-shih gave his own idea saying: 'The old lady claims that Chao-chou has only finished revolving a half of the Tripitaka. This is replacing the spurious for the genuine. The only thing that was needed at the time to say was this: Why not take the whole thing in before Chao-chou started to walk round the chair?'

To quote another Zen method of treating the problem of Prajñāpāramitā. Chieh-feng Ying,[1] of Ming dynasty, once had a caller in the person of Tai-tou An, who was a learned scholar. Ying asked: 'What is the sūtra you are most proficient in?'

An: 'The *Vajracchedikā*; and I have my understanding as to the meaning of "Nowhere to come and nowhere to depart".'

Ying: 'If "Nowhere to come and nowhere to depart", how is it that you have come over here?'

An: 'The very person who comes from nowhere and departs nowhither.'

[1] Op. cit.

Ying: 'Where is he this very moment?'

An burst out into a '*kwatz!*'

Ying: 'Let alone for a while this uttering a "*kwatz!*" or shaking a fist; where would you find your abode of peace when the four elements are dissolved?'

An: 'This entire earth—is it not myself?'

Ying: 'When all of a sudden the world-end fire breaks out and all the chiliocosms are reduced to ashes, where are you?'

An: 'I know not.'

Ying: 'The sixth patriarch has his "I know not" and went on preparing kindlings and pounding rice; Bodhidharma had his "I know not" and kept up his meditation for nine years. You have your "I know not" and what is your insight?'

An: 'Mine is simply "I know not".'

Ying: 'This blind fellow! Sit down and sip your cup of tea!'

II

The Religion of the Prajñāpāramitā

1. *Where the Prajñā Functions*

The Prajñāpāramitā may be said to be standing on the line which divides the absolute aspect of existence from its relative aspect, and this line is a geometrical one just marking the boundary and having no dimension. Even then we must not conceive the Prajñā as looking this way or that way when it wants to survey the two realms of existence. If the Prajñā were to take Śūnyatā alone without its Aśūnyatā, or Aśūnyatā alone without its Śūnyatā, it would no more be Prajñā. To symbolize this, the Indian gods are furnished with one extra eye cut straight up between the two ordinary ones. This is the Prajñā-eye. By means of this third eye the enlightened are enabled to perceive Reality *yathābhūtam*, without splitting it into two and then unifying them, for this splitting and unifying is the work of abstract thinking. The Prajñā-eye, placing itself on the boundary line of Oneness and Manyness, of Śūnyatā and Aśūnyatā, of Bodhi and Kleśa, of Prajñā and Karuṇa, Buddha and Sarvasattva, Enlightenment and Ignorance, Samādhi and Karma, takes in these two worlds at a glance as one Reality. 'Prajñā is not on this side, nor on that side, nor in the middle; when it is subjected to discrimination, it is lost, it is no more there.'[1]

The intellect represents the Prajñā as sitting astride of the two realms of existence, but as far as the Prajñā itself is concerned it is not conscious of such a division, it goes on with its own experience. Śūnyatā is not felt to be something separate from a world of Saṁsāra, and the latter from Śūnyatā. When the Prajñā asserts itself, the two, Śūnyatā

[1] *Hsiao-p'in*, 58b.

and Saṁsāra, are drawn up in one string. Hitherto, we have given ourselves up too much to abstraction, the Prajñā has been coloured too pale, and as the result the entire universe has come to assume too indifferent an aspect—probably not satisfying enough to the needs of our heart. When the landscape is painted with one daub of Śūnyatā, there is no room for mountains, rivers, rocks, chrysanthemums, etc., in the canvas called the universe. If this be the case, the fault is our own and not the Prajñā's.

When we wish to make ideas more comprehensible, we generally translate them into spatial relations. And then we take these relations for realities, forgetting that the spatial representations are symbols. The manipulation of symbols is not the same as grasping the original. The Prajñā ought to be released from these static complications. The realm of Śūnyatā ought not to be severed from the world of particulars; for the severance is merely to facilitate the analytical intellect. When it has served its utility the sooner it is put aside the better. One of the reasons why the *Prajñāpāramitā* is so tiresomely repetitive is to impress the reader with the fact that Śūnyatā is not an abstraction but an experience, or a deed enacted where there is neither space nor time. When Śūnyatā and everything else is declared to be merely a name, it is to be so understood.

Further, all human activities, mental and physical, are carried on in time; or, at least, when we try to describe them they are set in the frame of time. Even when we talk of eternity or beginninglessness, the idea has the background of time. It is very difficult to get rid of this form of thinking, and especially is this the case when the Prajñā is to be properly understood. The following question undoubtedly comes from the notion that Prajñā or Saṁbodhi is a child of time, while the fact is that time starts from the awakening of Prajñā, and Prajñā is where there is yet neither time nor space.

'Subhūti: Is Saṁbodhi to be attained by the awakening of a preceding thought or by the awakening of a succeeding thought? If it is by the preceding one, this does not concord with the succeeding one. If it is by the succeeding one, this does not concord with the preceding one. And when there is no concordance between the two, how can a stock of merit be increased? [And also how is the attainment of Saṁbodhi possible?]'[1]

According to Subhūti, what we call mind is a succession of thoughts, it can be cut up into so many thoughts and arranged in time-form, i.e. in terms of priority and posteriority. When thoughts are supposed to succeed one another in time-sequence, what is it that links two thoughts together, as their concordance (*samavahita*) is otherwise not possible? In the absence of such concordance, how can one single thought of enlightenment be construed to pervade a whole series of thoughts, which by definition is a mind? This is the central point in Subhūti's question.

The Buddha illustrates this by means of a flame and says: The burning takes place not by a preceding flame, nor by a succeeding one; yet it is not separated from either. It goes on through the succession of flames. When it is taken by itself, there is no burning. When it is cut up into flames, it is difficult to conceive its successive burning. But in point of fact there is a suchness of burning. When experience is described in terms of birth-and-death, coming-to-exist and passing-away, going-ahead and following-after, it is no more there, the suchness of things slips out of one's grasp.

The Prajñā thus escapes all our intellectual efforts to pin it down in the loom of time. The process must be reversed if it is to be judiciously orientated. Instead of placing it somewhere in our scheme of thought-constructions, let us begin with the Prajñā itself as the starting point of all our activities and thoughts, and the whole text of the *Prajñāpāramitā* becomes intelligible. Time- and space-compli-

[1] *Aṣṭa*, p. 352; *Fo-mu*, 49b.

cations rise from the Prajñā in which there is yet neither time nor space. With its awakening we really live, and a world of particulars reveals itself before us with its problems. These preliminary remarks will probably help us to pass on to the second part of this Essay, in which what the Mahāyāna philosophers technically termed Upāya ('skilful means') will be discussed.

2. *Upāya ('Skilful Means')*

As long as our point of view is confirmed to the absolute aspect of the Prajñāpāramitā, we stop there and no room is left for us to make further advances. In this case there will be no more of Mahāyāna Buddhism, or of Bodhisattvahood. If all things are like a vision (*māyā*), one may reason, and if there is no reality whatever in them, how can a Bodhisattva make progress towards the attainment of Sarvajñatā (all-knowledge)? How can the nature of Sarvajñatā itself be established? How can there be any turning over of merit to the realization of Sarvajñatā? These are the questions naturally asked by one whose understanding of the Prajñāpāramitā is made to fit into the scheme of time-concept. Śāriputra's answer is as follows:[1]

'If all things were not like a vision but had something of reality in them, it would be impossible for the Bodhisattva to turn his merit towards the attainment of Sarvajñatā, or to make progress towards its realization. It is just because there is nothing real in all things, which are like a vision, that the Bodhisattva can turn his merit over to the attainment of Sarvajñatā and advance towards realization; it is just because he perceives the unreality and the vision-like character of all things that he endures and untiringly practises the virtue of strenuousness.

'What is the reason of this endurance, of this untiring strenuousness?

[1] *The Mahāprajñāpāramitā*, Hsüan-chuang, Fas. 587.

'It is owing to the operation of "skilful means" (*upāya-kauśalya*) which is born of the Bodhisattva's great compassionate heart for all sentient beings. Because of this skilful means he is told that all things are empty; and also because of this skilful means he does not attempt to realize in himself the truth of absolute solitude. It is like a man who, firmly holding a huge umbrella in his hands, stands at the top of a high mountain. He may bend himself and look down into the gaping abyss at the foot of the precipice, but he cherishes no fears, does not tremble at the thought of being swallowed up in the bowels of the earth; for he is supported by the umbrella, which, by the aid of the wind, keeps him from falling. In like manner, by virtue of Prajñā which sees into the nature of all things, by virtue of a compassionate heart which keeps him among his fellow-beings in this world of tribulations, the Bodhisattva disciplines himself in all the Pāramitās, by degrees making his progress towards Sarvajñatā, so that he is finally enabled to mature all beings, to benefit and bestow happiness on all beings, and to establish a Buddha-land.'

'Skilful means' (*upāyakauśalya*), or simply 'means' (*upāya*), has a technical sense in the teaching of the Mahāyāna. It is the creation of the great compassionate heart which the Bodhisattva has. When he perceives his fellow-beings drowning in the ocean of birth and death because of their ignorance and passionate clinging to a world of particulars, he awakens his great heart of love and compassion for them and contrives all kinds of means to save them, to enlighten them, to mature their consciousness for the reception of the ultimate truth. The 'means' grows out of the Bodhisattva's clear perception of the truth of Śūnyatā (emptiness), though not out of Śūnyatā itself. The truth as such remains powerless, it must go through the consciousness of the Bodhisattva; for beings of the two vehicles, the Śrāvaka and the Pratyekabuddha, are unconcerned with the welfare of their fellow-beings. They are content with the intellectual understanding of the truth, they abide with the truth of absolute solitude, they do not venture out of their cell of self-sufficiency. Therefore, there is no 'skilful means' with them. The 'means' cohabits with the intuition (*prajñā*) in the mind of the Bodhisattva. It is his intellectual insight, as it were, into the nature of things when he sees that they are not real, they are like Māyā, they are 'empty'; but his is more than this insight, more than the intellect, more than a cold indifferent surveying of a world of turmoil and suffering from the viewpoint of absolute solitariness or of eternal serenity. As he perceives that a world of particularities is like Māyā, he is not attached to it; but he knows that this world is right before him, because it is the stage where all his activities are performed, that is to say, where all his ignorant and egoistic fellow-beings are actually suffering and harassed to the extreme. Hence the Upāya growing out of the Prajñā.

The chain linked with Prajñā, Karuṇā, and Upāya goes through all the systems of Mahāyāna Buddhism. This linking is the most characteristic feature of it. So says the *Prajñāpāramitā*:[1] 'The Mahāyāna consists in the practice of the six Pāramitās, and this practice is characterized with the raising of mind in conformity with Sarvajñatā (all-knowledge). This raising is headed with a great compassionate heart, which creates "means" (*upāya*); and the means is characterized with non-attainment (*anupalambha*), [that is, with non-attachment]. All things inside and outside are given up for the sake of directing all beings towards Sarvajñatā. And this merit of giving up is performed not only by oneself but by others. . . .'

The thesis of the *Prajñāpāramitā* is that the realization of the Prajñā comes foremost in thoroughly comprehending the spirit of the Mahāyāna, which constitutes the life of the Bodhisattva (*bodhisattvacaryā*). When his mind (*citta* or *manasikāra*) is abiding in perfect conformity (*pratiyukta*) day and night with the Prajñāpāramitā, he becomes the benefactor (*dakṣinīyata*) of all beings; for it is then that a great compassionate heart (*maitrīsahagatam cittam*) is awakened in him towards all beings. With his penetrating insight into

[1] Hsüan-chuang, Fas. 413, Chapter 'On Samādhi'.

the nature of Prajñā, he perceives that all beings are held in leash and far from being free masters of themselves. He is seized with a great feeling of pity (*mahākaruṇā*). Being also endowed with a spiritual eyesight, he perceives beings suffering from the evil karma they have committed or entangling themselves in the net of falsehood. He is intensely agitated over these facts and firmly makes up his mind to the effect that he will be a protector of and a refuge (*nātha*) for the world and release it from the bondage of ignorance and passion.[1]

We can thus see that there is an inevitable relationship between Sarvajñatā, Prajñā, Karuṇā, Upāya, and Saṁbodhi or Moksha. Theoretically stated, Sarvajñatā is the outcome or content of Saṁbodhi which is realizable by Prajñā; but Prajñā in itself is unable to achieve any practical result, it operates through Upāya, and this Upāya is born of Karuṇā. The *Prajñāpāramitā* illustrates these relations with the following similes:[2]

'Subhūti, it is like a man taking himself out on the sea; after a while his boat is wrecked; if he does not take hold of a life-buoy, or a piece of board or wood, he is sure to be drowned in the water before he reaches his destination. Subhūti, in like manner a Bodhisattva may have faith in the supreme enlightenment (*anuttara-samyak-saṁbodhi*), may accept it whole-heartedly, may have a strong longing for it, may have an understanding of it, may be pleased with it, may find great joy in it, may aspire earnestly for it, may have confidence, resignation, assiduity, vigilance, pure thought regarding it. In spite of these virtues on his part, the Bodhisattva is unable to attain Sarvajñatā unless he is taken care of by Prajñā and Upāya. For he is sure to retrogress in the middle of his career. By "the middle of his career" is meant the stage of Śrāvakahood and Pratyekabuddhahood; by "retrogression" is meant the losing sight of Sarvajñatā.

'It is otherwise with the man who takes hold of a life-

[1] Abstract from *Fo-mu*, Fas, 20, Chapter 'On Good Friends'.

[2] *Fo-mu*, Fas. 14, Chapter 'On Similes' (*aupamya*). Generally, four similes are given, but two of them are quoted here.

buoy or a piece of board when his boat is wrecked, for he can safely attain the other shore; and also with the Bodhisattva who, with all his virtues of faith, understanding, etc., in the supreme enlightenment, is taken care of by Prajñā and Upāya; for he attains Sarvajñatā without stopping in the middle of his career at the stage of Śrāvakahood and Pratyekabuddhahood.'

To give another simile: Here is an old man one hundred and twenty years old; being assailed by all forms of illness, he is kept to his bed and patiently endures his pain; as to his getting up and walking a few miles, not to say anything of a very much longer distance, he is unable even to dream of such an undertaking. Here to him come two strong men and tell him to get up, for they will support him and carry him along the road to whatever end he wishes to reach. He follows their advice. Weak as he is, he finally attains his destination.

In a similar way, whatever confidence, delight, resignation, etc., a Bodhisattva may have in the supreme enlightenment, he cannot reach the other shore of Sarvajñatā, unless he is helped by the two strong men, Prajñā and Upāya; for these are the supporters of the Bodhisattva in his progressive career towards the goal of his life, and without them he will assuredly break down in the midst of his progress and sink into the level of Śrāvakahood and Pratyekabuddhahood. Why? Because this is the suchness of things.

3. *The Bodhisattva and the Śrāvaka*

As was stated elsewhere, what characteristically distinguishes the Bodhisattva from the Śrāvaka and the Pratyekabuddha is that while the former is concerned with the welfare, spiritual and material, of all beings, the latter are content with their own enlightenment or deliverance; they keep up their meditation undisturbed and do not go out of their cell, so that they can do something to relieve other fellow-beings of their karma, ignorance, and suffering. This spiritual egotism stands in great contrast to the self-sacrificing impulses of the Bodhisattva. As far as the enlightenment goes, both the Bodhisattva and the Śrāvaka may be on the same level, but the former is ready whenever necessary to come down from his supreme position and mix himself with his unenlightened, bespotted, karma-bound fellow-beings, and live their life too if there are opportunities to benefit them in one way or another. The Bodhisattva would therefore very frequently abandon the life of an ascetic, or a monk, or a hermit, in order to be in the world, to live with the world, to suffer its sufferings, and thereby to bring it to a state of final enlightenment. To be thus in a world of particulars and passions and to follow the laws that govern it (that is to say, 'not to obscure cause and effect')—this is the Bodhisattva's way of living, this is the 'being taken care of by Prajñā and Upāya'. Sarvajñatā comes out of that.

For this reason, we read throughout the *Prajñāpāramitā* that the motive which prompts the Bodhisattva to realize within himself the supreme enlightenment is not for his own benefit but for all beings; he wishes to raise them from the bondage of karma and ignorance so that they are finally established in Parinirvāṇa. This is the most difficult achievement, especially for the Bodhisattva who lives in the realm of birth-and-death (*saṁsāra*). He is thus warned not to relax in his vigilance, not to become frightened.

The Bodhisattva's desire is to benefit the world (*lokahita*), to give happiness to the world (*lokasukha*), to stir within himself a compassionate heart for the world (*lokānukampā*).

Therefore, when he realizes in himself the supreme enlightenment, he vows to become the world's great benefactor, protector, refuge, dwelling-house, ultimate path, isle of reteat, illumination, leader, and passage-way.[1]

Thus the Bodhisattva is no retiring, negative soul always wishing to flee from the world for his own perfection and enlightenment; but he is a most aggressive rescuer of the world; he positively works upon it to yield the result he

[1] Ibid., Fas. 14, Chapter 'On Wise Men'.

PLATE XXIX

SAMANTABHADRA AS A COURTESAN

By Ókyo Maruyama

That the Bodhisattva frequently incarnated himself as a courtesan is told in Japanese literature although the necessary connection historical or otherwise between Samantabhadra and a woman of this class is difficult to establish. So far as we know, Mañjuśrì never appeared in history in this form. He represents wisdom, and wisdom is not regarded generally as the specific quality of womankind. But why the courtesan Samantabhadra? The latter stands for the principle of love, essentially spiritual, but also carnal, for the latter leads up to the former when properly guided. This may be the reason for his transformation in this particular function.

The woman here was known in history as Eguchi at the time of Saigyò, the monk-poet of the Kamakura era. When Saigyò in his wanderings all over Japan came to a certain place near Osaka, it was already dark, and not finding any house where he could pass the night, he knocked at the gate where Eguchi resided. She refused to take him in, for she was all alone. Saigyò then sent in a poem:

"Before my renunciation of the world,
Hard-hearted you might be to me;
But now why should you deny me
A night's lodging in this life of unreality?"

But the lady was firm in her refusal and wrote to him this poem in return.

"Knowing you to be a man who renounced the world,
To this life of unreality,
I should only think of you,
As not cherishing any attachment."

This incident was later made use of by a composer of a No-play with the title "Eguchi." In this a monk-pilgrim visits the old site where Saigyo and Eguchi had their romantic interview. The spirit of the lady appears to him and complains of her not being understood by the world. Her refusal was really a kindness to the poet, and not a deed of harshness, for she thereby wished to protect his reputation. The spirit disappears. Then the monk-pilgrim hears a fine chorus of women's voices travelling over the waves of the Yodo. As he listens to it, the music seems to ascend heavenward, and he observes Samantabhadra on a white elephant and with a retinue of fairies disappearing among the multicoloured clouds.

PLATE XXX

BODHIDHARMA AND THE EMPEROR WU OF LIANG

By Sansetsu Kano

This historical interview has been told in my *Essay in Zen Buddhism*, First Series, p. 189, from which the following is quoted:

The Emperor Wu of Liang asked Dharma:

"Ever since the beginning of my reign I have built so many temples, copied so many sacred books, and supported so many monks and nuns; what do you think my merit might be?"

"No merit whatever, sire!" Dharma bluntly replied.

"Why?" demanded the Emperor astonished.

"All these are inferior deeds," thus began Dharma's significant reply, "which would cause their author to be born in the heavens or on this earth again. They still show the traces of worldliness, they are like shadows following objects. Though they appear actually existing, they are no more than mere non-entities. As to a true meritorious deed, it is full of pure wisdom and is perfect and mysterious, and its real nature is beyond the grasp of human intelligence. Such as this is not to be sought after by any worldly achievement."

The Emperor Wu thereupon asked Bodhi-Dharma again, "What is the first principle of the holy doctrine?"

"Vast emptiness, and there is nothing in it to be called holy, sire!" answered Dharma.

"Who is then that is now confronting me?"

"I know not, sire!"

wishes from his active contact with it. His self-assertion consists in cherishing the thoughts of sameness (*samam cittam utpadya*) and not the thoughts of discrimination (*viṣamacittam*) towards all beings, in holding thoughts of compassion (*maitracittam*), of benevolence (*hita*), of good friendship (*kalyāṇa*), of not hurting (*nihatamāna*), of non resistance (*apratihata*), of not-injuring (*avihiṁsā*), of not-harming (*aviheṭhanā*). The Bodhisattva will also regard all beings as his mother, father, sons, or daughters.[1] Maitrī (friendliness), Karuṇā (compassion), Anukampā (sympathy), and others are terms we most frequently come across in all the Mahāyāna sūtras; for to regard all beings with these thoughts is the one desire (*praṇidhāna*) all the Bodhisattvas most heartily cherish.

The following dialogue between Pūrṇamaitrāyaṇīputra and Śāriputra quoted from the *Mahāprajñāpāramitā*[2] gives us an idea as to the reason why the Bodhisattva feels compassionate towards his fellow-beings who are not fully enlightened. In the feeling of fellow-love there is no thought of superiority, no thought of separation or of exclusiveness, which keeps one from another as distinct in some fundamental and irreconcilable manner. The Bodhisattva, even when he is distinguishable from the Śrāvaka and the Pratyekabuddha and their discipline, motive, morality, attainment, and wisdom, entertains no sense of superiority; he is not at all inclined to think slightingly of others; he maintains his attitude of reverence towards all beings as possible Buddhas and Tathāgatas.

'Pūrṇamaitrāyaṇīputra asks Śāriputra: Should the Bodhisattva pay respect only to other Bodhisattvas and not to all beings generally?

'Śāriputra answers: The Bodhisattva should respect all beings just as much as he does the Tathāgata. He should respect all the Bodhisattvas and all sentient beings without making any distinction between them. For it is for the Bodhisattva to cultivate towards all beings the feeling of

[1] Ibid., Fas. 16, Chapter 'On Tathatā'; *Aṣṭa*, p. 321.
[2] Hsüan-chuang, Fas. 387, Chapter 12 'On Morality'.

humility and reverence and not to look upon them with arrogance. He should in fact revere them with the same feeling of self-abnegation as he does the Tathāgatas.

'The Bodhisattva is to think in this wise: When I attain enlightenment I will instruct all sentient beings in the essence of the Dharma in order to make them cut off their evil passions and realize Nirvāṇa, or attain enlightenment and rest in peace and happiness, or become fully emancipated from the pain of the evil paths.

'The Bodhisattva should thus awaken a great compassionate feeling towards all beings and keep his mind completely free from arrogance and self-conceit, and let him feel in this wise: I will practise all the skilful means (*upāya*) in order to make all sentient beings realize that which is the foremost in themselves, i.e. their Buddha-nature (*buddhatā*). By realizing this they all become Buddhas, and I will by virtue of the skilful means lead them to this final realization which entitles them to the rank of Dharmarāja. The Dharamarāja is the highest and most honourable position, for here one becomes master of all things (*dharma*).

'Therefore, let the Bodhisattva respect all sentient beings, let his compassionate feeling pervade all around, irrespective of its objects; for the Dharmakāya of the Tathāgata pervades all things. . . .'

4. *Śūnyatā Seen but Not Realized*

We know now that the complex of Prajñā, Karuṇā, and Upāya constitutes the career of the Bodhisattva, but here lies the fundamental mystery of human life which is too deep for the intellect to fathom. By this I mean that the mystery involves contradictions which philosophers have failed to reconcile. What the author of the *Prajñāpāramitā* attempts, therefore, is not to give a logical account of his experiences but to narrate them in the plainest words he can command. If there is anything incoherent about his accounts, it is due to the inherent nature of the experience, and it is our duty to endeavour to comprehend them by looking into the inmost recesses of our own consciousness. This means that the *Prajñāpāramitā* is to be read through our own life and experience and not by means of the intellect. When we watch earnestly, deeply, and with patience the workings of our soul, we see the sūtra unroll its contents before our own eyes. Whatever difficulties we formerly had will now be thoroughly dissolved. Logical entanglements and intellectual incomprehensibilities exist no more. It is like seeing an apple as apple. The fruit lies before us, we see it, we handle it, we can eat it and taste it sweet, we find it in every way satisfactory. The chemist, the botanist, the medical scientist, the agricultural expert, etc., may find in the apple many questions still unsolved and go on discussing them and experimenting with it; but the practical man of the world is satisfied with the actuality of things of which he is assured of himself, not depending on anybody else, or on some process of analysis and abstraction which always interferes with the immediacy of perception and feeling.

The following passages quoted from the chapter entitled 'Skilful Means' in the *Aṣṭasāhasrikā* are full of difficulties and complexities, and our imagination is charged to the utmost to unravel them successfully. But as they make up the very essence of the Bodhisattva's life, they are given below.

'If,' says the Buddha, 'the Bodhisattva wishes to practise Prajñāpāramitā, he should regard (*pratyavekṣitavyam*) all things[1] as empty by seeing into their nature with a steady, uninterrupted mind (*avikṣiptayā cittasantatyā*); but at the same time he may not realize Emptiness[2] within himself.'

In our ordinary way of thinking, this is an impossible situation: to see things as empty, to abide in the Samādhi of Emptiness, and yet not to realize Emptiness in oneself. How can this be possible?

To this, the Buddha replies: 'While the Bodhisattva sees

[1] That is, the five Skandhas: *Rūpam, Vedanā, Saṁjñā, Saṁskāra*, and *Vijñāna*.

[2] *Na śūnyatām sākṣātkaroti.*

(*pratyavekṣate*) that all things thoroughly contain within themselves the reason of Emptiness, he refuses to follow this reason up to its practical conclusion; for he knows that the time is for him to discipline himself in Emptiness and not to realize it in himself.'[1] Thus he stops short before he reaps the legitimate fruit of the Samādhi, does not unreservedly abandon himself into the midst of Emptiness. Being guarded by the virtue of Prajñāpāramitā, he, while not realizing Emptiness, does not neglect the practice of the factors of enlightenment, nor does he sink, by destroying all his passions, into the abode of absolute extinction. It is for this reason that the Bodhisattva, in his practice of the Samādhi of Emptiness which leads to final emancipation, does not give himself up to the unconditioned realization of Emptiness; and that, while abiding in the Samādhi of no-form (*animitta*), he does not give himself up to the unconditioned realization of no-form, nor does he abide in form. His knowledge is deep, and his accumulation of merit is perfect, and, being under the protection of the Prajñāpāramitā, he perceives that his life here now is meant for maturing himself and not for realization. Thus he keeps himself from stepping into the reality-limit (*bhūtakoṭi*).

This explanation does not seem to be quite sufficient and is therefore not quite convincing as far as the unenlightened are concerned. Hence the following parable in which the Bodhisattva's will and insight are illustrated:

Here is a man handsome in features and strong in prowess; he is active and strenuous; as a solider he is well versed in all the arts of fighting; as a gentleman he is intelligent, virtuous, and an expert in various fields of life; he is thus highly revered by all who know him. One day he has business to transact in a distant region; to reach there he has to travel through wild mountainous districts inhabited by bandits and outlaws. His parents, wife, children, and others accompanying him are afraid of an assault from these villainous brigands. But the man full of valour and wisdom tells them not to cherish any anxieties over their journey,

[1] *Parijayasyāyam kālo nāyaṁ kālaḥ sākṣātkriyāyā.* P. 370.

because he knows how to outwit these highwaymen and to carry his party safely and comfortably over the mountains and across the wildernesses. They feel at ease with his assurances. They finish the trip unmolested, and are comfortably settled at the destination. This is altogether due to the man's intelligence, wisdom, dauntless courage, and unparalleled firmness of mind.

In like manner, the Bodhisattva's compassionate heart is ever bent on benefiting all beings; he is always ready to practise pity, compassion, loving-kindness, joy, impartiality towards all beings; he is protected by the power of the Prajñāpāramitā (*prajñāpāramitayā parigṛihitaḥ*); he is furnished with the skilful means; he turns all his meritorious deeds over to the attainment of Sarvajñatā. For this reason, the Bodhisattva, while disciplining himself in emptiness, no-form (*animitta*), and no-desire (*apranihita*), stops short of realizing Bhūtakoṭi[1] in himself. He is not in this respect like the Śrāvaka and the Pratyekabuddha.[2] For his mind is always occupied with the welfare of all beings, wishing to see them attain the supreme enlightenment of Buddhahood.

That the Bodhisattva does not realize in himself the actuality of Emptiness even while disciplining himself in it is like the bird flying in the air. It neither remains in the air, nor does it fall on the ground. The Bodhisattva wishes to practise all the teachings of Buddhism for the sake of all beings, and as to the fruit of his life he waits for the proper time to enjoy it.

It is again like the shooting of one arrow after another into the air by a man whose mastery of archery has attained a very high degree. He is able to keep all the arrows in the air, making each arrow support the one immediately preceding. He does this as long as he wishes. The Bodhisattva seeks the supreme enlightenment, and, being protected by

[1] *Na tveva bhūtakoṭim sākṣātkaroṭi. Bhūtakoṭi* is used throughout the sūtra as a synonym of *śūnyatā*. It literally means 'reality-limit'. It has quite a modern note.

[2] Cf. the *Gaṇḍavyūha's* description of the two Yānas, as *bhūtakoṭīpratiṣṭhitā* and *atyantaśāntaniṣṭhāṁgatā*. See supra, pp. 94 f.

the power of Prajñāpāramitā, he does not retreat into the doing-nothingness of Bhūtakoṭi. He waits for it until all his works are accomplished, although his deep insight penetrates even into the emptiness of all things. His compassionate heart for all beings who are groping in the dark for the truth that will release them from ignorance and suffering, and his skilful means which is generated from this all-embracing love and sustains him throughout the long and arduous course of his Prajñāpāramitācaryā—these are the forces which determine Bodhisattvahood.

However this may be, there is no doubt that this is one of the greatest mysteries in the spiritual life of the Mahāyānist—to be living Emptiness, to be abiding in Emptiness, to be attaining the Samādhi of Emptiness, and yet not to realize the reality-limit within himself. The Buddha himself acknowledges that it is an achievement of the greatest difficulty, of the most extraordinary nature.[1] The mystery indeed lies in the Bodhisattva's cherishing the most wonderful vows that he will not abandon all beings, that he will deliver them from ignorance and suffering. All the mysteries and

[1] *The Aṣṭasāhasrikā*, p. 375. 'The Buddha then said to Subhūti: So it is, so it is! It is difficult indeed; it is of the utmost difficulty that the Bodhisattva Mahāsattva, training himself in Śūnyatā, abiding in Śūnyatā, and in the attainment of Śūnyatā-Samādhi, should not yet realize Reality-limit (*bhūtakoṭi*). Why? Because he has made most wonderful vows (*praṇidhānaviśesāḥ*) not to abandon all beings, but to lead them to final emancipation. Having made these vows, he enters upon the Samādhi of Emancipation as regards emptiness, formlessness, and desirelessness; but in the meantime he does not realize Reality-limit since he is fully equipped (*samanvāgata*) with Skilful Means. Protected by Skilful Means, he knows how far to go in the realization of Reality-limit before he fulfils all the Buddha-dharmas. His mind is firmly made up not to enjoy the fruit of his discipline in Śūnyatā until all beings are delivered from attachment and suffering.'

In another place (ibid., p. 28) we have this: 'Śāriputra asks Subhūti: If I understand you right, the Bodhisattva is unborn; being unborn how does he ever come to conceive and undertake such a hard thing as to benefit all beings? Subhūti answers: I should not like to have the Bodhisattva think this kind of work hard to achieve and hard to plan out. If he did, there are beings beyond calculation, and he will not be able to benefit them. Let him on the contrary consider the work easy and pleasant, thinking they were all his father and mother and children, for this is the way to benefit all beings whose number is beyond calculation.'

incomprehensibilities of the Buddhist life are traceable to this awakening in us of the desire for universal emancipation. When this is firmly established in the mind of the Bodhisattva, he is said to be at the stage of Avinivartanīya (no-turning-back).

Incidentally, it may be interesting to see what are the specific qualities of the Bodhisattva who has attained this stage of the Buddhist discipline; for the psychology of the dream is brought in very much here in the determination of the Bodhisattva-mentality. In fact, it is not the psychologist alone who will read deeply into one's Unconscious. The spirit also works through it from the far deeper source.

'The Buddha said to Subhūti: If a Bodhisattva shows no desire whatever even in a dream for the position of the Śrāvaka and the Pratyekabuddha, or if he harbours no thought of being born in the worlds which they are inhabiting, he is said to be at the stage of Avinivartanīya. . . .

'If a Bodhisattva sees himself in a dream as sitting in the air and preaching to people, as emitting rays of light from his body and going around in the form of a Bhikshu in the other Buddha-lands in order to carry out works of Buddhism such as preaching, etc., he is said to be at the stage of Avinivartanīya. . . .

'If a Bodhisattva sees in a dream scenes of a hell where all beings are suffering all forms of pain, and having seen them, makes his mind up to attain supreme enlightenment, and by this attainment to keep the Buddha-land clean of all impurities and evil passions so that even the name of hell will be unheard of in his land, he is said to be at the stage of Avinivartanīya. . . .'[1]

The ever-recurring questions which rise while reading the *Prajñāpāramitā* are: How can the Prajñā which sees into the absolute aspect of all things known as Emptiness be made to generate out of itself Karuṇā and Upāyakauśalya, which have their meaning in a world of particulars only? How can the Bodhisattva whose wings are always soaring high up to the realm of Sarvajñatā be made to hover around

[1] *Fo-mu*, 43ab.

this earth filled with sufferings, iniquities, follies? More than that, how can he come to suspend his final flight which brings him to the ultimate goal of his discipline because his heart is called back to the welfare of his fellow-beings and he does not wish to abandon them to their own karma-hindrances? How can his eyesight be made to look in two opposite directions? According to the *Prajñāpāramitā*, he accomplishes this mystery just because he is ever aspiring after Prajñā and Sarvajñatā and disciplining himself in it.

And 'this is not difficult', according to Subhūti, although it has been so pronounced elsewhere. 'What is most difficult is to lead all beings, in number beyond calculation, and to make them safely abide in Mahāparinirvāṇa. The Bodhisattva wears the armour of energy and strenuousness. But beings (*sarvasattva*) are characterized like space with solitude (*viviktatva*) and unattainability (*anupalabdhatā*); they are ultimately unknowable.[1] The Bodhisattva, however, is not frightened to learn it, he is not taken aback, he is by no means depressed or dejected; for he is disciplining himself in the Prajñāpāramitā. . . . For he who is in the practice of the Prajñā gives the evil spirits no opportunities to interfere with his work if he observes two things: (1) Seeing into the truth that all things are empty, and (2) Never abandoning all beings.' Evidently there is no way to reconcile this contradiction except by unflinchingly leaping down into the abyss of Śūnyata itself.

5. *Some of the Significant Opposites*

The *Prajñāpāramitā* thus offers to us a set of opposites out of which we are to draw a higher synthesis, not by logical cleverness, but by actually living the life of the Bodhisattva who walks the way to Sarvajñatā. Some of the significant opposites may be formulated as follows:

(*a*) *Prajñā or Sarvajñatā versus Karuṇā or Upāya.* This

[1] *Te ca sattvā atyantatayā na saṁvidyante.—The Aṣṭasāhasrikā,* p. 445.

antithesis is fundamental in the *Prajñāpāramitā* and also in all the other teachings of Mahāyāna Buddhism. The contrast is, however, conceptual, and, therefore, superficial, as in all other cases; for in the actual life of a Bodhisattva this opposition is not felt and offers no obstruction in the execution of all the Buddha works. Or we may say that one is a Bodhisattva when these apparently contradicting notions disappear from one's religious consciousness. For instance, we read in the sūtra:[1]

'To practise Prajñā means to practise Sarvajñatā, which in turn means realizing Tathatā. For the title "Tathāgata" means one who has realized Tathatā, suchness of all things. And in this Suchness (*tathatā*) there is neither extinction (*kṣaya*), nor birth (*utpāda*), nor disappearance (*nirodha*), nor rising (*janaka*), nor manifesting (*vibhāvana*), nor defilement (*raja*), nor freedom from defilement, nor existing like space, nor being in any state. And yet in practising this Prajñā the Bodhisattva perfects his own virtues, affords a refuge for others, and performs all that comes forth from a loving compassionate heart, a joyous spirit, and a great charitable feeling towards all beings. Not only this, the Bodhisattva helps others to discipline themselves in the way of emancipation, and keeps the family of the Tathāgata in continuous prosperity. . . .'

(*b*) *Practising Dhyāna and yet Refusing its Fruits.*[2] 'Disciplining himself in the Prajñā, the Bodhisattva refuses to be born in the various heavens according to the various Dhyānas, in which he is a thorough adept. This is by virtue of the skilful means (*upāyakauśalya*) inborn of the Prajñā, for it is the Upāya that keeps him from giving himself up to the enjoyment of the heavenly pleasures. Adepts in the Dhyānas are destined to be born in the celestial abodes, where, free from worldly cares, they are recipients of all kinds of untainted pleasures. But the Bodhisattva has no

[1] *Fo-mu*, 59b (Hsüan-chuang, Fas. 552, 56b ff.; Kumārajīva, 77ab). Hsüan-chuang's version differs widely from the other two in that it negates what the latter affirm. I have drawn my own conclusion.

[2] Hsüan-chuang, Fas. 552, 57b (*Fo-mu*, 60a; *Hsiao-p'in*, 77b).

desire to leave this world of suffering where his fellow-beings are still kept in bondage. To be in the world, of the world, and yet not to be tainted by it—this is the Bodhisattva's discipline. In spite of his worldly life he is fully endowed with the purities.

'Subhūti asks: If all things are in their original nature pure and free from defilements—which is the Buddha's teaching—how does the Bodhisattva in any special sense attain the purities as if he were not by nature pure?

'The Buddha answers: Yes, all things, as you say, are primarily pure, and the Bodhisattva disciplining himself in this purity—which is the Prajñā—realizes all things pertaining to it. This is the Upāya inherent in and born of the Prajñā. He sees into this reality as it is, and is free from fright and despondency.'

(*c*) *The Bodhisattva versus the Śrāvaka.* In all the Mahāyāna texts this opposition is made the most of, for the life of the Bodhisattva stands sharply against that of the Śrāvaka. The latter is ready to quit this world for his own enlightenment and emancipation, he is willing to lend his ear to the advice of Māra the Tempter who would tell him: 'The heavenly pleasures are of the most exquisite and transcendent nature, and cannot be compared with those of this world which is characterized with transiency, suffering, emptiness, and dissolution. Train yourself so as to enjoy the fruits of the various religious disciplinary measures, so as not to suffer the karma of rebirth on this earth.' The course of the Bodhisattva is, however, otherwise destined, he wants to remain with us, to do something for us. Disciplining himself in the Prajñā, he accepts every spiritual advantage accruing from the life of the Śrāvaka, but rejects the idea of forever abiding with its fruits. He knows that the Prajñā is the mother of all the Buddhas and Bodhisattvas, and that what constitutes the reason of Buddhahood is Sarvajñatā, and further that Sarvajñatā is Prajñā and Prajñā is Sarvajñatā because each is born of the other.[1] Knowing this, he devotes himself to the study of the

[1] See Kumārajīva, 60b, 63b, 64b, 78b, etc.

Prajñā. But he never thinks of himself as studying and disciplining himself in the Prajñā, nor does he think that his study and discipline will bring him to the realization of the Prajñā. His Prajñā-life consists in neither seeing, nor hearing, nor thinking of, nor being conscious of, the Prajñā; for this is truly practising it, studying it, and disciplining himself in it.

Why? Because when you think, 'This is my mind', 'I am conscious of this', 'I take hold of the mind', etc., the Prajñā is no more there, for the Prajñā is no-mind (*acitta*).[1]

(*d*) *Realities versus Māyā.* Superficially, the Prajñāpāramitā seems to deny realities, declaring them to be Māyā-like existences; and Śūnya and Māyā are taken as synonymous. In the understanding of the sūtra this is perhaps one of the most difficult points, as has been repeatedly pointed out.

According to the Sūtra,[2] all things are Māyā, the five Skandhas are Māyā, since all things have no hindrances, i.e. no self-substance. Not only all things are Māyā, but the Buddha-dharmas are Māyā, Nirvāṇa is Māyā; even when there is something surpassing Nirvāṇa, it is Māyā; there is no distinction whatever between one thing and another (*sarvadharma*) including Nirvāṇa and Māyā. However this may be, Māyā is not to be understood in the sense of illusion or unreality as when we say that all is a dream. The Buddhist sense of Māyā is that the Prajñā is to be found neither in the five Skandhas nor away from it, that it is to be sought for 'where Subhūti moves about'. As long as the world is statically conceived, it has no reality behind it, it is Māyā; the world must be grasped as it 'moves about', as it becomes, as it passes from one state of being to another. When this movement is arrested, there is a corpse. When movement is thought of as something distinct by itself and apart from the things in which it is conceived as manifested it loses all its significance. To understand this, *yathābhūtam*, is Prajñā.

Most people are frightened when they are told that the

[1] Ibid., 46b. [2] Ibid., 47, 49a, and elsewhere.

world is illusion, and imagine that if it is so their life is of no value and they can do anything they like and are not responsible for their deeds. This is one of the greatest misinterpretations of the Māyā theory. When the Mahāyānists make this announcement, they do not mean to ignore certain laws regulating the Māyā. Even when all is Māyā there are laws in it, and nothing in it can escape them; all must conform to them. The Māyā does not release anybody in it from being controlled by them. Only those who have found a realm of reality in the Māyā, and yet are not conditioned by it, can be masters of it and its laws. That all is Māyā can be declared by such seers of the truth and by no others.

The Mahāyānists are, therefore, those who, in conformity with the truth of Śūnyatā, abide in the Prajñā, refusing to find their foothold in Rūpam, Vedanā, Saṁjñā, Saṁskāra, and Vijñāna, neither in a world of Saṁskritas nor in a world of Asaṁskritas. This abode is called an abode in which there is no abode. For this reason, abiding in the Prajñā must mean not abiding in it; to abide in the Prajñāpāramitā in any other sense means to have a fixed point of attachment, and this is to be avoided if one wishes to be the free master of oneself. When a point is fixed anywhere, even in the Prajñā, this has a binding effect on us, and we cease to be independent intellectually, morally, and spiritually. The *Prajñāpāramitā* thus teaches us to wipe off every possible point of fixture or reference in our consciousness. When a world of no references is obtained, this is a no-abode, or abiding in Śūnyatā. The Buddha or the Bodhisattva gives out his teaching from this abode of no references; therefore, in them there is nobody teaching, nothing taught, and no audience listening. This is the meaning of the Māyā.[1]

(*e*) *Prajñā versus Discrimination.* As soon as a thought that discriminates arises (*saṁjñāsyate*) we leave the Prajñā behind, we separate ourselves from the Prajñā.[2] Discrimination (*vikalpa*) or the awakening of consciousness is the destroyer of the Prajñā, it puts a stop to the triumphant

[1] See ibid., 49a, etc.

[2] *Aṣṭa*, pp. 189–190.

course of the latter. Discrimination is no doubt born of the Prajñā, for without it Saṁjñā itself is impossible. The only trouble with it is that it asserts itself at the expense of Prajñā. It takes no notice of Prajñā, in spite of the fact that its function prevails because of Prajñā. This one-sidedness is so characteristic of Saṁjñā that the latter always stands contrasted to Prajñā, and causes attachment (*saṁga*) to exercise its baneful influence over the entire field of consciousness. Discrimination itself is harmless, but when it is coupled with attachment—and this coupling takes place inevitably in all consciousness—it does a great deal of harm. So says the sūtra, 'Because of name (*nāma*) there is attachment; because of form (*nimitta*) there is attachment.' Naming is discrimination, so is recognizing form, and from this naming and recognizing there arises attachment. Intellection and conation always go hand in hand.

'When you declare Rūpam to be empty, this is attachment (*saṁga*). When you declare Vedanā, Saṁjñā, Saṁskāra, and Vijñāna to be empty, this is attachment. When you declare dharmas of the past, present, and future as belonging to the past, present, and future, this is attachment. When you recognize yourself to be a Bodhisattva in whom the desire for enlightenment has for the first time been awakened and who thereby has succeeded in accumulating so much merit, this is attachment. When you recognize yourself to be a Bodhisattva of long standing in whom much more merit has already been stored up, this is attachment.'[1]

Therefore, to practise the Prajñā means not to practise according to Rūpam, Vedanā, Saṁjñā, Saṁskāra, and Vijñāna, but to practise it as if practising nothing. Practising is doing something, and yet to be doing nothing—this is the Upāya born of Prajñā, this is the way the Mahāyānists describe the Bodhisattva's life as *sasaṁgatā cāsaṁgatā*, i.e. 'attached and not attached'. When this state of consciousness in which neither discrimination nor attachment obtains, the depths of Prajñāpāramitā are said to have been fully sounded.

[1] Ibid., p. 190; *Fo-mu*, 25b.

For this reason it is inevitable that Prajñā has come to be be defined in self-contradicting terms, and finally declared to be beyond the sphere of relative knowledge. The following are some of the terms we encounter everywhere in the *Prajñāpāramitā*, all of which tend to show that there is a deep cleavage between the intellect and the Prajñā experience: (1) Incomprehensible (*acintyā*); (2) Difficult to understand (*duranubodhā*); (3) Isolated [from all knowledge] (*viviktā*); (4) Not at all intelligible (*na kaścid abhirambudhyate*); (5) Not to be known by the intellect, not accessible to the intellect (*na cittena jñātavyā, na cittagamanīyā*); (6) Not a thing made (*akṛtā*), because no maker is obtainable (*kārakānupalabdhitaḥ*); (7) What is regarded as the original nature (*prakṛti*) of all things, that is no no-nature (*aprakṛti*), and what is *aprakṛti* that is *prakṛti*; (8) All things are characterized with oneness (*ekalakṣaṇa*), which has the nature of no-character (*alakṣaṇa*).

A quotation from a chapter in the *Mahāprajñāpāramitā*[1] will conclude this part of the Essay:

'Śāriputra asked Subhūti: When the Bodhisattva-Mahāsattvas practise the Prajñā, does this mean that they practise something which is firmly fixed (*sāra*) or something which is not firmly fixed?

'Subhūti said: They practise something which is not firmly fixed, and not something which is firmly fixed. Why? Because in the Prajñāpāramitā as well as in Sarvadharma (all things) there is nothing firmly fixed. Why? Because when the Bodhisattva-Mahāsattvas practise the deep Prajñāpāramitā, they do not perceive in it as well as in Sarvadharma even that which is not firmly fixed, much less anything that is firmly fixed and attainable.

'At that time there was a present a numberless crowd of the heavenly beings from the world of Kāma and from the world of Rūpa, and they thought: Those beings belonging to the Bodhisattva-vehicle cherish the desire for supreme enlightenment, practise the Prajñāpāramitā whose deep signification is beyond measure. Yet they do not in them-

[1] Hsüan-chuang, Fas. 558, 61a.

selves realize the reality-limit (*bhūtakoṭi*), thereby keeping themselves away from the state of the Śrāvaka and the Pratyekabuddha. For this reason, those Bodhisattvas are wonderful beings, they set for themselves a task most difficult to accomplish. Deep reverence is to be paid to them. Why? Because although they practise the truth of all things, they do not in themselves realize the reality-limit.

'Knowing what thought was being cherished by those heavenly beings, Subhūti then said: That those beings of the Bodhisattva-vehicle do not in themselves realize the reality-limit so as not to fall into the state of the Śrāvaka and the Pratyekabuddha is not anything so wonderful and difficult to accomplish.

'What is most wonderful and difficult to accomplish with the Bodhisattvas is this: even though they fully know that all things and all sentient beings, in their ultimate nature, are not to be regarded as being and attainable, they raise the desire for supreme enlightenment for the sake of all beings, innumerable and immeasurable; and, putting on the armour of strenuousness (*vīrya*), they bend all their efforts towards the salvation of all beings so that the latter will all be led finally to Nirvāṇa.

'This is indeed like attempting to put vacuity of space under discipline. Why? Because vacuity of space is by nature transcendental (*vivikta*), empty (*śūnya*), and not firmly fixed (*asāra*), and to be regarded as not being (*na saṁvidyate*); and so are all sentient beings transcendental, empty, not firmly fixed, and to be regarded as not being. And yet the Bodhisattvas attempt to convert all beings and lead them to final Nirvāṇa.

'They put on the armour of great vows (*mahāpraṇidhāna*) in order to benefit all beings, to discipline all beings. And yet they are fully aware of the truth that all beings as well as their great vows are in their ultimate nature transcendental, empty, not firmly fixed, and to be regarded as not being. With this knowledge, they are not at all frightened, or depressed, or mortified. They thus practise the deep Prajñāpāramitā. . . .'

III

Recapitulation

We are now in a position to summarize what has been stated as constituting the principal teachings of the *Prajñā-pāramitā*:

1. The object of the discourse is to exhort and extol the practice of the Prajñā.

2. The Prajñā is one of the six Pāramitās. Being the mother-body from which all the Buddhas and the Bodhisattvas issue, it is the vivifying spirit of all the other Pāramitās. Without it the latter remain inactive, are not at all productive of meritorious works.

3. The Prajñā leads us to the attainment of all-knowledge or Sarvajñatā, which makes up the reason of Buddhahood. Sarvajñatā is used synonymously with Prajñā. For it is from the Prajñā that Buddhas of the past, present, and future are born, and it is from Sarvajñatā that the Prajñā is born.

4. By means of the Prajñā the Bodhisattva sees into the nature of all things which is empty (*śūnya*).

5. Emptiness does not mean the state of mere nothingness. It has a positive meaning, or rather it is a positive term designating the suchness of things (*tathatā*). In a sense Tathatā and Śūnyatā are interchangeable notions.

6. Bhūtakoṭi is one of the technical terms used in all the Mahāyāna texts. It is here translated 'reality-limit', *bhūta* = reality, and *koṭi* = limit or end. As it is often used synonymously with Śūnyatā, it means the ultimate end of all realities. If Śūnyatā is identified with the Absolute, Bhūtakoṭi is also another term for the Absolute. It has a cold intellectual ring. Śrāvakas and Pratyekabuddhas are supposed, according to the Mahāyānists, to be finally so absorbed into it as to find their eyes wholly closed to the sufferings of their fellow sentient beings. They realize

Bhūtakoṭi. But the Bodhisattva refuses to identify himself with the Absolute, for the identification puts a stop to the pulsations of his heart which feels for a world of particulars and iniquities. In other words, with the eye of absolute purity he perceives the Tathatā (suchness) of all things, which is Śūnyatā, but keeps his other eye open, seeing into multiplicities, i.e. the world of ignorance and suffering. Technically, this is known as 'not realizing Bhūtakoṭi (reality-limit) within oneself'.[1]

7. Why and how can the Bodhisattva achieve this wonder—to be in it and yet not to be in it? This contradiction is inherent in the Prajñā, for the Prajñā is not only an intellectual seeing into the emptiness of things but an emotional plunging into realities as they appeal to the will. The Prajñā is thus found unifying in itself the seeing and the feeling. The feeling aspect is known as being 'skilful in means' (*upāyakauśalya*). The Prajñā harbours in it the Upāya that works out a complete scheme of salvation for all sentient beings. This logic of contradiction is what may be called the dialectics of Prajñā.

8. This Prajñā dialectics prevails through the entire system of Mahāyāna thought. The Bodhisattva being a living spirit lives this dialectics in his so-called Prajñāpāramitācaryā. This is his life (*caryā*), not mere behaviour conventionally regulated according to the logic of the philosopher. The two contradicting principles, Prajñā and Karuṇā, are found harmoniously living in the person of a Bodhisattva. This is the main teaching of the *Prajñāpāramitā*.

9. Readers are apt to make more of the philosophy of Śūnyatā or Tathatā than of the practical moral aspect of it. This in fact has been the case with some Buddhist scholars. But we must never close our eyes to the meaning of Praṇidhāna, the Bodhisattva's vow to enlighten and benefit all his fellow-beings. The Praṇidhāna is frequently lost sight of because of the too startling nature of the Śūnyatā. The Śūnyatā, however, is the chief qualification of the Hīna-

[1] *Aṣṭa*, p. 373. *Na bhūtakoṭiṁ sākṣātkaroti.*

yāna, and in this the latter is, according to all the Mahāyāna texts, placed in diametrical opposition to the Bodhisattva ideal.

10. When Sarvadharma or existence generally is regarded as empty and unattainable, all the means and vows which are cherished by the Bodhisattva seem to be really 'like waging war against the sky or vacuity of space (*ākāśa*)'. This idea is quite frightening or at least very depressing. Frightening because all our moral strivings seem to come to naught; depressing because, in spite of the vows and means, all the ignorance and suffering in the world are Māyā-like phenomena and do not substantially yield to the Bodhisattva's skilful treatment. This is the mystery of the religious life, that is, of the Prajñā life.

11. The Bodhisattva lives this mystery, which is regarded in the *Prajñāpāramitā* as *āścaryam*, as marvellous. His eye turns in two opposite directions, inwardly and outwardly; so does his life proceed in two opposite directions, that is, in the direction of Śūnyatā and in the direction of Sarvasattva (all beings). He does not immerse himself in the ocean of eternal tranquillity; if he does, he is no more a Bodhisattva; he somehow keeps himself on the wavy surface of the ocean, allowing himself to suffer the fate of an aspen leaf on the turbulent waters. He does not mind subjecting himself to the tyranny of birth-and-death (*saṁsāra*); for he knows that thereby he can be a good friend to all his fellow-beings who are also like him tormented and harassed to the extreme.

12. This Prajñāpāramitācaryā of the Bodhisattva corresponds to the *Laṇkāvatāra's* Anābhogacaryā. In both there is no thought of accumulating merit for oneself, every good performed by the Bodhisattva is turned over (*pariṇāmana*) to the general attainment by all beings of Sarvajñatā or Anuttara-samyak-saṁbodhi; but even in this he has no conscious feeling of elation, he cherishes no thought of having achieved something praiseworthy. This is also known as the life of no-discrimination (*avikalpa*), or, we may say, the life of the lilies of the field.

13. To understand the *Prajñāpāramitā* we must entirely abandon what may be called the 'this side' view of things, and go over to the 'other side' (*pāram*). The 'this side' view is where we generally are, that is, where a world of particulars and discrimination extends. The shifting of this position to the 'other side' of Śūnyatā, Tathatā, Viviktā, and Sarvajñatā is a revolution in its deepest sense. It is also a revelation. The *Prajñāpāramitā* reviews all things from this new position. No wonder that its expressions and demonstrations are full of paradoxes or irrationalities. Nothing else could be expected.

14. When this revolution is not complete, our position involves many complexities from which it is difficult to extricate ourselves. Because when we are imagining a complete about-facing, our legs are still carrying the ancient dust; each time we try to walk, the path of absolute purity (*atyantaviśuddhi*) is found bespotted. By this it is meant that the reasoning and wording we resort to are ever remindful of the 'this side' view. We are caught in the net we have ourselves set up. The *Prajñāpāramitā*, therefore, uses every possible cleverness to keep us away from this self-working snare. The *Aṣṭasāhasrikā*, 'the sūtra of 8,000 verses', has thus developed into the *Śatasāhasrikā*, 'the sūtra of 100,000 verses'.

15. One of the reasons why all these sūtras are so repetitious, so full of reiterations which are tiring to us modern readers, is due to the fact that all the Mahāyāna sūtras, especially the *Prajñāpāramitā*, are not meant to appeal to our reasoning faculties, that is, to our intellectual understanding, but to a different kind of understanding, which we may call intuition. When the *Prajñāpāramitā* is recited in Sanskrit or Chinese or Tibetan, without trying to extract its logical meaning, but with a devotional turn of mind and with the determination to go through masses of repetitions, the Prajñā-eye grows gradually more and more penetrating. Finally, it will see, through all the contradictions, obscurities abstractions, and mystifications, something extraordinarily transparent which reveals the 'other side' together with 'this

side'. This is the awakening of the Prajñā and the study of the deep Prajñāpāramitā. Herein lies the secret of the sūtra-recitation.

16. The mystery of 'not realizing Bhūtakoṭi although deeply immersed in it' may thus become comprehensible. As long as we are on 'this side', it is impossible to carry two diametrically opposed and mutually exclusive ideas; if we have a thing, we cannot not-have it; if we do a thing, we cannot not-do it; having and not-having, doing and not-doing, being and not-being—they exclude each other. Between these two sets of thoughts there is an impassable chasm. The Bodhisattva, however, has crossed this chasm and is setting himself on the 'other side', which is the realm of Tathatā. He finds here that things formerly impossible to accomplish are readily accomplished as if they were nothing extraordinary. There is a spade in his hands and yet the tilling of the ground is done by him empty-handed. He is riding on the back of a horse and yet there is no rider in the saddle and no horse under it. He passes over the bridge, and it is not the water that flows, but the bridge. The Śrāvaka still stays in spite of his realization on 'this side', and therefore his realization is something quite distinct from his experience. The very idea of Śūnyatā hinders his really living it. With the Bodhisattva Śūnyatā ceases to be Śūnyatā. He is just living his life, and is no more troubled with Śūnyatā and Aśūnyata, with Nirvāṇa and Saṁsāra, with Saṁbodhi and Avidyā. This is what is termed in the *Prajñāpāramitā* 'not realizing Bhūtakoṭi although already in the Samādhi of Śūnyatā'. And it is one of the most characteristic attitudes of the Bodhisattva towards existence.

17. That, by virtue of Upāya which is inherent in the Prajñā, the Bodhisattva suffers the miseries of birth and death with the rest of his fellow-beings is the description of his actual life. And it is because of this actual suffering on the part of the Bodhisattva that he is able to know what life means and what pain means. If not for this actual living, all his 'skilful means' would be no more than mere abstraction and productive of no effects whatever. His vows, too,

could not go beyond mere earnest wishing. In this connection reference may be made to the 'original vows' of the Bodhisattva Dharmākara, which constitute the foundations of the Pure Land teaching. The main idea expressed in those vows is that the Bodhisattva would not attain supreme enlightenment until all beings were also ready to cross over to the 'other side'. As he has disciplined himself for so many kalpas in all the Buddhist disciplines, he is fully qualified for the final attainment. But he cannot make up his mind to leave all his suffering fellow-beings behind. So he refrains in the meantime from enjoying the fruit of his work. This is exactly the position of the *Prajñāpāramitā* Bodhisattva, in fact of all the Bodhisattvas, as distinguished from the Śrāvakas and the Pratyekabuddhas.

18. The differentiation of Bodhisattvahood means that Buddhism has abandoned its ascetic monasticism. A religion which was perilously near to the point of appealing to the *élite* only has now been rescued from this exclusive aristocratic spirit, which is not at all in correspondence with the spirit of the founder. Although the teaching of Pariṇāmana is not quite definitely formulated in the *Prajñāpāramitā*, the idea already has its distinctive note here; for it is something inseparable from the secularization and democratization of so-called primitive Buddhism. The Bodhisattva-ideal is most intimately connected with the social development of the religious consciousness. The possibility of one's merit being turned over to others presupposes the fellowship of all beings. The social nature of the Mahāyāna is thus strongly reflected in the doctrine of Pariṇāmana.

19. The *Prajñāpāramitā* points out in what the detached life (*viviktaviharā*) of the Bodhisattva really consists. With the Śrāvakas, to be detached means to keep themselves away from the world, from city life, from living in society with other fellow-beings; so they fly away from the crowd, live in the wilderness where they think they are safe from worldly entanglements.[1] But the detached life of those who

[1] Ibid., p. 394 (*Fo-mu*, 55a).

practice the Prajñāpāramitā means to practise a great compassionate heart and loving-kindness towards his fellow-beings by living with them, among them, and for them. Mere physical detachment does not mean anything. The Bodhisattva is detached when he sees the Śūnyatā of all things. As far as his living is concerned, democratization sums up its essence.

20. With this spirit strenuously and persuasively inculcated by devotees of the Prajñāpāramitā, Mahāyāna Buddhism has spread all over Asia. It is doubtful if Buddhism in its so-called primitive form would have been able to accomplish this. The six Pāramitās are really the Mahāyāna categories of life, and followers of the Prajñāpāramitā have singled out this Prajñā category in order to give the six Pāramitās a directing unifying principle. Charity, morality, patience, strenuousness, and tranquillization have now come to have a definite meaning attached to their execution.

21. Mystic trends have no doubt been encouraged by the propagation of the Prajñāpāramitā teaching, especially in China. What is essential in religion is life and not philosophy, and this life—which means in Mahāyāna the life of the Bodhisattva (*bodhisattvacaryā* or *prajñāpāramitācaryā*)—is a great mystery. And when a man faces this mystery one day in his life, he is filled with the mystic sense which goes utterly beyond intellection. Its logical expression being impossible, the treatment of the subject is finally delivered up to the hands of the Zen master.

There are more topics which I wish to expound in the *Prajñāpāramitā*, but as I trust the foregoing has given the reader a general idea of what the sūtra purports to state, let me conclude this part again with quotations from the Zen masters, hoping that they will also illustrate the mysticism of the Prajñāpāramitā doctrine:

A scholar once came to Mu-chou[1] and the latter asked:

[1] See under Bokuju, *Zen Essays*, Series I, and Mu-chou, *Zen Essays*, Series II.

'I am told that you can discourse on seven sūtras and śastras; is that so?'

Scholar: 'Yes, master.'

Mu-chou without a word raised his staff and struck him.

Scholar: 'If not for you, master, I might have wasted my life.'

Mu-chou: 'What do you mean?'

The scholar was about to open his mouth when another blow was delivered by the master.

Scholar: 'I thank you for your repeated courtesy.'

Mu-chou: 'You talk wisely, but your monkhood is far from being finished.'

A scholar asked Nan-yang:[1] 'What is transmitted in your school?'

The master proposed a counter-question: 'What is transmitted in your school?'

Scholar: 'My transmission consists in the three sūtras and five śastras.'

Master: 'Indeed! You are a lion's son.'

The scholar respectfully bowed and was at the point of departure when the master called him back, saying: 'O scholar!'

The scholar responded: 'Yes, master.'

The master said: 'What is that?'

The scholar gave no reply.

Kuang-hui Lien asked a scholar: 'I am told that you are an expert in the three sūtras and the five śastras. Is that so?'

Scholar: 'Yes, master.'

The master held up his staff and asked: 'How do you discourse on this?'

The scholar hesitated, whereupon Kuang-hui struck him.

Scholar: 'How impatient you are!'

Master: 'O you humbug scholar who lives on others' drivellings! What did you say?'

The scholar made no reply.

[1] See under 'Chu the National Teacher' in my *Zen Essays*, Series I.

The master told him to come up nearer, which he did. Kuang-hui drew a line on the ground and said: 'Does this appear in the sutras or in the śastras?'

Scholar: 'No reference in the sūtras, nor in the śastras.'

Master: 'An iron bar with no hole! Go back to the Hall!'

The scholar-monk came up again to the master after some time and saluted him.

Master: 'Where do you come from?'

Scholar: 'I have already finished my salutation.'

Master: 'What do you think this place is? O this fellow!'

So saying, the master kicked him down. As soon as he regained his footing he exclaimed: 'I understand, I understand!'

The master took hold of him and said: 'This devil, what do you say? Speak out without delay!'

The scholar gave the master a slap.

The master still demanded: 'This purblind scholar, what do you mean by acting so? Speak again!'

The scholar reverently made a bow.

Concluded the master: 'Unless the son does not do better than his father the family dies out in one generation.'

The monk Fu, of T'ai-yüan,[1] was first a Buddhist scholar. When he was lecturing on the *Parinirvāṇa Sūtra* while in Yang-chou, a Zen monk happened to stay in his temple and attended the lecture. Fu began discoursing on the Dharmakāya, which incidentally evoked the Zen monk's laugh. Afterwards Fu invited the monk to tea and asked: 'My scholarship does not go very far, but I know I have faithfully expounded the meaning in accordance with the literary sense. Having seen you laugh at my lecture, I realize that there must have been something wrong. Be pleased to give me your kind instruction in this.'

The Zen monk said: 'I simply could not help laughing at the time, because your discourse on the Dharmakāya was not at all to the point.'

Fu asked: 'Where am I wrong?'

[1] See also Second Series of *Zen Essays*, pp. 258 and 261.

The monk told him to repeat his lecture, whereupon Fu began thus: 'The Dharmakāya is like vacuity of space, it reaches the limits of time, it extends to the ten quarters, it fills up the eight points of the compass, it embraces the two extremes, heaven and earth. It functions according to conditions, responds to all stimulations, and there is no place where it is not in evidence. . . .'

The monk said: 'I would not say that your exposition is all wrong, but it is no more than a talk about the Dharmakāya. As to the thing itself, you have no knowledge.'

Fu: 'If this be the case, tell me what it is.'

Monk: 'Would you believe me?'

Fu: 'Why not?'

Monk: 'If you really do, quit your lecturing for a while, retire into your room for about ten days, and, sitting up straight and quietly, collect all your thoughts, abandon all your discrimination as regards good and bad, and see into your inner world.'

Fu followed this advice wholeheartedly, spending all his night absorbed in deep meditation. In the small hours of the morning he happened to hear a flute, which suddenly opened his mind to a state of satori. He ran to the quarters where the monk was staying and knocked at the door.

The monk: 'Who are you?'

Fu: 'Myself.'

The monk burst out into a terrible scolding: 'I wanted you to have an insight into the Dharma so that you could be a bearer and transmitter of it. Why do you get drunk and snore away the night in the street?'

Fu: 'O Zen monk, listen. Hitherto all my lectures have been carried on with the mouth given by my parents,[1] but from now on there will be no more of them.'

[1] This is tantamount to saying that the ultimate truth of the Mahāyāna teaching is to be experienced and not to be made a mere subject of intellectual analysis. Also note a change of attitude on the part of the Zen monk after T'ai-yüan's actual seeing into the nature of the Dharmakāya. So we see that those apparently nonsensical remarks, impetuous vilifications, or biting insinuations which are so frequently met with in Zen literature are the natural outcome of a certain spiritual revolution that takes place at the moment of satori.

The monk: 'Begone for now. Come again during the day and I will see you.'

The poem then composed by Fu runs as follows:

In those days, I remember, when as yet I had no satori
Each time I heard the flute played my heart grieved;
Now I have no idle dream over the pillow;
I just let the player play whatever tune he likes.

The following will be a fit conclusion to the philosophy of the *Prajñāpāramitā*:

While still on his Zen pilgrimage, Chao-chou saw Tai-t'zŭ[1] and asked: 'What is the body of the Prajñā?'

Tai-t'zŭ repeated: 'What is the body of the Prajñā?'

Thereupon, Chao-chou gave a hearty laugh and went off.

On the day following Tai-t'zŭ saw Chao-chou sweeping the ground. Tai-t'zŭ asked, 'What is the body of the Prajñā?'

Chao-chou threw up his broom and with a hearty laugh went away. Tai-t'zŭ then returned to his quarters.

[1] See also First Series, p. 288.

VII. BUDDHIST, ESPECIALLY ZEN, CONTRIBUTIONS TO JAPANESE CULTURE[1]

BUDDHISM was introduced to Japan officially in A.D. 552, and ever since it has kept up a most intimate and vital relationship with the cultural history of the nation. In fact, every page of it records something achieved by Buddhism for the enhancement of the intellectual, the aesthetic, and the spiritual life of the Japanese. This was quite natural, seeing that at the time of its introduction to Japan Buddhism represented a superior civilization. It was backed by such highly advanced cultures as the Indian, Chinese, and Korean in the arts, industries, learning, and humane activities, which were then greatly in advance of the Japanese. Not only as a far-sighted statesman and a highly endowed mind, but as a deeply-devotional soul, Prince Shōṭoku (574–622) worked like a genius to create a new Japan by building Buddhist temples, writing commentaries on the Mahāyāna Sūtras, encouraging the arts, sending students to China, establishing hospitals and colleges, compiling histories, and laying down the principles of government. Buddhism, besides being a great religious system, was then the source of wisdom for every department of human activities. Those who have visited Nara and its vicinity will fully understand what I mean by these statements. Even at this late date, the Horyuji with all its treasures remains a great wonder.[2]

As I have a very limited time at my disposal I cannot describe the whole field of Buddhist contributions to the culture of the Japanese people. Let me, therefore, confine myself to what Buddhism, especially Zen Buddhism, has done towards their intellectual and artistic life—and this very briefly.

[1] This paper is based on the author's lectures delivered at the Summer School of Oriental Culture for Foreigners in Kyoto, 1931.

[2] See the Appendix.

I

To do this, it is necessary to understand first what kind of Buddhism it was that came over to Japan after centuries of its development on the continent.

We generally distinguish between Hīnayāna Buddhism and Mahāyāna Buddhism. Historically, the Hīnayāna is the more primitive form of Buddhism, and the Mahāyāna is a later and more advanced system of it. What characterizes each may most briefly be defined thus: the ideal of the Hīnayāna discipline is to realize Arhatship, while that of the Mahāyāna is Bodhisattvahood.

The Buddhist life aims at attaining enlightenment, technically known as 'Bodhi'. In this aim Hīnayānists and Mahāyānists are at one, but with the former there are no conscious efforts to impart the bliss of enlightenment to all other fellow-beings—if necessary, unconditionally.[1] A Hīnayānist remains satisfied if he is enlightened by his own untiring efforts. Of course he is full of missionary spirit, trying to convert his pupils or people generally to his own way

[1] By this I mean the doctrine of Tariki ('other-power') developed in the thirteenth century. According to this doctrine, first taught by Shinran (1173–1262), we are too sinful to deliver ourselves from the heavy burden of ignorance and karma by our own efforts, moral and intellectual. The power of faith is needed—faith in the so-called Original Vows of Amitābha Buddha. All that is needed on our part is to rely absolutely upon the omnipotence of Amitābha's spiritual power. He has accomplished in his past lives everything that is required for our deliverance, and what is now demanded of us is to give ourselves up unconditionally to the 'other-power' which is Amitābha's love for us.

The Hīnayānist or Arhat is a strong believer in the law of causation, and in this he may be said to be strictly scientific and individualistic. He does not believe in the mystery of faith and love which overrides the law. In the Mahāyāna the social aspect of the Buddhist life is most emphatically insisted upon, and naturally some power far stronger than merely individual comes to the front. This assertion of a super-individual power is the basis of Bodhisattvahood.

The development of the Bodhisattva-ideal means the secularization of the Samgha life. Or it is possible that secularization gradually led to the denouncement of monasticism which gave a fine shelter to the Śrāvaka and the Pratyekabuddha. This transformation was in full accord with the original spirit of Buddhism, which is to save the world from the universal bondage of ignorance and karma. In this Japanese Buddhists are real followers of the Buddha.

of thinking and feeling, that is, to make them embrace the teaching and follow the discipline of Buddhism, but all he does for others is more or less intellectual. If others fail to come up to the standard, the moral law of cause and effect follows, and if they cannot attain what they seek, they fall short of being enlightened. The Hīnayānist cannot, however, help them, for each has to achieve his own salvation—this being the view held by the Hīnayāna school of Buddhism. The Arhat is a solitary philosopher, he is absorbed all by himself in the bliss of enlightenment. He lacks in human sympathy and all-embracing love. When he sees suffering about him he coldly looks at it and tells the sufferers how to contrive by their own efforts to get out of the tribulation. This is all he does and can do for others, he can do no more for them; each reaps what he sows. The Arhat or Hīnayānist is an ultra-individualist.

The Mahāyāna ideal differs from this. The love-phase of religious life is more emphasized here than its rationalism. In order that his fellow-beings may increase or grow stronger in their spiritual power, the Bodhisattva wishes to extend towards them whatever merit he has acquired by his moral life. Although he is morally ready for it, he will even postpone his own enlightenment.[1] He does this because he knows that there are yet many suffering beings whom he

[1] As has already been noted, this doctrine is known as the doctrine of Upāya ('skilful means') and of Pariṇāmana ('turning over'). The Upāya is born of the Prajñā and Karuṇā, and connotes a more general idea than Pariṇāmana. The Pariṇāmana is characteristic of the Mahāyāna. Literally it means to turn the result of one's own merit over to somebody else. It goes directly against the individualistic idea of karma and also against the moral law of causation as ordinarily understood. For the Pariṇāmana is impossible so long as one is confined to a dualistic world of being (*astitva*) and non-being (*nāstitva*). By means of Prajñā and Karuṇā the latter is transcended and the Pariṇāmana is made to work out its mission.

The Pariṇāmana works in two directions. The *Prajñāpāramitā* refers to one of these directions when it makes the Bodhisattva give up all his stock of merit towards the realization of universal enlightenment (*saṁbodhi* or *sarvajñatā*). This we may call the upward moving of Pariṇāmana. The other one is from the Buddha or Sarvajñatā to all beings. The power that constitutes Buddhahood emanates, as it were, from its body and is transferred on to all sentient beings, and the latter are helped

feels he ought to wake up to enlightenment. However strong the chain of individual karma may be, the Bodhisattva's whole-souled endeavour is to break it in pieces. For by this he can achieve the grand scheme of universal enlightenment and the salvation of entire humankind. (In Buddhism salvation is not confined to human beings, it extends over all creation. Even animals, plants, rivers, rocks, mountains are included in the scheme of salvation, that is, in the attainment of Buddhahood.)[1]

Bodhisattva was originally the name given to the Buddha prior to his attainment of enlightenment while he was practising the six virtues of perfection (*pāramitā*). The Mahāyāna places great stress upon this stage of the Buddha's life. The practising of the Pāramitās means the assertion of humanity as a social being, the basic idea being that individuals cannot be perfect until society itself is made perfect. This will naturally mean that an individual becomes perfect when he loses his individuality in the All to which he belongs. By losing himself he gains something more than himself, for his perfection consists in being more than himself and not in being just what he is in himself.

The six virtues of perfection are characteristic of Mahāyāna Buddhism in many ways. They contain virtues commonly held up as cardinal by all religious systems, but there are some more which differentiate the Mahāyāna.

The six virtues are:

1. Charity (*dāna*). This does not merely mean to give away what one has in abundance, but involves even the giving-up of one's whole being for a cause.

2. Morality (*śīla*). The practising of all the Buddhist

thereby to quit their life of ignorance and passion. In Shin Buddhism this is called the 'power of Amida's original vow' and made the very foundation of its elaborate, though at first sight simple, system. In other schools of Buddhism, this power is known under the name of Adhishṭhāna, which means 'basis' or 'authority' or 'sustaining power'.

By this mutual working between Buddha and sentient beings, the world-scheme of enlightenment and emancipation is carried on without interruption and till the end of time.

[1] See Beatrice L. Suzuki's *Nōgaku*, in which she tells how the spirit of the butterfly, or of snow, or of the banana-plant, attains Buddhahood.

PLATE XXXI

MA-TSU, PAI-CHANG, AND HUANG-PO

By Sesshu

We can say that Chinese Zen really originated with Ma-tsu (died 788) and Shih-t'ou (700–790). From Ma-tsu we have Pai-chang (720–814) who is the founder of the Zendò system, that is, he is the one who initiated the Zen monastery life by minutely regulating its daily activities and various functions. Until his time the Zen monks did not have any special institution of their own. Realising that their life could not be passed anywhere else except in their own, he instituted the first Zen monastery. The principle that inspired him was the gospel of manual labour. The famous saying of his is, "A day of no work is a day of no eating." He faithfully followed this injunction himself. (See p. 316 ff. of my *Zen Essays*, First Series.) Huang-po (died 850) was one of the chief disciples of Pai-chang, and Lin-chi (Rinzai in Japanese) succeeded Huang-po, becoming founder of the Rinzai school of Zen Buddhism, which is still flourishing in Japan principally, but also in China. The Sòtò school follows the line of Shih-t'ou, Yüeh-shan (751–834), Yün-yên (died 841), and Tung-shan (807–869).

PLATE XXXII

A ZEN MASTER AND A LAYMAN

By Keishoki

Keishoki means "Kei the Secretary" who was a great Zen painter-monk at Kenchòji, Kamakura, in the Ashikaga period (roughly 1350–1550). He left many masterpieces. This picture has the simple title "Huang-lung" and it is difficult to know to which Huang-lung the reference is, for there were many Zen masters who were residents of the Huang-lung monastery. And so far as I can ascertain the subject does not fit any record left of any Huang-lung.

The most noted of the Huang-lung was Hui-nan (1002–1069), under whom there were many laymen as well as monks who took up the study of Zen. Perhaps the scene here represents one of such cases, while the swords under his rock-seat may symbolise the general powerlessness of the worldly weapon. In reality it does not matter who the Zen master is and what particular historical incident is referred to. Sufficient if we have a glimpse into the life of a Zen master whoever he may be.

precepts, or all the virtuous deeds that are conducive to the moral welfare of oneself and that of others.

3. Striving (*vīrya*). A constant application of oneself to the promotion of good. The Mahāyānists' life is one of utmost strenuousness not only in this life but in the lives to come—and the lives to come may have no end.

4. Humility (*kṣānti*). This is sometimes rendered patience, but humility is more to the point. Rather than merely enduring all sorts of ills of the flesh, it is the feeling of unworthiness, limitedness, and sinfulness.

5. Meditation (*dhyāna*). Not in the sense of meditating on a moral maxim or a philosophical saying, but the disciplining of oneself in tranquillization.

6. Transcendental knowledge (*prajñā*). This is what constitutes enlightenment; it is an intuition into the ultimate truth of things, by gaining which one is released from the bondage of existence, and becomes master of one's self.

2

Let us next see on what theoretical ground Mahāyāna Buddhism stands. The doctrine of Non-ego (*anatta* in Pāli, *nairātmya* in Sanskrit) is the foundation of both Hīnayāna and Mahāyāna Buddhism, but the latter has developed all the implications, ending finally in the doctrine of the Law-body, or Dharmakāya as it is better known in its Sanskrit original, for 'Law-body' is liable to be wrongly interpreted.[1]

[1] From the theory of Anatta or Nairātmya to this conception is a long jump, and a great deal of historical tracing is required to understand adequately how the Triple Body (*trikāya*) came to occupy an important position in the system of Mahāyāna Buddhism. Briefly stated, there are two forms of Nairātmya, Pudgala and Dharma. The teaching of no-ego-substance which is Pudgalanairātmya is held both by the Hīnayāna and by the Mahāyāna, while that of Dharmanairātmya is generally considered to be taught exclusively by the Mahāyāna. The Dharmanairātmya means the denial of the reality of an individual existence as holding in itself a permanent and free-moving agent. This is a psychological statement of the law of causation technically known as Pratītyasamutpāda. Or it may be said that the Dharmanairātmya is the extension of the Pudgalanairātmya. The ontological expression of the Nairātmya is the doctrine of Śūnyata which has been fully elucidated in the preceding pages.

To understand adequately the Mahāyāna conception of Dharmakāya requires a great deal of knowledge as regards the philosophy of Buddhism; for the Dharmakāya is one of the Triple Body and its significance is organically related to the other two Bodies called Sambhogakāya and Nirmāṇakāya, or Body of Enjoyment and Body of Transformation[1]

The positive statement of Śūnyatā from the religious and personal point of view is the Dharmakāya. The Dharmakāya was in the beginning contrasted with the Rūpakāya; that is, the body of the Buddha regarded as the Dharma itself was made to stand against his physical existence which is subject to the law of birth and death. The latter passed away from this earth like everything else, but the Dharma-body of the Buddha could not vanish like that, for the Dharma is a permanent abider. Later, this Dharma-body came to denote also Reality which is the Suchness of all things. It means at present not only the essence-being (*svabhāva*) of all the Buddhas but the ground and reason of all things. Śūnyatā, properly speaking, has no negative connotation. It is another name for Tathatā—that is, emptiness is suchness and suchness is emptiness. This is the intuitionalism of the *Prajñāpāramitā*. Now the suchness of the Buddha is, from the religious point of view, Dharmakāya, and this Dharmakāya is perceived when the egolessness (*nairātmyatā*) of individual things (*dharma*) and individual souls (*pudgala*) is experienced.

[1]The dogma of Trikāya may be summarily interpreted in the following manner: The Dharmakāya is the essence-being of all the Buddhas and also of all beings. What makes at all possible the existence of anything is the Dharmakāya, without which the world itself is inconceivable. But, specifically, the Dharmakāya is the essence-body of all beings which forever is. In this sense it is Dharmatā or Buddhatā, that is, the Buddha-nature within all beings. The Sambhogakāya is the spiritual body of the Bodhisattvas which is enjoyed by them as the fruit of their self-discipline in all the virtues of perfection. This they acquire for themselves according to the law of moral causation, and in this they are delivered at last from all the defects and defilements inherent in the realm of the five Skandhas. The Nirmāṇakāya is born of the great loving heart (*mahākaruṇā*) of the Buddhas and Bodhisattvas. By reason of this love they have for all beings, they never remain in the self-enjoyment of the fruits of their moral deeds. Their intense desire is to share those fruits with their fellow-beings. If the ignorant could be saved by the Bodhisattva by his vicariously suffering for them, he would do so. If the ignorant could be enlightened by the Bodhisattva by turning his stock of merit over to them, he would so do. This turning over of merit and this vicarious suffering are accomplished by the Bodhisattva by means of his Nirmāṇakāya, transformation-body. In this form, therefore, the Bodhisattva, spatially speaking, divides himself into hundreds of thousands of koṭis of bodies. He can then be recognized in the form of a creeping caterpillar, in a sky-scraping mountain, in the saintly figure of Francis of Assisi, and even in the shape of a world-devouring Evil One, if he thinks it necessary to take this form in order to save a world that has passed into the hands of ignorance, evil passions, and all kinds of defilements and corruptions.

Briefly, the Dharmakāya is the final reality making up the being of all things; this is what is popularly misconceived as an ego-substance.

Psychologically, the Dharmakāya may be regarded as the Ālayavijñāna, 'all-conserving mind', of which the Yogācāra school of Buddhism talks so much. The Ālayavijñāna is something akin to what may be called the transcendental or universal consciousness which lies behind our ordinary relative empirical consciousnesses. The purification of this universal consciousness, where all things are conserved in their essence or in their seed-form (*bīja*)—the purification taking place through its individually manifested consciousnesses—is the aim of all Buddhist discipline. But we must not forget that as long as we are on the psychological plane and referring to the Ālayavijñāna, we are yet far from the Dharmakāya whose realm lies much deeper than our consciousness.

From another point of view the Ālayavijñāna is Śūnyatā (emptiness). If Ālayavijñāna is a psychological term, Śūnyatā is an ontological conception, or would it be better to regard it as epistemological? Because when the notion of logical relativity is to be finally transcended in order to reach something ultimate, the human intellect inevitably comes to Emptiness. So long as Emptiness is conceived relatively we cannot go beyond logic, and logic is not something in which the soul finds its abode of rest. Emptiness must be, after all, our last shelter. It is needless to say that Emptiness does not mean mere nothingness.

Emptiness is, however, a word greatly abused, suffering all kinds of maltreatment. Mahāyāna Buddhism has another term with an affirmative connotation. I mean 'Suchness' or 'Thusness' (*tathatā* in Sanskrit). The Mahāyānists would thus describe existence to be in a state of suchness, and they insist that, as it is not so perceived, the result is a state of ignorance from which follow prejudices and passions in all their possible complications. To regard existence as this or that, as being or non-being, as eternal or transient, is our thought-construction, and not Reality as it is in itself. It requires the highest degree of intellectual perspicuity to look into Reality in its suchness and not to weave around it subjectively-constructed meshes. This is, then, a realm of intuitions. When we enter into this realm, we realize what Śūnyatā or Tathatā really means.

All these general syncretic statements are liable to be grossly misinterpreted when we do not fully realize the relative positions held by the different schools of Buddhist thought. The psychological school known as the Yogācāra attempts to explain the world from the point of view of consciousness or idea, while the ontological school represented by the Mādhyamika insists on reducing reality to Śūnyatā by negating the finality of all particular existences. The conception of the Dharmakāya, on the other hand, has followed still another line of development. And as these general currents of thought have never been thoroughly systematized, students of Buddhism are often at a loss as to how to relate these notions harmoniously to one another. My brief explanations are meant to help them only tentatively.

Being more or less philosophical, the Buddhist ideas are pronounced by many people to be difficult to grasp. Some European scholars of Buddhism who try hard to understand its profound concepts fail to perceive, especially, the meaning of 'Emptiness' and 'Suchness'. One of the commonest criticisms against Buddhism is that, because it denies existence, it teaches nihilism or negativism. Superficially this is true. Emptiness seems to be the negation of existence. But what is taught by Buddhism is to go beyond even this negation, for this is where there is what is known as the Śūnya; and when we get into this realm of absolute solitude (*viviktā*) the meaning of Emptiness and Suchness is grasped, for it can after all be grasped, though not in the relative sense. And when this is grasped, this world of particular objects is accepted in its proper signification.

When Wei-k'uan (*Chuan-têng Lu*, VII) was asked, 'What is the Way?', meaning the ultimate truth of Buddhism, he said, 'What a fine mountain this is!', referring to the mountain where he had his retreat.

The questioner said, 'I am not asking you about the mountain, but about the Way.'

'As long as you cannot go beyond the mountain, you cannot reach the Way,' replied the master.

Another time the same master was asked about the Way, and he said, 'It lies right before your eyes.'

'Why do I not see it myself?'

'You do not, because of your egoistic notion.'

'If I do not because of my egoistic notion, do you?'

'So long as you have dualistic views, saying "I don't" and "you do" and so on, your eyes are bedimmed by this relativity view.'

'When there is neither "I" nor "you", who is it that wants to see?'

I may comment on this conclusion of the master. Just because there is no one wanting to see what the Way is, this mountain is a quiet retreat for the monks, and these wild flowers are blooming even if no city people come out so far to admire them.

Another criticism made against Mahāyāna Buddhism is that it is pantheistic. When the Mahāyānist sees the Buddha-nature in everything, even in things inanimate, he seems to be pantheistically inclined in his philosophy. But read the following carefully and see where the whole trend of the discourse is:

Wei-k'uan (*Chuan-têng*, VII) was asked, 'Is there the Buddha-nature in the dog?'

'Yes.'

'In you too?'

'No, not in me.'

'How is it that there is no Buddha-nature in you when all beings are endowed with one?'

'I am not one of "all beings".'

'If you are not, are you Buddha himself?'

'I am not Buddha.'

'What are you, then?'

'I am not a "what" either.'

'Is it then something at all tangible or thinkable?'

'No, monk, it is altogether beyond thought, beyond comprehension. Therefore, it is called the unthinkable.'

When we go over this dialogue carefully we see that the Mahāyānist sees something beyond individual realities which cannot be wholly included in them, or that, according to the Mahāyāna, the Buddha-nature is manifested in every particular object—in the dog, in the plant, in a piece of rock, in a stream of water, in a particle of dust, in you, in me, in the ignorant, as well as in the Buddha; but at the same time it goes beyond them and cannot be grasped by our thought and imagination. This view of reality cannot be called pantheistic.

There is another point we have to make against the pantheistic interpretation of Buddhist philosophy. This corresponds to what is known in the Avatainsaka school as the doctrine of perfect mutual fusion of individual objects. When the Zen master T'ien-lung[1] held his index finger up to the question 'What is the Buddha?' he did not mean that his finger was the Buddha or his expression or manifestation. If he did, we might say that there is something of pantheism in it. But there was no such indication even hinted at in his finger. If I may add an altogether unnecessary and unwarranted comment, just because I wish to point out the non-pantheistic attitude of T'ien-lung, his finger stands here all by itself, with no reference whatever to the Buddha, to his revelations, or to its space-and-time relations; the finger is to be perceived in its aspect of absolute solitude; the finger is not to be subjected to any form of determination, logical, metaphysical, or theological, or what not; just the finger held out before you is the most threatening reality, and when you even begin to stir you are despatched instantly into the abyss which is bottomless.

3

Roughly there are three means of realization by which the Buddhists come to the suchness-view of reality: 1. Practical, 2. Intellectual, and 3. Intuitional.

[1] See my *Zen Essays*, First Series, p. 35–36 fn.

The practical method is followed by all the Buddhists; but the Shingon may explain my point more graphically. The method consists in arranging the environment in such a way as to make the mind harmoniously respond to the general atmosphere thus created; that is to say, the ear listens to a solemn air, the eye perceives the holy images of Buddhas and Bodhisattvas, the nose smells odours reminding one of a heavenly kingdom, the hands are engaged in forming secret mudrās, and the mouth repeats sacred mantrams of deep signification. When these arrangements are completed, the mind is naturally influenced by them, and, without realizing how, becomes deeply permeated with the subtle *vāsanā* emanating from them.[1] When this is repeated regularly for a certain space of time, the devotee may ultimately come to a realization.

The second method of reaching the final goal of the Mahāyāna discipline is to appeal to the intellect. This is done by training oneself in the philosophy of the Avataṁsaka school or in that of the Tendai. The Avataṁsaka teaches a highly abstract system of the so-called fourfold Dharmadhātu, while the Tendai has the contemplation of the threefold view of existence known as Emptiness, Relativity, and the Middle Way. All these are meant for a highly developed and well-trained intellect. Without many years of philosophic discipline, one cannot comprehend the deep spiritual meaning therein involved.

The third method, appealing to our intuitive faculty, is Zen. Possibly the Nembutsu is classifiable under this head. This is a direct method, for it refuses to resort to verbal explanations, or logical analysis, or to ritualism. Whatever

[1] *Vāsanā,* meaning 'perfuming', 'impression', 'memory', 'habit-energy', is an emanation issuing from every deed, good or bad, which has the power to affect others. And inasmuch as the entire world with all its individual objects symbolizes deeds of the past, there is also an emanation from them, collectively as well as individually. These emanations are also loaded with the power to affect or 'perfume' any sentient being who may be in the position to come in touch with them. The conception of Vāsanā belongs to the psychological school of Buddhism, according to which the Ālayavijñāna is the depository of all such emanation-germs, as it were.

reality there is to take hold of, Zen proposes to grasp it directly without any mediatory tools such as intellection, imagination, accumulation of merit, etc. It straightway awakens the highest spiritual power which may be called intuition, and by this enlightenment is attained.

It goes without saying that along with all these methods of spiritual training Dhyāna (meditation, so called) is practised, for without this no amount of discipline, whether intellectual or intuitive or ritualistic, can produce the result desired. Wherever Buddhism is put into practical use, let us therefore understand that Dhyāna is the one thing indispensable to it. Only in Zen this is more systematically exercized; in fact, the practice of Dhyāna is regarded in Zen as the means essentially in correspondence with an ultimate realization. Historically the term 'Zen' comes from 'Dhyāna' (*zenna* in Japanese).

Thus, of the three methods whereby to bring about a state of enlightenment in Buddhist life, Zen has so far proved the most generally practical and efficient to the Oriental mind. As it has contributed much to the appreciation of a certain artistic taste in the life of the Japanese people, I will devote the rest of my lecture to Zen and its cultural value.

The Shingon knows how to appreciate the value of form and as the result it has helped much in the creation of beautiful objects of art. The Tendai, the Kegon (*avataṁsaka*), and the Yuishiki (*vijñaptimātra*)—three of the intellectualist wing of Mahāyāna Buddhism—have no doubt stimulated the growth of the ratiocinative faculty:[1] and when Japan faced he streaming-in of the Western thought, she knew well how

[1] The teaching of Śūnyatā is closely associated with Zen. In fact, Zen developed from the intuitions of the *Prajñāpāramitā*. In the beginning of its history Zen had much to do with the *Laṅkāvatāra*, but it gradually detached itself from this sūtra and took up the Prajñā teaching for its fundamental tenets. Perhaps the *Laṅkāvatāra* offers a too-complicated system of thought to be easily digested by the Chinese mind. The *Prajñāpāramitā* on the other hand is simple and straightforward in its statements, which fact appeals quite readily to the compatriots of Lao-tzŭ and Chuang-tzŭ.

to discriminate and assimilate it according to her needs. That she took in with the proper frame of mind the invasion of modern idealism and Hegelian dialectic is no doubt due to the fact that her intellect has been under a severe training at the hands of the Buddhist philosophers.

Strangely, Zen had its share in promoting the study of the Chinese classics. If Zen did not countenance the study of Buddhist philosophy, as being a hindrance to the growth of the intuitive power, it acted as a missionary for Chinese learning in general, which included poetry, history, ethics, philosophy, calligraphy, painting, etc. This is an unusual phenomenon in the history of Buddhism, that a teaching which is so against the letter became a strong, efficient agency in the preservation and encouragement of scholarship.

4

In one sense, Zen is the Chinese interpretation of the doctrine of enlightenment. When Buddhism passed through the prism of the Chinese mind it was differentiated into many schools, with Zen as one of them. But it was evidently Zen that was in the best conformity with the Chinese psychology, for of all the Buddhist schools that flourished in that land during the twenty centuries of its growth Zen is one of the two currents of Buddhist thought which have successfully survived; indeed, as far as the official name of a school is concerned, Zen is the only school of Buddhism now in existence in China; for the Pure Land Teaching has never become a separate school in China, finding its shelter in the Zen monasteries as a sort of boarding guest.

Historically, Zen no doubt started with the coming of Bodhidharma to China early in the sixth century. But as a matter of fact, Zen, properly to be so called, dates from the appearance of Yeno (Hui-nêng, A.D. 637–714), who was a native of Southern China. The history of Zen from Bodhidharma down to Yeno, the Sixth Patriarch, is told in my *Essays in Zen Buddhism*, Series I.[1]

Apart from its insistence on the all-absorbing importance of personal experience in the realization of a final fact, Zen has the following characteristics which have exercised a great deal of moral influence in the moulding of what may be designated the spirit of the East, especially of Japan.

1. Neglect of form is generally characteristic of mysticism, Christian or Buddhist or Islamic. When the importance of the spirit is emphasized, all the outward expressions of it naturally become things of secondary significance. Form is not necessarily despised, but attention to it is reduced to a minimum, or we may say that conventionalism is set aside and individual originality is asserted in its full strength. But because of this there is a forceful tone of inwardness perceivable in all things connected with Zen. As far as form is concerned, nothing beautiful or appealing to the senses may be observable here, but one feels something inward or spiritual asserting itself in spite of the imperfection of the form, perhaps because of this very imperfection. The reason is this: when the form is perfect, our senses are satisfied too strongly with it and the mind may at least temporarily neglect to exercise its more inner function. The efforts concentrated too greatly in the outwardness of things fail to draw out what inner meaning there is in them. So Tanka (Tan-hsia) burned a wooden image of Buddha to make a fire, and idolatry was done away with. Kensu (Hsien-tzŭ) turned into a fisherman against the conventionality of monastery life. Daitō Kokushi (1282–1337) became a beggar and Kanzan Kokushi (1277–1360) was a cowherd.

2. The inwardness of Zen implies the directness of its

[1] As I stated elsewhere, my view of the history of Zen in China down to Hui-nêng and his disciples has undergone certain changes, owing to the discovery of new materials which have been kept away from the public for over a thousand years in the desert of the north-western Chinese borderland. As soon as practicable, my intention is to write a newly constructed history of Zen with Hui-nêng as the central figure. The significance of the Prajñā teaching in connection with Zen will then be brought out in a broader light than before.

appeal to the human spirit. When the intermediary of form is dispensed with, one spirit speaks directly to another. Raise a finger and the whole universe is there. Nothing could be more direct than this in this world of relativity. The medium of communication or the symbol of self-expression is curtailed to the shortest possible term. When a syllable or a wink is enough, why spend one's entire life in writing huge books or building a grandiose cathedral?

3. Directness is another word for simplicity. When all the paraphernalia for expressing ideas is discarded, a single blade of grass suffices to stand for Buddha Vairochana sixteen feet high. Or a circle is the fullest possible symbol for the immeasurability of the truth as realized in the mind of a Zen adept. This simplicity also expresses itself in life. A humble straw-thatched mountain retreat, a half of which is shared by white clouds, is enough for the sage.[1] The potatoes roasted in the ashes of a cow-dung fire appease his hunger, as he casts a contemptuous look upon an envoy from the Imperial court.[2]

4. Poverty and simplicity go hand in hand, but to be merely poor and humble is not Zen. It does not espouse poverty just for the sake of poverty. As it is sufficient with itself, it does not want much—which is poverty to others, but sufficiency to oneself. Rich and poor—this is a worldly standard; for the inwardness of Zen poverty has nothing to do with being short of possessions, or being rich with the overflowing of material wealth.

5. Facts of experience are valued in Zen more than representations, symbols and concepts—that is to say, substance is everything in Zen and form nothing. Therefore, Zen is radical empiricism. This being so, space is not something objectively extending, time is not to be considered a line stretched out as past, present, and future. Zen knows no such space, no such time, and, therefore, such ideas as eternity, infinitude, boundlessness, etc., are mere dreams to Zen. For Zen lives in facts. Facts may be considered

[1] See *Essays in Zen Buddhism*, Second Series, p. 352.

[2] Lan-tsan, late eighth century in the reign of Tê-tsung, of T'ang.

momentarily, but momentariness is an idea subjectively constructed. When Zen is compared to a flash of lightning which disappears even before you have uttered the cry 'Oh!', it is not to be supposed that mere quickness is the life of Zen. But we can say that Zen eschews deliberation, elaboration. When a roof leaked, a Zen master called out to his attendants to bring in something to keep the *tatami* dry. Without a moment's hesitation, one of them brought in a bamboo basket, while another went around and, searching for a tub, took it to the master. The master was immensely pleased, it is said, with the first monk with the basket. It was he who understood the spirit of Zen better than the one who was deliberate, though his wisdom proved far more practical and useful. This phase of Zen is technically known as 'non-discrimination'.

6. What might be designated 'eternal loneliness' is found at the heart of Zen. This is a kind of sense of the absolute. In the *Laṅkāvatāra Sūtra* we have what is known there as the 'truth of solitude' (*viviktadharma* in Sanskrit). The experience of this seems to wake the feeling of eternal loneliness. This does not mean that we all feel solitary and long forever for something larger and stronger than ourselves. This feeling is cherished more or less by all religious souls; but what I mean here is not this kind of solitariness, but the solitariness of an absolute being, which comes upon one when a world of particulars moving under the conditions of space, time, and causation is left behind, when the spirit soars high up in the sky and moves about as it lists like a floating cloud.

7. When all these aspects of Zen are confirmed, we find a certain definite attitude of Zen towards life generally. When it expresses itself in art, it constitutes what may be called the spirit of Zen aestheticism. In this we shall then find simplicity, directness, abandonment, boldness, aloofness, unworldliness, innerliness, the disregarding of form, free movements of spirit, the mystic breathing of a creative genius all over the work—whether it be in painting, calligraphy, gardening, the tea-ceremony, fencing, dancing, or poetry.

5

As I said before, Zen, of all the schools of Mahāyāna Buddhism, has given great impetus to the cultivation of the arts peculiar to the Japanese, and the above delineation may help somehow to understand the spirit of this phase of Japanese culture. To illustrate, let me choose Japanese painting known as 'Sumiye' and Japanese poetry called 'Haiku' and also a Zen master's instruction given to a great Samurai expert in swordsmanship.

Zen came to Japan in the twelfth century[1] and during the eight hundred years of its history it has influenced Japanese life in various ways, not only in the spiritual life of the Samurai but in the artistic expressions of it by the learned and cultured classes. The Sumiye, which is one of such expressions, is not painting in the proper sense of the word; it is a kind of sketch in black and white. The ink is made of soot and glue, and the brush of sheep's or badger's hair, and the latter is so made as to absorb or contain much of the fluid. The paper used is rather thin and will absorb much ink, standing in great contrast to the canvas used by oil-painters, and this contrast means a great deal to the Sumiye artist.

The reason why such a frail material has been chosen for the vehicle of transferring an artistic inspiration is that the inspiration is to be transferred on to it in the quickest possible time. If the brush lingers too long, the paper will be torn through. The lines are to be drawn as swiftly as possible and the fewest in number, only the absolutely necessary ones being indicated. No deliberation is allowed, no erasing, no repetition, no retouching, no remodelling, no 'doctoring', no building-up. Once executed, the strokes are indelible, irrevocable, not subject to future corrections or improvements. Anything done afterwards is plainly and painfully visible in the result, as the paper is of such a nature. The artist must follow his inspiration as spontaneously and abso-

[1] See the Appendix.

lutely and instantly as it moves; he just lets his arm, his fingers, his brush be guided by it as if they were all mere instruments, together with his whole being, in the hands of somebody else who has temporarily taken possession of him. Or we may say that the brush by itself executes the work quite outside the artist, who just lets it move on without his conscious efforts. If any logic or reflection comes between brush and paper, the whole effect is spoiled. In this way Sumiye is produced.

It is easily conceivable that the lines of Sumiye must show an infinite variety. There is no chiaroscuro, no perspective in it. Indeed, they are not needed in Sumiye, which makes no pretentions to realism. It attempts to make the spirit of an object move on the paper. Thus each brush-stroke must beat with the pulsation of a living being. It must be living too. Evidently, Sumiye is governed by a set of principles quite different from those of an oil-painting. The canvas being of such strong material and oil colours permitting repeated wipings and overlayings, a picture is built up systematically after a deliberately designed plan. Grandeur of conception and strength of execution, to say nothing of its realism, are the characteristics of an oil-painting, which can be compared to a well-thought-out system of philosophy, each thread of whose logic is closely knitted; or it may be likened unto a grand cathedral, whose walls, pillars, and foundations are composed of solid blocks of stone. Compared with this, a Sumiye sketch is poverty itself, poor in form, poor in contents, poor in execution, poor in material, yet we Oriental people feel the presence in it of a certain moving spirit that mysteriously hovers around the lines, dots, and shades of various formations; the rhythm of its living breath vibrates in them. A single stem of a blooming lily apparently so carelessly executed on a piece of coarse paper—yet here is vividly revealed the tender innocent spirit of a maiden sheltered from the storm of a worldly life. Again, so far as a superficial critic can see, there is not much of artistic skill and inspiration—a little insignificant boat of a fisherman at the centre of a broad expanse of waters; but as we look we cannot help being deeply impressed with the immensity of the ocean which knows no boundaries, and with the presence of a mysterious spirit breathing a life of eternity undisturbed in the midst of the undulating waves. And all these wonders are achieved with such ease and effortlessness.

If Sumiye attempts to copy an objective reality it is an utter failure; it never does that, it is rather a creation. A dot in a Sumiye sketch does not represent a hawk, nor does a curved line symbolize Mount Fuji. The dot is the bird and the line is the mountain. If resemblance is everything with a picture, the two dimensional canvas cannot represent anything of objectivity; the colours fall far too short of giving the original, and however faithfully a painter may try with his brushes to remind us of an object of nature as it is, the result can never do justice to it; for as far as it is an imitation, or a representation, it is a poor imitation, it is a mockery. The Sumiye artist thus reasons: why not altogether abandon such an attempt? Let us instead create living objects out of our own imagination. As long as we all belong to the same universe, our creations may show some correspondence to what we call objects of nature. But this is not an essential element of our work. The work has its own merit apart from resemblance. In each brush-stroke is there not something distinctly individual? The spirit of each artist is moving there. His birds are his own creation. This is the attitude of a Sumiye painter towards his art, and I wish to state that this attitude is that of Zen towards life, and that what Zen attempts with his life the artist does with his paper, brush, and ink. The creative spirit moves everywhere, and there is a work of creation whether in life or in art.

A line drawn by the Sumiye artist is final, nothing can go beyond it, nothing can retrieve it; it is just inevitable as a flash of lightning; the artist himself cannot undo it; from this issues the beauty of the line. Things are beautiful where they are inevitable, that is, when they are free exhibitions of a spirit. There is no violence here, no murdering, no twisting-about, no copying-after, but a free, unrestrained, yet self-governing display of movement—which constitutes the principle of beauty. The muscles are conscious of drawing a line, making a dot, but behind them there is an unconsciousness. By this unconsciousness nature writes out her destiny: by this unconsciousness the artist creates his work of art. A baby smiles and the whole crowd is transported, because it is genuinely inevitable, coming out of the Unconscious. The 'Wu-hsin' and 'Wu-nien'[1] of which the Zen master makes so much, as we have already seen elsewhere, is also eminently the spirit of the Sumiye artist.

Another feature that distinguishes Sumiye is its attempt to catch spirit as it moves. Everything becomes, nothing is stationary in nature; when you think you have safely taken hold of it, it slips off your hands. Because the moment you have it it is no more alive; it is dead. But Sumiye tries to catch things alive, which seems to be something impossible to achieve. Yes, it would indeed be an impossibility if the artist's endeavour were to represent living things on paper, but he can succeed to a certain extent when every brush-stroke he makes is directly connected with his inner spirit, unhampered by extraneous matters such as concepts, etc. In this case, his brush is his own arm extended; more than that, it is his spirit, and in its every movement as it is traced on paper this spirit is felt. When this is accomplished, a Sumiye picture is a reality itself, complete in itself, and no copy of anything else. The mountains here are real in the same sense as Mount Fuji is real; so are the clouds, the stream, the trees, the waves, the figures. For the spirit of the artist is articulating through all these masses, lines, dots, and 'daubs'.

It is thus natural that Sumiye avoids colouring of any kind, for it reminds us of an object of nature, and Sumiye makes no claim to be a reproduction, perfect or imperfect. In this respect Sumiye is like calligraphy. In calligraphy each character, composed of strokes horizontal, vertical, slanting,

[1] *Mu-shin* and *mu-nen* in Japanese. See p. 23 et seq. of the present book.

flowing, turning upward and downward, does not necessarily indicate any definite idea, though it does not altogether ignore it, for a character is primarily supposed to mean something. But as an art peculiar to the Far East where a long, pointed, soft hair-brush is used for writing, each stroke made with it has a meaning apart from its functioning as a composite element of a character symbolizing an idea. The brush is a yielding instrument and obeys readily every conative movement of the writer or the artist. In the strokes executed by him we can discern his spirit. This is the reason why Sumiye and calligraphy are regarded in the East as belonging to the same class of art.

The development of the soft-haired brush is a study in itself. No doubt it had a great deal to do with the accidents of the Chinese character and writing. It was a fortunate event that such a soft, yielding, pliable instrument was put into the hand of the artist. The lines and strokes produced by it have something of the freshness, tenderness, and gracefulness which are perceivable in animated objects of nature, especially in the human body. If the instrument used were a piece of steel, rigid and unyielding, the result would be quite contrary, and no Sumiye of Liang-kai, Mu-ch'i, and other masters would have come down to us.

That the paper is of such a fragile nature as not to allow the brush to linger too long over it is also of great advantage for the artist to express himself with it. If the paper were too strong and tough, deliberate designing and correction would be possible, which is, however, quite injurious to the spirit of Sumiye. The brush must run over the paper swiftly, boldly, fully, and irrevocably just like the work of creation when the universe came into being. As soon as a word comes from the mouth of the creator, it must be executed. Delay may mean alteration, which is frustration; or the will has been checked in its forward movement; it halts, it hesitates, it reflects, it reasons, and finally it changes its course—this faltering and wavering interferes with the freedom of the artistic mind.

While artificiality does not mean regularity or a symmetrical treatment of the subject, and freedom mean irregularity, there is always an element of unexpectedness or abruptness in Sumiye. Where one expects to see a line or a mass this is lacking, and this vacancy instead of disappointing suggests something beyond and is altogether satisfactory. A small piece of paper, generally oblong, less than two feet and a half by six feet, will now include the whole universe. The horizontal stroke suggests immensity of space and a circle eternity of time—not only their mere unlimitedness but filled with life and movement. It is strange that the absence of a single point where it is conventionally expected should achieve this mystery, but the Sumiye artist is a past master in this trick. He does it so skilfully that no artificiality or explicit purpose is at all discernible in his work. This life of purposelessness comes directly from Zen.

6

Having seen something of the connection Sumiye has with Zen, let me proceed to make my remarks on the spirit of 'Eternal Loneliness'. I know that my lecture is altogether inadequate to do justice to what Zen has really done in its peculiar way for the aesthetic side of Japanese life. So far we can say, Zen's influence in Far Eastern painting has been general, as it is not limited to the Japanese, and what I have described may apply equally to the Chinese. What follows, however, can be regarded as specifically Japanese, for this spirit of 'Eternal Loneliness' is something known pre-eminently in Japan. By this spirit, or this artistic principle, if it can be so designated, I mean what is popularly known in Japan as 'Sabi' or 'Wabi' (or 'Shibumi'). Let me say a few words about it now, using the term 'Sabi' for the concept of this group of feelings.

'Sabi' appears in landscape gardening and the tea-ceremony as well as in literature. I shall confine myself to literature, especially to that form of literature known as 'Haiku', that is, the seventeen-syllable poem. This shortest possible form of poetical expression is a special product of the Japanese genius. This made a great development in the Tokugawa era, more particularly after Bashō (1643–1694).

He was a great travelling poet, a most passionate lover of nature—a kind of nature troubadour. His life was spent in travelling from one end of Japan to another. It was fortunate that there were in those days no railways. Modern conveniences do not seem to go very well with poetry. The modern spirit of scientific analysis leaves no mystery unravelled, and poetry and Haiku do not seem to thrive where there are no mysteries. The trouble with science is that it leaves no room for suggestion, everything is laid bare, and anything there is to be seen is exposed. Where science rules the imagination beats a retreat.

We are all made to face so-called hard facts whereby our minds are ossified; where there is no softness left with us, poetry departs; where there is a vast expanse of sand no verdant vegetation is made possible. In Bashō's day, life was not yet so prosaic and hard-pressed. One bamboo hat, one cane stick, and one cotton bag were perhaps enough for the poet to wander about with, stopping for a while in any hamlet which struck his fancy and enjoying all the experiences, which were mostly the hardships of primitive travelling. When travelling is made too easy and comfortable, its spiritual meaning is lost. This may be called sentimentalism, but a certain sense of loneliness engendered by travelling leads one to reflect upon the meaning of life, for life is after all a travelling from one unknown to another unknown. In the period of sixty, seventy, or eighty years allotted to us we are meant to uncover if we can the veil of mystery. A too smooth running over this period, however short it may be, robs us of this sense of Eternal Loneliness.

The predecessor of Bashō was Saigyō of the Kamakura period (1168–1334). He was also a traveller-monk. After quitting his official cares as a warrior attached to the court his life was devoted to travelling and poetry. He was a

Buddhist monk. You must have seen the picture somewhere in your trip through Japan of a monk in his travelling suit, all alone, looking at Mount Fuji. I forget who the painter was, but the pictures suggests many thoughts, especially in the mysterious loneliness of human life, which is, however, not the feeling of forlornness, nor the depressive sense of solitariness, but a sort of appreciation of the mystery of the absolute. The poem composed by Saigyō on that occasion runs:

> The wind-blown
> Smoke of Mt. Fuji
> Disappearing far beyond!
> Who knows the destiny
> Of my thought wandering away with it?

Bashō was not a Buddhist monk but was a devotee of Zen. In the beginning of autumn, when it begins to rain occasionally, nature is the embodiment of Eternal Loneliness. The trees become bare, the mountains begin to assume an austere appearance, the streams are more transparent and in the evening when the birds, weary of the day's work, wend their homeward way, a lone traveller grows pensive over the destiny of human life. His mood moves with that of nature. Sings Bashō:

> 'A traveller—
> Let my name be thus known—
> This autumnal shower.'

We are not necessarily all ascetics, but I do not know if there is not in every one of us an eternal longing for a world beyond this of empirical relativity, where the soul can quietly contemplate its own destiny.

When Bashō was still studying Zen under his master Bucchō, the latter one day paid him a visit and asked, "How are you getting along these days?'

Bashō: 'After a recent rain the moss has grown greener than ever.'

Bucchō: 'What Buddhism is there prior to the greenness of moss?'

Bashō: 'A frog jumps into the water, hear the sound!'

This is said to be the beginning of a new epoch in the history of Haiku. Haiku before Bashō was a mere word-play, and lost its contact with life. Bashō, questioned by his master about the ultimate truth of things which existed even prior to this world of particulars, saw a frog leaping into an old pond, its sound making a break into the serenity of the whole situation. The source of life has been grasped, and the artist sitting here watches every mood of his mind as it comes in contact with a world of constant becoming, and the result is so many seventeen syllables bequeathed to us. Basho was a poet of Eternal Loneliness.

Another of his Haiku is:

> A branch shorn of leaves,
> A crow perching on it—
> This autumn eve.

Simplicity of form does not always mean triviality of content. There is a great Beyond in the lonely raven perching on the dead branch of a tree. All things come out of an unknown abyss of mystery, and through every one of them we can have a peep into the abyss. You do not have to compose a grand poem of many hundred lines to give vent to the feeling thus awakened by looking into the abyss. When a feeling reaches its highest pitch we remain silent, because no words are adequate. Even seventeen syllables may be too many. In any event Japanese artists more or less influenced by the way of Zen tend to use the fewest words or strokes of brush to express their feelings. When they are too fully expressed, no room for suggestion is possible, and suggestibility is the secret of the Japanese arts.

Some artists go even so far as this, that whatever way their strokes of the brush are taken by the viewer is immaterial; in fact the more they are misunderstood the better. The strokes or masses may mean any object of nature; they may be birds, or hills, or human figures, or flowers, or what not; it is perfectly indifferent to them, they declare. This is an extreme view indeed. For if their lines, masses, and dots are judged differently by different minds, sometimes altogether unlike what they were originally intended for by the artist, what is the use at all of attempting such a picture? Perhaps the artist here wanted to add this: 'If only the spirit pervading his product were perfectly perceived and appreciated.' From this it is evident that the Far Eastern artists are perfectly indifferent to form. They want to indicate by their brush-work something that has strongly moved them innerly. They themselves may not have known how to give expression to their inner movement. They only utter a cry or flourish the brush. This may not be art, because there is no art in their doing this. Or if there is any art, that may be a very primitive one. Is this really so? However advanced we may be in 'civilization', which means artificiality, we always strive for artlessness; for it seems to be the goal and foundation of all artistic endeavours. How much art is concealed behind the apparent artlessness of Japanese art! Full of meaning and suggestibility, and yet perfect in artlessness—when in this way the spirit of eternal loneliness is expressed, we have the essence of Sumiye and Haiku.

7

That the Zen form of Buddhism has influenced Japanese life, especially in its aesthetic aspect, to such an extent as has never been attained by the other forms, is due to the fact that Zen directly appeals to the facts of life instead of to concepts. The intellect is always indirect in its relation to life, it is a generalizing agency, and what is general lacks in instinctive force, that is, in will-power. Zen is not solely the will, it contains a certain amount of intellection too, inasmuch as it is an intuition. Standing in contrast to the conceptualizing tendency of the other schools of Buddhism,

Zen's appeal to life is always more fundamental. This is the chief reason why Zen takes hold so strongly of Japanese life.

The art of fencing, to master which was one of the most absorbing occupations of the governing classes of Japan since the Kamakura era, achieved a wonderful development, and many different schools of it have been prospering until quite recently. The Kamakura era is closely related to Zen, for it was then that as an independent school of Buddhism Zen was first introduced to Japan. Many great masters of Zen ruled the spiritual world of the time, and in spite of their contempt of learning, learning was preserved in their hands. At the same time the soldiers thronged about them, eager to be taught and disciplined by them. The method of their teaching was simple and direct; not much learning in the abstruse philosophy of Buddhism was needed. The soldiers were naturally not very scholarly; what they wanted was to be not timid before death, which they had constantly to face. This was a most practical problem on their part, and Zen was ready to grapple with it, probably because the masters dealt with the facts of life, and not with concepts. They would probably say to a soldier who came to be enlightened on the question of birth and death that 'There is no birth and death here: get out of my room as quick as you can.' So saying they would chase him away with a stick they generally carried. Or if a soldier came to a master saying, 'I have to go through at present with the most critical event of life; what shall I do?' the master would roar, 'Go straight ahead, and no looking backward!' This was how in feudal Japan the soldiers were trained by Zen masters.

Since the soldiers were constantly threatened as regards their lives, and since their swords were the only weapons that turned their fate either way to life or to death, the art of fencing developed to a wonderful degree of perfection. It is not strange, then, that Zen had much to do with this profession. Takuan (1573–1645), one of the greatest figures in the Zen world of the Tokugawa period, gave full instruction in Zen to his disciple, Yagiu Tajima-no-kami (died 1646), who was fencing teacher to the Shōgun of the day. The instructions are not of course concerned with the technique of the art itself, but with the mental attitude of the fencer. To follow them intelligently must have cost a great deal of spiritual training on the part of his illustrious disciple. Another great fencing master of the Tokugawa period was Miyamoto Musashi (1582–1645), who was the founder of the school called Nitōryū. He was not only a fencer but a Sumiye artist, and as such as he was equally great. His pictures are very highly valued and have 'Zen flavour', so to speak. One of his famous sayings on fencing is:

> Under the sword lifted high
> There is hell making you tremble;
> But go ahead,
> And you have the land of bliss.

Not mere recklessness, but self-abandonment, which is known in Buddhism as a state of egolessness. Here is the religious significance of the art of fencing. This was the way that Zen got deeply into the life of the Japanese people—their life in its various aspects, moral, practical, aesthetic, and, to a certain extent, intellectual.

As was stated somewhere else, it may be better to regard the Buddhist teaching of Non-ego as the practical method of expounding the philosophy of the Unconscious. The Unconscious evolves silently through our empirical individual consciousnesses, and as it thus works the latter takes it for an ego-soul free, unconditioned, and permanent. But when this concept takes hold of our consciousness, the really free activities of the Unconscious meet obstructions on all sides. Emotionally, this is the source of torments, and life becomes impossible. To restore peace in the most practical manner, Buddhism now teaches us to abandon the thought of an ego-soul, to be free from this clinging, to dry up this main spring of constant annoyance; for it is thus that the Unconscious regains its original creativity. Great things so called seem to be achieved always by our direct appeal to the Unconscious. Not only great spiritual events but great moral, social, and practical affairs are the results of the immediate working of the Unconscious. Egolessness is meant to direct our attention to this fact.

To the Japanese mind, 'Muga' and 'Mushin'[1] signify the same thing. When one attains the state of 'Muga', the state of 'Mushin', the Unconscious, is realized. 'Muga' is something identified with a state of ecstasy in which there is no sense of 'I am doing it'. The feeling of 'self' is a great hindrance to the execution of a work. Although absence of self-consciousness does not guarantee the greatness of an achievement, to be conscious of it, especially in the sense of self-pride or self-conceit, at once depreciates from the spiritual point of view the value of the accomplishment. Not only that, the accomplishment itself is doubted as to its final success. There is always a taint of self attached to it. We instinctively turn away from it as not directly coming from the Unconscious. Anything from the latter seems to go beyond moral judgments; it has a peculiar charm of its own as being a first work of the Unconscious. That we can feel this charm bears testimony to the Unconscious. The aim of all the artistic discipline in Japan gathers around the self-appreciation of it, which is at once its own realization. 'Muga' or 'Mushin' or effortlessness is thus the consummation of art.

8

This is the gist of Takuan's Zen instruction given to Yasyū Tajima-no-kami on fencing:

'What is most important in the art of fencing is to acquire a certain mental attitude known as "immovable wisdom". This wisdom is intuitively acquired after a great deal of practical training. "Immovable" does not mean to be stiff and heavy and lifeless as a rock or a piece of wood. It

[1] In Chinese, *wu-wo* (non-ego) and *wu-hsin* (no mind); in Sanskrit. *anātmya* and *acitta*. See p. 352, and p. 23 of the present work.

means the highest degree of motility with a centre which remains immovable. The mind then reaches the highest point of alacrity ready to direct its attention anywhere it is needed—to the left, to the right, to all the directions as required. When your attention is engaged and arrested by the striking sword of the enemy, you lose the first opportunity of making the next move by yourself. You tarry, you think, and while this deliberation goes on, your opponent is ready to strike you down. The thing is not to give him such a chance. You must follow the movement of the sword in the hands of the enemy, leaving your mind free to make its own counter-movement with your interfering deliberation. You move as the opponent moves, and it will result in his own defeat.

'This—what may be termed the "non-interfering" attitude of mind—constitutes the most vital element in the art of fencing as well as in Zen. If there is any room left even for the breadth of a hair between two actions, this is interruption. When the hands are clapped, the sound issues without a moment's deliberation. The sound does not wait and think before it issues. There is no mediacy here, one movement follows another without being interrupted by one's conscious mind. If you are troubled and cogitate what to do, seeing the opponent about to strike you down, you give him room, that is, a happy chance for his deadly blow. Let your defence follow the attack without a moment's interruption, and there will be no two separate movements to be known as attack and defence. This immediateness of action on your part will inevitably end in the opponent's self-defeat. It is like a boat smoothly gliding down the rapids; in Zen, and in fencing as well, a mind of no-hesitation, no-interruption, no-mediacy, is highly valued.

'So much reference is made in Zen to a flash of lightning or to sparks issuing from the impact of two flint-stones. If this is understood in the sense of quickness, a grievous mistake is committed. The idea is to show immediateness of action, an uninterrupted movement of life-energy. Whenever room is left for interruption from a quarter not in vital relation with the occasion, you are sure to lose your own position. This of course does not mean to desire to do things rashly or in the quickest possible time. If there were this desire in you its very presence would be an interruption. When it is asked, "What is the ultimate reality of Buddhism?" the master answers without a moment's delay, "A branch of plum-blossom", or "The cypress tree in the courtyard". There is something immovable within, which, however, moves along spontaneously with things presenting themselves before it. The mirror of wisdom reflects them instantaneously one after another, keeping itself intact and undisturbed. The fencer must cultivate this.'

A life of non-interruption here described as necessary to the mastery of fencing is the life of effortlessness (*anābhogacaryā*) or of desirelessness (*apraṇihita*), which is the essence of Bodhisattvahood. Artistically, this is the art of artlessness. The Confucians would say: 'What does heaven say? What does the earth say? But the seasons come and go and all things grow.' The followers of Lao-tsŭ would paradoxically declare, 'Benevolence and righteousness are products of human artificiality when the highest truth no more prevails in its own way.' Or, 'It is the principle of non-action that makes all things move.' Or, 'Just because the axle moves not, the spokes revolve.' All these remarks tend to show that the centre of life-gravity remains immovable, and that when this has successfully taken hold of all the life activities, whether artistic or poetic or religious or dramatic, whether in a life of quietude and learning or in one of intense action, a state of self-realization obtains, which expresses itself in a most exquisite manner in the life and acts of the person.

9

To conclude: the spirit of Eternal Loneliness (*viviktadharma*) which is the spirit of Zen expresses itself under the name of 'Sabi' in the various artistic departments of life such as landscape gardening, the tea-ceremony, painting, flower arrangement, dressing, furniture, in the mode of living, in nō-dancing, poetry, etc. The spirit comprises such elements as simplicity, naturalness, unconventionality, refinement, freedom, familiarity singularly tinged with aloofness, and everyday commonness which is veiled exquisitely with the mist of transcendental inwardness.

For illustration, let me describe a tea-room in one of the temples attached to Daitokuji, the Zen temple which is the headquarters of the tea-ceremony. Where a series of flagstones irregularly arranged comes to a stop, there stands a most insignificant-looking straw-thatched hut, low and unpretentious to the last degree. The entrance is not by a door but a sort of aperture; to enter through it a visitor has to be shorn of all his encumbrances, that is to say, to take off both his swords, long and short, which in the feudal days a samurai used to carry all the time. The inside is a small semi-lighted room about ten feet square; the ceiling is low and of uneven height and structure. The posts are not smoothly planed, they are mostly of natural wood. After a little while, however, the room grows gradually lighter as our eyes begin to adjust themselves to the new situation. We notice an ancient-looking kakemono in the alcove with some handwriting or a picture of Sumiye type. An incense-burner emits a fragrance which has the effect of soothing one's nerves. The flower-vase contains no more than a single stem of flowers, neither gorgeous nor ostentatious; but like a little white lily blooming under a rock surrounded by in no way sombre pines, the humble flower is enhanced in beauty and attracts the attention of the gathering of four or five visitors especially invited to sip a cup of tea in order to forget the worldly cares that may be oppressing them.

Now we listen to the sound of boiling water in the kettle as it rests on a tripod frame over a fire in the square hole cut in the floor. The sound is not that of actually boiling water but comes from the heavy iron kettle, and it is most appropriately likened by the connoisseur to a breeze that passes through the pine grove. It greatly adds to the serenity of the room, for a man here feels as if he were sitting alone in a mountain-hut where a white cloud and the pine music are his only consoling companions.

To take a cup of tea with friends in this environment, talking probably about the Sumiye sketch in the alcove or some art topic suggested by the tea-utensils in the room, wonderfully lifts the mind above the perplexities of life. The warrior is saved from his daily occupation of fighting, and the businessman from his ever-present idea of money-making. Is it not something, indeed, to find in this world of struggles and vanities a corner, however humble, where one can rise above the limits of relativity and even have a glimpse of eternity?

Satyasiddhi (Jōjitsu), Vinaya (Ritsu), Yogācāra (Hosso), Mādhyamika (Sanron), and Avataṁsaka (Kegon). Teachers belonging to these schools wrote many commentaries on sūtras and śastras. It is wonderful to note that they were all products of learned scholarship, showing how eagerly those Japanese Buddhists took up the study of Buddhism which was to them a new philosophy, a new science, a new religion, a new culture, and an inexhaustible mine of artistic impulses.

The building of many temples and monasteries, the maintenance of monks and nuns, the erection of a gigantic bronze image of Vairochana (finished in 749)—all these were defrayed from the government exchequer. We may wonder how a government came to engage in such undertakings. The truth is, however, that we ought not to judge this religion in a modern light, for in those days the Buddhist temples were schools, hospitals, dispensaries, orphanages, refuges for old age; and the monks were schoolmasters, nurses, doctors, engineers, keepers of free lodges, cultivators of land, explorers of the wilderness, etc. When the community was still in a primitive stage of evolution the Buddhists were leaders in every sense, and the government naturally encouraged their activities.

Among other things to be mentioned here there is one which concerns the movements of Buddhist women in the Nara era. The Empresses Kōmyo and Kōken and the nun Hōkin are some of the names to be long remembered by the Japanese as typifying the Buddhist life of love and compassion.

THE SHADOWS CAST

Perhaps the growth of Buddhism was fostered in the beginning too lavishly or too artificially. Although it aided immensely the development of Japanese culture, it tended to become too heavy a burden for the nation of the eighth century, especially financially. The favoured monks behaved too selfishly. The distinction between secular power and religious attainment began to be wiped out. Even in the latter the unessentials were brought out at the expense of the essentials. The time came for Buddhism to change direction. Nara Buddhism was to be replaced by Heian Buddhism.

The Emperor Kwammu moved his capital from Nara to Kyoto towards the end of the eighth century. Against the tradition that had prevailed until then, he left all the old temples in Nara, and established new ones on Mount Hiei and in the south of the capital. The new leaders represented the Tendai and the Shingon. Dengyō (767–823) and Kōbō (774–835), the two greatest stars that illuminated the heavens of the new regime, stepped forward boldly on the stage.

DENGYŌ DAISHI

Every visitor to Kyoto will easily recognize where Mount Hiei stands, for it is the highest, towering up in the north-east of the city. This was the site selected by Dengyō to establish his Tendai school of Buddhism. He was one of the first Buddhist monks to realize the dangers of city-life, which was too well enjoyed by his predecessors. He was not only a perfect master of the abstruse philosophy of the T'ien-tai, but a profound student of the mystic rites and the Dhyāna practice. His ambition was to synthesize all the schools of Buddhism that were known in his day. All the new sects of Buddhism that were unfolded later in the Kamakura era can be traced back to Mount Hiei, the headquarters of Dengyō.

The old schools of Nara were inevitably opponents of the new leaders, not only for sentimental reasons but mainly from the point of doctrinal differences. For Dengyō belonged to the T'ien-tai school which upheld the absolutism of the One Vehicle, whereas the old Nara school defended the Yogācāra doctrine. The issue was concerned with the ultimate character of the teaching of the *Puṇḍarīka* (*Hokkekyō*).

Dengyō also wanted to have a special Mahāyāna ordination platform which was to be independent of Nara. He fought strongly against an overwhelming opposition, and only succeeded in having his plan carried out after his death.

KŌBŌ DAISHI

Kōbō was a younger contemporary of Dengyō by seven years and survived him by twelve years. He belonged to a different type of genius, and was one of the most versatile of great men; a profound scholar, an ascetic, an extensive traveller, an artist of the first class, a man of affairs, and a most experienced calligrapher. His chief object of study was the *Dainichi-kyō* (*Mahāvairocana Sūtra*) and the *Kongōchōgyō* (*Vajraśekhara Sūtra*), the two great textbooks of the Shingon sect. While in China he became a disciple of Keikwa (Hui-kuo) and was his orthodox successor as the Eighth Patriarch of the Shingon.

He opened up Mount Kōya as the headquarters of Shingon mysticism, and is regarded by his disciples as still living there in a state of Samādhi. He liked to have a monastery in the mountains but did not forget to keep up his connection with the world. The Tōji in the south of Kyoto marks his deep footprints in the capital. Dengyō seems to have kept himself away from the world too much, and Hiei remains solitary in spite of its nearness to the city. Kōya is quite an inaccessible place compared to Hiei, but how many pilgrims congregate there every year! The mountain itself is a little town.

The Heian period was chiefly taken up by the Shingon and the Tendai, which almost overshadowed the old Buddhism of Nara, but at the same time there were signs that they, too, had to give way to a new force which had quietly but steadily been lifting its head.

ARISTOCRATIC BUDDHISM

The Tendai in its pure form is too deeply philosophical, and for its popularization it was necessary to come down from speculative flights and to find some way down into the hearts of the masses. The way was the performing of mystic rites which properly belonged to the Shingon. The Japanese Tendai is thus a mixture of Chinese T'ien-tai metaphysics with the practical ritualism of Shingon. We can say that the Buddhism of the Heian period was ritualism pure and simple. To put a stop to evil influences the ritual called 'Sokusai Ho' was performed; to increase happiness the 'Zoyaku', to invite good powers the 'Kujo', to overturn enemies the 'Gōfuku', to pray for the loving protection of the Buddhas and Bodhisattvas the 'Kyōai', and to achieve prolongation of life the 'Yemmei'. All these mystic rituals were considered thoroughly effective to bring about what the devotee desired.

Besides these there were all kinds of ceremonies performed for different occasions, auspicious or otherwise, and at various chief temples in the land. The performance sometimes lasted a week, and could be attended only by people of the leisured classes, that is, by the nobility of the time. In those days, when there were not many and varied social entertainments, it was natural enough for those noble classes to turn some of the Buddhist ceremonials into a type of refined amusement whereby to pass their Sundays and holidays. That the present-day Buddhism still wears an air of aristocracy is no doubt traceable to the traditions of those begone days.

AGAINST THE SPIRIT OF BUDDHISM

The aristocratic and ritualistic Buddhism is not Buddhism. When it undergoes such transformation it is high time for it to go back to its original form, that is, democratic and practical Buddhism. While the Shingon was enjoying its heyday of prosperity, there was another movement going on undermining its apparent influence. This was the rise of the Pure Land school, whose principal teaching consists in repeating the Buddha's name (*nembutsu*) and being born in the country of Amida.

Buddhism was so far confined to the upper classes of society who had enough intelligence and leisure to master its abstruse philosophy and its extraordinarily complicated system of ritualism. This was inevitable. It first came to Japan through official channels, it aided the court and those who surrounded it in carrying out their programme of policy. Buddhism became solidly amalgamated with all that was symbolic of power, culture, knowledge, and morality. It was all well as far as it went, but aristocracy is a one-eyed child; it sees the refined surface but lacks solidity. Real power must grow from life itself. The Buddhism of the Heian period could not continue any longer in the way it used to go, and had to become the Kamakura Buddhism.

CREATIVE BUDDHISM

I. COMING OF KŪYA SHŌNIN

The one who in the Heian period struck the first note of reformation for democratic Buddhism was Kūya Shōnin (902–972), known as the 'market sage'. He left the mountains and monasteries and palatial temples, and came among the masses saying his Nembutsu. He never stayed in one place; a real wandering monk he was. Ryōnin (1072–1132) followed him, but from the Avataṁsaka point of view, which is founded on a philosophy of identity. Aristocracy and democracy were to be united in the Nembutsu.

The great leader of the Nembutsu was Hōnen Shōnin (1133–1212), who not only expounded his doctrine in numerous writings, scholarly and popular, in classical Chinese and vernacular Japanese, but was the perfection of religious genius. His teaching was simple; that is to say, if we believed in Amida and his Original Vow with a devotional heart and wished sincerely to be born in his Land of Purity and Happiness, saying, 'Na-mu-a-mi-da-bu-tsu' (*nembutsu*), we should surely be taken up by Amida and relieved of the oppressive burden of worldly cares. No elaborate ritualism, no mystifying philosophy, no labyrinthian complexity of technical terms, but a simple, straightforward invocation of Amitabha Buddha—was this not a wonderful leap from the Nara and Heian Buddhism?

Hōnen's worthy successor was Shinran (1173–1262). In Shinran the Pure Land Buddhism reached its culmination. In Hōnen's Nembutsu there was still something of 'self-power' but in Shinran's all is given up to the 'other-power', although in practice we can never get away from 'self-power' as long as we are relatively-conditioned individuals. Shinran frankly admitted not only in theory but in practice that we are all sinful beings, and made no pretension to escape the outcome of our sinfulness. It is, he stated, in the very constitution of our being that we are sinful; therefore let us take refuge in the 'other-power', and let alone our ignorance and sinfulness. This was, in a way, a dangerous doctrine. When it is not carefully balanced by reason and morality, it will surely turn into antinomianism.

Ippen Shōnin (1239–1289) was a wandering monk like Kūya, who went around all over Japan, saying his Nembutsu and telling others to follow his example. As he came after Hōnen and his disciples and also studied Zen, his Nembutsu has its own note. His sect never attained the popularity of Shin or Jōdo, because he was a rolling stone which gathered no moss. He burned all his writings just before he died. What is left of them is a short collection of his letters and sayings and poems.

One of the reasons why the Nembutsu school prevailed in this period was owing to the idea, which then gained currency, that the age belonged to the declining age of Buddhism as predicted by the Buddha. All the moral and ascetic rules given to the monks would be neglected, the people would not be wise enough to follow the profound teaching of the Buddha, the monks would be quarrelsome in every way, and even engage in warfare, etc. The era just preceding the Kamakura showed every indication of this degeneracy, and the wise men thought that the time had come for the entire reconstruction of Buddhism to enable it to adapt itself to the requirements of the time. They found this in the Nembutsu doctrine.

CREATIVE BUDDHISM

2. NICHIREN APPEARS

Along with the Nembutsu there was another current started by Nichiren Shōnin (1222–1282). Unlike most great Buddhists he rose from among the lower strata of the community, his father being a mere fisherman in a remote village in Awa. He thus exhibited his aggressive and pugnacious spirit throughout his religious career. His followers even now are more or less militaristic and do not mix well with other Buddhists.

Nichiren's teaching is founded on the *Puṇḍarīka Sūtra*, and may be said to be the practical application of Tendai philosophy. He believes in Śākyamuni Buddha and his eternal life; that he is still teaching as in his former days on Mount Holy Vulture. This eternal Buddha is revealed in us who are living in this world. Amida's Pure Land is not of this world, nor is the Lotus World of Vairochana; but, says Nichiren, his Śākyamuni is here, and we are so many revelations of him. Of this revelation we become conscious by reciting 'Na-mu-myo-ho-ren-ge-kyo' with singleness of purpose and sincerity of heart, as the *Myōhōrengekyō* (*Puṇḍarīka*) has grown out of our religious yearnings. Thus the Nichiren sect is strongly characterized with this-worldliness. Its association with the patriotic spirit was a natural consequence.

THE RISE OF ZEN BUDDHISM IN KAMAKURA PERIOD

The Buddhism of Kamakura was the affirmation of religious consciousness itself against the externalism and intellectualism which characterized the Buddhism of the preceding period, but was at the same time a sort of re-assertion which consisted in the unfolding of the spiritual yearnings which had been suppressed by historical conditions. When, towards the end of Nara Buddhism, there was a tendency to cast off all the intellectual complications which highly coloured the study of Buddhism at the time, it was superseded by the ritualism of Shingon. This tendency now came up to the surface in the introduction of Zen into the Japanese Buddhist world of Kamakura.

There were more than twenty streams of Zen that poured into the thought realm of Buddhism from China. The aim of Zen is to throw off all the external paraphernalia which the intellect has woven around the soul and to see directly into the inmost nature of our being. Man is not a simply constructed creature; he requires many appendages, but when they grow too heavy he wants to unload himself, and sometimes to include his own existence.

The military class of Kamakura had a great liking for simplicity in every form. They were tired of and averse to ornate aristocracy and effeminate refinement. Zen supplied their wants to a nicety. If Shingon and Tendai were meant for the nobility, and the Nembutsu for the commoner, Zen was assuredly for the soldier. Zen was in those days represented by Eisai (1140–1215) and Dōgen (1200–1253).

AFTER KAMAKURA

Everything that could be drawn out of Buddhism in the course of Japanese history unfolded itself in the Kamakura period, and what followed was more or less the filling up and working out of details. There were no more new schools possible so long as there was no new development of ideas and no shifting of values in the community where Buddhism thrived. From Kamakura down to the fall of the Tokugawa Shōgunate, which meant roughly six hundred years of peace and uneventful life for Buddhism, there was nothing that would stimulate the growth of a new life in it except that the new schools of the Kamakura era continued to flourish in every direction: more temples were built either under the patronage of the powerful princes and lords or by the contributions of the public; and then the organizations grew stronger, priestly hierarchy more elaborate and complicated, traditional authorities more autocratic, faith and devotion more formal, scholarship and speculation more ossified. In other words, Buddhism was gradually losing its vitality because of the non-stimulating character of its surroundings.

The Buddhists were, however, rudely awakened from their long narcosis when the downfall of feudalism took place towards the end of the nineteenth century. Shintoism, which had been kept under the yoke ever since the completion of the Ryōbu Shinto doctrine, shook itself off from official interference; and what may be called a mild form of persecution overcame Buddhism. Whatever patronage in the form of estates or donations it used to receive from the authorities, local and central, was taken away, and the temples and monasteries, including all their occupants, were thrown out into the streets, leaving only their past dreams of comfort and prosperity.

Since then more than half a century has elapsed and the Buddhists are growing more and more keenly alive to the situation; for if they were not, there would be no choice left for them but to resign themselves to the fate of annihilation. Besides, Christianity, backed by its modern methods of propaganda and its full grasp of modern ideas, has been living among them for some years now. With these stimulations Buddhism has to draw more intensely and deeply than ever upon those vital sources which are still its own.

CONCLUSION

Whatever faults and follies Buddhism may have committed in its history in Japan, there is no doubt that it is a mighty spiritual power by which the Japanese as a nation as well as individually have been sustained and nourished in the general works of civilization. Without Buddhism, Japan could hardly have reached the present stage of culture and enlightenment.

If the East is one, and there is something that differentiates it from the West, the differentia must be sought in the thought that is embodied in Buddhism. For it is in Buddhist thought and in no other that India, China, and Japan, representing the East, could be united as one. Each nationality has its own characteristic modes of adapting the thought to its environmental needs, but when the East as a unity is made to confront the West Buddhism supplies the bond. What then are those central ideas of Buddhism which sweep over Asia and which have been asserting themselves either openly or covertly in Japan? They are the immanent conception of the Buddha-nature, the transcendentality of Prajñā (intuitive knowledge), the all-embracing compassion and the eternal vows of the Bodhisattva.

Japanese Buddhism has left its permanent impression on the arts, customs, culture, such as the tea-ceremony, flower-arrangement, Nō-drama, etc., ways of thinking, and ways of looking at the world and life, and these marks will be the perennial fountain of inspiration to the Japanese now and hereafter. Let those who grow tired of mechanical industry, economical struggles, scientific wonders, or achievements of egotism, visit one of the ancient Buddhist monasteries, sit before the image of a Bodhisattva, be it Kwannon, Jizō, or Yakushi, and pass an hour of meditation, and I am sure that their worn-out souls will once more expand to the limits of the chiliocosm and be vivified enough to come back to the world of finitudes.

VIII. THE ZEN LIFE IN PICTURES

THE Mahāyāna is pre-eminently the religion of the Bodhisattva, and the Bodhisattva's life of devotion (*bodhisattva-caryā*) is the ideal of the Zen life. In India this life was depicted with exuberant imagination as well as with philosophical intuitions. As the result we have such great Mahāyāna sūtras as the *Avataṁsaka* (or *Gaṇḍavyūha*), *Prajñāpāramitā*, and *Saddharmapuṇḍarīka*, and such great Bodhisattvas as Mañjuśrī, Samantabhadra, Maitreya, and Avalokiteśvara. The spiritual insight penetrating all the mysteries of being, the feeling of love awakened from the depths of the soul, the grand scheme of universal salvation which includes the most insignificant and down-trodden creatures, and the inexhaustible resource of energy and 'means' (*upāya*) to be employed for the carrying-out of the scheme, all these which we see exhibited by those grand supernatural and superpersonal figures are the basic factors of the Mahāyāna consciousness.

When the religion of the Bodhisattva came to China and was assimilated by her people, it became what is now known as Zen Buddhism. It took off its Indian raiment; its highly metaphysical intuitions were replaced by the practical statements of our daily life, and its richly variegated fantasies gave way to the matter-of-fact activity of gathering kindling and planting pine-trees. And yet there was no vulgarity, no philistinism. On the contrary, wherever the spirit of Zen moves, everything that comes in touch with it acquires something of mystery about it. The oil jar carried by T'ou-tzŭ[1] emits an ineffable glow; the ladle

[1] Ta-tung, of T'ou-tzŭ (819–914), was a great Zen master towards the end of T'ang. While he was living in a straw-thatched hut in T'ou-tzŭ Shan, Chao-chou called on him. Chao-chou met him on his way to the hut, and finding out who he was, Chao-chou asked, 'Are you not the master of the T'ou-tzŭ Shan?' T'ou-tzŭ without answering him said, 'Pray give me a penny for my tea and salt.' Chao-chou gained the hut

in the hand of Hsüeh-fêng[1] is incalculably more than a wooden stick; the straw-sandal on the head of Chao-chou[2] is worth sharing a corner in the temple treasure-house. Not only that, every shrimp consumed by Hsien-tzŭ[3] is still alive with us and in us; the pork that filled the stomach of Chu-t'ou[4] has duly attained its Buddhahood. Tosui[5] is said to have eaten with relish from a beggar's bowl while his disciple could hardly swallow it. The master said: 'Your mind is still choked with ideas of what is sweet and what is spoiled. Hence this mess!' Although it is doubtful in this particular case how far we can go the way of Tosui, his absolute idealism or his understanding of Śūnyatā must be said to be of the most practical kind. In any event, we cannot deny the fact that wherever there is genuine Zen life there takes place a transmutation of value, and one begins to live in a realm unreachable by the senses and the logic based on them.

That there is another realm for Zen adepts even while living the prosaic facts of their everyday life is demonstrated by their eccentric, unsociable, bizarre mannerisms. Their behaviour does not allow prediction or inference or rationalization. It is generally unexpected. Strangely, however, there is something in it both refreshing and stimulating. When we read the biographical accounts of the Zen masters, or come across the Sumiye pictures illustrating their lives,

before T'ou-tzŭ came back from his errand; he entered and quietly waited for the host. Asked Chao-chou, seeing him approach with an oil-pitcher, 'I heard so much of T'ou-tzŭ, and what do I see now but an old oil-pedlar?' T'ou-tzŭ said, 'You just see an oil-pedlar, but no T'ou-tzŭ.' 'Where is T'ou-tzŭ?' 'Oil, oil!' was the response of the old monk-pedlar. (*The Chuan-têng Lu*, XV.)

[1] Hsüeh-fêng (822–908) is said to have carried a ladle or dipper all the time on his Zen pilgrimage. His idea was to serve as a cook in every monastery he visited. Cooking is one of the most important but laborious tasks in the Brotherhood. Hsüeh-fêng purposely wanted to submit himself to this onerous drudgery, which is avoided by most people.

[2] See *Zen Essays*, Series I, p. 277.

[3] See Plates XXI and XXII.

[4] See Plate XXI.

[5] Died 1683. He used to preside over a prosperous Zen temple in Kyūshū, Japan, but one day, after attending a great celebration, he left and became a wandering mendicant.

we realize what an iron chain of moral and intellectual conventionalism we are all the time dragging along. The chain is not always made of iron; it is sometimes of the thinnest possible material such as the lotus filament—just an idea slumbering deep in the darkest nook of consciousness; yet how strong, how heavy it is! Our legs, our arms are so securely tied! When we feel we are the most free we fail to kick off this lotus filament of the ego-consciousness. The realm symbolized by the dancing Pu-tei, the Bodhidharma crossing the ocean on a reed-leaf, the pair of lunatic poets with a broom and a writing brush, and others, seems to be utterly beyond the attainment of ordinary mortals. Yet how alluring and irresistible this realm is!

This inner world is frequently represented objectively, that is, impersonally. Nature is left to sketch her own images without reference to persons. She has her moods, and they are expressed by means of her rocks, mountains, rivers, logs, birds, people, and weeds. Her spirit moves among them. The Zen artist catches her—which is possible when the artist loses himself in nature, or rather when he becomes the most willing instrument in her hands, and the result is so many landscape paintings left by the Sumiye artists. Having nothing to do with so-called realities appealing to the senses, these landscape pictures are devoid of colour and perspective. And yet we are conscious of a certain spirit hovering over the mountains and waters and whatever other objects there are. Recently we hear much from the West of 'conquering' nature, but the idea is quite foreign to us of the Far East, because to us nature is a friend and not an enemy. Not to understand her is our fault and not hers. Even when she looks most threatening, she never betrays ill-feeling towards us, as human evildoers do. Therefore, the artist knows nature best when he is in a state of the unconscious (*mu-shin*, *wu-hsin*, or *acitta*); and naturally we observe that constant references are made to nature by Zen masters throughout the history of Zen Buddhism.

Lastly, the Zen masters are not mere nature-lovers, nor are they intoxicated with their own 'God' which they hold within themselves. They are social workers, they serve society in their own way.

When Bodhisattvas are in the realm of their Sambhogakāya, 'Self-enjoyment Body', they are attired in what may be called their ceremonial dress, fully decorated and in formal posture. In the Shingon Maṇḍalas all the Buddhas and Bodhisattvas are so represented, and this takes place to a certain extent also in the Pure Land paintings. When the Bodhisattva-ideal is brought nearer down to the earthly human life, that is, when he comes to be seen in his Nirmāṇakāya, 'Transformation Body', engaged in his actual service to sentient beings, his transcendental attitude, so stiff and unapproachable, becomes gradually softened, as it were, and goes through a 'secularizing' transformation. That is to say, the Bodhisattva assumes an easier posture and appears in a simple loose-fitting robe, divested of all the ornamental effects. He is a more familiar figure now. He is not to be enshrined in a sanctuary as an object of worship, but he is made to live among us as one of our kind.

When this 'Transformation Body' idea undergoes a further transformation, the Bodhisattva is actually our neighbour. He—or maybe she—goes to the market for the provisions, he chops the wood, he copies the sūtras, he works in the factory, he is a clerk in the office; she was in ancient days even a courtesan.

Expressed in another way, this means that the Buddha-nature (*buddhatā*) is in every one of us, in every sentient being. Only when we see it, we recognize the Bodhisattva in one of his transformations. When a Mañjuśrī (Monju), or a Samantabhadra (Fugen), or an Avalokiteśvara (Kwannon) is thus brought to our own social level, we meet him or her every day and everywhere in our daily walk of life. The meanest thing we do, the most insignificant deed we perform, is the Bodhisattva's *vikurvita*, his *lalita*, and all the wonders achieved by the Indian Mahāyānists and recorded so grandly in their various sūtras have also been performed by Hui-nêng and Hung-jên, Han-shan and Shi-tê;

more than that, by every Tom, Dick, and Harry. What is needed to become aware of this, to see how it is done, is just to open our own Prajñā-eye.

With these preliminary remarks, and with what has already been stated in the foregoing pages of the present book, as well as in the two preceding Series of Essays, the reader will be able to understand the significance of the illustrations, and find out for himself where lies the messages of Zen in the age of science and machine, industrialism and self-aggrandisement.

The following 'dialogues' (*mondō*) will further illustrate the points I have repeatedly noted in my Essays about the practical turn of Chinese psychology in the demonstration of the truth of Zen Buddhism, and also furnish the reader with a key which will successfully open the treasure-house of the Zen life:

The venerable Yên-yang, of Hsin-hsing,[1] was asked by a monk:

'What is the Buddha?'

'A mass of Clay.'

'What is the Dharma?'

'The earth moves.'

'What is the Samgha?'

'One who eats gruel (*chou*) and rice (*fan*).'

When the venerable master was asked what is the meaning of the Buddha's manifesting himself in accordance with conditions, he said:

'O monk, pass that stool over to me, please.'

Hui-chiao, of Yang-chou,[2] was imploringly requested by a monk:

'I have come from a far-off district to receive your instruction. Will you kindly tell me the truth of Zen as you understand it?'

[1] *The Chuan-têng Lu*, XI.
[2] Ibid.

'The official regulations are so strict, and there is no room for private arrangements,' answered the master.

'There must be some contrivance (*upāya*), master!'

'[As you come from so far away,] pass the night by the fireplace.'

Fêng the master, of the Kuo-ch'ing Inn,[1] was asked by a monk:

'What are the characteristic features of your household [that is to say, of your school, or of your teaching]?'

'A table, a tray, a chair, a fireplace, and windows.'

'What is monkhood?'

'In early morning, "How do you do?" At night, "Good Night".'

'What is the teaching of Buddhism?'

'The Śākya is a bull-headed jail-keeper, and the Patriarchs are horse-faced old maids.'

T'ang-sheng, of Yün-yen,[2] was sweeping the ground when Kuei-shan[3] came up to him and remarked:

'You keep yourself very busy, don't you, Brother?'

'You must know that there is one who never gets busy.'

'In this case, I must say that there is a second moon.'

T'ang-sheng held up the broom and said, 'What moon is this?'

Kuei-shan nodded his head and went off.

Another time T'ang-sheng was engaged in making straw-sandals, when Tung-shan came and asked:

'I wish to get an eye by your kind instruction; is it possible for me to have one?'

'To whom did you give yours away?'

'I have had none, Master.'

[1] Ibid.

[2] 782–841. Ibid., XIV.

[3] This is pronounced in Japan *I-san*, and I have so far had Wei-shan for it. But recently I have been informed by a Chinese scholar that Wei-shan is wrong and it should be Kuei-shan.

'If you have, where would you set it up?'

Tung-shan made no reply, whereupon the master remarked:

'The one who asks for an eye—is he the eye?'

'That is no eye,' said Tung-shan.

The master burst into a terrible scolding, exclaiming, '*Ch'ua!*'

INDEX

Abaddhāmukta, 283
Abhāva, 262
Abhāva-śūnyatā, 258
Abhibudhyote, 287
Abhijñā, 100
Abhiniryāta, 83
Abhisheka,[1] 124, 135
Abhiśraddhā, 249
Abhyātmā-bahirdhā-śūnyatā, 255
'Abrupt' school (or teaching), 36, 37
'Abruptness', 30
Abysmal, the, 30
Acintya, 77 fn., 82, 88, 248, 319
Acintyavimokṣa, 71, 159
Acitta (*mushin*), 362
Acittatva, 36 fn.
Adhimukta, 163
Adhimukti, 180, 249
Adhipateyata, 94
Adhiṣṭhāna, 82, 94, 100, 149, 156 157, 335 fn.
Adhyāśayasarvajñatāpraṇidhānaprasthāna, 83
Adhyāśayata, 249
Adhyātmā-śūnyatā, 255
Agada, 189
Akanishṭa Heaven, 274
Ākāśa, 315
Akṛtā, 319
Akṣaya, 152 fn., 158, 283
Alakṣaṇa, 319
Alaṁkāra, 287 fn.
Alaṁkāras, 74, 149, 154
Ālayavijñāna, 274, 340, 345 fn.
All-knowledge, 92, 97, 157, 244
Amanaskāra, 36 fn.
Amida, 335 fn., 373, 374, 375
Amitābha, 155, 332 fn.
An Shih-kao, 239
Anābhāsa, 77
Anabhilāpya, 77 fn., 82
Aṇabhinirvṛitta, 266
Anabhisaṁskāra, 36 fn., 100

[1]*Sh* and *ṣ* are somewhat indiscriminately used in this book.

Anābhoga, 36 fn.
Anābhogacaryā, 323, 364.
Anantacitta, 179
Anāśrāya, 283
Anātman, 258
Anātmya, 167, 362 fn.
Anatta, 338
Anavakāra-śūnyatā, 255
Anavarāgra-śūnyatā, 255
Anāyūha, 100
Animitta, 30, 309, 310
Aniruddha, 91
Anirvṛittamūla, 188, 194
Añjana, 205
Anubhāva, 83
Anujāta, 252 *et seq.*
Anukampana, 168
Anupalabdha, 248, 272, 280, 283
Anupalabdhatā, 313
Anupalambha, 262
Anupalambha-śūnyatā, 258
Anuraja, 72
Anuśaya, 187, 188, 190, 203
Anutpāda, 36, 155
Anutpādānirodha, 283
Anutpannatvāt, 265
Anuttarasamyaksaṁbodhi, 167
Apada, 283
Aparāmṛiṣṭā, 251, 280 283
Apatha, 283
Aprakṛti, 319
Apraṇihitā, 30, 36 fn., 310, 364
Apratihata, 306
Archery, 310
Arhat-ideal, 84–5
Arhatship, 123, 334
Asadbhūtatvāt, 265
Asambhinnajñāna, 183
Asaṁga, 182, 281, 283
Asaṁgacitta, 179
Asaṁskṛita, 259
Asaṁskṛita-śūnyatā, 255
Aśara, 320
Aścaryam, 323
Aśeṣajñāna, 182
Aśleṣa, 281, 283

INDEX

Aṣṭaśāhasrikā, 36 fn., 234, 242
Aṣṭasāhasrikā-Prajñāpāramitā, 114
Asthita, 283
Asti, 155, 282
Astitva and *nāstitva*, 270, 271, 273, 276, 278, 281, 283, 334 fn.
Asura, 135, 206
Asvabhāva, 155, 281
Atmakārya, 96
Attachment, 317
Atyantaśānti, 96
Atyanta-śūnyatā, 255, 286
Atyantaviśuddhi, 282, 283, 324
Atyantavivikta, 283
Aupamya, 300 fn.
Avalokiteśvara, 86 fn., 223, 226, 227, 234, 235, 237, 379
Avataṁsaka, 343, 344
Avataṁsaka Sūtra, 20, 21, 29, 61, 70, 71, 72, 73, 75 fn., 154, 155, 180 fn., 379; and six contemplations, 73; as philosophy of Identity, 19; Fa-tsang's interpretation of, 73; Shên-hsiu on, 20 fn.
Avihethanā, 306
Avihiṁsā, 306
Avikalpa, 284, 323
Avikṣiptayā cittasantatyā, 308
Avinivarta Stage, 254
Avinivartanīya, 312, 313
Āyatanas, 123 *et passim*

Bahirdhā-śūnyatā, 255
Bashō, 356, 357
Being and non-being, 216 *et passim*
Bhadracaryā, 170
Bhūmis, 162, 163
Bhūtakoṭi, 85, 96, 250, 310, 320, 322, 325
Bīja, 340
Birth-and-death, 26, 48
Bodhi, 38, 41, 44, 51, 67
Bodhicaryā, 170
Bodhicitta, 163; as abbreviation, 174; variously defined by Buddhas, 174, 175
Bodhicittotpāda, 171, 172, 173, 184
Bodhidharma, 18, 20, 23, 30, 41, 46, fn., 69, 346, 381
Bodhisattvacaryā, 162, 240, 287, 327, 379
Bodhisattvādhyāśayāpariśuddhi, 83
Bodhisattvahood versus Śrāvakahood, 91, 95
Bodhisattva-ideal, 79 *et seq.*
Bodhisattva-life, 249
Bokuju, 327
Brāhma, 134, 135
Buddha, 76, 77, 121; as conceived in *Gaṇḍavyūha*, 101; as mere name (*nāmadheyamātram*), 266; is the universe, 76; of Suchness, 56
Buddhabhadra, 71, 72
Buddha-body, 275
Buddha-knowledge, 126, 181
Buddha-lands, 88, 95, 115, 121, 125
Buddha-nature, 44, 342
Buddha-realm, 124, 130
Buddhatā, 307, 339 fn., 382
Buddhi, 173

Caitya, 190
Cakravada, 187
Calligraphy, 353
Campaka, 200
Caraṇa, 180
Caritavikurvita, 94
Caryā, 83, 243, 322
Chao-chou T'sung-shên, 32, 44, 45, 47, 48, 53, 105, 106, 292, 331, 380
Charm, known as Invincible, 191; known as Sudarśana, 191
Chêng, 19
Chêng nien, 41
Ch'i yün shêng tung, 129
Chieh-fêng Ying, 293
Chien-na-p'iao-ho, 32
Chih Ch'ien, 72
Chih Lou-chia-ch'an, 71–2
Chih-chang, 53, 103
Chih-fêng, 60
Chih-mên, 106
Chinese: genius, 32, 36, 68, 106; imagination,, 102; mind, 52, 74 164
Ching, 110, 111, 114
Ching-ch'ên of Chang-sha, 116, 117
Ching-chieh, 39 fn.
Ch'ing-hsi, 111
Ching-hui, 80
Ch'ing-ling Peak, 86
Chin-lun K'ê-kuan, 59
Chi-yen, 151
Chu Fo-nien, 72

Chuang-tzŭ, 29, 52, 345 fn.
Ch'u-shih Fan-ch'i, 291, 292
Chu-t'ou, 380
Cintamāni, 188, 196
Citta, 53, 114, 173, 300
Cittāśaya, 173
Cittotpāda, 170, 172, 173
Compassion, 122
Confucians, 364
Consecrated-to-fire-god, 197
'Cypress-tree in the courtyard', 47

DAITŌ Kokushi, 347
Daitokuji, 365
Dakṣinīyata, 300
Dāna, 163, 335
Daśabala, 181
Daśabhūmika, 71, 180, 181
Dayācitta, 179
Dengyō, 371
Devil's talk, 68 fn.
Dhāraṇa, 249
Dhāraṇi, 127, 227
Dharma, 116, 121, 122, 125, 127, 131, 135, 137, 141, 147, 171, 261, 338 fn., 339 fn.; wheel of the, 84, 89, 101
Dharmacakrapravarta, 182
Dharmadhātu, 69, 71, 72, 74, 78, 82, 84, 85, 88, 92, 99, 120, 121, 124, 125, 127, 130, 148, 149, 150, 151, 154, 155, 164–5, 178, 183, 187, 198, 199, 201, 204, 250, 344; fourfold, 150
Dharmadhātupraveṣa, 72, 78
Dharmākara, 326
Dharmakāya, 28, 31, 43 fn., 49, 94, 307, 330, 338, 339 fn., 340, 341
Dharma-king, 205
Dharmakośa, 247
Dharmameghā, 218
Dharma-ocean, 131
Dharmapada, 21, 28
Dharmarāja, 307
Dharmaraksha, 72
Dharmarati, 186
Dharmatā, 250, 339 fn.; entered through various avenues, 254
Dharma-wheel, 84, 89, 101
Dhātus, 124, 163, 174
Dhyāna, 31, 120, 124, 127, 163, 338, 345; and its fruits, 314; four, 122
Diamond Cutter, the, 242
Diamond Sūtra, 289
'Die Prajñāpāramitā-literatur', 242
Discrimination, 317
Dōgen, 149, 376
Dṛiṣṭa-śruta-mata-jñāta, 24 fn.
Duranubodhā, 319

EGO, soul, 75, 84, 115, 163
Egolessness (*anātmya*), 214
Ekacitta, 151
Ekadhātu, 151
Ekalakṣaṇa, 319
Ekavyūha-Samādhi, 38
Emancipation, 120, 122, 124, 130, 135, 136; triple, 123
E-mei, 86 fn.
Emperor Wu of Liang, 305
Emptiness (*śūnyatā*), 28, 29, 36, 51, 79, 100, 115, 120, 122, 214, 225; absolute, 259; and Māyā, 263; doctrine of, 272; eighteen forms of, 255–8; is *anupalabdha*, or *acintya*, 263; not nothingness, 262; not to realize, 308; not relativity, 262, 274; philosophy of, 255; realm of, 274; the King of, 45
Engaku-kyō, 18
Enjoyment- and Transformation-Buddhas, 51
Enlightenment, 51; and the Unconscious, 26; attainment of, 70, 169; desire for, 70, 169, 319; elements of, 181–3; factors of, 163; in the *Gagaṇdavyūha*, 167 *et seq.*; like Māyā, 259; variously identified, 250
Eternal Loneliness, 349, 355, 356, 357
Evil paths, 101, 122, 125
Excitements, exhilarating (*prativega-vivardhana*), 96
Experience, Chinese psychological, 63

FA-TSANG, 19, 70, 72, 73, 87, 150, 156; his commentary, 70
Fa-yen, of Wu-tsu Shan, 105
Fa-yen Wên-i, 19, 23, 54, 103, 111 fn.
Fencing, 360 *et seq.*
Five Aggregates, the (*pañcaskandhāḥ*), 264 fn.

INDEX

Fo-mu Prajñāpāramitā, 242
Forty-two Chapters. The Sūtra of, 239
Fu, of T'ai-yüan, 329

Gambhīra-prajñā-pāramitā, 267
Ganda, 180 fn.
Gaṇḍavyūha Sūtra, 18, 19, 68 *et seq.*, 180 fn., 379; acclimatized, 106; and abode, 108; and miracles, 83; as a philosophical treatise, 150; background of, 99; mystery of the, 85; original Sanskrit text of the, 70 fn.
Gandhamādana, 187
Garuḍa, 126, 203
Gocara, or *viṣaya*, 110, 114
Gradual School, 31, 37
Gurukāra, 249

HAIKU, 350, 356, 359
Han-shan, 160
Hastigarbha, 210
Haṭakaprabhāsa, 200
Hetupratyaya, 155, 272
Himālaya, Mount, 187
Hita, 306
Hitācitta, 179
Hōnen Shōnin, 373
Hōryuji, 306 fn., 332, 367
Hosso, 369
Hṛidaya, 224 *et seq.*
Hsiao-ch'un, of Ling-ch'uan temple, 90 fn.
Hsiao-p'in, 242
Hsieh nien, 41
Hsien-tzŭ, 347, 380
Hsing-nien, of Shou-shan, 105
Hsing-szŭ, 19, 117
Hsiu, 116, 117
Hsüan-chiao, 54
Hsüan-chuang, 222, 234, 239
Hsüan-fa, of the Lo-han, 61
Hsuan-sha Shih-pei, 57
Hsüeh-fêng, 380
Hsüeh-tou, 103
Huang-lung, 337
Huang-po, 110, 336
Hua-yên, 70, 71, 72
Hu-ch'i, 273
Hui-chao, 103
Hui-hai, of Pai-chang Shan, 40, 41, 43 fn., 67, 103
Hui-k'ê, 18, 20, 21
Hui-nan, 337
Hui-nêng, 18, 21, 30, 31, 35, 37, 41 fn., 63, 66, 68, 104, 116, 117, 346, 382
Hung of Tai-lung, 103
Hung-jên, 18, 382
Hu-shih, 37 fn.; on Zen, 74

I, of Pa-chiao, 105
Identity, the theory of, 150
Idzumi Hōkei, 70 fn.
Immeasurables, the, 122, 135
Indra, 187; fire of, 190; net of, 190
Indra-gem-treasure, 197
Indṛiyas, 136
Interpenetration, in Zen, 102; perfect, 152
Ippen Shōnin, 374
Ita, 244 fn.
I-tuan, 54

Jagat, 168
Jambudvīpa, 142, 194, 198, 199, 203
Jambūnada, 133, 139, 190, 198, 202, 204
Jamnabhūmī, 159
Janaka, 314
Jetavana, 75, 77, 82, 83, 88, 91, 92, 95, 96, 100
Jñāna, 149, 156, 181
Jñānacakṣus, 83, 97
Jñānacitta, 180
Jōdo, 374
Jōjitsu, 369
Ju-ching, 149
'*Jyo gu bo dai, ge ke shu jo*', 169

KALAPA, 187
Kalavinka, 202
Kalpa, 121, 122
Kalyāṇa, 306
Kalyāṇamitra, 170, 180
Kalyāṇamitraparigraha, 83
Kanzan Kokushi, 347
Kapphiṇa, 91
Kārakānupalabhita, 319
Kāraṇasamutpāda, 274, 275

Karma, and passions, 205, 206, 213; and passion-hindrances, 123, and time, 215; -hindrances, 26, 97, 121
Karpāsa, 188
Karuṇā, 73, 168, 181, 215
Kātyāyana, 91
Kegon (*avataṁsaka*), 345, 369
Kegon-gyō, 71, 180
Keishoki, 337
Kleśa, 45, 187, 190
Knots, 93
Knowledge, 120; transcendental, 98
Knowledge-hindrance, 168
Koan exercise, 235–6
Kōbō, 370
Kokoro, 129
Kongōchōgyō, 371
Kovidāra, 199
Kripākaruṇā, 182
Kritsuāyatana, 135, 144
Kṣaṇa, 121
Kṣaṇabodha, 182
Kṣānti, 338
Kṣaya, 152 fn., 314
Kṣetra, 121, 155
Kṣetrapariśuddhi, 94
Kshāntis, 134, 135, 163
Kuang-hui Lien, 328
Kuei-tsung, 103, 109
Kumārajīva, 235, 239
K'ung (*śūnyatā*), 62
Kuśala, 178, 180
Kusha, 367
Kūya Shōnin, 374
Kwannon, 53

LAKSHANA, 261
Lalita, 382
Lankāvatāra, 18, 19, 20, 21, 53 fn., 69, 75, 253, 273, 323, 345 fn., 349
Lan-tsan, 348 fn.
Lao-tzŭ, 29, 52, 345 fn.; followers of, 364
Lekhana, 249
Liang, 53–4
Liang Kai, 354
Li-ao, of Lang-chou, 56
Light and Dark, 19
Lin, of Ts'ang-ch'i, 110
Lin-chi, 19, 44, 52, 86, 108 fn., 110, 116
Ling-hsün, of Fu-jun Shan, 103, 109
Ling-shu Ju-min, 109
Lokadhātu, 78, 85, 121, 148
Lokahita, 303
Lokānukampā, 303
Lokaraksha, 239, 242
Lokasukha, 303
Loving Kindness, 123

MĀDHYAMIKA, 341
Maghi-herb, 191
Mahākaruṇā, 83, 100, 168, 301, 339 fn.
Mahākaruṇācitta, 179
Mahākāśyapa, 91
Mahāmaitrī, 100
Mahāmaitrīcitta, 179
Mahānāga, 196, 203
Mahāprajñāpāramitā, 239, 242
Mahāprajñāpāramitā Sūtra, the, 233
Mahāpraṇidhāna, 320
Mahā-śūnyatā, 255
Mahāvairocana-Buddha, 101
Mahāvaiśāradya, 182
Mahāyāna, 83, 84, 90, 99, 100, 124, 147, 155, 162, 163, 265; differentia of, 91; ideal, 119; sutras, 22
Maitracittam, 306
Maitrāyanāputra, 91
Maitreya, 85, 100 fn., 119, 124, 132, 134, 140, 141, 143, 185, 190, 217, 379
Maitrīsahagatam cittam, 300
Makara, 205
Manasikāra, 36 fn., 300
Mandalas, 382
Mañjusri, 38 fn., 62, 75 fn., 86, 109, 170, 185, 379, 382, a verse on, 86
Mantram, 224
Māra the Evil One, 93, 123, 188, 213, 215, 220; the Tempter, 315
Masters and Disciples of the Lankā, the, 21, 22 fn., 28 fn.
Mati, 173
Ma-tsu, 47, 53, 54, 104
Matsumoto, Tokumyō, 242
Maudgalyayana, 91
Māyā, 92, 282; against Śūnyatā, 269; is Suchness, 267
Māyā-knowledge, 144, 146
Māyāvāda, 267

INDEX

Māyāvadin, 264
'Means' (see *Upāya*)
Merit, stock of, 97, 134, 178, 180
Miao-hsi, 291 *et seq.*
Mind, 50, 56, 57, 73, 104, 106; has no form, 50
Mind-only, 74, 79; doctrine of, 20
Ming, of Hsiang-t'an, 111
Miraculous Powers, 120
Mirror for Zen Students, 68 fn.
Miyamoto Musashi, 361
Moksha, 41
Mondō, 63, 104, 383
Mu-chi, 354
Mu-chou, 108, 290, 355–6
Muga, 362
Mukha, 83
Muller, Max 111 fn., 242
Mushin, 362, 381

Na cittena jñātavyā, na cittagamanīyā, 319
Na kaścid abhirambudhyate, 319
Na manyeta, 36 fn.
Na saṁvidyate, 320
Nādikerī, 200
Nāga-gem, 188
Nāgārjuna, 255, 261, 268
Nairātmya, 338
Nairātmyatā, 339 fn.
Nāma, 281, 318
Nāmadheya-mātram, 266
Nan-ch'an Ch'i-fan, 59
Nan-ch'üan, 48, 117
Nandika, 91
Nan-yang, 328
Nārāyana, 138, 212
Nāsti, 155
Nātha, 301
Nature mysticism, and Zen, 73
Nembutsu, 344, 373, 374, 375
Nêng, of Tao-wu, 105
Nêng, of Yün-chü, 104
Niao-k'ê, 368
Nichiren Shōnin, 375
Nieh Ch'êng-yüan, 72
Nihatamāna, 306
Nimitta, 281, 318
Nirmāṇa, 100
Nirmāṇakāya, 49, 159, 339 fn., 382
Nirmita, 134
Nirodha, 314
Nirvāna, 26, 44, 51, 259, 260; is Māyā, 266, 316
Nirvāṇa Sūtra, 68, 68 fn.
Nirvikalpā, 116
No-birth, 36
Noble paths, the eight, 123, 124
Noble truths, the four, 123
Noble wisdom (*Pratyātmāryajñānagocara*), 69
No-fixation, 114, 119
No-mind, 106
Non-achievement, 28
Non-attachment, 251, 280
Non-ego, 79; and the Unconscious, 361
Non-interruption, 363–4
Nothingness, 38

OCEAN-array-womb, 198
'Ode on Identity', 20
Opposites, significant, 313 *et seq.*
Original Vows, 326
Orthodox Transmission of the Śākya Doctrine, The, 66–67
Otani Kanjur Catalogue, Sakurabe's, 72 fn.

PAI Lê-t'ien, 368
Pai-ma T'an-chao, 54
P'ang, 86
Pantheistic, 342
Pāragata, 237
Pāram, 244 fn., 285, 324
Paramārtha-śūnyatā, 255
Pāramitā, 72, 89, 135, 137, 138, 141, 162, 188, 213, 238, 243, 244, 327, 335
Pāramitā-virtues, 124
Parāmṛikśa, 251
Paranirmita-vasavartin, 218
Parāvṛitti, 273, 274, 280
Paricodana, 168
Parijñā, 163
Pariṇāmana, 323, 326, 334 fn.
Parinirvāṇa, 75
Paripāka, 168
Pariśuddhi, 168
Paritrāṇa, 168
Pariyātraka, 200
Paryavāpti, 249
Paryupāsita, 180
Passion-hindrances, 123

Passions, 93, 125,; evil, 26, 120
Paths of existence, 131
P'ien, 19
Pi-yen-chi, 103
Poshadha, 141
Powers, inconceivable, 98; the ten, 92
Prabhāva, 94
Prajñā, 29, 30, 31, 35, 43 fn., 171, 225, 233, 243 *et seq.*, 338; and *Bodhisattvas*, 245, 246; and Karuṇā, 312, 334 fn.; and Karuṇā in the Citta, 218, and Māyā, 267; and the intellect, 319; and Upāya, 245; and Vijñāna, 363, constitutes all-knowledge, 246; fire of, 196, is *janayitri*, 247; is like the earth, 247, is the eye, 244, its relation to time, 295; like life, 244; personifying, 247; recapitulation, 264; seeing things *yathābhūtam*, 250; sees minds of sentient beings, 252; versus Karuṇā or Upāya, 314; with Karuṇā and Upāya, 300
Prajñā-eye, 268, 285, 294, 324, 383
Prajñāpāramitā, 170, 223, 252
Prajñāpāramitā Sūtra, 21, 69, 71, 115, 118, 120, 170, 171, 339 fn., 345 fn., 379; in Sanskrit, 242; Nāgārjuna's commentary on the, 71
Prajñāpāramitācaryā, 322, 323, 327
Prajñā-Samādhi, 35
Prajñopāya, 100, 162 fn.
Prakrita-śūnyatā, 258
Prakṛiti, 260, 319
Pramuditā, 184
Praṇidhāna, 84, 100, 127, 158, 159, 172, 322
Prāpti or *labdhi*, 227
Pratāpacandra Ghosha, 242
Pratibhāna, 136
Pratihārya, 94
Pratiśaraṇa, 136
Pratiyukta, 300
Pratyaveksitavyam, 309
Preta, 97
Pudgala, 338 fn., 339 fn.
Pūjā, 249
Puṇḍarīka Sūtra, 68, 367, 370, 375
Pure Land teaching, 326, 346
Pure-light, 197
Pūrṇa, 91
Purposelessness, in Zen, 355
Purvaṅgama, 83
Pūrvapraṇidhāna, 83
Pūrvasukṛitakśalamūla, 83
Pu-tei, 381
P'u-t'o-lo, 86 fn.

RAJA, 314
Rājendralāla Mitra, 242
Rasāyana, 206
Ratilambhya, 194
Ratnakūṭa, 27
Realism, 268
Reality, 22, 28, 107, 118, 155; limit of, 45, 99, 123; summit of (*bhūtakoṭi*), 85
Reality-limit, 320
Relativity, not emptiness, 262
Revata, 91
Ritsu, 369
Romakūpa, 89
Rūpakāya, 34, 339 fn.
Rūpaloka, 168
Rūpam, 317, 318
Ryōbu Shintō, 377
Ryōnin, 373

'SABI', or 'Wabi', or 'Shibumi', 355
'Sacred Mirror Samādhi', 19
Saddharma-puṇḍarīka, 20, 21, 22, 75, 379
Sāgaramegha, 178
Saigyō, 357
Śakra, 134, 196, 206
Śakrendra, 98
Śākyamuni, 49, 75, 101, 375
Samacittatā, 39
Samādhi, 76, 96, 120, 127, 130, 131, 134, 135, 178; and the spiritual powers, 82; as miracle, 83; of Avālokiteśvara, 86
Śamam cittam, 306
Samantabhadra, 75 fn., 84, 85, 86, 89, 91, 96, 99, 109, 217, 379, 382; his arms, 85
Samāpattis, 120, 136; formless, 122; nine successive, 123
Samatabuddhadharma, 182
Śamatha, 73, 122
Sambhogakāya, 49, 339 fn.
Sambodhi, 229, 273, 334 fn.

INDEX

Saṁa, 318
Samgha, 332 fn.
Saṁgraha, 168
Saṁjñā, contrasted to Prajna, 318
Saṁjñāsyate, 317
Saṁsāra, 323
Saṁskṛitas, 259, 317
Saṁskṛita-śūnyatā, 255
Sanron, 369
San-shêng, 116, 117
Santāna, 194
Śaptaśatikā-Prajñāpāramitā, 39 fn.
Śara, 319
Śāriputra, 223, 228
Śārira, 83
Sarvadharma, 261, 323
Sarvadharmasya śūnyatā, 155
Sarvajagatparitrāṇa, 182
Sarvajñata, 97, 173, 216, 245, 246, 271, 281, 284, 287, 334 fn.; as void space, 267
Sarvajñatācittotpāda, 195
Sarvākārajñatācaryā, 334 fn.
Sarvamaṇiratnasamuccayam, 195
Sarvaprabhāsasamuccaya, 195
Sarvasattva, 159, 168
Sasaṁgatā casaṁgatā, 318
Śatasāhasrikā-prajñāpāramitā, 233
Satkāra, 249
Satkāyadriṣṭi, 244
Sattva, 121, 168
Sattvabalabuddhi, 183
Satya, 136
Selections from T'ang Poetry, 118
Self-nature (*svabhāva*), 124, 131
'Self-power', 235
Shên-hsiu, 31, 37, 66
Shên-hui, 18, 37, 38, 39, 43 fn.
Shih Hu, 242
Shih-chin of Jui-yen, 60
Shih-tê, 382
Shih-t'ou, 19, 45, 55, 57, 117
Shin, 235, 335 fn.
Shingon, 222, 229, 344, 345, 370, 371, 372, 373, 376
Shinran, 332 fn., 374
Shintoism, 377
Shōtoku, Prince, 332, 367
Shou-ch'u, of Tung-shan, 105
Shou-shan, 106
Shu, of Pao-fu, 105
Śikshananda, 71
Śīla, 100, 163, 335
Siṁhanāda, 90
Siṁhavijṛimbhita, 88
Skandhas, 124, 125, 163, 174, 223, 225, 277, 278, 309 fn.; 316; the five grasping, 123
Sōtō School, 58
Śraddhāyajñānvisuddhi, 83
Śraddhotpāda, 20
Śrāvakahood, versus Bodhisattvahood, 91, 93, 95,–6
Śrāvaka-ideal, 79
Śrāvakas, in the *Gaṇḍavyūha*, 91
Śri, 187
Śrīmālā, 367
Sthāna, 285
Studies in the Lankāvatāra Sūtra, 82 fn.
Subhūti, 91, 253
Suchness (*tathatā*), 34, 35, 40, 43, 73, 85, 116, 123, 220, 250, 340
Sudarśana, 98, 87
Sudhana, 84, 85, 100, 119, 120, 124, 134, 156, 159, 178, 185, 191, 217
Śukhacitta, 179
Sukhāvatīvyūha, 75
Sukladharma, 180
Sumana tree, 200
Sumeru, Mount, 98, 187, 199
Sumiye, 351, 359, 361, 365, 380
Śūnyatā (emptiness), 30, 39, 62, 69 235, 242, 250, 276, 320, 338 fn., 340, 380; and *Aśūnyata*, 295; associated with Zen, 345 fn.
Śūnyatā-śūnyatā, 255, 286
Supreme Sovereign, 198
Śūrangama, 115
Sustaining power, 96
Svabhāva, 99, 107, 251, 262, 339 fn.
Svakārya, 98
Svalakṣaṇa, 261
Svalakṣaṇa-śūnyatā, 258
Svapna, 266
Svayambhūjñāna, 183

TAI-AN, 109 fn.
T'ai-ch'in, 110
Tai-chu Hui-hai, 40
Tai-hui, 290, 291
Tai-mei, 104
Tai-sui Fa-chên, 109
Tai-t'zŭ Huan-chung, 54, 331

Takuan, 360, 362
Tan-ching, 31 fn., 68
Tan-hsia, 347
T'an-hsüan-chi, 70 fn.
Tao-chên, 72
Tao-ch'ien, 61
Tao-ch'üan, of Kuei-tsung, 105
Tao-hsin, 21, 29, 30; on the Abandoning of the Body, 28
Tao-hsing Pan-jê, 239, 242, 274
Taoism, 36
Tariki, 332 fn.
Tathā, 237
Tathāgata-family, 95
Tathāgatagarbha, 174, 253
Tathāgata-guhyaka, 174
Tathāgata-tathatā, 253
Tathatā, 237, 238, 250, 252, 253, 321, and *śūnyatā*, 263; not sameness or oneness, 252
Tendai, 222, 344, 345, 370, 372, 375, 376
Têng-kuan, 18, 150
'Thou art it', 85
T'ien-lung, 343
Tōsui, 380
T'ou-tzŭ, 379
Traces (*pada*), 116
Trikāya, 338–9 fn.
Truth, the twofold, 124
Tsang-yung, of Chang-ching, 60
Ts'ao-tung branch of Zen Buddhism, 19
Tsê-t'ien, the Empress, 87
Tso-i, 36 fn.
Tsung-chien, of Kuan-yin shrine, 62
Tsung-ching-lu, 20
Tsung-mi of Kuei-fêng, 18, 19, 23
Ts'ung-yüeh, of Tou-tsu, 107
Tuan of Têng-hui, 105
Tung-shan Liang-chieh, 19, 58, 237, 384
Tun-wu, 36
Tun-wu Ju-tao Yao-mên Lun, 41
Tushāra Sūtra, 72
Tushita, 134, 159
Tu-shun, 19, 21, 151

Udārādhimuktyavabhāsapratilambha, 83
Udhāna, 136
Ultimate truth, 255
Unattainable, the, 272, 278, 279, 280–1
Unconscious, the, 22, 24 fn., 30 *et seq.*, 46 fn., 73, 74, 381; and enlightenment, 26–7
Unobstructedness, 154
Upasthāna, 136
Upāya, 104, 158, 163, 252, 298, 299, 301, 325, 334 fn., 379, 384
Upāyakauśalya, 314, 322
Utpāda, 314

Vācana, 249
Vairocana-alaṅkāra-vyūha-garbha, 147
Vairocana-garbha, 214
Vairocana-vyūha-alaṅkāra-garbha, 119
Vairochana, 174, 348, 369, 375
Vairochana Tower, 74, 85, 119 136, 150, 156, 185, 217; described, 132–3
Vaiśravana, 187
Vajra, 174, 206, 210, 211, 212, 213
Vajracchedikā, 18 *et seq.*, 27, 42, 43 fn., 75, 111, 233, 242
Vajragarbha, 218
Varsha, 200
Varuna's chain, 190
Vāsanā, 344
Vaśavartin, 134, 135
Vastu, 151
Via negativa, 228, 234, 238
Vibhāvana, 314
Vidyā, 136, 226, 227, 234
Vigama, 187, 194
Vihāra, 120
Vijñāna, 173, 258; and Prajñā, 262
Vijñāptimātra, 20, 234
Vikalpa, 281, 317
Vikrīdita, 94
Vikurvita, 83, 84, 94, 142, 159
Vimalacitta, 179
Vimalakīrti, 21, 26, 29, 35, 62, 115, 367
Vimoksha (emancipation), 127
Vinaya, 168
Vipaśya, 122
Vipaśyanā, 73
Vipulacitta, 179
Vipulādhyāśaya, 180
Vīrya, 163, 320, 338
Viṣamacittam, 306
Viśuddhacitta, 179

Viśuddhāśaya, 180
Viviktā, 319, 320, 324, 341
Viviktadharma, 349, 364
Viviktatvāt, 265
Viviktavihāra, 326
Vṛiṣabha, 94
Vyūha, 69, 74, 94, 148, 154, 156, 180 fn., 287 fn.
Vyūhālaṅkāra, 156
Vyūhavikurvita, 159

WALLESER, Max, 242
Wang-chin-huan-yüan-kuan, 72 fn.
Wei-k'uan, 341
Wei-shan (for *Kuei-shan*), 47
Wên, of Chên-ching, 104
Wên-yen, of Yün-mên, 105
Wisdom-eye, 89, 95, 96, 97, 290
World-embellishing-receptacle, 196
Wu-hsin, 23, 30, 41, 106 fn., 262 fn., 381
Wu-kuang-yung, 36
Wu-ming, 18
Wu-nien, 30, 31, 36 fn., 37, 38, 40, 41
Wu-shêng, 36
Wu-tai Shan, 86
Wu-tso, 36
Wu-tso-i, 36 fn.
Wu-wei, 36
Wu-wo, 362 fn.
Wu-yêh, of Fên-chou, 105
Wu-yüan, 36

YAGIU Tajima-no-kami, 360–1
Yāma, 134
Yāna, 123
Yang-shan Hui-chi, 55, 68 fn., 109
Yao-shan Wei-yen, 56, 57, 58
Yathābhūtam, 85, 234, 238, 250, 251, 252, 254, 271, 271, 273, 277, 278, 287, 316
Yathābhūtatā, 251, 271, 276
Yên-jui of Yang-lung, 32–3
Yên-shou of Yung-ming, 20
Yogācāra, 340, 341, 370
Yüan-chih, 58
Yuishiki (*vijnaptimatra*), 345
Yün-chü, 58
Yung-chia Hsüan-chiao, 287
Yün-mên, 111 fn.
Yün-yên, 57, 58.

ZEN, 222, 349, 350, 355, 359, 360, 376; and Chinese genius, 22 fn.; and fencing, 360–1; and soldiers, 360; and sutras, 90; and the *Gaṇḍavyūha*, 90, 102, 118, 119; in a Chinese poem, 118, in a Japanese popular song, 117–18; not a philosophical system, 20, 90; on Buddha, 102; asks, 'Where do you come from?' 107, 108; your self-nature, 107
Zen master, and his residence, 108
Zen sayings, enigmatical, 116